ROUND IN CIRCLES

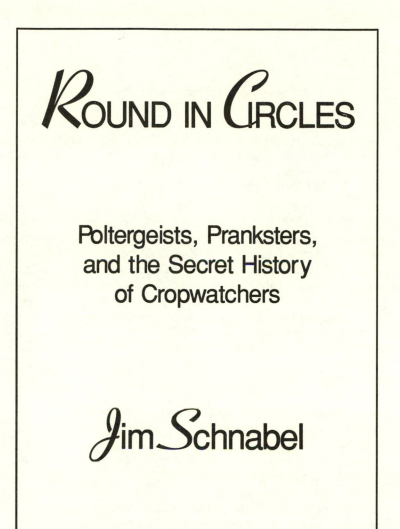

ROUND IN CIRCLES

Poltergeists, Pranksters, and the Secret History of Cropwatchers

Jim Schnabel

 **Prometheus Books**

59 John Glenn Drive
Amherst, New York 14228-2197

Published 1994 by Prometheus Books

98 97 96 95 94   5 4 3 2 1

Library of Congress Cataloging-in-Publication Data

Schnabel, Jim.
    Round in circles : poltergeists, pranksters, and the secret history of the cropwatchers / Jim Schnabel.
        p.   cm.
    Originally published: London : Hamish Hamilton, 1993.
    Includes bibliographical references.
    ISBN 0-87975-934-8 (hard : alk. paper)
    1. Crop circles. 2. Curiosities and wonders—England. 3. Curiosities and wonders—North America. I. Title.
AG243.S35   1994
031.02—dc20   94-26225
                                                                      CIP

Printed in the United States of America on acid-free paper.

We wait for light, and behold, darkness, and for brightness, but we walk in gloom.

– Isaiah 59:9

Contents

Preface to the American Edition

They came from England, tended to provoke hysteria wherever they appeared, and, for many, were the greatest things since Jesus. Yet they were not the Beatles. They were the "crop circles," strange swirled patterns that appeared mysteriously overnight in ripening fields of grain.

The crop circles are now also a North American phenomenon, for on this continent at least fifty formations have been reported each summer since 1990. Circles researcher Chris Rutkowski tells me that in the summer of 1993, they turned up in such places as Amherst, Massachusetts; Kanata, Ontario; and Granum, Alberta. They sowed consternation and mystery across Oklahoma, Texas, and California, and there were even rumors of some two dozen, in grass or dirt or god knows what, in downtown Vancouver. In Syracuse, New York, four circles linked by straight and sinuous corridors drew a storm of gawkers and media types. And in Kennewick, Washington, a symbolic wheatfield formation measuring 120 feet by 200 feet inspired one W. C. Levengood, a plant physiologist from Grass Lake, Michigan, to analyze stalk samples from the formation and declare it "genuine," that is, not man-made.

The vast spread of North America, and the unfocussed nature of the circles phenomenon here, make research somewhat more difficult than it is in the British Isles, where about half of the annual total occur within a six- or seven-mile radius of the hospitable and relatively accessible village of Avebury in Wiltshire. Still, devotees such as Levengood, and a scattered band of UFO enthusiasts, New Age millennialists, and anomaly aficionados from Manitoba to New Mexico, have ensured that crop circles wherever they appear are likely to get a going-over, radiologically and electromagnetically and plant-physiologically, and with techniques yet unembraced by orthodox science, such as meditation and dowsing.

Such a social and scientific and religious reaction, on a massive, national scale, drawing into its vortex Parliament, prime minister, and the monarchy itself, is what occurred in England during the 1980s, and it is this story that *Round in Circles* records. For some, this story is an embarrassing one, and shortly after its UK publication I was told that the London-based Centre for Crop Circles Studies, the world's largest organization devoted to this phenomenon, actually discussed buying up every copy before it could reach bookstore shelves and the innocent public.

Unfortunately I escaped such a windfall; but in any case, apropos of embarrassment, I note that I have included in these pages even some of my own mortifying crop circle experiences. The reader might be interested to know that the original title of this book, rejected by my British publishers as sounding a bit vague and New-Ageish, was *Waiting for Light*. It had been meant to capture, affectionately, the central, hopeful enterprises of circles research: waiting for UFOs, for descending electrified vortices, for spiritual or scientific illumination, for the warm glare of fame and fortune, or merely for the heartrendingly lovely midsummer dawn that brings to tired eyes the circular gifts of the night. Those who dismiss the subject as so much human folly miss the point that such folly is, to a great extent, what makes us human.

Even so, these days in Britain it seems that most of the people who flock to see new circles formations, to absorb their invisible energies, are continental Europeans or Australians or Asians or— the largest contingent of all—North Americans. The British themselves seem to have developed a collective amnesia about the pandemonium that the crop circles once set loose among them.

But never mind. Each summer continues to bring a bountiful harvest of those interested in the circles. There are special week-long excursions organized by firms in the United States and Europe. For the less devoted, day-trip buses roam in comfort from southern cities such as London and Oxford, disgorging passengers with their cameras and sunglasses and dowsing rods and floppy tourist hats into the picturesquely circles-prone villages of Avebury, Alton Barnes, Bishops Cannings, and Stanton St. Bernard, and providing a rustic, exhilarating alternative to the Tower of London, or the dreaming spires of Oxford, or the Elizabethan fineries of Stratford-on-Avon.

Dedicated bands of artists continue to visit the fields, perhaps spurred on by the words of John McEwen, art critic for the *Sunday Telegraph,* who several years ago commented of the circles that "whoever or whatever made them is an artist of genius," and disparaged by comparison less elusive landscape-shapers as Andy Goldsworthy and Richard Long.

More scientific and spiritually minded participants also continue to make the crop circle pilgrimage. I understand that last summer, for example, a German group arrived at Alton Barnes and encircled a wheatfield with copper wire, forming a giant magnetometer that should have registered the passage of any circles-swirling energy. The dowsers are still out there, too, and the meditators and prophetesses and channellers and healers. In the depths of summer, on the hills of north Wiltshire, the faithful still gather by their tents and campervans to await the inevitable visitation from above, the glorious second coming. However imminent or distant that coming will be, the circles are there—and here—and fourteen years after their public genesis in southern England, they continue to arrive, like presents at Christmas, like eggs at Easter, echoes of forgotten ritual and wonder.

Jim Schnabel
May 1994

Foreword

I first became aware of the crop circle phenomenon on a hot morning in the late summer of 1989, in America, when I read a front-page story in the *Wall Street Journal* headlined 'Mysterious Circles in British Fields Spook the Populace'. Flying saucers, earth energies, helicopters, whirlwinds, hedgehogs, rutting deer, over-fertilization, underfertilization, rogue viruses and pranksters were mentioned as possible explanations, pranksters being made to seem the least likely. Whatever had swirled the several hundred eerily symmetrical formations that summer, and in summers past, had never been seen, had never been heard, and had never left any tracks. England was in an uproar. Journalists and tourists were wading in their thousands through the circles-prone cornfields. The Ministries of Agriculture and Defence were investigating. The Queen was said to have 'sharply questioned' Mrs Thatcher on the subject.

I was mildly interested, and even considered the problem in spare moments for a day or two − before it was eclipsed, as most news-paper stories are, by the grey haze of workaday worry. Somehow, though, the mystery continued to simmer within some dark layer of my cortex, for on a Saturday morning in June of 1991, while I was a postgraduate student living in England, an otherwise obscure story leapt out at me from several of the London newspapers: the crop circles were back, and this time modern science was hot on their trail. Thirty-nine British and Japanese scientists, equipped with 'radar, an automatic weather station, thermal imaging equipment, and other monitoring equipment', were gathering at 'a secret site in Wiltshire'.

A secret site . . . Despite its cool technological context, the term seemed to throb with ancient evocations: of mystical rites and gatherings in the wild, of midnight and magic, of collective awe at ineffable Nature. I found the irony intriguing. Moreover, I wanted to see the thirty-nine scientists catch a circle in the act. I had twisted visions of cherubim and howling seraphim, trapped at last within the cage of Reason, in an arc-lit wheatfield, in a busy Spielbergesque tableau featuring jumpsuited scientists, geodesic radomes, sirens, cameras, technicians, special military detachments ... I went out and bought a book on the crop circles by the apparent ringleader of the thirty-nine scientists – a freelance meteorologist named Terence Meaden. I devoured the book, then phoned Meaden and asked if I could help out at the secret site. He wanted to know my perspective on the phenomenon. I assured him that my perspective was scientific. He said hurry down to Wiltshire.

What I found, on a chilly, windy hilltop near Devizes, was a cheap marine radar antenna on makeshift scaffolding, a myopic video camera wired to an inert yellow generator, a spiderlike miniature weather station, and a small towable caravan within whose musty interior two elderly volunteers sat worrying over the absences of batteries for the radar, fuel and parts for the cantankerous generator, and Dr Meaden – who with a visiting Japanese physicist amounted to two scientists occasionally present at the site, not thirty-nine.

Meaden eventually made a brief appearance, providing batteries for the radar and a pep talk; and around midnight a Japanese TV crew, which had loaned much of the equipment, arrived to fix and fuel their generator. But the generator died of thirst at two, and the batteries of cold at five, and by the time the secret site emerged from its thick morning fog, my Spielbergesque vision had evaporated and I was on my way home to a warm bed.

I never gave up hope that some kind of scientific advance would result, directly or serendipitously, from the study of crop circles. But the brief glimpse I'd had of Meaden, of his volunteers, of the assortment of other characters who had visited the secret site that day and night, convinced me that the most interesting aspect of the phenomenon was the human one – the obsession with anomaly, the longing for meaning, the would-be scientists and the would-be shamans, the paradigm shifts and conspiracy theories, the intrigues, scandals, love affairs, libel suits, con games, hoaxes, pagan rituals, demonic possessions, midnight epiphanies ... and countless press releases.

Foreword

And so I returned to Wiltshire, and without immediately knowing it, began this enterprise – a backstage look, as it were, at one of the strangest popular mysteries of our time.

The White Horse

The practice of cutting white horses in Wiltshire seems to have started with the restoration of the Westbury horse by Gee in 1778 ... [D]uring a period of seventy or eighty years, the fashion spread, and it is easy to imagine the motives of those farmers, landowners, doctors, parsons, and others responsible – how they must have seen and admired in every case some other white horse elsewhere, and conceived the pleasant idea of enriching their own district in a similar way, perhaps in commemoration of some great event, perhaps for the mere joy of artistic creation and achievement.

– Morris Marples, *White Horses and Hill Figures*

Beneath its rumpled verdure, southern England consists largely of chalk – the crushed, calcium-carbonate detritus of some long hot diluvial summer. In most areas, it lies only a few feet beneath the surface, and on many hill-slopes it peeks out naturally, exposed by landslides. Somewhere, at least a few millennia ago, a human being exposed it creatively, and the practice of cutting hill-figures began.

The Uffington white horse in Oxfordshire is probably the oldest surviving example, and is widely thought to have been made a few hundred years BC. The Long Man of Wilmington and the phallically fantastic Cerne Abbas giant also seem to have a pre-Christian significance. But most of the ancient chalk figures have long been obscured by grass and neglect, and almost all of the ones now on display were made comparatively recently. The white horse between Westbury and Bratton, where Salisbury Plain drops down to the Pewsey Vale, was cut on the site of an earlier horse-figure by a man named Gee, a steward to the then landowner, Lord Abingdon. Gee's work itself was soon improved upon by a series of anonymous locals, and as the historian Morris Marples has suggested, the practice spread: in the next few years, two more white horses were made, at Cherhill and Pewsey, and by the late 1930s another seven had been carved into the nearby hills, all by local artists – the descendants of pagan chalk-cutters and the forerunners, aesthetically speaking, of such modern exterior decorators as Christo and Andy Goldsworthy.

As with any art form, the white horses were something to admire and ponder, and they attracted tourists. Above the Westbury horse there was also an Iron Age camp known as Bratton Castle, and sightseers could walk around the old earthworks to the edge of the hill and look down over the horse and the lovely Vale of Pewsey.

One day in early August 1980, a tourist walked along the earth-works and looked down and saw the white horse and the lovely view, and . . . in a field just below the hill-slope, three strange circles which had been swirled into the grain with a remarkable precision.

The tourist phoned the offices of a nearby weekly newspaper, the Trowbridge-based *Wiltshire Times*, which duly sent a photographer and a reporter to check it out. In the next issue, next to KILLED HIMSELF AFTER A ROW and HI-FI SO LOUD CONVERSATION STOPPED AND KITCHEN SHOOK, there was a photograph of one of the swirls, and an accompanying story:

MYSTERY CIRCLES – RETURN OF THE 'THING'?

The Warminster 'Thing' could be back. Speculation that the UFO, which hundreds of people claimed to have seen in the mid and late 1960s, began again this week after three circular depressions appeared in cornfields near Westbury White Horse.

The depressions have mystified local farmers and tourists to the White Horse, and the Army could come up with no immediate explanation ... Inside the circles, the grain has been flattened, with the stalks all lying in a clockwise direction ...

At first sight they appear to be spots where helicopters have landed, but the circles seem too well-defined and regular to be caused that way. They are all in the middle of fields, with no tracks leading from them.

One farmer told the *Wiltshire Times* on Wednesday, 'I have never seen marks like it before. It certainly cannot be wind or rain damage, because I have seen plenty of that and it is just not that regular.

'If it is not a helicopter, then it is very mysterious,' he added ...

The 'Thing' was an odd name for what had gripped Warminster fifteen years before. Evocative of some Godzilla-like beast from a horror film, it had actually been applied to a wide variety of sounds and shapes and lights which residents of the Wiltshire market town had reported during a series of 'waves' beginning in 1964. According to the stories, there had been zig-zagging orange globes, and white tubes, and roaring black cones, and silent silvery discs, and disembodied humming noises which had knocked birds out of the sky.

The Warminster UFO waves, in terms of numbers and types of sightings, were not substantially different from those which had occurred, or were occurring, in other places around the world. But in Warminster the combination of a mysterious phenomenon, a hospitable town, and a highly mobile 1960s counter-culture made the social impact that much greater. Bohemians, millenarians, and proto-New Agers from Britain and beyond flocked to the town, parts of which seemed to become one big skywatching commune.

To many, the Thing had a mystical aspect, and the strange lights, noises and silvery discs were just as likely to be considered manifestations of some ancient deity, or of some alternate reality – a shimmering astral plane – as they were to be nuts-and-bolts visitors from another planet. And even among the nuts-and-bolts believers there was a growing sense of spiritual mystery. The concept of 'orthotenic lines' – or imaginary lines across the globe which seemed to link certain UFO sightings – had just been introduced through the writings of mainstream UFO researchers Aimé Michel and Jacques Vallée. Orthoteny seemed remarkably similar to the concept of 'ley-lines' – ancient trackways which apparently linked all manner of ancient sites in Britain, from towns to temples to tumuli. Several important ley-lines, it was noted, passed through Cley Hill and Cradle Hill, two popular Warminster skywatching spots.

In any case, the Warminster episode converted young people from all over Britain to belief in the UFO phenomenon, and by the time the craze faded in the late 1970s – well after the end of the Warminster UFO waves themselves – it had given birth to dozens of UFO groups, many of which carried on investigating the sporadic reports that continued to come in.

Thus it was that, the day after the *Wiltshire Times* story appeared, three young men and a woman arrived at John Scull's farm beneath the Westbury white horse, and explained that they were UFO researchers. They went out into the circles, measured them, photographed them, took some samples of soil and cropstalks, and asked Scull and his neighbour Geoff Cooper some questions. When exactly had the circles been found? Had there been any strange lights in the sky? Any strange noises heard? Any disturbances of domestic or farm animals?

It emerged that the first circle had been in one of Cooper's fields of winter wheat, and had appeared some time in May. By the time the *Wiltshire Times* story had run, it had already been harvested. The second circle had been found on the morning of 21 July, and the third on the morning of 31 July. They both were in one of Scull's oatfields. Scull had neither seen nor heard anything, and the same was true of Cooper; but on the night of the 30th, Cooper's housekeeper had heard strange humming sounds coming from the fields, on for twenty minutes, then off for ten, then on for twenty again. And Cooper's dogs had barked all night. The young UFO researchers thanked the farmers for the information and left.

The researchers were Ian Mrzyglod, Mike Seager, Terry Chivers, and Julie Blake, members of a small Bristol-based UFO research group called PROBE. They were amateurs, of course – they all held down jobs during the week – but even so, they took their work quite seriously. They called themselves 'ufologists'. And in fact, although they had had their interest kindled in the later years of the Warminster craze, they were far from being stereotypical flying-saucer cultists. They considered themselves to be fairly sceptical, and liked to cite the statistic that upwards of 90 per cent of UFO sightings could always be explained as shooting stars or planets or aircraft or satellites, or some other well-known natural phenomenon.

In this case they decided to entertain four possibilities regarding the circles: the first, obviously, was that an extraterrestrial spacecraft had done it; the UFO lore included numerous cases in which a flying saucer (meaning usually a glowing blob or disc) had apparently left behind a swirled 'nest' or some other ground marking. The second possibility was helicopters; the third was hoaxers; and the fourth was some kind of meteorological effect – the spiral pattern of the laid crop suggesting to Mrzyglod the swirling flow of a whirlwind.

Mrzyglod and his colleagues tested their four hypotheses as best they could. For the first one, they took the soil and stalk samples to a friend who worked as a technician at Bristol University. The technician laid a Geiger counter on the samples and also performed some spectroscopic analyses. (These for some reason were among the tests preferred by ufologists to establish whether an alien craft had landed.) Nothing unusual was found in the soil or the stalk samples, and there were no differences between samples taken from within the circles and 'control' samples taken from outside the circles. For the second hypothesis, photographs of the circles were sent to the Royal Aeronautical Society for comment. The Society balked at giving an official opinion, but privately advised – just as the Army had advised John Scull – that a helicopter downwash wasn't to blame. For the third hypothesis, Mrzyglod and his friends relied on their own inspection of the circles for signs of hoaxing, and on their interviews with Scull and Cooper. The farmers said they hadn't seen any suspicious trails through the stalks, and there were no clear tractor-paths (or 'tramlines', as the locals called them) along which hoaxers could have easily crept. Moreover, Mrzyglod and his friends had noticed that the laid stalks seemed to be bent at the root, not broken or crushed – as if they had been swept down gently.

Finally there was the meteorological hypothesis, and on this point, Mrzyglod knew just which expert to contact. There was a meteorologist living in Trowbridge, a Dr Terence Meaden, who ran an amateur research organization concerned with tornadoes and other odd weather. A few months previously, a Swindon UFO research group had received a report from an individual who had seen a strange reddish light in the sky at dusk, near the sun. Someone who knew of Meaden's organization had sent the report to him, and Meaden had studied it and had promptly written back, arguing that the UFO was only a mock sun – a reflection of the sun off high-altitude ice particles – because the reported angle between the UFO and the sun had been about twenty-three degrees, which was where mock suns typically appeared. Case closed, as Mrzyglod liked to say. Anyway, this time Mrzyglod sent Meaden a letter, referring to the *Wiltshire Times* story and enclosing his own research results, and asking for comment on the possibility that tornadoes or whirlwinds might have swirled the mysterious circles beneath the Westbury white horse.

The Westbury white horse had been a white speck across the Pewsey Vale, in the view from Terence Meaden's boyhood bedroom window. It was one of those Wiltshire wonders, he says, that had always mesmerized him, calling him towards a life of science.

Meaden was born in 1935, in Trowbridge, and grew up an only child. His mother, who had lost three others in childbirth, naturally doted on him. His father spent most of his time in nearby Bradford-on-Avon, at the auto-repair workshop he owned and managed. Meaden apparently never wanted to follow in his father's footsteps. He enjoyed physics and maths, and archaeology, and astronomy, and ornithology. And when he was about fifteen, he fell deeply in love with meteorology.

This love began, or at least began to manifest itself, when Trowbridge Boys High School decided to acquire an amateur weather station, as a kind of ongoing science project. Someone was needed to keep accurate and regular records of rain-gauge readings, barometer readings, anemometer readings, and so on. Whoever initially had the job made a mess of it, and soon Meaden, then in the fifth form at the school, found himself in charge. Within a year he had another station running at his parents' home, and had begun subscribing to *Weather*, one of the journals of the Royal Meteorological Society.

When university loomed, Meaden was torn between his various interests. He eventually decided on physics, long known as 'the Queen of the Sciences' – a fundamental and broad subject which kept the most career options open. In 1953 he took the entrance exams for Oxford and Cambridge, and was accepted by St Peter's Hall, Oxford (now St Peter's College), matriculating in autumn 1954. St Peter's didn't have the reputation of, say, Balliol or Merton, but it was relatively strong in the sciences, and after three undergraduate years Meaden had done well enough there – an upper second – to gain admission as a doctoral student.

Meaden had kept his interest in meteorology during this period, and had seen to it that his mother maintained his weather station back home in Trowbridge. But in his final undergraduate year he developed an enthusiasm for low-temperature physics, and it was in this area that his doctoral research was concentrated. He worked at the University's Clarendon Laboratory and at the government's Atomic Energy Research facilities in nearby Harwell, under the émigré physicist Kurt Mendelsohn, and wrote a thesis on the cryogenic properties of the heavy metals thorium, uranium, neptunium, and plutonium.

He received his doctorate in 1961, and stayed on for a few years under a postdoctoral fellowship, but by 1963 he felt that he was in a rut. Mendelsohn arranged a place for him in the French centre for low-temperature studies at the University of Grenoble, where he taught classes and worked in a low-temperature metals laboratory run by a Professor Weil. In 1964 he wrote a book for a series Mendelsohn was editing, and married an attractive young woman who had been a secretary at the university. He was beginning to like France. But in 1965 Professor Weil became seriously ill, and the laboratory began to deteriorate. Casting about for academic posts elsewhere, Meaden was eventually offered an assistant professorship at the University of Dalhousie in Nova Scotia, and moved there in early 1967 with his wife and, by now, two young children.

Meaden was given tenure and an associate professorship after a few years, but he soon grew bored of the academic life . . . the lectures and seminars and committee meetings and conferences and thesis supervisions and mind-numbing paperwork. And Nova Scotia was a bit remote, for almost everything except North Atlantic storms. Southern England seemed dry and bright and cosmopolitan by comparison, France a sunny paradise.

For most academics, financial considerations would have been paramount, but by now Meaden's ageing father had given him a substantial portion of the auto-repair workshop. It was a profitable business, and Meaden's share provided enough income to support himself and his family, independent of whatever else he decided to do for a career.

He decided initially to become a consultant. That he had been a university professor, he decided, was a solid credential, and a physicist with verve and imagination and broad interests should be able to find enough clients – engineering firms, oil companies, government agencies – to keep himself busy. Not that he would become too absorbed in a consultancy, for he would also set aside some time to write. He had enjoyed writing the book for Mendelsohn, and felt that there was more where that had come from. Perhaps a textbook on low-temperature physics. Perhaps something lighter – perhaps he would rekindle his interests in archaeology, astronomy, ornithology, meteorology . . .

Meaden and his family moved to the south of France that year, 1973. They rented a place in Nice, on the Riviera. But after a few months, it was clear that Meaden wasn't easily going to find work. The family packed again and moved to Trowbridge.

In England the prospects seemed much better. Not so much for consulting, but for writing. Meaden hadn't been in the country long when he hit upon the idea of writing books on British climatology. He imagined a fifty-book series – *Wiltshire Weather, Hampshire Weather, Oxfordshire Weather,* and so on – that one could buy in ordinary bookstores, like little Baedekers for the weatherwise. He had drafted much of the first volume, on Oxfordshire, when something else occurred to him. In his researches, he was coming across hundreds of fascinating historical anecdotes concerning British tornadoes: cows hoisted atop church steeples, cornstalks driven like nails into tree-trunks, and so on. He realized that he could throw together a few dozen of the stories for a book more quickly than he could finish *Oxfordshire Weather.* So he set aside the Oxfordshire material, and began digging into tornado accounts.

Somehow Meaden never managed to finish the book on tornadoes, nor any of the Baedekers, but even so, he was now completely immersed in meteorology. By the end of 1973, he had become relatively knowledgeable on the subjects of tornadoes and whirlwinds, and was sending in papers regularly to the journal *Weather*. Tornado reports were fairly rare in Britain, and didn't feature heavily in the modern British meteorological literature, but as time went by a few of Meaden's papers were accepted and published. He seemed to have found a niche.

In 1974 Meaden began contacting other amateur meteorologists with similar interests, and before the end of the year he announced the formation of an official group – to pool information on British tornadoes and other strange weather, and to publish it. He decided to call the group the Tornado and Storm Research Organization, or 'TORRO'. Its journal, which he would edit, would be called *The Journal of Meteorology* – *J. Met.*, to aficionados – after a peer-reviewed monthly that had perished in the late fifties, and would feature mostly amateur anecdotes, plus the occasional serious paper by a professional researcher. After the launch in late 1975, *J. Met.*'s subscribership rose to 300 or so, and Meaden, living again in his boyhood home, began to establish himself in a modest way as a scientific authority on the weather. He had, so to speak, come full circle.

Meaden and his family were in France, on their annual holiday, when the letter from Ian Mrzyglod arrived. By the time he returned, a few weeks later, the fields had been harvested and the stubble burnt, and the 'mystery circles' had largely been forgotten.

He read the letter, and the *Wiltshire Times* piece, and went out for a look at the charred fields. By then it was mid September, but the dimensions of the two later circles were still perceptible in the swirled stubble. Meaden wrote back to Mrzyglod and agreed that whirlwinds might have done it. Not tornadoes, which were too rare in England to strike the same place thrice within a few weeks, and left winding trails of destruction – but common whirlwinds, land-devils, minor vortices that originate as updrafts on hot windless days.

Meaden was moderately excited. He could find nothing in the

meteorological literature about such circles, and he was as unfamiliar with stories of 'UFO-nests' as he was dismissive of the UFO phenomenon in general. Mrzyglod could have enlightened him, but didn't. He saw Meaden as an impartial arbiter, a tool of his own ufological investigation. He worried that to acquaint Meaden with UFO-nest stories would be to bias his opinion.

Meaden thus believed that he would be the first to describe the phenomenon. He also felt that he had a strong hypothesis to explain it: checking the meteorological records, he noted that the probable days of formation had been largely hot and windless at Westbury, favourable for the development of thermal updrafts. These in the presence of some wind-shear condition could become whirlwinds, which might be stabilized briefly by a low-pressure pocket in the lee of the steep hill. As for why there seemed to be nothing else in the literature, Meaden had a ready answer: the circles were exceedingly rare. It was only their chance proximity to the tourist-prone Westbury white horse that had brought them to public attention.

Meaden published a report in a subsequent issue of *J. Met.* – 'Mystery Spirals in a Wiltshire Cereal Field' – describing the circles and briefly sketching out his whirlwind theory. Then he sat back and waited.

2

The Vortex

●　●　●

A few weeks after describing the Westbury circles in *J. Met.*, Meaden received a letter from Michael Hunt, a TV weatherman in East Anglia. Hunt reported having seen crop circles in the late 1950s, during frequent train trips through farmland between Yorkshire and London. Hunt was a friend of Meaden's, and a reputable source. Which meant that for Meaden, who remained unaware of the UFO lore, the mysterious circles now seemed to have a past.

But as the summer of 1981 progressed without incident, Meaden began to wonder whether they would have a future. After all, as editor of *J. Met.* he was often sent reports of strange phenomena – from waterspouts to odd-looking clouds to mysterious falls of fish or frogs. *J. Met.* had become almost a meteorological version of *Fortean Times*, the famous journal for anomaly-lovers; and an anomaly was hardly an anomaly if it popped up every day. Meaden might not see another report of circles in his lifetime.

But on 19 August, just before that year's harvest began, three more circles arrived, at a place called Cheesefoot Head.

'Cheesefoot Head', meaning God knows what, is the name of a hilltop a few miles east of Winchester. The A272 roadway snakes past, and tourists can park their cars at a scenic overlook and admire the natural amphitheatre – called 'the Devil's Punchbowl' – just beneath them. It is all farmland, most of it owned by a septuagenarian former naval officer, a Lt.-Commander Henry Bruce.

On the morning of 19 August, a passer-by spotted three clockwise-spiralled circles aligned along one of the tramlines in the middle of the Punchbowl. The first and third circles were each about twenty-five feet in diameter, the middle one about sixty feet. Reporters and photographers from the local papers scurried out to Cheesefoot Head to see the photogenic swirls, and to interview Farmer Bruce. But instead of perplexed head-scratching, Bruce gave them a lecture on the evils of property damage, and how the vandals – 'grown-up children' – were presumably trying to create a flying saucer scare. Another farmer, Giles Rowsell, backed the chopper theory. He told the reporters he'd experienced some similar damage in one of his fields nearby, and had put in a claim for compensation with the RAF.

Meaden, meanwhile, relying again on data from Ian Mrzyglod, stuck with the meteorological vortex theory. He noted that, as with the previous year's circles, the weather conditions around the time of the circles formation had been just right for the development of whirlwinds. Except that this time, the prevailing winds would have put the circles formation not to leeward of the Punchbowl slope, where eddy currents might have been expected to spawn vortices, but to *windward*. Writing in *J. Met.*, he suggested that some kind of windward trap, where the slope obstructed an oncoming frontal system, might have formed and allowed stationary whirlwinds to develop:

> Possibly, moreover, after the life and death of the first whirlwind, the frontal boundary twice advanced some 25 metres before halting and permitting the thermal to re-establish itself as a new whirlwind. We infer that the three damage patterns lay close to one another, not because of chance coincidence, but because of the special position of their site relative to the adjacent hill.

The next year brought more circles, and again they were beneath a hill – this time Warminster's Cley Hill, which in the sixties and seventies had been a favourite haunt of the Thing. Someone had written in to a paranormal enthusiasts' journal, *The Unexplained*, to report one circle; and Mrzyglod and his friends, following it up, had found five more, ranging in diameter from fifteen to sixty feet.

One was slightly oval, suggesting to Mrzyglod a short-lived, slow-moving whirlwind. Nearby farmers told Mrzyglod they agreed with the whirlwind theory, since they had seen stationary whirlwinds appear suddenly on hot windless days and carry tons of new-mown hay into the air. Mrzyglod passed this on to Meaden, who noted in *J. Met.* that the continued 'high frequency of near-circular patterns close to hillsides' appeared to confirm his proposed connection between whirlwinds and hills. He now elaborated his theory slightly, arguing that the sharp divide between laid and standing stalks occurred because 'dry stalks, when bent beyond a critical limit, are irreversibly damaged' – the perimeter representing the line where the inflowing wind velocity had reached this critical limit.

In that summer of 1982, Meaden also saw his first UFO-nest story, when a Scottish subscriber to *J. Met.* sent him an account of a famous old case: it had happened at about nine o'clock in the morning on 19 January 1966 – midsummer in Tully, tropical Queensland, about eighteen degrees below the equator in north-east Australia. A worker on a banana farm, George Pedley, had been driving a tractor past a reed-filled lagoon on a neighbouring sugar-cane farm when he heard a hissing noise. He thought one of his tractor tyres might have sprung a leak, but the hissing noise grew louder and suddenly he saw its origin: rising from behind a clump of trees in the lagoon, about forty yards away, was an oblong shape, silver-grey, and about as big as a bus. To Pedley, the thing looked like two stacked, upside-down saucers. The object hovered over the trees for a few moments, apparently spinning like a top, before jumping up about twenty feet and then soaring off towards the south-west, disappearing into the distance in seconds.

It was a classic UFO close-encounter, except for one thing. Behind the trees in the lagoon, Pedley found an elliptical area about thirty by twenty-five feet, in which the swamp reeds had been swirled clockwise – most of them ripped from their roots. Pedley also noticed an odd smell about the place – a 'sulphur smell', and later the cane farmer who owned the land told him that his dogs had acted strangely that morning. Within another few days, locals had found two more swirled patches in the lagoon, each about ten feet in diameter, one clockwise and the other counter-clockwise. Samples of the reeds from the first patch were taken to Queensland

University for radioactivity tests, which proved negative; nevertheless the 'flying saucer nest' story hit all the big Australian papers.

The Tully case impressed Meaden as further evidence that the crop circles were a recurrent phenomenon, and not merely a one-off by pranksters. Had he explored the UFO literature further, he would have seen that Queensland was by then famous for its waves of UFO sightings and the apparently related nests in swamp reeds and canefields, many of which predated the Tully case. Indeed, the UFO lore was full of reports of strange ground-markings left by UFOs; and though relatively rare, such reports had come in from all over the world.

The only problem, as far as Meaden's theory was concerned, was that UFOs didn't look like whirlwinds. Whirlwinds didn't glow and buzz and flit about hypersonically. But, fortunately for his theory, Meaden had been given an account of the Tully case which contained an error: indicating that the incident had occurred at 9 *p.m.* rather than 9 a.m. This allowed Meaden neatly to turn the Tully UFO into a whirlwind. In *J. Met.* he speculated:

> As for the Australian banana grower at Tully who saw a bluish-grey 'spaceship' rising from a circular flattened reed-bed when he was going home in the evening (tired? poor eyesight?), it seems possible that he was observing a whirlwind rising and then literally 'disappearing into thin air' as it moved off in a south-westerly direction.

Crop circles were, as Meaden confidently put it, 'a mystery no longer'.

In early 1983, Ian Mrzyglod wrote a piece on the circles for *The Unexplained*. He more or less dismissed the idea that alien spacecraft were at work, and pushed Meaden's whirlwind theory instead. Afterwards, a reader from a rural area near Ross-on-Wye, Herefordshire, wrote to the magazine to say that one afternoon back in August 1981, he and his neighbours had briefly heard a mysterious noise 'not unlike an express train'. The next morning, walking his dog, he had found two twenty-five-foot circles swirled into a nearby field of barley. Later he encountered a farmer who said he'd seen the cause of the noise – a whirlwind which had formed over a roadway, had tossed some of the farmer's haybales, and had eventually headed towards a nearby field ... where the circles had been found.

That was just the kind of report Meaden wanted to hear: nice, simple, single circles, with evidence for a thermal vortex connection. Nothing complicated.

But then the summer of 1983 came, and suddenly things did become complicated. It was the year of the quintuplets – big circles surrounded by four 'satellite' circles, just like the 5-side on a die. There was one down in the Punchbowl at Cheesefoot Head, and another beneath Cley Hill at Warminster, and two beneath the white horse at Westbury, and one beneath the ancient hilltop-following Ridgeway, near Wantage in Oxfordshire. There were also a few singletons scattered around Hampshire and Wiltshire, and tracks which seemed to have been made by whirlwinds through a field at Westbury. But of nine major circles 'events' that summer, five were quintuplets. Moreover, on some old photos from 1980, Meaden noticed what looked like symmetrical damage patterns surrounding one of the Westbury circles – as if that one had been a quintuplet, too, albeit an abortive one.

Now, for the Cheesefoot three-in-line circles of 1981, Meaden had proposed three separate whirlwinds forming along an advancing wind-shear zone, almost like bombs dropped from a passing jet. But that kind of explanation obviously wasn't going to cover the quintuplets; he was going to have to expand his theory yet again.

Meaden noted from the meteorological literature on tornadoes and other whirlwinds that satellite vortices had occasionally been seen orbiting the main twister. He suggested that the quintuplets, like the triplet two years before, were the images left by such 'whirlwinds in the multi-vortex state'.

> ... we can at any rate suppose, from the nature of the observed 2-fold and 4-fold symmetry, that all of the circles of the quintuplet formations are linked to one another (through the air of the atmosphere) by a sort of standing-wave system with nodes and anti-nodes ... We suggest therefore that, when a major thermal is sustained in a typical dynamic state which

is quasi-stationary relative to the ground and rotation about it then commences giving birth to a standing whirlwind, then the forces in the general inflowing circulation can be such as to stabilize minor whirlwinds in 2-fold or 4-fold symmetric positions about the major [axis] . . . we predict that the patterns so far observed are simply part of a larger and more general scheme displaying multiple nodes . . . Systems based on 8-fold, 6-fold, or 3-fold symmetry may be found in the future, and also systems in which satellite whirlwinds trace out arcs that link up with the main circle.

It sounded plausible, sort of. But by now Mrzyglod and his friends had virtually given up on the whirlwind theory. The apparent year-by-year jump from singlets to triplets to quintuplets suggested that the formations were being made by intelligent beings – which to them could mean only humans. The key piece of evidence came from Westbury, where the second quintuplet formation, though largely identical to the first, had been shown to be a hoax. Alan and Francis Shepherd, a local farmer and his son, revealed that they had been paid by Robert Maxwell's tabloid, the *Daily Mirror*, to swirl the five circles. On camera, they had measured out the circles with a pole and rope, had indicated the angles for the satellites with a compass, and had swirled the crops down with a heavy chain. The entire operation, from measuring out the circles to swirling them, had taken the two men twenty-four minutes. The *Mirror*'s idea had been to tempt their rival, the *Daily Express*, into running a story on the fake formation, and then to run a 'gotcha' story on the *Express*'s blunder. But the *Express*, though it raved over other formations, somehow ignored the Shepherds' handiwork, and the eager farmers eventually leaked word of their feat to the local press.

There were also the hoaxing trails. Since the *Wiltshire Times* story on the 1980 circles, virtually every commentator had remarked upon the absence of such trails, insisting that every circle lay pristine in its respective field. But in the summer of 1983 Bob Rickard, the editor of *Fortean Times*, sent Mrzyglod a newspaper photo of the first Westbury quintuplet, the one the Shepherds claimed to have copied theirs from. In the photo, a thin ring was obviously visible outside the central circle, running in an arc from satellite to satellite – as if one hoaxer had been at the centre of the main circle, holding one end of a piece of string, and another hoaxer had been out in the wheat holding the other end, using it to guide him in the radial spacing of the satellites. In fact, that was exactly how the Shepherds had made their quintuplet – which also had a faint ring joining the four satellite circles.

The Shepherds' quintuplet at Westbury, assumed Mrzyglod, was only a one-time prank; he doubted that the farmer and his son would have vandalized anyone else's property. But it seemed clear to him that the same basic mechanism, the human being, was probably at work in other circles. And if humans had made some of them, then humans could have made all of them.

That summer, the hoaxing theory appeared here and there in the press, in various forms. One of the Wiltshire papers reported the Shepherds' stunt, and another expressed the opinion that the quintuplet near Wantage was a man-made copy of the ones further south. But few wrote off the phenomenon entirely. The evidence so far was inconclusive, and it was just too good a story for editors to throw away.

Meaden, for one, was sure that the circles were genuine. He shrugged off Mrzyglod's defection, believing that he now had fairly solid eyewitness accounts – the Ross-on-Wye case, and the Tully case – plus Michael Hunt's report of circles from the 1950s. Moreover, the circles that had appeared in the summers of 1980–83 had all done so beneath hills, precisely in accordance with his theory.

Even so, in the media frenzy over the 1983 quintuplets, Meaden was largely absent. It wasn't that he disdained to lower himself into the fray – on the contrary, he was regularly contacting reporters to tell them about his theory. It was just that he wasn't really the kind of authority the press – at least the national press – were looking for. If a reporter wanted a meteorological expert, he could always call the UK Meteorological Office. In fact, for a story about the Westbury quintuplets, the *Daily Star* had talked both to Meaden and to the Met Office, and although Meaden had obviously been working on the problem longer, only the Met Office had received mention in the story:

The five flat patches look as if a heavy object, supported by four legs, dropped into the field at Westbury, Wiltshire. But yesterday at the Met Office in Bracknell, Berks, a weather expert said it was all hot air. He explained: 'A bare patch in a cornfield will heat up to a higher temperature than the surrounding corn and send a column of hot air up to 200 feet in the air. The hot air is then caught by a breeze and it begins to spin, causing a small local whirlwind that flattens the corn.'

Another authority the press turned to for crop circles stories was the British UFO Research Association. With about 500 members, BUFORA was the largest such group in Britain, and like Mrzyglod's PROBE and other affiliates, it considered itself the representative of the conservative, semi-sceptical, scientific wing of British ufology. BUFORA's Director of Investigations was a former science teacher named Jenny Randles. She had contacted both Meaden and Mrzyglod on the circles issue in the summer of 1980, and Meaden's arguments had convinced her that whirlwinds were to blame, not alien spacecraft. She had already published a few UFO books, and tabloid reporters often called her for comments on oddball stories, so when the national media got involved after the quintuplets of 1983, she embarked upon what she would later call 'a crusade against this stupid idea that the circles were caused by landing spaceships'.

Her crusade started out well enough. The *Daily Star* reporter who phoned her up for the Westbury quintuplet story expected her to back the flying-saucer theory. But she gave him an earful of the whirlwind theory, and suggested he talk to Mrzyglod, Meaden, and Bracknell. In the end, the *Star* decided to skip the UFO invasion theme, and to ridicule it instead with the headline, 'IT's ALL HOT AIR'.

The *Daily Express* was less cooperative. They gave Randles a long interview, but her comments wound up on a back page, half-hidden among the eccentric speculations of the Earl of Clancarty, chairman of the House of Lords' All-Party UFO Study Group.

In fact, the *Express* and many similar papers wasted no time in whipping up UFO hysteria. At the level of tabloid journalism, editors loved UFO-type stories, as they loved anything that was unusual, shocking, horrific, apocalyptic. One had only to consider

Orson Welles's famous *War of the Worlds* radio broadcast, which for an evening in 1938 had induced the very deepest shivers in hundreds of thousands of ordinary citizens. And those shivers had been touched off by nothing more than the human voice. The crop circles were a visual phenomenon, and thus had an even more immediate impact. It also helped that Steven Spielberg's blockbuster film *E.T.* was playing in the cinemas, in that hot summer of 1983.

'Has E.T. responded to public demand and made an unannounced flying visit?' asked the *Daily Express* on its 11 July front page. The eleventh of July was a Monday, and the *Express* ran something on the 'white holes' of Wiltshire and Hampshire every day that week. A picture of E.T. himself was usually featured somewhere nearby. On the Friday, the *Express* ran a piece by columnist Jean Rook, who had spent an afternoon in the first Westbury quintuplet and had emerged to gush about her experience. 'So what in the name of Heaven . . . made that, if it wasn't a four-legged spaceship?'

The summer of 1983 had been one of the hottest in centuries. The summer of 1984 was wetter and cooler, more English. Meaden heard reports of only three quintuplets – from Alfriston in Sussex, from Cley Hill outside Warminster, and from a farm near Cheesefoot Head. Four singlets were also reported, from Bratton, Trowbridge, Marlborough, and Vienne in southern France.

The Alfriston quintuplet occurred in a field near the country cottage of the shadow Foreign Secretary, Denis Healey. Healey photographed the formation for the *Daily Mail* and told their reporter, 'I am the last person to believe in UFOs, but trying to find a rational solution to this problem is a bit difficult. I'm totally baffled.' His wife apparently had seen a strange light in the sky the night before. Meaden decided from Healey's photographs that the formation was genuine, although the BUFORA investigator for Sussex, Philip Taylor, pointed out suspiciously that the formation had occurred beneath a hill with the same name – 'Cradle Hill' – as a famous UFO skywatching spot in Warminster.

The Cheesefoot Head quintuplet was also noteworthy because it had only been discovered by several farm managers inspecting their crops by helicopter. It wasn't easily visible except from the air, a fact which seemed to rule out a hoax. It also wasn't to windward or to leeward of a hill – it was on top of one. Which forced Meaden to expand his theory again:

> [I]n some way local vorticity in the air mass triggered the whirlwind. Such vorticity could have been engendered by a sea-breeze front ... It does ... now appear that whirlwind patterns, in crops or grass, may form on almost any terrain, provided that the necessary meteorological stimuli are present. Doubtless, more would be found on open terrain if suitable vantage points were available.

The 1984 circles, though undoubtedly valuable in reinforcing the impression of a continuous phenomenon, were nevertheless overshadowed by two eyewitness cases that Meaden came across. The first was from Arthur Shuttlewood, a local journalist who had made a small fortune writing books about the Warminster Thing. In an interview with a short-lived magazine, *Now!*, just after the first circles had been found at Westbury in 1980, Shuttlewood described a circle he had seen swirled near Warminster a few years before.

> One evening there were about 50 of us skywatching along the Salisbury Road. Suddenly the grass began to sway before our eyes and laid itself flat in a clockwise spiral, just like the opening of a lady's fan. A perfect circle was completed in less than half a minute, all the time accompanied by a high-pitched humming sound. It was still there the next day.

And then there was the Melvyn Bell case. Bell was a beefy, amiable Wiltshireman, a motor mechanic who happened to work part-time at Meaden's garage. One afternoon in the summer of 1984, Bell was in the garage office for a moment and Meaden, who knew that Bell often went horseback riding in the countryside, casually asked him if he had ever seen any crop circles from his horse. As a matter of fact, said Bell, he had seen one – the previous summer, at Lavington. He hadn't considered it anything special. He'd seen the stories in the papers about flying saucers, but he knew it was only whirlwinds that did it. At least, the one at Lavington had been made by a whirlwind. He'd seen it happen: it had been about half past seven in the evening, after a calm and sunny August day. He and his wife had been out riding along the ridge of a hill, at the northern edge of Salisbury Plain. He had noticed something out of the corner of his eye, something moving in a field below them – a little whirlwind, like the dust-devils one sees in a supermarket car-park on a hot day, picking up sweet wrappers and ragged plastic bags and so on, only this one was carrying dust and loose wheatstalks up into the air.

'Hey, look at that,' he said to his wife, but she, riding the horse in front, didn't hear him, or was looking at something else. Anyway it didn't seem important, and it was over in a few seconds, without any noise as far as he could tell, though it was a good quarter of a mile away. Later he guessed that the circle had been about fifteen or twenty feet in diameter. But he had never gone down into it. It just hadn't seemed important.

Meaden wanted to hug the man. The story confirmed everything he'd been saying. Nothing could shake him now from the view that the circles were swirled by whirlwinds – 'sunset whirlwinds', he now decided to call them, since they all seemed to happen at dusk.

Nineteen eighty-five brought another comparatively damp, cool summer. Quintuplets were found at Cley Hill and Fonthill Bishop near Warminster, at the white horse near Westbury, at Gander Down and Charlton Woods near Winchester, and at Goodworth Clatford, south of Andover. Another set appeared in Sussex, this time near Findon, west of Brighton: a farmer and a gamekeeper were out for their morning chores at 6 a.m. when they saw what appeared to be a cloud of steam above a nearby field. Approaching the field, the farmer noticed what he later described to the *Daily Express* as 'a hazy mist from the centre circle, smoky, dewy, coming up from the ground, almost as a series of fountains. There were no signs of anyone walking through the field. I am convinced it was not a man-made thing.' Several locals later claimed to have seen, a few days previously, a pulsating yellow light hovering near the field, then shooting off at an incredible speed.

Other odd reports came in from around the globe. A French correspondent sent Meaden an account from 1963 of a circle in a spinach patch at St-Souplet. A Spanish correspondent sent a report from 1935 of a spherical vortex which roared and glowed. And Bob Rickard of *Fortean Times* passed on a report from a timber grower in Wisconsin who had recently found a circular area in his neighbour's forest, about 90 feet across, in which the trees had been bent low or snapped near the bottom of their trunks. Such stories continued to strengthen Meaden's conviction that the circles were genuine, and in that summer of 1985, although he was also helping to manage the auto-repair workshop and (at long last, as a consultant) was writing a report for the government on tornado risk at nuclear power plants, he made frequent visits to circles-prone areas, recording the details of anything he found – dimensions, probable time of formation, weather conditions at formation, proximity to hills, and so on. His contacts with journalists increased, and the press paid him increasing attention. In the local papers, on local television, in the London tabloids, his quotes began to mingle with those of Jenny Randles, and Bracknell spokesmen, and other authorities – although in the fields, it seemed, he remained alone.

3

The Delgado Effect

In the late 1970s, in a small house, in a small town near Winchester, lived a retired gentleman named Pat Delgado. He was tall and bespectacled, and wore a faint grey pencil moustache, and he seemed to have a trace of something foreign in his accent – perhaps Spanish, or perhaps a bit of Australian, for Australia was where he had spent much of his career, working on the Woomera Tracking Range in the 1960s, in the deserts north of Adelaide, helping to maintain large radar antennae for ballistic missile tests and several of the Gemini, Apollo, and Mariner missions.

Earlier in his career he had helped to invent an automatic tea-making machine, and later, a dissolved oxygen meter for nuclear power plant cooling systems. Indeed, he thought of himself above all as a designer; he was always coming up with an idea for some new device. Now, retired and with time on his hands, he spent long hours developing ideas for his latest project: an efficient power-generating windmill.

One day in August 1978, he was working on a miniature windmill he'd built to study a vertical-axis design. It was a paper cut-out, propped by a needle, with the needle anchored in a heavy base. As he pondered some problem or other and awaited inspiration, he rested his hand near it, unconsciously curling his hand around the needle, beneath the little paper rotor ... And the rotor began to spin.

He moved his hand away, and the rotor slowed and stopped. He put his hand next to it again, and it started up again. He took it away and it stopped again. Then he put his other hand next to it. Now it began spinning in the opposite direction. He tried different materials for the rotors: tissue paper, parcel paper, notecard paper, kitchen foil, plastic. All but plastics were susceptible to the effect – the Delgado Effect, he decided to call it.

To eliminate the possibility that the Delgado Effect was merely due to warm air rising up from his hand and exerting uneven pressure on the rotor, he experimented with a little aluminium foil cap from a milk bottle, smoothing it into what he believed would be a convection-resistant dome shape. It rotated at 35 r.p.m. when he cupped his hand beneath it. Next he tried putting both hands round the little foil cap and needle set-up, and the rotor didn't seem to know which way to turn, as if the forces from his hands were in opposition. Then he put both hands together on one side and . . . 60 r.p.m. The force had doubled.

Months of tinkering and experimenting went by. Little paper and aluminium rotors lay everywhere. Delgado believed that he was definitely on to something. A new kind of energy, which emanated from the body. Without one of his hands cupped around it, the little foil windmill would stop spinning every time. And it had polarity to it. His left hand made the little rotor spin clockwise, the right hand anti-clockwise. It seemed as if it was something that radiated outwards from the body, and cupping one's hand might . . . curve the field of energy, so that one was generating a kind of vortex.

He had a sense, though, that things didn't end there. He suspected that the energy might radiate from other things: the earth, the air . . . So that his body was merely a collector. Perhaps other materials could be used as collectors. He cut some strips of cardboard, and curved them around the rotor, and . . . the little rotor began to drift around at 3 or 4 r.p.m. It wasn't much, but it was definitely spinning. Cardboard was a collector. Which meant that cheap, clean, unlimited energy had become a very real possibility.

Within a short time Delgado had dug a hole in his backyard, a foot and a half on each side, and about eight inches deep. Inside it a tin-foil rotor balanced on a needle, with two cardboard collectors curved round the needle, so that the entire apparatus looked like a stylized S. He put a plate of glass over it, sealed the edges of the glass with dirt, and watched it go ... slowly ... drifting ... 0.25 r.p.m. ... for a full day and night ... before it gradually stopped.

He scraped the dirt away and lifted the glass and found that two cobwebs had tethered the foil rotor to its base. He cleared them away and it started off at a good 0.25 r.p.m. clip, but then the cobwebs got it again. The third time a spider or some other insect knocked the rotor off-centre. The fourth time a slug climbed up and pulled the whole rotor down. The fifth time ... the little rotor reached 0.28 r.p.m., and ran for a whole week. Delgado would go out to check it every so often, to note the r.p.m.s. Sometimes he would get out of bed in the middle of the night, and putting on his slippers and his bathrobe and an overcoat, would go out into the backyard and note the r.p.m.s. And afterwards he would linger to watch the thing ... rotating ... slowly ... Day or night it was relaxing, soothing, just to watch the little rotor turn on its own.

Eventually he constructed a larger hole in his backyard, bug-proofing it and draught-proofing it, and letting it run forever, in perpetual motion. And after a while he noticed that the r.p.m. count would suddenly jump up at around dawn, then gradually dip down to the original level, drop further at dusk, and then return to the middle level until dawn again. It was obviously some kind of energy emanating out of the earth, with its own circadian rhythm, its daily pulse, as if the earth were one gigantic organism.

Delgado believed that the cheap-and-clean power prospects were just the beginning of his discovery. This energy, this omnipresent earth-energy, could possibly explain a lot of hitherto inexplicable phenomena: such as dowsing, telepathy, ghosts, poltergeists, and spiritual mediumship. It promised a revolution in science. Though of course not immediately. His investigations would take time to bear fruit ...

One afternoon in the summer of 1981, almost exactly three years after his discovery, Delgado was playing a round of golf at Alresford Golf Club. A couple of occasional golfing partners, who knew of his interest in things unexplained, happened to mention to him the crop circles triplet over at Cheesefoot Head. What did he make of it? In fact, he hadn't heard of it, but a few days later he drove out for a look.

He first saw the formation on a Saturday. On Monday he started phoning the TV stations. On Tuesday the first story on the circles ran, on ITV, and on Friday two more stories appeared, in the *Hampshire Chronicle* and the *Southern Evening Echo*. None of the stories mentioned Delgado, and yet it occurred to him that . . . *he* had caused these stories to happen, to be researched, recorded, written, filmed.

Delgado sat down and wrote a short account of the triplet in the Punchbowl and the reaction to it by the locals. He took particular pains to note that he had alerted the press to the story. He stayed away from committing himself too strongly to any one theory, but it was obvious where his sympathies lay. Besides noting the sharp symmetry of the formation, and the absence of any hoaxers' trails, he pointed out that Cheesefoot Head and the sites of several other reported circles lay mysteriously in a straight line, and that Cheesefoot Head was not far from where a locally-famous UFO close-encounter had been reported in 1976. He suspected that the circles were the result not merely of Delgado Effect earth energy – but of Delgado Effect earth energy being manipulated, in some fashion, by some kind of unknown intelligence, probably extra-terrestrial. He sent his account in to *Flying Saucer Review*.

Gordon Creighton, the editor of *Flying Saucer Review*, read the report, phoned Delgado with some questions, and published it the following spring. The response was impressive – old stories of 'UFO-nests' flooded in, including the Tully case which *Flying Saucer Review* had written about in the 1960s. In the summer of 1983, when the quintuplets appeared, Delgado sent in a second report, again emphasizing his media-notification activities, and hinting that the phenomenon was not of this earth. He noted especially that quintuplets had appeared near Winchester, Westbury, and Wantage:

> . . . these three locations form an equilateral triangle on a map. (Is it purely coincidental that all three place-names, Winchester, Westbury, and Wantage, commence with a 'W'?)

The circles had by now begun to occupy Delgado's thoughts almost as much as the Delgado Effect had. Almost every day he would go out driving around Cheesefoot Head, to see if any new circles had arrived. If they had, he would photograph them and note their dimensions – most often from a distance, but occasionally from within the formation itself. Sometimes he would be accompanied by Chris Wood, a *Daily Express* photographer, or Omar Fowler, a ufologist from the Surrey Investigational Group on Aerial Phenomena, and one of the few dozen 'consultants' to *Flying Saucer Review*. But usually he worked alone, and as the years went by, the newspapers, radio networks, and television stations began to turn to him for quotes. *Flying Saucer Review* added him to the ranks of their consultants. He was sixty-five years old, and yet . . .

The last quintuplet of 1985 appeared in a wheatfield at a place called Goodworth Clatford, a little village south of Andover in Hampshire. Busty Taylor, a small-plane pilot out for a jaunt with friends, discovered it as he flew over on approach to a nearby airfield. He made a few passes, then landed and got hold of a video camera, and since one of his friends was a helicopter pilot, they all went up again in a helicopter and hovered a few hundred feet above the formation, while Taylor videotaped it. After landing again, Taylor telephoned the local *Andover Advertiser*, which soon announced:

THE GREAT ANDOVER FLYING SAUCER MYSTERY

There were no obvious hoaxers' trails in the field. In fact, Taylor told the *Advertiser*, 'The circles are so neat that it looks as though something has punched them out of the corn . . . I've never seen anything like it before.'

Which was not to say that the circles didn't vaguely evoke an ancient memory. In fact, when he later became a circles celebrity Taylor would describe that first quintuplet at Goodworth as 'something I recognized but couldn't place'.

Born during the Second World War, Taylor had been christened Frederick Charles. But his mother ran the cinema ticket office at an Army base near Salisbury, and when she was on duty, baby Fred's pram would be parked by the window. The soldiers would feed him sweets as they queued for tickets, and when he consequently began to fatten up, they nicknamed him 'Busty'. Now in 1985 he was only about five foot six, and of medium build, but the name still seemed apt, somehow – for beneath the hard carapace of his class, there was something else . . . a sense of infinite possibility . . . a biblical grandeur . . . which could bust into even the most commonplace communication. 'I could take a car apart and put it back together again in a few days,' he once told me, by way of describing his early skill with machines.

Mostly he had handled agricultural machines, though, working 'the grain side and the beef side' as a young farmhand. In the sixties, he quit the farm life, became a driving instructor in Andover, got married, and settled down in a little house to raise a family. And he decided that he wanted to fly. Not for a living, but as an avocation, a recreation, a soul-filler – for there was something about being up in the sky, free, busted loose from the myriad bonds of earth, looking down on all the tiny hills and dales and rills and houses, and indistinct people. He bought a cheap hang-glider kit, sweated over the plans and built it, and on the sixth attempt became airborne – only to meet the side of a hill at fifty miles an hour. He broke one of his legs in three places, and cracked four or five vertebrae. He was about a month in hospital. After that he decided to graduate to fully-powered flight. He scrimped and saved again, took the courses, and within a few years had his regular pilot's licence. On weekends he would often hire a single-engine plane out of a small airfield near his home in Andover, just to take her up and meander around, up above the rest of the world.

Taylor also had an interest in archaeology, and occasionally when he went flying he would look for crop marks – patterns of discoloration in a ripe grain field, which could give away the presence of buried structures. Wiltshire and Hampshire had made up the bulk of the kingdom of Wessex, and the two counties were riddled with ancient sites, many of which still waited to be unearthed. Whenever Taylor happened across anything of interest, he would report it to local archaeologists, and often would check back to see what they'd made of it.

The Goodworth quintuplet was not an archaeological crop mark, however. Taylor could see that the formation had been swirled by some descending force. He wondered whether UFOs could be involved. UFOs had been another hobby of his; he had seen several in his life – never anything with this kind of quintuplet pattern, but enough to take seriously the possibility of, say, a descending aerial machine with four legs and a central pod.

Something within the formation itself also seemed unearthly. When he first entered the quintuplet, with a reporter from the *Advertiser*, he noticed a white, jelly-like goo at the centre of the main circle. As he neared it, it began to play havoc with his mucous membranes. 'It gave me stinging sinuses, and eyes,' he remembers. 'I also suffered a terrific head cold within a matter of hours ... It was one of the worst head colds I've ever had in my life.'

In the wake of the *Advertiser*'s coverage, Taylor had been contacted about the circle by Pat Delgado and Omar Fowler. Fowler took some samples of the jelly-like substance to two nearby laboratories. One lab, at the University of Surrey, noted a high starch content and a smell of honey and suggested that the stuff was 'some kind of confectionery which had gone off'. The other lab noted soil bacteria and 'coliform organisms'. But neither lab really knew what it was, and the results were deemed 'inconclusive'.

Taylor wasn't particularly worried over that. If the substance wasn't of terrestrial origin, one shouldn't expect a terrestrial laboratory to come up with the answer right away. In any case, Taylor spent August and September flying around Wessex – over Stonehenge, Avebury, Winchester, Cheesefoot Head – trying to find new circles in the waning season, trying to figure it all out. He noticed, for example, that an average-sized crop circle would fit within the dimensions of Stonehenge. So would Bronze Age round barrows, also known as tumuli. Fowler and others introduced him to the concept of ley-lines, which seemed to connect various ancient and sacred sites. And he began to notice what had eluded him at first: that the quintuplets looked like Celtic cross patterns.

These clues all seemed to come together in a bright Eureka flash. 'I was dancing up and down,' he remembers. 'I couldn't sleep. I went to museums – the Salisbury museum, the London museums.' He brought Pat Delgado and Omar Fowler down to Stonehenge to explain his theory, and they seemed to agree with him ... that Stonehenge, and the tumuli, and Celtic crosses, and somehow the crop circles, were all artistic representations of the same ancient and recurrent phenomenon – UFOs.

*

Colin Andrews lived in Andover, too, and worked as the communications officer for the Technical Services department of the Test Valley Borough Council. Still only in his late thirties, he enjoyed tinkering with electronics and radios and gadgetry, and seemed to have, like Taylor and Delgado, a restless interest in anomalous phenomena. On the night of Saturday, 6 July 1985, Andrews happened to hear on his home VHF scanner a police report of a UFO sighting by an elderly couple driving on the A272 at Stockbridge Down near Winchester. He jumped in his car and drove to the site, and watched the police searching the downs with torches. They found nothing, but some time later he managed to track down the couple that had seen the UFO. They described the thing to him as a big yellow-white 'funfair wheel' hovering over the downs, a few hundred yards away from them.

The sighting occurred a day after a quintuplet had been found at nearby Gander Down, and four weeks before the Goodworth quintuplet. Andrews in retrospect believed that there might be a connection. He wrote an article for *Flying Saucer Review* (for which he was made a consultant) describing the sighting, and in the article he drew a little map, noting that the sighting lay more or less on a straight line from Goodworth Clatford to Gander Down.

Andrews was still unknown on the circles scene at the end of that summer, and thus didn't receive an invitation to Pat Delgado's first meeting of circles enthusiasts, held on a Saturday in October at the Arlebury Park Sports Centre near his home in Alresford. About a dozen people attended, including Busty Taylor, Omar Fowler, a ufologist colleague of Fowler's named Paul Whitehead, a farmworker named Martin Payne and his wife Petronella, and a Lt.-Col. Edgecombe from a nearby Army Air Corps base.

Delgado presided, and began by mentioning some recent Canadian cases of circles in grass. He also suggested that the apparent recentness of the circles phenomenon might only be an illusion created by increased reporting; he gave an example from a Hampshire district called Cheriton Woods, where, a friend had told him, farmers for some superstitious reason kept silent about the circles.

Delgado argued that hoaxing was probably impossible. He suggested that the pole-and-chain method – the presumed hoaxing technique – would require enormously heavy chains, and would cause obvious damage. Meaden's whirlwind theory was brought up, but Delgado dismissed it, noting the impossible complexity of the quintuplets, and the fact that whirlwinds he'd seen in the Australian desert never stood still. Someone explained how electromagnetic fields from alien craft might have swirled the crops flat. Someone else said that psychokinesis might be responsible. Paul Whitehead described a theory of parallel universes, and how the circles could have been swirled by rising columns of earth energy. Omar Fowler discussed the jelly-like substance and the lab tests. Lt.-Col Edgecombe argued that any hoaxers would have left tracks in the wheat, and there clearly were no such tracks. The Colonel's air-crews, who liked a mystery as much as anyone, were showing increasing interest in the formations, and the Colonel himself was sending a report to the UFO Investigation desk at the MoD. Delgado noted that Westbury, Stonehenge, Goodworth Clatford, Alresford, and Findon . . . all lay along a straight line.

Towards the end of the meeting, a motion was proposed, which said, in effect: the circles are a genuine phenomenon, not a hoax.

The Ayes had it.

4

Critical Mass

Paul Fuller's call to ufology occurred at the age of seven, when he saw a UFO in the sky from his bedroom window. When he was eighteen he joined BUFORA, and a few years later became a local investigator for the organization in Hampshire, where he lived and worked as a statistician for the County Council. Fuller was thin, with a sparse brown beard, and he lived in a small flat in Romsey amid piles of UFO reports which he collected and investigated – to such a distracting extent that the circles phenomenon largely passed him by during those early years. It was only when Pat Delgado unexpectedly invited him to the Alresford meeting in October of 1985 that he became involved at all. But by the summer of 1986 he had become one of the major figures of crop circles research, fielding reports of new circles, investigating them with Meaden, commenting on them in the press, and acting as a liaison to the subject for the Cheshire-based Jenny Randles, with whom he soon was writing a short BUFORA press-briefing booklet, 'Mystery of the Circles'.

Fuller and Randles kicked off publication of the booklet that July with a news conference in a hired lecture room at the London Business School. Only one or two tabloid reporters turned up, but a few dozen circles enthusiasts attended, and the conference served to bring Meaden, Delgado, Fuller, and Randles together for the first time. They all gave short talks or slide-presentations, and the atmosphere was cordial, with a particular respect being paid to the ex-professor Meaden, who had been professorially reluctant to appear in public with people who believed in UFOs.

Colin Andrews had somehow heard about the meeting, and he attended, sitting inconspicuously at the back. A few days later he phoned Meaden, introducing himself and remarking on a circle with a counter-flowing outer ring that Meaden had mentioned at the conference. He'd just been to see it beneath the Westbury white horse, he said, and it was nice, though it wasn't as impressive as the first ringed circles, at Cheesefoot Head. Meaden agreed. They chatted some more about the circles and the things they'd seen, and agreed to keep in touch, and a few days after that, Andrews phoned Meaden again to tell him about a strange new circle out at Headbourne Worthy, a village north of Winchester. Until then all circles had been swirled clockwise, but this one at Headbourne Worthy had reportedly been swirled anti-clockwise. Meaden and Andrews went out to investigate, and eventually wrote up their findings in back-to-back articles in Meaden's *J. Met.* Andrews also passed to Meaden a number of reports from Hampshire farmers and from his own relatives, describing simple circles from 1936–40 and 1982, and an apparent quintuplet from 1978. Andrews seemed thrilled to collaborate with the ex-professor, and for his part Meaden was glad to have assistance from someone with Andrews's energy and resourcefulness.

At the same time, Busty Taylor was regularly flying over circles-prone areas, often with Pat Delgado in the co-pilot's seat and Don Tuersley sitting behind them. Tuersley was a kindly, grey-bearded sign painter who had been a devoted skywatcher during the days of the Warminster Thing. A back injury early in 1986 had forced him into retirement and freed him for circles research.

Soon Andrews and Meaden and Fuller joined Delgado, Taylor and Tuersley, and for the first time the major circles researchers were all working together. 'If a circle appeared,' recalls Fuller, 'either Delgado would find out, through his network of friends, or Meaden would find out, and they'd just swap info. In those early years, I'd do the same.' They would all drive over to the new circle, or perhaps overfly it with Busty Taylor, and take measurements and photographs and note the swirl patterns and any unusual features or witnessed events. It helped that, despite their different views on what caused the phenomenon, they were still engaged in the same basic investigatory activities – measuring, photographing, diagramming, interviewing – so that Delgado could make sense of data collected by Meaden, and vice versa. It was an efficient way to work, and the men also enjoyed having someone else to talk to about the phenomenon. For the most part, their wives had already become bored with the subject.

The ideological strains within the alliance soon became apparent, however, as 1986 brought a bumper harvest of crop formations and media attention. Fuller and Randles argued in their 'Mystery of the Circles' booklet that flying-saucer believers were 'fanatics', with 'no theoretical justification'. Delgado and Andrews were less antagonistic in their public statements, but merely by pronouncing their beliefs they posed a threat to the others – more so than vice versa because their beliefs were less orthodox. Delgado and Andrews were in a sense honoured to work with a former professor of physics, whereas Meaden, sensitive to the loss of his academic authority, had reservations about working with people whom his former physicist colleagues might have dismissed as cranks.

In that summer of 1986, Delgado told the *Southern Evening Echo* that he favoured as an explanation for the circles 'some electromagnetic power, either from the earth or the atmosphere, reacting in some way with the wheat'. He told the *Winchester Extra*: 'We have ruled out whirlwinds and a helicopter's downwash and we have ruled out hoaxing in many cases because of the impossible position of the circles. Some are only accessible by aeroplane. It has nothing to do with sink holes or anything conventional. The whole thing is unconventional and does not conform to any known science. It is possibly an unknown force field manifested in an unknown manner by an unknown intelligence . . . We should not be so arrogant as to try to explain this mystery with only the forces we know today.' And according to the *Hampshire Chronicle*, 'the favourite and most likely theory of local expert Mr Pat Delgado is that the circles are formed by an 'iuff' or an invisible unknown force field. This he believes is in the form of a vertical rotating force field, from either below the ground or above it, which creates unexplained activity similar to that caused by poltergeists.'

In his report of the year's events for *Flying Saucer Review*, Delgado went even further: 'UFO's could be manipulating *Earth-Forces* to create these circles with such clean precision. This same precision may be responsible for the animal mutilations.'* He went on to describe an unusual formation he had seen one day in August, while flying over Cheesefoot Head: 'Busty Taylor and I were very surprised to see words had been formed in the same field that contained the three circles. The words were joined up and appeared thus: WEARENOTALONE ... The shape of the letter N in ALONE was formed backwards ... *I am undecided about this creation. At first sight it was an obvious hoax, but prolonged study makes me wonder.*'

Andrews's unorthodoxy was also becoming explicit, if not in statements to the press, then in a series of claimed unusual experiences. When they met for the first time at Headbourne Worthy, Andrews told Meaden, 'Just five minutes before you got here, I saw something strange. It was like a silver spot in the sky, moving along ... It went into a cloud. I watched and watched but it didn't come out.'

'Well,' Meaden remembers responding, 'it sounds as if it could have been a high-flying aircraft, on its approach to Heathrow.'

'You *might* say that,' replied Andrews. 'But it might also have been ... a UFO.'

And Andrews's subsequent commentary on the Headbourne Worthy circles in *J. Met.*, despite its dutiful profession of the core belief he shared with Meaden ('*we are not looking at a hoax*'), had a subversive hint of gleaming, spinning metal about it:

For many weeks I had been troubled by what I had seen ...
The whole structure appeared to be formed as if by two
separate plates rotating anti-clockwise, and, while in motion,
oscillating in a spiral-like wave-form.

---

*Although not otherwise linked to the circles phenomenon, animal mutilations were a prominent element of UFO lore. A typical case would involve farm animals which had died for no obvious reason, or were apparently deliberately mutilated in some odd way. One fairly typical report from Wales described several dozen sheep whose bodies, when discovered, each had a single hole near the neck, about an inch in diameter.

Then there was the Wantage poltergeist incident. It began with an unusual crop formation that had been swirled that summer near Wantage in Oxfordshire. It was more or less an ordinary ringed circle, but jutting from the outer, anti-clockwise swirled ring was a twenty-foot spur of laid stalks, terminating in a kind of arrowhead shape. Within the arrowhead lay a bare cylindrical hole in the dirt, about nine inches deep and a foot in diameter.

The formation was discovered in late July by the farmer who owned the land, James Matthews, but no one told the circles network about it until early September. Delgado was notified, but couldn't go at once, and so Taylor and Andrews went out for a look. By that time, the field where the circle lay had already been harvested, but the two were able to interview Farmer Matthews, who reported that the police had come and taken measurements and that some of his farmer friends had come and taken some photographs. No one had seen or heard anything in connection with the thing being made, but Farmer Matthews gave his opinion that the hole had been excavated with some kind of tool.

Andrews scooped a sample of dirt from the hole, brought it home, and deposited it in what he would later describe as 'an office specially prepared for this research', in a little wooden shed in his backyard. Andrews had wired the shed with motion sensors, heat sensors, and for some reason even a microwave detector. In fact, according to an account Andrews gave later, his modest little property on the quiet outskirts of Andover was virtually a fortress, in which not only the office, but the house and 'the perimeter' had 'very intricate burglar alarm systems'. Tuersley remembers it being 'like Fort Knox – barbed wire on the gate, all sorts of alarms and lights'.

But alas, Andrews's electronic fortress was no match for the demon that inhabited that sample of dirt from Wantage. Busty Taylor recalls Andrews phoning him the morning after their visit to Wantage. 'He rang up here panicking, about twenty past seven, wondering what the hell was going on at his house. He had all these strange things happening, all these sophisticated burglar alarm systems going off, and he couldn't understand it. He was worried about it.'

What had happened, according to the account Andrews published later, was this:

I locked the office door and set the alarms. Minutes later an infra-red detector had sensed movement inside the office and activated one of the alarms . . .

At 4.15 the following morning another alarm sounded. This time it was the system protecting the perimeter. I found a time clock, which is mains voltage operated, had stopped at 4.15 a.m. and was now faulty. I found no cause for this, but the next day the clock was working again. Again, several nights later, it stopped working at 4.15 a.m. And the office alarm, which is separate from the perimeter system, was also sounding, and had been activated at 4.15 a.m. My wife guarded the side door to the house as I walked to the office and unlocked the door. A microwave detector had been activated and the battery-operated wall clock had stopped at 4.15 a.m.

After further occurrences around the house in the following weeks, my wife suggested I end my research work. She is not interested in the paranormal or the fringes of science, but even she thought that some entity appeared to be behind these events which might be connected with the mysterious circles.

In public, Andrews never mentioned why these strange events seemed to cluster at 4.15, but according to colleagues familiar with the episode, there was a significance to the number which was particularly disturbing to Andrews. It seems that to go out to Wantage to examine the formation, he had left work early, without official permission. He had been out in the field, taking the sample from the strange cylindrical hole, when suddenly he had felt a pang of guilt for not being back at the office. He had glanced at his watch: 4.15.

5

Flash, Crackle, Knock

One time when no one else was listening, Delgado said to Tuersley:
'I had a letter the other day, addressed to The Circles Man at
Alresford, and . . . it got to me: *The Circles Man . . .*'

Tuersley knew what he meant. Delgado would often relate such
stories, and even if he would chuckle simultaneously in gentle self-
deprecation, his anxious message shone through: he liked being
Number One on the circles scene, and wanted to stay that way.

Delgado could not have been too worried about Tuersley, whose
manner was always deferential. Nor did he seem particularly
concerned about the amiable Busty Taylor. Delgado's primary
concern, as quickly became obvious, was Colin Andrews.

The conflict was partly ideological. Delgado believed that alien
intelligences, perhaps parked out of sight in earth orbit, were
remotely controlling Delgado Effect energies to make the circles.
Andrews was certain the effect was more direct. 'There is an aerial
component,' he would insist grimly. And Delgado would shake his
head and reiterate the importance of the Delgado Effect and earth-
energy, and how the remote manipulation of such force fields
would surely lie within the grasp of any star-travelling race. And
Andrews would respond by cataloguing the UFO sightings which
appeared to be linked to the circles, and so on, back and forth – and
occasionally the arguments became heated. Tuersley remembers
they once had 'quite a tiff', with Delgado heaving the Delgado
Effect around and Andrews hurling back aerial components.

Of course this would probably have amounted only to a minor disagreement, a friendly difference of opinion, had there not been beneath it a much more fundamental tension. This tension became apparent for the first time when Andrews invited the others over to his house, one afternoon in the summer of 1986. He guided them in past the perimeter wire, then through the house, through the backyard, and into the backyard shed, where he kept his office. 'He had the maps and coloured pins,' remembers Tuersley. 'He had a computer and all the equipment to go with it, and I think it rather shook Pat – how Colin had got organized, how he was really going for it. I could see the look on Pat's face. It was going to slip away from him.'

Andrews's energy, moreover, extended beyond matters technical and scientific, for in that first season of his he had managed to have two significant paranormal experiences – the UFO in the cloud at Headbourne Worthy, and the poltergeist in the clump of dirt from Wantage. The poltergeist incident had brought Andrews an enviable amount of attention from his colleagues, and had even attracted the interest of Archie Roy, the chair of the Astronomy faculty at Glasgow and a prominent member of the Society for Psychical Research – a relatively reputable group that looked into parapsychology, spiritualism and other occult phenomena. According to Andrews, Roy had agreed with him that 'no rational explanation' could be found for the incident.

In any case, by the end of the summer of 1986 Delgado was obviously concerned about the upstart newcomer. According to Tuersley, if Delgado and Andrews and the rest of them were busy inspecting a new circle, and a reporter happened along, Delgado would often hustle over to the reporter and announce his credentials, saying something like: 'I'm Pat Delgado. I'm the one who brought this phenomenon to the world.'

His colleagues also noticed that, as the summer wore on, Delgado became a good deal less willing to share information, frequently neglecting to mention to the others, say, reports of circles he had received from correspondents who had come across his name in the media. Indeed, for Delgado information had begun to acquire a certain proprietary value.

This should have provided a clue not only to Delgado's anxiety, but to his growing ambition, although he soon made that ambition clear enough in a letter – accompanying that year's crop circles report – to Gordon Creighton of *Flying Saucer Review*: 'Naturally I could have written many reams more about all the complexities of the various configurations that we have found. Maybe I'll save it all for a book.'

The idea of a book seemed to hang in the air that summer of 1987, and whatever lay behind the circles phenomenon seemed to be aware of it. Not only were the circles much more numerous that season, but ... very odd things began to happen in the fields: strange flashes, crackles, knocks, roars, balls of light, which would later serve to make a book on circles much more interesting than it otherwise would have been.

In early June, at South Wonston in Hampshire, at a beautiful circle in a field of yellow-flowered oilseed rape, Colin Andrews and his father were taking some measurements, while his mother sat in the car nearby. Andrews suddenly saw a bright flash. He turned to his father, who had simultaneously heard a loud crackling noise. In the car, his mother Elsie had heard it too.

Similar phenomena attended a formation in a field at Kimpton, beneath the approach to Thruxton Airport near Andover. The formation was just a clean ring, without an inner circle, and it seemed to have been formed on 13 June, the same night that a local teenager claimed to have seen an orange glowing object hovering in the vicinity. A few elderly villagers also said they'd heard strange 'warbling, humming-like noises' in the area around the same time. A few weeks later Andrews was within the ring, dictating his observations into a tape recorder, when suddenly – as he recounted later in the best-selling book, *Circular Evidence* – he experienced a 'black flash'.

I flinched and for a fraction of a second the sun was blotted out. At once I looked up into the sky. There was nothing in front of the sun.

That afternoon, Andrews brought the family dog into the field. Apparently Gordon Creighton of *Flying Saucer Review* had suggested some sort of canary-in-a-coal-mine experiment, using animals to detect any residual energies in the circles. The experiment was a success. Andrews's father coaxed the poor animal along the tramlines into the centre of the ring, and 'within minutes it was vomiting and became quite ill'. They took the dog home, and it returned to normal.

Andrews came back for more that evening, walking into the field near the ring and praying silently: 'God, if you would only give me a clue as to how these are created.' And at that moment, an 'electrical crackling noise' erupted from about ten feet away. It quickly grew louder, until Andrews was ready to turn and run. But somehow he forced himself to remain still, and after a few seconds, the noise ceased.

The noise returned on 4 July, when Andrews was visiting a circle at Dog-leg Field on Longwood Estate, across the A272 from Cheesefoot Head. This time the crackling seemed to emanate from the heads of the standing wheat. It sounded like a static electric discharge – but pulsating, and gradually fading away.

On 5 July, he put a tape recorder into the circle at Dog-leg Field and let it record for forty-five minutes. He took the tape home and listened to it. For about thirty minutes, he heard only a light background hiss and a slight hum, and the oceanic sounds of passing cars. Then 'a peculiar roaring sound of fairly low frequency' started up, grew louder, and faded. It happened three times. He returned to the field several days later to repeat the experiment, but heard nothing unusual.

On 6 July, Andrews and Delgado took Archie Roy and one of Roy's psychic friends, Helen Tennant, out to see the circle at Dog-leg Field. According to Andrews's later account, the energies were so strong that Tennant refused to go near the centre. Afterwards, Andrews tried to play back a tape he had made of a conversation with Roy and Tennant. But . . . the tape was blank.

The circle at Dog-leg Field seemed to play havoc with other kinds of equipment. While loading film into his camera one day, standing just outside the circle, Andrews heard his film winder jam. He opened the back and found that the shutter curtains had 'buckled' irreparably. At the same time, Busty Taylor's video camera seemed mysteriously to expire – although after a few minutes it somehow revived.

On 9 July, Martin Payne and his wife Petronella reportedly saw a row of bright lights hovering over the Punchbowl at Cheesefoot Head. On 28 July, Delgado and Andrews were measuring a pair of circles beneath the Westbury white horse when the compass they were using suddenly began to spin wildly for a moment. On 3 August, Delgado and Andrews were at Westbury again, and Andrews placed his tape recorder in the centre of a circle, recording ambient sounds for ninety minutes. When he listened to the tape a few months later, he noticed 'a peculiar knocking . . . similar to a wooden box being tapped' – and also similar to a 'loud knock' they both heard, unaided by tape recorders, in the same field on 8 August.

To make things even stranger, a photograph taken at the same site and at about the same time shows Delgado, standing at the edge of a circle, and a small white object near the centre. In the photo published in *Circular Evidence*, the object looks remarkably like a piece of paper, or a notebook, but when Andrews examined the image he saw a 'disc-shaped object, bright white in colour and with well-defined edges'. He could find 'no rational explanation' for it.

Nor could Andrews find any rational explanation for the black darts of Chilcomb. Chilcomb, near Winchester, was the site of a big single circle that appeared in mid August. Whatever had made it had come down hard, because the stalks were splayed outwards, explosively, as much as they were swirled. There were no flashes or crackles or knocks around the Chilcomb circle, but a few weeks later, Andrews was looking at some photos Busty Taylor had taken of the formation when he noted that 'on one of the prints were what looked like two black ribbon darts, similar to the head of the forked spear usually associated with the devil. One was clearly focused, but the second was blurred as if by rapid movement.' Andrews says he consulted experts, who ruled out foreign objects in the camera or on the lens.

Late in August, just before the harvest, Busty Taylor was flying with his son Nigel, Terence Meaden, and Meaden's daughter Isabel over Salisbury Plain when they spied a new group of circles – one ringed, three ordinary – in a field next to the busy A303 roadway near Winterbourne Stoke. They landed, drove out to the site, made their measurements, returned home, and eventually reported their discovery to Delgado and Andrews, who might have simply buried the report in their files for ever had not a very unusual incident occurred eight weeks later. At about five o'clock in the afternoon on 22 October, a British Harrier jet took off from a base in Surrey, on a routine flight heading west. The plane had only been airborne for a few minutes when radio contact was suddenly lost. Other aircraft along the flight path were alerted, and eventually, somewhere over the Irish Sea, a US transport plane made visual contact. The American crew noted that the Harrier's cockpit canopy, and its pilot, were missing. The Harrier finally ran out of fuel and went down in the Atlantic.

'For some reason which I cannot explain,' Andrews wrote later, 'I had a strong inner feeling that the finding of the pilot might in some way be associated with the phenomenon of the circles. And I had that feeling even before I heard where the accident had happened.'

The pilot's body was found the next day, next to his reserve parachute and life-raft, in a field near Winterbourne Stoke, a few hundred yards from where the group of circles had appeared two months before.

Andrews felt strongly enough about the possible connection to write to the RAF: 'What I feel to be significant is that this very field in which four circles were recently found lies directly below the area in Space where it seems that this pilot was taken out of his £13.5 million pounds' worth of Jet-fighter.' Andrews also wrote an article about the incident for *Flying Saucer Review* – his byline bulging with the unusual professional suffix of 'MASEE, AILE'. The headline of the article read:

THE LOST HARRIER JET AND THE CORNFIELD RINGS: EXCLUSIVE!

That month, Andrews phoned up the others – Delgado, Taylor, Tuersley, and even Meaden – with some particularly bad news. A total stranger had written him a letter, the essence of which was that this person wanted to write a book about the circles, and would Colin and the rest of them please turn over their information to him to facilitate his research.

The five of them met at Andrews's house to talk it over. Obviously they weren't going to write someone else's book for them, said Andrews. 'We'd have to be daft.' And most likely this wouldn't be the first such request they would receive from someone trying to cash in on the phenomenon. Andrews proposed that they write their own book, before someone else came along and beat them to it. Andrews offered to do much of the writing.

Delgado, who hadn't yet got his own plans off the ground, said that he liked the idea of a book, and also offered to do some of the writing. Taylor, too, was enthusiastic about the project, but backed away from committing to a big writing load. He promised to contribute some of his photos to the book, and perhaps a page or two of text besides. Tuersley said he didn't mind not being one of the authors, but still wanted to continue as a member of the research team.

When it was Meaden's turn to give his opinion, he explained that he had been working on a book for several years already. It had been more or less a secret, but now he felt it was only right that they should know where he stood. They did, and although Meaden would continue to stay in touch with all of them, officially he was no longer a member of the group.

Andrews must have regarded this outcome with some satisfaction. In the space of a year, he had risen to the top of the circles fraternity. He had become co-author on a book, he had a published article to his credit, he had become a consultant to *Flying Saucer Review*, and by extending his network of press contacts, he was becoming almost as well known for circles expertise as Delgado. Meanwhile Taylor and Tuersley had been effectively neutralized as possible literary adversaries. Meaden was still a problem, but he had been edged out of the group, and it seemed clear that whatever he would write would be aimed at a relatively small audience of fellow scientists.

The rules of the game had been drawn, and Andrews knew them better than anyone. Finding out about circles first, measuring and photographing them before they became marred and trampled by tourists, interviewing potential eyewitnesses, experiencing associated paranormal events – these had become the goals. Andrews had even set up a hotline scheme that summer of 1987, in which the five of them, Meaden included, had worn telephone pagers (provided gratis by Andrews, the Borough Council communications man) so that whenever a report of a circle came in, they would all be notified. The system had required a central operator who would man the hotline and call all five pager numbers whenever a report came in. Andrews's father had been the central operator.

After the decision to write a book, Andrews was also the driving force behind the official formation of Circles Phenomenon Research, or CPR. Meaden had TORRO, Andrews explained to the others, and a big acronymic name like that provided a certain amount of legitimacy – particularly if one planned to be an author. In fact, Meaden was increasingly being referred to in the press as: 'Dr Terence Meaden of TORRO'. It would be nice if the rest of them could be: 'Mr Colin Andrews of CPR', and 'Mr Pat Delgado of CPR', and so on. So CPR was formed, comprising just the four of them – Andrews, Delgado, Taylor, and Tuersley – and eventually they even had official notepaper with an official CPR logo: a stylized quintuplet formation.

Of course, throughout all of this, as the circles phenomenon grew in intensity and apparent strangeness, other researchers were drawn in, and inevitably they wanted to join Andrews and Delgado and the others at the centre of things. The first such applicant was George Wingfield, from Somerset. Wingfield had a handsome, long-nosed, square-jawed, patrician look to him, and his accent was unmistakably upper-class. His house was his 'hice'. He had been at Eton, and then at Trinity College, Dublin, where – after a year's rustication for planting a smoke bomb at a college debate – he'd received a broad BA degree in Natural Sciences. Afterwards he had worked at an observatory in Sussex for a while, had married a nice girl from a good family, and then had settled down to town and country life, commuting between his big house in Somerset and his office in Bristol, where he worked as a systems analyst for IBM. He was roughly the same age as Andrews and Taylor, and despite the obvious class differences, shared with them a general curiosity about UFOs and the paranormal, a sense that there was something else out there . . .

One day in August of 1987, Wingfield took his wife and two teenage boys out to see the new double-ringer beneath the Westbury white horse. As it happened, Andrews and Delgado and Taylor and Meaden were in a circle nearby, measuring and photographing and looking at swirl patterns. Wingfield recognized Andrews and came over, and tried to strike up a conversation. Andrews was polite but terse, and after a few minutes Wingfield and his family left. After a while, Andrews and the others moved over to the double-ringed circle, which was just below the white horse. They began photographing and measuring and checking out the swirl patterns –

'Oh God, not again,' Meaden remembers someone groaning. They all looked up to see Wingfield and his wife and two sons coming down the path from the white horse towards them. But in a minute or two, Andrews and the others were listening raptly while Wingfield and his wife, Gloria, told them what had just happened.

They had been up on the ridge, over the white horse, looking down at the double-ringer, and they had seen the four of them in the circle and had decided to go down to inspect the circle up close, and to ask Delgado and Andrews a few more questions. Wingfield and his sons had started hurrying down the path from the top of the hill, and Gloria had followed, but soon had fallen behind. The path was steep, and rocky in places. She felt uneasy . . . and then –

Flash-Flash . . . She was seeing flashes on the ground . . . Flash-Flash . . . Pulsating. Throbbing blue. Flash-Flash . . . They seemed to reflect off something on the ground, or something low to the ground . . . Flash-Flash . . . Something invisible –

Then suddenly the flashes ceased, and Gloria hurried to catch up with the rest of them.

Now Gloria and George stood in the double-ringer telling Andrews and Delgado and Taylor and Meaden the story. Meaden listened quietly, remembering that there had been a narrow break in the clouds to the west of them, and the sun had suddenly and brilliantly come through it and he had taken some photographs with the brief period of good light before the sun had gone back behind the clouds, and George and Gloria and their boys had come running down.

Meaden's scepticism notwithstanding, the event proved to be George Wingfield's entrée with Delgado and Andrews, and he kept in touch with them as the summer continued, exchanging information and anecdotes. One day in September of that year, he visited

Andrews, who showed him the black dart photos from Chilcomb. Wingfield remarked that he had seen similar marks on photographs of circles at Bratton. Sharing an anecdote like this was a classic way to build up a working relationship, but when Andrews asked to see the photo, Wingfield couldn't find it. According to Andrews in *Circular Evidence*, Wingfield phoned and told him, 'I don't have a print with those marks on. I'm usually very methodical and have a good memory. But I've checked all my prints and negatives and they don't show the black darts. I was so disturbed by this that I checked with my son. He didn't know what I was talking about. I'm beginning to doubt my sanity and can only conclude I dreamt this.'

But oddly enough, the event did help to forge closer ties between the two – because apparently Andrews interpreted it as just another example of the paranormal incidents that were plaguing them all. Delgado too had once claimed to have similar marks on his photos, but after checking, hadn't been able to find them . . .

It wasn't long before Wingfield indicated that he wanted to work on a more or less formal basis with Delgado and Andrews – to join the club, so to speak. It was true that he was based down in Somerset, which was a long way from the centre of things at Cheesefoot Head, but then he was closer than they were to Westbury and Warminster, where many other things were happening. He had the energy, he had money, he had connections, he could write –

Andrews headed him off easily. Just before he convened the meeting to discuss writing the book, he sent Wingfield a letter, thanking him for his interest in the circles phenomenon, and leaving open the door to continued cooperation on an informal basis, but, in effect, refusing him membership in the club.

Next at the door was Richard Andrews. A former farmer, seed-breeder, and government crop inspector, he was pushing sixty, and a few years before had suffered a major heart attack, but he looked vigorous enough; he was tall and muscular, with biceps that stretched the sleeves of his polo shirts. And he was brimming with enthusiasm for the circles. He had something to offer the group, too. For he was a dowser.

To most people, the word 'dowsing' probably evokes a forked birch branch, quivering when its bearer passes over a buried water source. The idea of it is vaguely mystical, but in the British Isles, at least, it has managed to acquire a certain down-to-earth authenticity – for dowsers have been credited with discovering many if not most of the wells in the country. There is even a British Society of Dowsers, which takes itself very seriously.

The techniques of dowsing can differ dramatically from dowser to dowser, involving variously birch branches, pieces of coat-hanger wire, special metal rods, crystal pendulums, or just bare feet or hands. But there are two main schools of thought on the subject. One holds that a direct physical force – presumably electrical or magnetic, or both – acts upon the dowsing tool, strongly enough to be sensed by its wielder. The force either emanates from the thing being dowsed, or the thing being dowsed somehow alters the local electric or geomagnetic field and the change is sensed as a change in force on the tool. The other school believes that the thing being dowsed can somehow effect neurological changes, which then cause subconscious muscle contractions, which in turn can be amplified by a combination of good concentration and a sensitive indicator – such as rods resting in your hands, or a rotating pendulum.

The first school's approach is thought of as somehow more traditional, more orthodox, but at the same time its underlying assumptions have never been confirmed – no one has ever conclusively linked dowsing to electric or magnetic fields. The second school, which more or less avoids the problem of mechanism, has been embraced by most New Age dowsers, who like it especially because it doesn't restrict them to finding water. In fact, proponents of this school believe that they can find anything – water, oil, gold, lost car keys, even spiritual infirmity. By forming an image of the thing in one's mind, by *asking for it*, one extrasensorily connects with the aura or the field of the thing . . . Many dowsers take the logical next step, and don't ever bother traipsing around fields; they simply use maps, and suspend tiny dowsing rods over them, or more usually a pendulum, and then concentrate their minds and start to ask for whatever they seek . . . And in principle, by this method, they should be able to discover, say, the location of all of the world's untapped oil fields – from the comfort of their living-rooms. No one yet claims to have done this, but many dowsing aficionados swear it's possible, and legend has it that the famous psychic Uri Geller has made a lot of money map-dowsing mineral deposits for big companies.

In the past decade or so, dowsers have begun to look for earth-energy, a feature of the environment which is said to have been discovered and rediscovered not only by seekers after the *perpetuum mobile*, such as Delgado, but by many ancient cultures. The Druids are said to have built temples around it. The Buddhists are supposed to have represented it by their omnipresent serpent-figure, Kundalini. The Chinese are said to have recognized it in their mysterious science of *feng-shui*, in which yin and yang currents of earth-energy are mapped out, built around, harnessed, harmonized.

As the dowsers see it, earth-energy flows around or inheres in the landscape. It usually flows underground but is also usually detectable, by dowsers at any rate, above the surface. What kind of energy it is no one seems to know, but it is said to be real enough to cause headaches, or nausea, or euphoria, or just about any kind of pain or pleasure. It is said to be associated often with 'sacred sites' such as stone circles and tumuli* and holy wells and the churches that the Christians built over pagan shrines. Thus earth-energy has also come to be associated with, and in fact is often confused with, the invisible straight lines – 'ley-lines' – that are believed to criss-cross the landscape.

In modern Britain the ley-line concept came first, being developed by a Herefordshire businessman, Alfred Watkins, in the 1920s. Watkins's popular book, *The Old Straight Track*, illustrated some of the networks that seemed to exist across the English landscape, apparently indicating relatively mundane things such as trading routes. He called the lines ley-lines because many of the towns along the routes had the suffix '-ley'.

But the etymology of '-ley' is said to show links to 'light', which of course is a manifestation of energy. In the sixties and seventies, British counter-culture writers such as John Michell rediscovered Watkins's work, and the ley-line concept began to be incorporated

---

*Busty Taylor once explained to me: 'Tumuli are built like batteries, so that if you drop water on 'em, they will run with electrical charge. And if you stand on 'em when it's been raining, and you've got a lot of teeth fillings, it'll make your teeth ache.'

into the growing neo-pagan, neo-New Age worldview. Michell, for example, without wholeheartedly embracing the earth-energy connection, saw the lines as integral parts in a 'sacred landscape'.

At the same time,* he and others were noting the apparent links between ley-lines and UFO sightings. Warminster lay along several of the apparent lines, and so did the sites of many UFO encounters around Stonehenge in Wiltshire, and Winchester in Hampshire. The ley-lines began to be seen as some sort of beacon for incoming extraterrestrials. Other writers began to suggest associations between ley-lines and haunted houses, or between ley-lines and geologic faults. The concept of earth-energy, when it was developed by dowsers and other fringe-science writers in the seventies and eighties, seemed to tie it all together.

Crop circles, too, seemed to fit into the picture. A well-known ley-line near Winchester was known to run through Danebury long barrow, a tumulus, Woodbury Ring, a crossroads, several more tumuli, and ... the Devil's Punchbowl beneath Cheesefoot Head. And of course the Warminster circles were all on or around ley-associated sites such as Cley Hill.

Thus, the circles hadn't been around long when the dowsers began to get involved. Soon they were detecting residual energies within the crop circles. Some dowsers would detect rings of energy spreading like ripples from a circle's centre, and some would detect spikes of energy flowing outward radially, and some would detect both. Often a local ley-line would cross through the centre. But almost invariably the dowsers detected something.

Richard Andrews would go out with Colin and Pat and Busty and Don, and sometimes Terence, and he would dowse the circles they visited and he would map out all of the energy rings and lines, and perhaps link them with nearby ley-lines. The rest of them were fascinated. Even Meaden was impressed, and tried his hand occasionally. Before long, Richard Andrews was encouraging Pat and Colin to adopt him into the group, to let him in on things. Not that he wanted to make the size of the group unwieldy. In fact, he wanted to shrink the group, to make it more efficient: for instance, he

---

*And while Jacques Vallée and Aimé Michel were developing the related concept of 'orthoteny', as mentioned earlier.

suggested that Busty and Don could be . . . shifted to the sidelines . . . kept in reserve . . .

Pat and Colin shrugged him off, and afterwards he came to Busty and talked about the phenomenon and how important it was for mankind, and so on and so forth. But Busty had been warned by Pat and Colin, and soon Richard was talking to Don.

Don and his wife Peggy remember the day Richard visited them at their home near Winchester. They had coffee and talked and talked about the phenomenon and its wider significance . . . Richard used what the others had begun to call his 'vicar's voice', a low, earnest, pious voice; yet seductive, even hypnotic. Anyway, he talked and talked, about the energies, and the planet, and mankind's treatment of the planet, and finally he worked himself around to the point. He paused, looking intently at Don and Peggy, and said. 'There's a lot of money in this.'

'I think he expected us to jump up and down,' remembers Peggy. 'But we didn't.'

And although Richard Andrews would continue to court the Tuersleys, and Busty Taylor, and Delgado and Andrews, the door of CPR was for ever closed to him.

6

The Pregnant Goddess

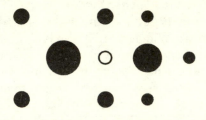

As his Majestie departed from Avbury to overtake the Queen, he cast his eie on Silbury Hill about a mile off: which he had the curiositie to see, and walked up to the top of it, with the Duke of Yorke.

– John Aubrey, Monumenta Britannica

Silbury Hill is a large grassy mound that lies beside the A4 roadway, a few miles west of Marlborough in north Wiltshire. Built in sturdy layers of chalk and dirt and stone, and radio-carbon dated to roughly 2500 BC, it covers more than five acres and is said to be the largest man-made prehistoric mound in Europe.

There is no obvious reason why it is there, but there are theories. One is that it is a burial mound, a Wessex pyramid, a king-sized version of the tumuli that dot the countryside. The seventeenth-century antiquarian John Aubrey noted that 'The countrey folk doe call it Zelbury Hill, and tell a story that it was rayzed over King Zel's grave.' More modern local legends tell of a buried solid-gold statue of a king on horseback, or of the glowing ghost of King Zel, or Zil, or Sil, who supposedly rides around the base of the hill on certain nights. But the burial-mound idea has its flaws: the round barrows of the surrounding countryside all date to the Iron Age, which began at least 500 years after the hill was raised. And major excavations in 1776, 1849, and 1967, plus a radar-like electrical resistivity survey in 1959, have uncovered no evidence of ancient human remains or Tut-like treasures. The 1967 survey, which was sponsored by BBC-2 TV, generated a certain amount of excitement when it unearthed a kind of pot from the heart of the hill; but the object turned out to be only a time capsule from the 1849 dig, containing among other things a leaflet advertising a Bible Society meeting.

Another theory suggests that the hill was built as a beacon or a fortress, but that seems unlikely, since it squats on low, wet ground in the Kennet river valley, and its peak, 130 feet above its base, remains well below the surrounding hills. Other theories suggest that the hill is an astronomical observatory; or a giant sundial meant to cast its shadow on the broad flat fields immediately to its north; or some kind of temple, possibly related to the stone circle a mile to the north, at Avebury. But the theory that seems to excite most New Age writers on the subject, if not professional archaeologists, is that Silbury Hill is a giant female fertility symbol, a pregnant belly – a monument to the ubiquitous 'Great Goddess' of early agrarian societies. 'The key to the Silbury Hill treasure,' wrote Michael Dames in a 1976 book, *The Silbury Treasure*, 'is the neolithic age of the monument, and the key to the Neolithic Age is the Great Goddess. From her womb, and from her eye, came Neolithic common sense.'

And much more, according to Hamish Miller and Paul Broadhurst, who in their classic earth-energy dowsing book, *The Sun and the Serpent*, argue not only that Silbury was a goddess-figure ('Silbury is, of course, a goddess image without comparison, its enormous rounded form projecting from the gentle curves of an otherwise rolling landscape') but also that she sat astride one of the hot currents of earth-energy associated with the 'St Michael line' – a famous ley-line which supposedly runs from Penzance in Cornwall, through the hilltop tor at Glastonbury, through Avebury, past Wantage in Oxfordshire, and on out through East Anglia into the North Sea, along the way hitting a remarkably high number of churches and other sites named after St Michael.

By the late 1980s, Silbury Hill had become a kind of New Age mecca. It was associated with Goddess symbolism, earth-energy, and ley-lines; and a wealth of other sacred, energy-imbued sites lay within a short driving distance: Avebury, the West Kennett long barrow, the East Kennett long barrow, the Stone Avenue, the Sanctuary, Swallowhead Springs, half a dozen chalk white horses, and of course tumuli as far as the eye could see. Only crop circles were needed to complete the picture.

On the night of 18 July 1988, a young woman named Mary Freeman dined with a friend at Winterbourne Monkton, a town a few miles north of Avebury. Shortly after 11 p.m., according to the story, she left for her flat in Marlborough. She drove south along the A361 and then, at Avebury, turned south-east on to the Stone Avenue passing about a half-mile east of Silbury Hill. It was a moonless night, and overcast, and in any case, the glow that suddenly appeared in the base of a cloud to her right seemed much brighter than even a full moon could have been. It was golden-yellow, a huge warm spot of light on the underside of the cloud, and as she watched, it emitted a white beam – an energy beam, she thought – at an odd angle towards the ground. Towards Silbury Hill.

Actually, it looked to her as if it had come down some way beyond Silbury Hill, to the south of it. She couldn't tell precisely, because the hill itself was obscured from view. But she could tell that the beam was tubular, and that it was as wide as a football pitch. As she watched the thing, a surge of energy seemed to pass through her little Renault, and several items jumped out on to her lap from the dashboard. Somehow the beam remained illuminated long enough for her to turn on to the A4 and head west, for a closer look. But the road dipped behind some trees, and by the time Mary Freeman regained a clear line of sight, the energy beam had gone.

Mary immediately contacted Isabelle Kingston, a middle-aged woman who lived in the nearby village of Ogbourne St Andrew. Isabelle Kingston was a medium and a channeller. Some years before, in the wake of a divorce, she had been directed by the spirit world to move to the Avebury area. She had been told to wait for a sign. So she moved to the area with her mother and son and set up spiritual shop, performing psychic readings for people, for modest fees, and gleaning truths about the future in general. Often, to better commune with her spirit guides, she would climb Silbury Hill and, seated at the summit, slip into a trance, as a small group of friends watched respectfully. Among these friends were usually several young people from the area, men and women in their twenties who were interested in matters spiritual and the coming New Age. Mary Freeman, it seems, was one of them.

Mary Freeman explained to Isabelle what she had seen. She knew that Isabelle had been waiting for a sign, and she felt sure that . . . this was it.

Isabelle thought so, too, but to be sure, she consulted her spirit guides. To her surprise, they explained to her that this was not the sign, but that the true sign would arrive very soon.

It arrived a day later, on the morning of Friday the 20th, in the form of a giant crop circle quintuplet in a wheatfield across the A4 from Silbury Hill. Three of the satellites had been swirled clockwise, the fourth anti-clockwise.* Within a few days, another quintuplet appeared at Firs Farm at Beckhampton, a mile to the west.

Richard Martin, a reporter for the local weekly newspaper, the *Marlborough Times*, lived in a flat beneath Mary Freeman's on Marlborough High Street, and mentioned to Mary the story he was writing about the crop circles at Silbury Hill. Apparently unaware of the circles, she reacted with astonishment and told Martin about her sighting of the energy beam. Martin's story about the energy beam and the circles ran in the next edition, on the front page – STRANGE SIGHTING AT SILBURY HILL – and soon the Silbury area was crawling with tourists and circles-researchers.

Colin Andrews and Busty Taylor were among the first to arrive, and they immediately went to work measuring and photographing and examining the swirl patterns. Andrews sensed a change in the

---

*Perhaps a hint of the mystical 3 + 1 motif, which according to Jung is often associated with quintuplet or 'quincunx' patterns, as an (unconscious) symbol of the complementarity within wholeness. In his book *Flying Saucers* Jung wrote: '[The quincunx] is a symbol of the *quinta essentia*, which is identical to the Philosopher's Stone. It is the circle divided into four with the centre or the divinity extended in four directions, or the four functions of consciousness with their unitary substrate, the self . . . The [3 + 1] motif appears . . . in the four gospels (three synoptic, one 'Gnostic') and in the four Persons of Christian metaphysics: the Trinity and the devil. The 3 + 1 structure . . . runs all through alchemy and was attributed to Maria the Copt or Jewess.'

phenomenon. The Cheesefoot Head and Westbury areas were still going strong, with eleven circles so far that summer. But now suddenly this new area around Silbury Hill was active. Something was going on. 'These things are rising at one hell of a rate,' he told Richard Martin. He refrained from asserting that spaceships had done it, but according to Martin's story in the *Marlborough Times*, 'Mr Andrews said that some sort of aerial component is responsible.'

The aerial component idea, of course, had always irked Delgado. And George Wingfield wasn't happy with it, either. How, wondered Wingfield, could some solid object have landed? The quintuplet across from Silbury Hill lay beneath several 11,000-volt power lines, and the local Electricity Board insisted that there had been no outages in the area during the period when the quintuplet had been formed. Wingfield's thinking in general was much closer to Delgado's. The way he saw it, there probably had been a build-up of energies in the ground, almost certainly under some kind of intelligent control ... building up and building up, until suddenly the circle had been swirled – with a terrific release of pent-up energy, so that Mary Freeman's beam of light might have been going *up*, not down. Alternatively, the beam might have been some kind of control beam from a spaceship in the cloud, initiating the build-up of energy in the ground, which would explain the day's gap between the sighting of the beam and the arrival of the quintuplet.

In any case, Wingfield was excited about it. He took his wife and his sons out to see the quintuplets at Silbury and Beckhampton, and they walked around and took pictures. They were driving home down the A361 towards Devizes when one of Wingfield's sons spotted a third quintuplet – missing a satellite, apparently – tucked between two groups of tumuli on North Down, spot on the St Michael ley-line.

On 26 July a fourth quintuplet appeared, this time in the same field as the first. Colin Andrews was there again with Busty Taylor, and again they set about taking measurements and photographs and studying swirl patterns, and the tourists stopped to gape, and helicopters and small planes filled with press photographers swooped overhead, and it was generally a fine day, although there was one sour note. Andrews and Taylor discovered small ...

shoe-prints . . . running between the seedlines from the main circle to two of the satellite circles.

'It might be that someone is playing around,' Andrews confided to the *Marlborough Times*. 'There is always the danger that someone will do this.'

And brows began to furrow. Even Taylor started to think the sudden rash of circles at the Silbury circles scene might be the work of pranksters. But then Brian Ashley arrived. Ashley ran a tourist shop in Avebury, and was enthusiastically interested in earth-energies and dowsing and ancient sacred sites. As Andrews and Taylor watched, Ashley began to dowse the new quintuplet. Richard Martin wrote later, in another front-page story:

> [Colin Andrews's] scepticism turned to clear surprise when local dowser Mr Brian Ashley arrived at the site and used dowsing rods to measure hidden energies at the circles.
>
> The rods clearly followed the clockwise lines of the flattened corn within the circles, and moved violently as Mr Ashley reached the centre of the large circle. Mr Ashley conducted many of his tests with closed eyes.
>
> The rods displayed many traits which Mr Andrews described as 'absolutely consistent' with similar experiments at sites in Hampshire. 'I am overwhelmed,' he said. 'No practical joker could do this.'

Wingfield was impressed, too, though in truth he had never really given much credence to the idea that practical jokers could be behind the Silbury circles. The gentle swirling effect, and the way the wheat had been laid flat, with a weird veining effect, would have been almost impossible to hoax.

And there was young Mary Freeman. Wingfield and Andrews tracked her down and spoke to her in her flat in Marlborough. They found her thoughtful, well-spoken, and thoroughly believable. She had felt honoured to see the energy beam. It had been 'ethereal'.

Wingfield came away from the interview convinced that the thing was no hoax. Even so, there were those shoe-prints. One couldn't simply explain them away . . . Was it possible that humans, perhaps an organized, serious group of them, could have been responsible for laying down those circles? If so, they couldn't possibly have done it in any conventional way. Could they have found a way to manipulate earth-energy themselves? In a subsequent report in *Flying Saucer Review* (for which he was then made a consultant), Wingfield suggested that:

> ... we should not, perhaps, be thinking in terms of our preconceived idea of a hoaxer: the mischief maker and his chums who have hoaxed the odd circle in previous years, using a post and chain, and whose clumsy efforts were certainly recognizable as a hoax. Here we are talking of people whose methods and motives are far more obscure and quite possibly sinister. *Alternatively, one could speculate that the 'shoe-prints' were not of human origin at all.*

Wingfield spent the night of 3 August on Silbury Hill watching the field across the road with an electronic night-sight a friend had brought. They watched the field most of the night, and nothing happened, but in the morning, tantalizingly, the final quintuplet of the year was discovered only a few miles to the south, on Allington Down.

Colin Andrews, meanwhile, was now completely satisfied that the Silbury circles were genuine. In fact, he began to wonder whether the connection with the 11,000-volt power lines might be significant. An increasing number of circles, he noticed, were appearing near such power lines ...

Taylor, whose aerial reconnaissance and photography had been the backbone of CPR's work that year, had his own stories to tell, several of which he related in a short summary of the recent summers' events for *Flying Saucer Review* (for which he, too, now became a consultant). His anecdotes lacked the supernatural intensity of Andrews's tales, or even Delgado's, but they were a start. For instance, there had been the strange objects on his 1987 photographs, and the fact that his 1988 photos, when he had gone to collect them from the photo-shop, 'appeared to have been copied' – the shop assistant claiming mysteriously that she had not been satisfied with the quality of the photos, and had therefore reprinted them. And then there had been the time when, flying over Cheesefoot Head and admiring a quintuplet, he had suddenly found himself dangerously amid a flock of model aeroplanes, all flying around under radio control by invisible individuals below ...

7

Your Client, Our Client

From the day that they had first met in 1986, outside the anti-clockwise circle at Headbourne Worthy, Terence Meaden and Colin Andrews had had an agreement. If one of them heard about a new circle he would tell the other. Each would thereby have access to the other's network of contacts – which was almost essential, since neither the Meadenite nor the Delgadonian network alone could cover the increasingly broad territory over which circles were occurring.

And as time went by, another deal was agreed to. Whenever one of them was contacted about television coverage, he would tell his interviewers about the other. Thus, when the BBC wrote to Meaden in the summer of 1988 about filming a documentary on the circles, he told them about some researchers he knew down in Hampshire. And when the Southampton-based network TVS contacted Delgado and Andrews that same summer, for the same reason, Meaden received a call, too . . .

The TVS crew went out to Beckhampton first, to film some circles in a field at Firs Farm. While they were there, the farmer, Steven Horton, mentioned that a friend of his over towards Yatesbury had a farmhand who had apparently seen a circle being swirled one morning a few days before. Delgado and Andrews found that interesting, because Busty Taylor had flown over that area recently and had seen more than a dozen small circles. Everyone was excited now, and the TVS crew packed their gear into their

vans and cars and everyone drove a few miles west to Manor Farm
at Yatesbury. They found the farm manager, who confirmed that he
did have a number of circles on the farm, and that he did have a
farmhand who had seen something. But the farmhand, Roy Lucas,
turned out only to have seen some kind of a whirlwind, and hadn't
actually seen a circle being swirled – although he was sure the two
things were connected. He had been out on a tractor at a little past
eight in the morning, almost two weeks before. It had been a fine
summer morning, humid and calm with a high mist and the feeling
of a hot day about to burn through it. He was driving along, towing
a grass-cutter, clipping the grass at the edge of a path near the A4,
when he noticed something odd in a field about a hundred yards
away. It looked like a puff of smoke, but as he watched it he saw
that it was a column of spinning vapour, about fifteen feet wide and
fifteen feet high, with a slow-spinning outer shell and a fast-spinning
core. It disappeared after a second or two, leaving a slight fog-like
wisp to drift and dissipate in the wind. A few seconds later another
little spinning vapour-puff appeared and disappeared at more or
less the same place, and then five minutes later another one winked
on and off in a field further away. He checked to see if any circles
had been formed, but couldn't see any from his tractor cab. In any
case, he told the TVS crew: 'After seeing what I saw I am quite
convinced that this is what causes the circles.'

Meaden was also convinced. 'What Mr Lucas observed,' he
would write later in *J. Met.*,

> were the lower ends of spinning, columnar vortices made
> visible by the condensation of water droplets in the cores as a
> result of reduced air pressure. The visible height of the spinning
> fog-cloud, about 4–5 metres, corresponds to the depth of
> nearly-saturated air in the inversion. The opacity and constric-
> tion of the core testify to the intensity of the rotation . . .

Meaden noted the proximity of the field to Windmill Hill, a half-
mile to the north-east – where the wind had been blowing from, that
morning – and the fact that the area, where an RAF camp had
existed during the war, had once been notorious for its tricky air-
turbulence and high incidence of aeroplane crashes. In an
unconscious echo of Colin Andrews's Harrier Jump-jet worries,

Meaden asked: 'Can this be tragic testimony to the high frequency and unusual character of the clear-air vorticity in the lee of Windmill Hill and Cherhill Down?'

Delgado and Andrews, by contrast, remained vague in their conclusions, at least in front of the TVS camera. The circles phenomenon was still a mystery, they said. And when Meaden had the camera, and began to assert in his confident, somewhat headmasterish manner that the circles were definitely caused by whirlwinds, and that any other theory was foolish and misguided and unscientific, they cringed. Delgado wasn't the only one to wonder why they had arranged for Meaden to come along.

A few days later, according to Meaden, he received a call from a reporter on the *Leicester Mercury*. A new circle formation – a ringed circle, surrounded by a triangle of three small satellites – had appeared in a wheatfield near Oadby, just south-east of Leicester. Delgado and Andrews had already been up to see it. Had Dr Meaden seen it?

Well, no, he hadn't, he told the reporter, but he was on his way. And as he made the long drive up to Leicestershire the thought gnawed at him: Andrews hadn't called. He had breached the agreement.

A few afternoons later, back in Wiltshire, Meaden decided to drive over to Bratton to see if there were any new circles. He was surprised to find a pair just off the road, beneath the white horse, and a linear triplet further along the road to the north-east. He went back to the pair and had started to photograph them from the road, when suddenly Andrews and Delgado and Taylor drove up.

'I've just discovered these,' Meaden remembers telling them. 'I thought I'd phone you.'

The others shrugged. 'We already knew about them.'

Well, it was obvious what was going on. Still, Meaden could hardly believe they would abandon him so callously . . . just like that. 'Why didn't you tell me about the Oadby circle?' he asked Andrews.

'Well, you know,' said Andrews, 'it all happened so quickly. There wasn't time . . .'

And for Meaden that was the end of it.

In fact, a split had probably been unavoidable. The cooperation had been strained by the public divergence of the Meadenite and

Delgadonian ideologies, and anyway it no longer seemed to provide a mutual practical advantage. For by now, the summer of 1988, it was becoming clear to Delgado, Andrews, Taylor, and Tuersley that their growing network of farmers and farmhands and lorry-drivers and pub-keepers and private pilots and dowsers and journalists could stand on its own. They didn't need Meaden's network any more. It was too small to provide them with anything they didn't already have. In fact, the chance meeting at Bratton provided a perfect example: as far as Delgado and Andrews and Taylor and Tuersley knew, Meaden had only just discovered the circles there, despite their having known about them for days. Either that, or Meaden had known but hadn't told them. In any case, there was no point in collaborating further. Information, or at least *new* information, was only flowing in one direction – away from them.

If Meaden had sensed the others' resentment at the time, he hadn't shown it. No matter what he had thought of Delgado and the others, he had wanted to maintain his access to their network. And to keep the connection going he had continued to phone them, had continued to meet them in the fields, had continued to exchange pleasantries, as if they were all in this together, all for one, one for all. Good to see you, Pat. How's the wife, Colin? And after a while . . . it had begun to grate on one or two of them. Taylor remembers a sequence recorded by one of his pole-mounted video cameras as far back as 1987, at Bratton, oddly enough on that very day that they all had been groaning at the approach of Wingfield, the hopeful newcomer:

ANDREWS: Terence just said, 'Isn't nature full of wonderful surprises?'
DELGADO: (inaudible)
ANDREWS: (laughing) That's just what I thought, too.

In any case, it became clear to Meaden, after the events of July 1988, that the time for cooperation had ended. And that summer, the ideological differences between the two sides took on a harsher, more personal tone in the media. 'The whirlwinds theory is far too simplistic,' Andrews told the *Leicester Mercury*. 'It is ridiculous to keep harping on about it.' Wingfield, whose *Flying Saucer Review* piece about the Silbury Hill circles contained numerous favourable references to Colin Andrews, made sure also to denounce 'such fanciful notions as "stationary whirlwinds".' Delgado told the *Winchester Extra* that 'We are so disgusted that [Meaden] is so adamant that the rings are caused by whirlwinds that we don't want anything to do with him.' Delgado went on to allege that when he briefed the Meteorological Office at Bracknell about Meaden's theory, 'they fell on the floor laughing'. And in perhaps the unkindest cut of all, Delgado suggested to both the *Extra* and the *Observer* that Meaden had once agreed with him that UFOs caused the circles.

But Meaden gave as good as he got. 'They believe these circles were caused by UFOs,' he told the *Leicester Mercury*. 'That is nothing but pie in the sky which is wasting a lot of people's time – although it looks good in newspapers. They have their own fantasy explanations for it and rule out all other possibilities. That is just not scientific.' Describing the upcoming BBC documentary in *J. Met.*, he referred to:

> amusing sequences [that] are to be included of interviews with believers in UFOs and the paranormal who choose to reject any natural origin for the circles from within our atmosphere and some of whom fantasize that the circles are 'created by an unknown force, possibly manipulated by an unknown intelligence' or are 'caused by high-energy fields within the earth' possibly 'linked to ancient world-wide energy paths (ley-lines)'. Although crop specialists are more usefully questioned as well, much of the film is likely to overemphasize wholly unscientific and irrelevant topics.

Meaden's most successful attack, however, was indirect. An *Observer* reporter named Andrew Stephen set out to write a piece about Colin Andrews's quest to get to the bottom of the mystery of the circles. He spoke with Andrews at length, and seemed impressed by his stories of lights in the sky and crackles and flashes. Then he spoke with Meaden, who together with Paul Fuller gave the journalist such a lengthy briefing on Andrews's background, his far-out beliefs, his links with *Flying Saucer Review*, his dismissal of eyewitness cases that supported the whirlwind theory, and so on, that the piece became decidedly less sympathetic. Referring to Andrews's peculiar obsession with the circles, Stephen concluded: 'The instinct to make our lives exciting, relevant, crucial to history is a strong one – overwhelmingly so for some.'

In the early years, while they were all still working together, meeting in circles and sharing information, Paul Fuller also tried to limit his public attacks against the Delgadonians, and privately tried to convert them to the Meadenite cause. He would send them long, earnest letters, pleading with them to take another look at Meaden's theory, for the sake of a respectable ufology, for the sake of science, for the sake of their own reputations. For instance, in a six-page single-spaced letter to Andrews in February 1988, Fuller wrote:

> I was concerned to read your recent article in *FSR* about the circles and feel I must write to you to warn you about the damage you are doing to your own credibility and that of ufology's credibility in general . . .
>
> Surely you must appreciate that by unquestioningly accepting these reports [associating circles with flying saucers] as 'real' or 'paranormal' UFOs you are giving the [sceptics] of this world all the material they need to discredit ufology? This is why ufologists have always failed to persuade scientists to look at our data with an open mind – too many people in the UFO field . . . adopt extreme views without trying to find realistic explanations for sightings, this weakens our cause and we become associated with the irrational para-religious element in our movement . . .
>
> I wonder why you deliberately ignored the eyewitness accounts of stationary vortices creating circles? Terence cites two in his *Journal of Meteorology* (the Melvyn Bell report and the Arthur Shuttlewood report), [and] I remember that last year a correspondent wrote to the *Daily Telegraph* and described their observation of a vortex bouncing across a field close to their home in the Malvern Hills creating two circles . . .
>
> I cannot stand by and allow you to misrepresent BUFORA's work or Terence's theory. Certainly I cannot imagine that your views would be printed in any magazine other than *FSR*.

Surely you realize that Gordon Creighton['s] . . . unquestioning and uncritical approach to the study of UFO reports may well represent some covert intelligence operation to discredit ufology . . .

Andrews didn't respond, but a month later Fuller wrote again, enclosing the results of a (mostly fruitless) survey they had all done the previous summer – asking farmers in circle-prone areas whether they had seen any circles, or had seen what caused them – and requesting a response to the points raised in his earlier letter. Andrews wrote back, thanking Fuller for the documents, but refusing to be drawn into an argument:

It is not my intention to comment on the contents of your letter of 9th February.

I am receiving more reports of similar ground markings from other countries, hitherto not known. I have two new sites in this country and a superb eyewitness report of a clockwise circle forming within a few metres of a person out for a walk with the dog.

It has been a very busy winter. We await summer with baited breath.

Fuller gave up trying to convert Andrews after that, and instead concentrated on discrediting him. In a series of articles that year in the BUFORA *Bulletin*, *Magonia*, and the *Journal of Transient Aerial Phenomena*, Fuller set out the case, as he saw it, for Meaden's vortex theory – that most of the circles were created by whirlwinds, and the rest by hoaxers – and belittled the Delgadonian camp. In *Magonia* he wrote:

I must say how frustrated I have been to see that some ufologists still continue to pander to sensationalism by promoting their wildly speculative theories about 'paranormal' UFOs (?), 'invisible earth forces' and 'ley-lines'! These ufologists dismiss my more rational approach to the study of the circles with a wave of their hand as if *they* were experts in vortex generation and we were fools just released from the asylum. Their obsession with finding an exotic explanation for the mystery circles can only result in the dismissal of *all* the UFO data by our detractors and the assumption that *all* ufologists are equally willing to discover incredible causes for anomalous events.

One day late in that summer of 1988, Fuller sat down and wrote another letter, this time to Ann Druffel, an American who was both a contributing editor to *MUFON UFO Journal* – the primary organ of American ufology – and a consultant to *Flying Saucer Review*. Druffel had herself written a letter to the editor of *MUFON UFO Journal*, complaining about a letter from Jenny Randles that had appeared in the same space a few issues before. Randles's letter had lamented the British ufology community's apparent espousal of the circles phenomenon, and had blamed *Flying Saucer Review*, which, she said, had 'grossly misled its readers into thinking those who adhered to the "wind" as the cause were both mad and uninformed ...' Druffel had responded with a spirited defence of *FSR*, and with some ridicule of the whirlwind theory: 'Incidentally, the explanation by the consulting meteorologist gave my family a hearty laugh ...' Fuller decided that Druffel needed straightening out; so he sat down and wrote directly to her:

> I am writing to you to express my concern at the sentiments you have been expressing in *FSR* and your view that atmospheric vortices are incapable of creating 'mystery circles' ... I must inform you that, regretfully, *FSR*'s 'honoured consultants' [meaning Delgado and Andrews in particular] are guilty of blatant misrepresentation of what has been occurring here, of failing to adequately evaluate the Vortex Theory, and of damaging everything ufologists have been trying to achieve ...
>
> Pat and Colin ... just *love* to see their names in the press and on TV and they repeatedly make claims like 'The circles are formed by an unknown intelligence by an unknown force in an unknown manner'! This year they have repeatedly appeared on local TV, bringing further ridicule down on ufology, and their tactics are beginning to verge on the unpleasant ...

Both Andrews and Delgado have begun making claims about themselves which are patently untrue. Delgado has never worked for NASA, although he did work for the British nuclear testing range in Australia; Andrews is not the Chief Electrical Engineer at Test Valley Borough Council, he is the emergency planning officer. Both men are completely obsessed with their wild ideas about these circles and they have led a lot of people down the garden path with their lies and selective use of evidence.

Fuller sent Druffel the letter on 4 September. Druffel received it in California a week or so later, and sent a copy to Gordon Creighton back in England. Creighton sent copies to Delgado and Andrews. Creighton, Delgado, and Andrews each sent further copies to their respective solicitors. And on 21 October, Fuller got his first response, from the firm of Dutton, Gregory & Williams in Alresford:

Dear Sir:
We act for Mr Patrick Delgado of 4 Arle Close, Alresford. Mr Delgado has passed to us a letter from you to a Mrs Ann Druffel dated 4 September 1988. . .

Dutton, Gregory & Williams stated that Fuller's allegations had been false and defamatory. They wanted a letter of retraction and apology, and another letter in which Fuller would promise not to repeat the allegations, plus £115 to cover Delgado's legal costs. Creighton's solicitors wrote next, demanding the letters plus £51.75. Then Andrews's solicitors contacted him, demanding the letters plus 'our client's legal costs, in full', the amount left ominously unspecified.

Fuller found a firm of solicitors in Winchester, and the negotiations began. Fuller's solicitor asked Delgado's and Andrews's solicitors for evidence that their clients had valid claims. Delgado made several phone calls, and managed to reach his old supervisor from Woomera Tracking Range, who sent a nice support letter certifying that Delgado, whose technical skills and integrity were beyond reproach, had worked for the Australian Commonwealth Public Service at the NASA Deep Space Network tracking station

at Island Lagoon, Woomera, South Australia, between 1962 and
1966.

Andrews's solicitors stated that Andrews was the Test Valley
Borough Council's Technical Support Services Officer. This wasn't
the same as the Chief Electrical Engineer, a position which apparently didn't exist; and the evidence put forward by Delgado's
solicitors clearly showed that their client, while having worked at a
NASA facility, had not been an actual employee of the space
agency. But the waters were becoming murkier, and although
Meaden had quietly sent Fuller a cheque for £115 to pay his initial
legal retainer fee, a defence against a libel suit would cost thousands.
Fuller wrote six apology letters — two for each potential plaintiff —
and sent them off. But he refused to pay any fees; he had already
run up a substantial legal bill of his own, and as his solicitors put it
in a final letter to Andrews's solicitors, Andrews's costs 'represent
the cost to your client of having broken a confidence by reading his
private and confidential letter'. Fuller's solicitors closed with a
defiant catalogue of alleged Delgadonian sins:

> Our Client has no wish to discuss the origin of cornfield circles,
> or the validity of your Client's theories about UFOs in Court,
> although he accepts that your Client has a right publicly to
> discuss his beliefs. Our Client was particularly disturbed at
> your Client's implication in the magazine *Flying Saucer Review*
> and on the BBC TV programme 'Country File' that the death
> of a Harrier pilot was due to invisible UFOs.
>
> We are instructed that your Client and his colleagues have
> repeatedly defamed our Client and his colleagues in their
> public announcements about the cornfield circles ('It's a sad
> fact that even the most stubborn believers in the Tornado and
> Storm Theory are beginning to see that in fact their theories
> won't work and they won't hold up!'), and that your Client
> falsely implied that the well known meteorologist Dr Terence
> Meaden — Editor of the prestigious *Journal of Meteorology* —
> used to be in agreement with him about the UFO theory
> (The *Observer*, September 1988). Dr Meaden has in fact
> promoted a natural weather-based solution to the mystery since
> 1981.

Your Client, Our Client

We are instructed to accept service of proceedings on behalf of our Client.

No writ ever came, but Delgado and Andrews and Creighton found a way to get back at Fuller. Nine months later, his allegedly libellous letters, and his forced apologies, were splashed embarrassingly across the pages of *Flying Saucer Review*, under the headline: A DOCUMENTATION OF PARANOIA AND CONSPIRACY COMPLEX.

8

The Electric Wind

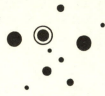

Some time in late 1988, Meaden told Paul Fuller about the book Delgado and Andrews were writing. Fuller told Jenny Randles, and the two decided to write their own book. They were pressed for time, knowing that Delgado and Andrews were likely to publish in the summer, but they also knew that they could publish something quickly through BUFORA, and could therefore pre-emptively attack whatever Delgado and Andrews had to say.

They began to write their book, *Controversy of the Circles*, that winter. The idea was to build on the theme of their 1986 *Mystery of the Circles* booklet, with a brief history of the circles phenomenon plus discussions of the three main theories – hoax, UFO, and vortex. They were, of course, particularly interested in the latter theory, and to write about it they needed help from Meaden. They wanted to know all the latest refinements.

Meaden was happy to oblige. In fact, his theory was now undergoing a transformation which would take it beyond ordinary whirlwinds to the edge of atmospheric physics.

As his erstwhile colleagues in Hampshire had often pointed out to the press, an ordinary whirlwind sucks things upwards. Yet the stalks in circles lay flat. Whatever was making the circles seemed to possess a downward momentum, as if it were a spinning mass of air that was rapidly descending.

The problem began to be resolved when Meaden contacted a Purdue University physics professor named John Snow. During

1988, Snow had been on sabbatical at a French atmospheric research centre at Puy de Dôme, in the mountains west of Lyon, where bonfires were set alight on disused airport runways and the resulting thermal whirlwinds were filmed. That summer, Meaden invited Snow across from France to a TORRO conference on whirlwinds. Snow came over, and presented a paper on dust-devils. Meaden also presented a paper – on crop circles and the presumed minor vortices which made them. Snow took an interest, agreeing with Meaden that the circles were worth studying. He referred Meaden to some theoretical work then being done which might be relevant: another American professor of atmospheric physics, Ted Fujita at the University of Chicago, had recently been arguing that the leading edge of air 'downbursts' (which had been blamed for several otherwise inexplicable air crashes) included a ring-vortex rotating about a horizontal circular axis – something like a smoke-ring. When it neared the ground, the ring's diameter would spread outwards, and the wind speeds between the ring and the ground surface would rise suddenly, potentially to well over 100 m.p.h. Subsequent work by Snow and others suggested that such a ring could have its origin in 'vortex breakdown' – where a spinning column of air develops something like a kink, the kink widens into a vortex ring, and the vortex ring is discharged downward along the axis of the column.

Meaden didn't immediately embrace the ring vortex concept, and his theorizing would thereafter usually refer only to columnar vortices, but he quickly incorporated the vortex breakdown idea into his theory, and by the end of the summer of 1988 was writing in *J. Met.* that:

> All the evidence gathered over the years about the circular areas of damage found in crops proves that a phase must be reached in which the vortex breakdown leads to the plunging of the damaging winds into the crop.

Fuller and Randles used the new material in their book, and BUFORA eventually published it, in the same low-budget dot-matrix printer format that had been used for *Mystery of the Circles*, only with more pages. But when it came off the presses that June, it was almost obsolete. Only in a few pages, written at the last minute by Jenny Randles, did the book indicate the further strange twist that Meaden's theory had suddenly taken.

The circle-making whirlwind was now . . . electric.

In retrospect, the evidence had been there all along. The blue-grey ellipsoid that George Pedley had seen rising from the marsh-grass at Tully. The tube of light that Mary Freeman had seen over Silbury Hill. The ball-lightning cases that Meaden himself had collected and printed in his *Journal of Meteorology* – cases which often involved glowing, descending spheres of roughly crop-circle diameter. And the endless reports from the UFO literature – balls of light, discs, tubes, car-stops, burnt patches in the garden – that CPR, and BUFORA, and increasingly Meaden himself, had been sent in apparent connection with crop circles. Meaden had seemed to ignore or dismiss them all, as irrelevant, as fantasy, or in George Pedley's case, as 'poor eyesight'.

But the cases wouldn't go away. They continued to come in, and Meaden eventually was forced to acknowledge that . . . something was wrong here. It was all reminiscent of a psychology experiment famously referred to by Thomas Kuhn in his book, *The Structure of Scientific Revolutions*. In the experiment, subjects were shown a series of playing cards. Most of the cards were ordinary, but some were not – a black queen of hearts, a red five of spades, and so on. When given short glimpses of the anomalous cards, most subjects failed to notice the anomaly; a black queen of hearts would be seen as a 'queen of hearts', or as a 'queen of spades'. In other words, the images would be squeezed into whatever conceptual category made the best fit, with the unassimilable elements simply ignored. Only at longer exposures would the anomaly become apparent – and with this, the subject might become distinctly unnerved.

> I can't make the suit out, whatever it is. It didn't even look like a card that time. I don't know what colour it is now or whether it's a spade or a heart. I'm not even sure now what a spade looks like. My God!

It is doubtful that Meaden ever experienced such a crisis, but clearly there came a day when he could no longer ignore the evidence that more than a whirlwind was involved. He is vague on when this occurred, but suggests that reports associating luminous flying objects with swirled or flattened ground-cover, plus the observations of thin rings connecting the satellites of quintuplets (which Mrzyglod and others considered to be evidence of hoaxing), began to stir his thinking in this area as early as 1983–5. But no public mention of this new thinking was made until the spring of 1989, suggesting that it may have occurred as late as that year, or perhaps after the summer of 1988, in the wake of the Mary Freeman energy-beam sighting, or after the case from Suffolk in which, according to the account in *J. Met.*, 'a 13-metre circle was found in a field of sugarbeet at the exact spot where the previous evening a strong bright light had "come down like a bullet" and hovered there'.

Anyway, Meaden's theory shivered and shook and underwent another mutation, and the circles-swirling vortex became the circles-swirling 'plasma vortex'.

A plasma is a gas a significant fraction of which has been ionized –meaning that some of its electrically neutral atoms have been separated into negatively-charged electrons and positively-charged ions. This loss of uniform electrical neutrality introduces a host of new and complicated factors which significantly alter the behaviour of the gas. For example, electric fields exist around the separated electrons and ions, and each field exerts force on every other charged particle nearby. Accelerating charges create magnetic fields, which in turn exert their own force on moving charges. Hydrodynamics – the motion of neutral particles – thus becomes complicated by electrodynamics and magnetodynamics, the whole forbidding vortex of equations going by the name of electromagnetohydrodynamics, to which could be added, for the sake of completeness, such things as the ponderomotive force, which is exerted on moving charged particles by electromagnetic radiation, which radiation in turn is emitted by charged particles as they are accelerated by changing electric or magnetic fields, and so on.

A plasma may be luminous, since the occasional recombination of electrons with ions, and the collision of ions with ions, among other processes, release electromagnetic photons of visible light (and potentially also thermal infra-red radiation, radio waves, gamma rays, and X-rays). A plasma may also be audible, either as the crackle of coupling groups of electrons and ions, or as the low-frequency hum of pressure waves given off by an oscillating mass of ionized air. The nocturnal glow and buzz around high-voltage wires is a classic example of a plasma, as is the gas within a turned-on fluorescent light, as is the gas at the edge of a candle flame, as is the aurora borealis. Plasmas are everywhere, in fact, but they are so complex that they are not yet very well understood and, as such, can seem capable of anything – which is ideal, if one is trying to explain as broad and mysterious a phenomenon as the crop circles.

Single circles, according to Meaden's plasma vortex theory, were swept more to less conventionally, mainly by the pressure of ions and neutral atoms against grainstalks. Outer rings might result when:

> the charge flow within the inner vortex circle induces a charge-flow of opposite sign beyond the perimeter; motions as a counterflowing current would naturally follow . . .

Triplets and quintuplets were of course more difficult to explain, but Meaden proposed that they might be:

> the consequence of electromagnetic wave interference resulting in antinodal extrema at the satellite positions, thus leading to secondary rotating plasmas at these locations . . .

And as for the thin rings connecting the satellites of a quintuplet:

> We suggest that the ions are fed into the satellites along a narrow ring, a race-track or 'ion race', which we know by photography and site inspection interlinks them.

In any case, argued Meaden, an association between meteorological vortices and electromagnetic effects was not a new one. Tornado funnel clouds had been seen and filmed emitting sparks or luminous balls, or flashing with rotating bands of blue light. Some old accounts described tornadoes that had appeared to be 'towers of flame'. Tornado eyewitnesses had also reported radio and TV interference, or sulphurous smells which Meaden attributed to the high-voltage creation of ozone and nitrogen oxides. Even dust-devils had been reported in the meteorological literature as being able to generate strong electrostatic fields.

Meaden wasn't too specific on how his plasma vortex would actually originate, but the scenario seemed to be something like this. A vortex would be spun to life a few hundred feet above ground, like a small whirlpool in a stream. The vortex would sink, like a deepening whirlpool, or perhaps from vortex breakdown, possibly assuming the shape of a ring vortex. As it sank, the vortex might collect and concentrate charged particles from the upper atmosphere which were attracted to the oppositely-charged earth, like a kind of slow lightning bolt, and as the vortex neared the ground it might pick up even more charge – from chalk dust or from the heads of wheat – and the ionization would eventually be great enough to make the vortex glow and hum. More charge, as needed, would be channelled down the vortex tube to keep the thing in the plasma state over relatively long periods.

It was only a short step from there to an explanation of the UFO phenomenon. Meaden reasoned that when a section of the vortex entered the plasma state, a surface tension would exist along the boundary between plasma and ordinary air. Any such boundary would be unstable until it had reached the point of minimum surface area – corresponding to a sphere.

> Therefore, although the spinning wind may be set going in the shape of a funnel or cylinder or sheath, then as the ionization content intensifies the naissant plasmoid tends to adopt a spherical form in the absence of other constraints.

> This hypothesis answers for the large number of low-level globular light forms reported in the scientific literature and the popular press as ball lightning, balls of light, and 'unidentified flying objects', etc. Rapid translation and simultaneous spin would tend to distort such forms, giving rise to non-globular shapes like 'cigars', ellipsoids, and, for very high spin rates, strongly flattened forms that appear discoidal.

Moreover, frequent reports of orange or red or bluish-white UFOs could be explained by the fact that 'Red is the colour of the emission spectrum of nitrogen, the dominant gas in our atmosphere, and accompanies the discharge process as nitrogen molecules fall back from excited energy states. A bluish-white light is seen instead if nitrogen is energized to even higher energy levels.'

During the day, the brightness of the sun would probably obscure the luminosity of most plasma vortices, and indeed, there had been comparatively few reports of luminous phenomena during daylight hours. On the other hand, the UFO literature was brimming with daytime reports of 'shiny', 'metallic' globes, cigars, discs, and flying saucers. But Meaden could explain those, too. The discontinuity at the boundary between plasma and ordinary air, he reasoned, was analogous to the one between an air bubble and surrounding water. 'The consequence is an evenly reflecting surface with the illusion of metallic lustre ... This may suffice to account for world-wide reported observations of such reflective, vaporous entities.'*

Meaden's theory to explain the crop circles had now acquired an extraordinary breadth. And it seemed to match the evidence perfectly. The Mary Freeman UFO sighting was now 'a case of an angled columnar vortex illuminated by a discharge current, in which the pipe served to provide a conducting path between cloud and earth'. The Melvyn Bell case was probably just a simple plunging vortex, with low plasma density. The Arthur Shuttlewood case, in which the grass had been swirled to the accompaniment of a high-pitched humming noise, was probably an example of an invisible, but audible, higher-density plasma vortex. Famous UFO cases where car ignitions had been shut off could be explained by the ionization of ambient air, which would short the battery leads;† while reports of radio and TV interference from UFOs could be explained by the presumably intense plasma vortex emission of radio frequency energy.

Even the Ray Barnes case could be explained.

'I have been meaning to write to you for some time on the subject of corn circles,' Barnes, a local Wiltshireman, wrote to Meaden in early 1989.

> About six or seven years ago I was fortunate to see one of these form in a field at Westbury. It happened on a Saturday in early July just before six in the evening after a thunder-

---

* It should be noted that the American UFO-debunker Philip Klass, in his 1968 book *UFOs – Identified*, also theorized that many UFOs might only be atmospheric plasmoids.

† The 1969 Condon report, commissioned by the US Government to investigate the UFO phenomenon, concluded after intensive vehicle tests that such car-stop cases could not reasonably have been caused by high magnetic fields, as had once been thought the likeliest explanation.

storm earlier that afternoon; in fact it was still raining slightly.

My attention was first drawn to a 'wave' coming through the head of the cereal crop in a straight line at steady speed; I have since worked this out to be fifty miles an hour. The agency, though invisible, behaved like a solid object throughout and did not show any fluid tendencies, i.e., no variation in speed, line, or strength. There was no visual aberration either in front, above, or below the advancing line. After crossing the field in a shallow arc the line dropped to a position about 1 o'clock and radially described a circle 50–75 feet radius in about four seconds. The agency then disappeared.

Meaden interviewed Barnes, extracting a few more details, and then sat down to figure the case out. He noted first of all that the apparent solidity of the agency was characteristic of 'a mass of air or ionized air spinning rapidly like a top'. And secondly,

From the behaviour and motion of the 'line' that crossed the top of the cornfield we may deduce that the axis of the vortex was angled so far from the vertical that it was literally flying parallel to the surface of the hillside . . . the proximal end of the spinning column dug into the crop and pivoted about a point which became the centre of the naissant circle. What had been until then a vanishing line on the surface of the corn was instantly transformed into the radius of the sector of the circle of rapidly increasing angle. This instantaneous transition between linear and circular geometrical states was plain proof of the existence of a pivoting vortex, resembling in its action a child's spinning top as it topples on its side and rolls around in a circle.

Q.E.D. Meaden had done it. After nine long years, he had explained the crop circles. Moreover, he had explained UFOs, at least some cases of ball-lightning, and probably a good deal of related modern and ancient folklore.

On the other hand, he would have liked to have kept his theory under wraps a bit longer, to develop his ideas more fully. The only reason he told Fuller and Randles anything about the plasma aspect was that he was about to publish it himself, in his own book – *The Circles Effect and Its Mysteries*.

He had been working on it, and on some other books relating crop circles to stone circles and tumuli, for the previous few years, adding bits and pieces here and there, mostly in a kind of diary format. He hadn't been in any particular rush. In 1987, when Pat Delgado had begun to express literary yearnings, he had made discreet inquiries, as a result of which he decided that Delgado was so far only dreaming. Even later that year, when Colin Andrews sat them all down and said they should write their own book, he wasn't worried. The correspondence he had received from Delgado and Andrews suggested to him that neither could write very well. They would never get a publisher. And in fact the following summer, in 1988, Andrews had told him that they were having problems selling the book.

Then in the autumn of that year Meaden heard that Andrews and Delgado *had* found a publisher – Bloomsbury, one of the hottest publishing houses in the UK.

He understood that the book would be out in late June. And like Fuller and Randles, he decided that he should publish something of his own before then. The fact that Delgado and Andrews were being published by such a major publisher as Bloomsbury might even be a blessing in disguise – for it might prove irresistible for newspapers and magazines to review his book alongside theirs. He could slipstream behind them, and then when people saw how much more sensible his ideas were, he would have his final triumph.

He began to write that winter, distilling from his files a concise, 100-page thesis that would authoritatively describe the circles phenomenon, the vortex theory, and the theory of plasmas and balls of light. He phoned up Ian Mrzyglod, explaining that he had solved the mystery of the circles, and was writing a book about it, and asked if he could please borrow some of Mrzyglod's old photographs. He told Mrzyglod that he had a publisher, and indeed he did – a small concern known as Artetech Publishing Company, located at 54 Frome Road, Bradford-on-Avon, Wiltshire. Which, since he had moved from Trowbridge three years before, was his own address. Meaden knew that it would take hopelessly long to sell his book to an established publisher. He had the money and the resources, and the connections as editor of *J. Met.*, to publish it himself. To help things along, he also published it as *J. Met*'s May/June edition, to ensure that every subscriber received a copy. He also sent review copies to the press. And then, as it had been after he had published his first report on the circles nearly a decade before, he sat back and waited.

And waited . . .

9

The Shamans

The natives believed this to be an incredibly malignant spirit belonging to, or possibly part of, the [shaman] from whom it emanated. It might take physical form, as we had just witnessed, or be totally invisible. It had the power to introduce insects, tiny mice, mud, sharp flints, or even a jelly-fish or baby octopus, into the anatomy of those who had incurred its master's displeasure. I have seen a strong man shudder involuntarily at the thought of this horror and its evil potentialities. It was a curious fact that, although every magician must have known himself to be a fraud and a trickster, he always believed in and greatly feared the supernatural abilities of other medicine-men.

— E. Lucas Bridges, *Uttermost Part of the Earth*

For Colin Andrews, the oppression took many forms. In 1986, it had manifested as the clock-stopping poltergeist from Wantage. In 1987, it had made itself known by the awful crackles and knocks and black flashes in the fields. And now in 1988, there were the headaches.

Occasionally the headaches were so bad that Andrews wondered to his colleagues whether someone, or something, might have planted some device inside his skull, covertly, while he slept. And even if . . . whoever it was . . . had failed to get that close to him, he felt certain that they had followed him, on at least several occasions. He had seen them in his car's rear-view mirror.

It was all very disturbing. And of course there were the dissonant worries of his job at the Test Valley Borough Council. And the hassles at home ... where his wife had been pleading with him to get out of crop circles research, to confine himself instead to repairing Test Valley Borough Council radios and procuring Test Valley Borough Council computers and taking out the rubbish and attending to the thousand other safe details of small town civil service and family life. Andrews was so completely absorbed in his research, he seldom saw his wife any more. And when he did, the arguments could be horrendous.

Andrews began to wonder, privately, and occasionally to his CPR colleagues, whether crop circles were really worth all this trouble. He even began to drop hints in the press. For instance, in August of 1988 the *Marlborough Times* reported:

MYSTERY CIRCLES EXPERT TAKES BACK SEAT

After a season of high-pitched activity ... Mr Colin Andrews this week stated his intention to take a back seat in future investigations ... Mr Andrews stated that he was 'very sorry' about his decision to take a less active role in the investigation, but that the importance of the circles was now 'of global importance'. As such, he said, it was better that 'more intellectual people' took up the reins.

Andrews might not have been consciously aware of it, but complaints of mysterious oppression, followed by professional withdrawal, were common among researchers into the paranormal – and particularly among UFO researchers. Since the 1950s, in America, Australia, and Great Britain, dozens of prominent flying saucer enthusiasts had reported receiving threats by phone, by letter, or in person, from mysterious individuals who might have been government agents, and might have been aliens, but who always demanded one thing: that the researcher in question immediately cease all UFO investigations. In one famous case, that of Albert K. Bender, an American who founded the International Flying Saucer Bureau in 1952, three men 'dressed in black' allegedly seized his just-completed monograph on the origin of UFOs, and while complimenting him on the acuity of his insight, warned him never to reveal his findings. Bender, it seems, did as he was told, and aside from telling the story of the Men in Black, withdrew completely from UFO research, shutting down the IFSB in 1953.

As the years went by and the Men in Black cases mounted, certain refinements were added to this basic motif. The hapless UFO researcher was occasionally afflicted and/or monitored remotely, by an *implant* – a device which had been inserted, somewhere in his or her body, by the mysterious Men in Black. A recent testimonial in *Flying Saucer Review* by its editor Gordon Creighton is typical of the genre:

> I have personally observed, over a period of many years, the presence of one of these immensely hard little balls just below the skin of a human body. *It had been there for at least 40 years.* Then, one day, the person, in whose body it was, 'woke up', and realized what the thing might be. The man at once rushed to inspect – and lo, the ball was already gone! It would be interesting if we could hear of other such cases where an *'implant' vanishes as soon as its significance is perceived.* [Creighton's emphases]

Other aspects of Men in Black-style oppression included confiscated mail, purloined photographs, debilitating bombardment by microwaves, and covert removal from library shelves of books dealing with the deeper aspects of the UFO subject. To a reader's complaint about the latter in 1984, Creighton responded:

> ... more than twenty years ago, when I was still working in the Ministry of Defence in Whitehall and held a regular reader's ticket at the big Westminster Central Library round the corner from Trafalgar Square, one of their young lady librarians more or less admitted to me that there was in existence a directive to clamp down on the reading of UFO books and to encourage the dissemination of only the more stupid ones ...

Sociologists tend to characterize such conspiracy theories and tales of harassment as a set of ingenious, if disingenuous, defensive measures, designed to explain why the esoteric knowledge in question – in this case, the knowledge of the existence of intelligent extraterrestrials – has been rejected by the rest of the society: the esotericist's excuse is that the government, or some other omnipotent entity,* fears the release of the special knowledge and has taken measures to prevent it.

But the standard sociological view misses something which should be more readily apparent to folklorists and anthropologists – that is, the remarkable universality of the Men in Black-style story, which in its basic form appears everywhere from tales of persecution by voodoo demons to complaints of covert surveillance by MI5 or the CIA. In some cases it may serve only as a standard psychological reflex for excusing failure or rejection, or for drawing attention. But in other cases it seems to have gone beyond this function to a much more elaborate and interesting one, in which oppression is a prelude not to failure or withdrawal, but to apotheosis, and the emergence of a spiritual superman: the shaman.

'The shaman,' according to Joseph Campbell's *Historical Atlas of World Mythology*,

> is a particular type of medicine man, whose powers both to cause illness and to heal the sick, to communicate with the world beyond, to foresee the future, and to influence both the weather and the movements of animals, are believed to be derived from his intercourse with envisioned spirits; this inter-course having been established ... by way of a severe psychological breakdown of the greatest stress and even danger to life. The extraordinary uniformity in far-separated parts of the earth of the images and stages of this 'shamanic crisis' suggest that they may represent the archetypes of a psychological exaltation, related on the one hand to schizophrenia and on the other to the ecstasies of the yogis, saints, and dervishes of the high religions.

The word 'shaman' comes from the 'samán' of the Tungus, a tribe of Siberian hunters and herdsmen who, when they were visited by researchers in the early part of this century, represented one of the few remaining anthropological laboratories for the study of

---

*'The conspiracy theory of society,' wrote the philosopher Karl Popper, 'comes from abandoning God and then asking "Who is in his place?"'

pre-agrarian society. In such societies, the shaman appears to have played a central role since palaeolithic times, and the instinct to become a shaman – to overcome affliction by spirits or poverty or general bad luck by reaching a valuable *modus vivendi* with the spirit world – must therefore have become deeply entrenched in the human psyche, to the extent that it continually manifested in certain individuals (St Paul, Joan of Arc) even after, as Campbell and others have argued, the rise of agrarian society signalled the end of shamanism as the primary form of religious expression:

> ... the individualistic shamans, in their palaeolithic style of magical practice, were discredited by the guardians of the group-oriented, comparatively complex organization of a seed-planting, food-growing community.

Of course, agrarian culture is now almost everywhere being rapidly eclipsed by industrial and post-industrial culture, in which social complexity has spawned not communalism, but an extraordinary individualism. The highly ritualized religions mediated by highly organized priesthoods now seem to be giving way to much more individualistic, idiosyncratic modes of religious life – in which gurus, mystics, prophets, mediums, channellers, dowsers, healers, fortune-tellers, psychoanalysts, and similar shamanic figures again play a central role.

And Colin Andrews was about to join their ranks. Indeed, by the autumn of 1988, Andrews had regained much of his confidence, and no longer planned to withdraw from crop circles research. That he and Delgado had just sold their book to Bloomsbury might have had something to do with it, for as Joseph Campbell noted, 'The healing of the shaman is achieved through art.'

One day in late November or early December of 1988, Andrews received a phone call from a man named George de Trafford, who said he lived in Malta and was a member of something called the Maltese Esoteric Society. De Trafford's accent was upper-class English, and his tone was mesmerizingly confident. He was calling about the crop circles. He felt he should explain to Andrews how they were made.

It all had to do with energies and a higher consciousness, said de

Trafford. And as far as that went, Andrews could hardly disagree. He had long been suggesting that an extraterrestrial higher intelligence lay behind the circles. And like most UFO enthusiasts, Andrews knew about earth-energy and ley-lines, which together might constitute a beacon system for incoming alien craft. Some time in the 1988 season he had even taken up dowsing, and had often been seen out in the fields with his little metal rods, checking the energy patterns of circles and ley-lines.

De Trafford was aware of the connections that had been suggested between the circles and UFOs and ley-lines, and he was gratified to know that Andrews, a scientist, had enough spiritual awareness to take them seriously. But he was talking about something much greater. He would send Andrews some literature through the post.

Andrews received the material a short time later, in the second week of December. And reading through it all, he began to understand what de Trafford was saying. According to the well-spoken man from Malta, matter was simply energy slowed down, and consciousness was inherent in both. Higher consciousness meant higher energy levels, or 'higher vibrations', within matter. To raise consciousness was therefore to raise the vibrations of our bodies – to become less dense. Unfortunately, the story of human civilization was a story of ... increasing density, away from energy and spirit, and towards the sclerosis and solidification of the lower natures – greed, envy, hate, and pollution. Which explained why we and the planet – which had its own planetary consciousness – were in such terrible shape.

Nevertheless, according to de Trafford, all consciousness is connected, so that even the rudimentary and dense are potentially able to communicate, on a spiritual level, with higher consciousness. In times of great distress, even the Cosmic Consciousness could be called upon – subconsciously, by the atrophied remnants of our spiritual nature – to lift earth and its people out of their present darkness. And when that happened, the Cosmic Consciousness would respond, by infusing energy into the planet. And as this energy went in, it would form ... circles ... on the planet's surface.

But there was more. The energy wasn't merely infused at random. It was infused at certain special points within a system of interpenetrating and multidimensional lines that covered the earth, like a gigantic Grid.

It was like something out of that Umberto Eco novel, *Foucault's Pendulum*, where the protagonists struggle to find the global map of the telluric currents. But de Trafford already had the map – the map of the Grid. The circles always lay along the Grid, and interestingly, so did the tumuli, and Silbury Hill, and Stonehenge, and Avebury, and the Great Pyramid at Giza, and Alexandria on the Mediterranean, and Knossos on Crete, and Venice, and Manicougan in Canada, where a large meteorite once impacted, and the Texas–Mexico border, and Malta. All of these places were nodes, valves, chakras for the infusion of Energy and Cosmic Consciousness. The ancients had realized this, of course, and the tumuli and Silbury Hill and the megalithic sites were actually energy-amplifying shrines erected at the sites of previous such infusions – although no infusion had ever been as powerful, or as necessary, as the one occurring now.

There was still more to the story, involving the angle of the Great Pyramid at Giza, and the Lost Hall of Records on the Giza Plateau, and the etheric pyramid that dangled over the southern counties of England, and the coming coincidence between the plane of the earth's ecliptic and that of the sun, when seasons would be abolished and the continents would shift and Atlantis would rise again and the Cosmic Consciousness would descend on wings of light. But as far as crop circles were concerned, the matter was fairly straightforward: the circles were merely the places where a beam of extraterrestrial energy had flowed into the earth.

Some of that energy seemed to reside within the circles, so that they glowed invisibly with spiritual radiation. Thus the wildly spinning rods of circle dowsers. But what these dowsers failed to realize was that this residual energy corresponded to a residual consciousness. De Trafford's people in the Maltese Esoteric Society had analysed several crop circle photographs in a British New Age magazine, *Kindred Spirit*, and had determined their energy/consciousness levels. For instance, a quintuplet in a field at Westbury in Wiltshire the previous summer corresponded to a Causal entity. A double-ringer nearby had been a Divine entity – one rung higher – while a quintuplet on Allington Down in 1988 had been a Cosmic mental heavyweight. A single-ringer in Cheesefoot Head radiated the most energy, however, and appeared to exist in the highest dimension of consciousness, the Adi Plus.

Of course, with all of this energy humming and throbbing in the fields, a crop circle researcher had to be careful. Towards the close of the letter, de Trafford warned Andrews: 'Be aware of your own physical self. You are dealing in very high energies which can manifest in various aches and pains. These are not problems. Just recognize them for what they are. It must surely be that your psychic structures are being stepped up through the focus you have in the work you are doing.'

Well, for Andrews that must have been a relief. The headaches weren't because of a neuralgic implant. They were because of the energies. They were a good sign. A sign of progress. No pain, no gain.

De Trafford arrived in England a few months later, in February. He stayed in Hampshire, and took Andrews and Delgado to dinner one night. To Andrews and Delgado, his appearance was a little unnerving. Though he was only in his forties, de Trafford's face seemed much older. His extremities occasionally quivered, as if recalling the passage of tremendous, unbearable energies. Apparently his otherworldly intercourse had left him the worse for wear. And yet . . . he spoke with a remarkable smoothness and confidence about the energies and the ley-lines and sacred sites and megaliths, and of course the circles.

A few days later Andrews and Delgado brought de Trafford down to Cheesefoot Head, to show him one of the hotspots of the crop circles phenomenon, and to introduce him to his colleagues. Busty Taylor was there, and Don Tuersley and his wife Peggy. They all met in the Cheesefoot Head car-park, and then walked along the side of the A272 roadway towards the Punchbowl, as de Trafford began to discourse about energy and consciousness and the circles.

As they walked, Andrews and Delgado each crouched in front of de Trafford with video cameras, backpedalling, filming the man from Malta as he walked and talked along the side of the A272 roadway. Occasionally a car would pass by, its occupants staring at them curiously, but Andrews and Delgado continued to crouch and backpedal and aim their video cameras. In truth, they regarded it as a historic moment. Before de Trafford had flown in from Malta, the word had spread somehow that he had something to do with the mysterious order of the Knights Templar, which had been reputed, before its sudden disappearance in the fourteenth century, to hold many secrets of ancient wisdom. Andrews and the others also had it on good authority that de Trafford was a friend of both the Prince of Wales and the Duke of Edinburgh. Which meant that he could be highly influential in the growing New Age movement, a movement which was rapidly beginning to take an interest in the phenomenon of crop circles.

So they crouched and backpedalled and filmed their way down along the A272, until –

'I can't go further,' de Trafford announced suddenly, the vibrations of his limbs increasing.

He seemed to be in pain. His hand went to his forehead. The rest of them weren't sure what was going on. Was he having a heart attack?

But in another moment, they all knew what it was ... *The energies.*

A big ley-line crossed the road at that point, having passed through a tumulus in a field on the other side of the road. The associated energy line snaked along the ley, down over the road into the Punchbowl. De Trafford, goaded by the video cameras before him, had walked slap into it.

Fortunately, he had his Aurameter with him. The Aurameter appeared to be a little metal box with a spring attached, but in de Trafford's hands it was a sensitive instrument which could detect any energy beam in which it was immersed. De Trafford, backing up to get out of the main beam, held out the little Aurameter and verified that the energy was coming across the road. It was very intense.

They moved back a few dozen yards and then crossed the road, walking up into the field where the tumulus lay. They approached the tumulus, stood next to it – and undoubtedly the energy was roaring through it, roaring all around them, but de Trafford seemed to be all right now. He was talking about the sclerosis and solidification of humanity and the need for less density and higher vibrations, and about the Cosmic Consciousness and the subconscious cry of the planet for help, and the Grid, and the infusions of energy, and the crop circles, and how each one was merely the place where the energy had come in, and though each had a residual energy and consciousness there wasn't much more to it than that, and the only thing to do was to soak up the energy, as far as one could stand it, of course, and –

It started to dawn on a few of them now what de Trafford was really saying. He was saying, 'Don't bother to measure the circles, or to photograph them, or to diagram the swirl patterns, or the dowsable energy patterns. Because none of that matters. What matters is what the circles mean for humanity, and that's what I'm here to tell you about.'

Delgado and Andrews weren't sure they wanted to go along with that. They had spent the past several years measuring circles and photographing them and mapping out their swirl patterns and their dowsable energy patterns. In fact, their book would be full of photographs and measurements and diagrams. And on the subject of what the circles meant for humanity – well, when you got right down to it, de Trafford's guess was only as good as anyone else's.

De Trafford was talking about the Grid and the Cosmic Consciousness and the Great Pyramid at Giza and the need for spiritual awareness in science when Delgado abruptly spoke up.

'Well, I think I'll be off. I don't see the point in another meeting.'

And off he went to the Cheesefoot Head car-park, as the rest of them stood around in embarrassed silence.

Andrews's attitude towards de Trafford might have been the same as Delgado's, but even so, he didn't disparage the man. That would have been simply rude, and perhaps foolish, given de Trafford's connections. No, any resistance to de Trafford would have to be accomplished subtly.

There was another meeting with de Trafford a few days later, at Colin Andrews's house. Delgado seemed to have had a change of heart, for he was there, along with Busty Taylor and Don Tuersley. De Trafford told them some more about the Grid, and the megalithic sites, and the plane of the earth's ecliptic, and the internal chambers of the Great Pyramid at Giza, and he gave them diagrams of the Grid, and diagrams of the internal chambers of the Great Pyramid, and monographs about vibrations and energy and sclerosis and solidification and consciousness, and they all thanked him for the material and listened politely. Then they took de Trafford out to Silbury Hill, where he met Richard Beaumont, the editor of *Kindred Spirit*, and Beaumont's business partner Patricia Yates, and the medium Isabelle Kingston, and Mary Freeman. They all climbed the narrow chalk path that spiralled around the Hill, and stood on the ancient summit, and Isabelle Kingston spoke about the significance of Silbury, and de Trafford discussed the Grid, and the need for spiritual awareness, and the terrible state of the planet, and the significance of the circles. And the wind blew, and it was bitterly cold atop Silbury Hill. The meeting ended soon, and they all went back to Isabelle Kingston's house for dinner and more talk about the circles, and the Great Pyramid, and the awful state of the environment, and the Grid.

De Trafford left the country soon afterwards, but he had said a great deal that was new and interesting, and his influence seemed to linger. Many who had been interested in the circles seemed to take an interest in him, too. Spiritually, he was telling them what they wanted to hear – what they had wanted to hear from Delgado and Andrews, but hadn't been hearing, at least not as clearly, not as smoothly . . .

In his original letter to Colin Andrews, de Trafford had proposed that Colin conduct a small experiment, an illustration of the kinds of energies involved in the Grid. In effect, he had suggested that Colin build a miniature Stonehenge in his backyard:

> If for example a horseshoe of stones is formed on a correct position in relation to the Grid and with the correct orientation i.e., the open end facing 50 degrees East, a pattern of energies is immediately manifested. They manifest to an apparent ratio which could I am sure be calculated mathematically from information I can provide. These energies form rings at varying distances beyond the horseshoe and also establish a microcosm of the Cosmic Grid with nodal points at set intervals. The heelstone at Stonehenge is one such nodal point. There are others that have either not been found or have disappeared.

However, psychically it is simple to pinpoint exactly where they should be . . .

I suggest you build yourself a small horseshoe using ordinary small pebbles. Orientate it correctly 50 degrees East and you may find that your scientific sensing equipment can pick up the presence of different energies.

At the time of the letter, Andrews hadn't seemed to take the suggestion too seriously. But eventually both Andrews and Delgado decided to try the experiment. They went out and found ten little pebbles of granite – during his visit de Trafford had suggested they use sedimentary stone – and brought them back into their gardens, and placed the little pebbles in a horseshoe shape, a few feet wide, the open ends orientated 50 degrees east of true north. And finally . . . there they were: two little horseshoes made of pebbles, sitting in two little Hampshire gardens.

According to the story that later made the rounds, Andrews decided to verify that the horseshoe had, in fact, created a microcosm of the Grid . . . He took out his scientific sensing equipment – that is, his dowsing rods – and went to work. And . . . it was very strange . . . There were now in his garden two lines of energy, each more powerful than he had ever dowsed before. One of them went through his house, and the other . . . headed for the little wooden shed in the backyard where he kept his office, his computer, his crop circle files and maps . . . Andrews zig-zagged along the line, the rods twisting in his hands whenever he crossed it. And within minutes he had established that the line did in fact go through the little office, passing directly beneath his office chair. The chair where he did most of his work.

And right away it was clear what de Trafford had done.

You are dealing in very high energies which can manifest in various aches and pains . . .

Andrews phoned up Delgado, warned him not to do it, but he was too late. Delgado had already placed the stones, and the evil energy line whipped and bucked through his modest little house in Alresford. No one was hurt yet, but even so – clocks stopped, refrigerators rattled, floors creaked, light bulbs blew . . . And they both realized what they had to do . . .

Destroy the horseshoe!

They went out into their gardens, hastily scattered the stones –

And things returned to normal . . . Although throughout the crop circles community, there was now a good deal less enthusiasm for the teachings of George de Trafford. Richard Andrews, who still hoped to gain favour with Colin and Pat, was quick to follow their lead, and upbraided Don and Peggy Tuersley when they later built their own little microlithic horseshoe. No adverse effects were apparent in the Tuersleys' house, and the neighbours didn't complain, but even so, Richard Andrews worked himself into a high dudgeon.

'You've done terrible harm to the planet,' he told Peggy.

This considerably perplexed her, for she considered George de Trafford to be a genuinely good and kind man, incapable of evil. She couldn't understand what all the fuss was about.

Nevertheless, the tide had turned. Many now suggested, in retrospect, that George de Trafford was a sinister character, with his ravaged features and occult oscillations. Perhaps he was some horrible Maltese vampire, or some undead Templar, with strange black powers. Word also spread about the night he had dined with Delgado and Andrews in Hampshire . . . and how throughout the meal, throughout all the talk about the Great Pyramid and Manicougan and Venice and the Cosmic Consciousness and the ethereal pyramid over the southern counties and the tragedy of man's solidification and greed and the plane of the ecliptic and the need for higher vibrations and spiritual awareness and the awfulness of man's depredations of the earth . . . de Trafford had been staring at Andrews, staring right at him, as if out of his pupils had come two energy beams, burning, biting, gnawing, drilling . . . into Andrews's skull . . . giving him the most intense *headache* . . .

10

White Crow

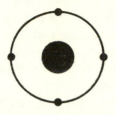

The shaman's vocation is normally announced by an initially uncontrolled state of possession: a traumatic experience associated with a hysteroid, ecstatic behaviour ... The less well qualified by birthright the aspiring shaman is, the more violent and dramatic will be the possession by which he seeks to demonstrate the efficacy of his calling.

– I. M. Lewis, *Ecstatic Religion*

I cannot bring it upon myself to describe the fine detail of what happened.

– Colin Andrews, recalling the White Crow 'trilling noise' incident in *The Latest Evidence*

Some time that spring, Colin Andrews sent a letter to Terence Meaden. It contained a few old reports of circles that Meaden hadn't yet seen, but more importantly, it had an unmistakable tone of conciliation, hinting that they, Meaden and Andrews, should start working together again. Meaden wasn't sure how to respond, but a few weeks later, as the 1989 season got under way, he received a call from Paul Fuller about a circle out on Longwood Estate, next to Cheesefoot Head. It seemed like a good opportunity to show Andrews that he was prepared to share information again, so he phoned Colin, told him about the report of the circle, and they made plans to meet one evening at Cheesefoot Head to investigate. Andrews arrived first, and found only a water tank in a distant wheatfield that might have looked like a circle from the road. He was waiting at the Cheesefoot Head car-park when Meaden arrived. He explained to Meaden that the circle was only a water tank. Meaden was disappointed, and apologized for having passed on the false alarm. Andrews said it didn't matter. The two of them stood uneasily in the country dusk . . .

So, said Meaden, I understand you want to collaborate again.

Andrews nodded vaguely.

Well, then, said Meaden, why did you stop sharing information the previous summer? Why didn't you tell me about the Oadby circle? Why didn't you tell me about the ones at Bratton? I would have told you if I'd found them first.

Oh, said Andrews. Well, that was all Pat's idea, really. He didn't like how . . . dogmatic you were being, especially when TVS was filming us all at Yatesbury. He didn't feel that he could work with you any more.

I see, said Meaden, softening a bit.

Anyway, said Andrews, I'm organizing a big cropwatch in June, here at Cheesefoot. We'll have night-vision cameras, video recorders, a caravan. You're welcome to join us.

Above all, Meaden wanted to tap into Andrews's network again. But the more he thought about it, the more he also wanted to participate in this upcoming cropwatch. It would be a big one, the first of its kind, and he worried that unless he were connected with it in some way . . . well, he could just imagine what would happen if a circles-swirling plasma vortex came down in front of the cameras. Andrews and Delgado would declare it a visitation from outer space, and all the world's press would suddenly rush out to Cheesefoot Head, baying for dramatic video clips and photo spreads. Serious scientists would be crushed in the stampede . . .

But if he had at least recorded the local meteorological conditions, he could forestall any UFO hysteria, or at least divert it, with his barograph and his thermograph . . . which together would prove, presumably, that a microfront had passed over the area, spinning to life the electroluminescent vortex that to unscientific eyes might have looked like a glowing spaceship.

And so the cropwatch had one of Meaden's small meteorological stations. It also had two video cameras, and two low-light short-wave infra-red cameras, and scaffolding on which to mount them, and a van in which the video monitors and recorders and volunteer cropwatchers would sit, and a nearby caravan, camouflaged, in which the cropwatchers could huddle for coffee or a nap when off duty. The operation was well equipped, and well planned, and Andrews had managed to recruit the support not only of Meaden, but of Archie Roy, the Astronomy Professor at Glasgow. Meaden's support was necessarily wary, given his well-publicized opposition to the extraterrestrial hypothesis; but Roy was a well-known proponent of the paranormal, and the cropwatch had his full blessing. The cameras had been provided by a businessman friend of his who manufactured electro-optical devices.

Roy himself had thought up the name for the operation: White Crow. It had a certain ring to it, and it meant something as well: the 'white crow', a purely hypothetical animal, was the epistemological bane of the scientist who, having seen thousands of black crows, smugly assumed them all to be black. It was a symbol of the essential indeterminacy of the universe, of the illogic in scientific discovery, of anomaly, of anything rare or strange. As such it was a perennial mascot for erudite enthusiasts of the paranormal. Every-one agreed it was a fine name for a cropwatch.

Of course, the cropwatch itself had been Colin Andrews's idea and he was its main figure, its driving force. He seemed to have a knack for organizing this kind of thing, assembling the equipment, the manpower, the big names like Archie Roy. And when he was like this, it was as if the other Colin Andrews — the harassed proto-shaman with his black flashes and neuralgic implants and poltergeists and Templars from Malta — didn't even exist. There was only strait-laced, hard-nosed, down-to-earth Colin Andrews, MASEE, AILE, electrical expert and intrepid investigator.

Pat Delgado could be down-to-earth, too, but he wasn't quite as smooth as Andrews when it came to dealing with the press, and these days he was increasingly prone to slip into supernatural mode. In fact, despite a late start, he seemed to be discovering his own shamanic vocation. Certainly his stories were beginning to rival any that Andrews had told. For instance, Delgado would now often talk about the time, one evening in the early part of the summer, when he had been out in the field above the Punchbowl, dowsing the big tumulus, watching the rods swerve and spin in his hands, and suddenly a disembodied voice had said to him: *Pat . . . You don't need the rods . . .*

And . . . the voice was right. He didn't need the rods. They were just an aid, for beginners. He threw aside the rods, held his bare hands out over the tumulus. He could *feel* the energy . . . like a warm fire . . .

Since then he had been a bare-hands dowser. *He didn't need the rods.* He explained to his envious colleagues that he had returned to basics, to primordial sensitivities, to ancient wisdom. Of course it went without saying that he had one-upped not only Colin Andrews, but also the dowser Richard Andrews, who had been lately acquiring quite a lot of influence with circles enthusiasts and the press.

According to Delgado, the voices didn't stop there, though. One night while he had been lying in bed they had descended upon him, and had explained to him what was causing the circles. Then they had sworn him to silence. He was allowed to tell other people, such as his CPR colleagues, that he had been given the answer to it all — but he was emphatically forbidden from telling them what that answer was. For the present, anyway.

The publication date for the book, *Circular Evidence*, was to be 13 July. The cropwatch, Andrews decided, should be held beforehand, close enough to help publicize the book, but not too close to interfere with the rest of the publicity-making that Bloomsbury had planned. He chose the third week in June, Saturday the 10th through Saturday the 17th. The area under surveillance would be the Devil's Punchbowl beneath Cheesefoot Head. It was a natural choice. The Punchbowl had been the site of dozens of crop circle formations over the years. This year the Bowl was planted unusually with peas, a non-cereal crop, but even so, the place was the hottest of the circles hotspots. If circles appeared anywhere, they would appear there, no matter what the crop.

Of course Farmer Bruce wasn't about to let anyone on to his

land, whether tourist or scientist. But the A272 snaked past Cheesefoot Head, and on the south side of the roadway, on Longwood Estate, the fields rose sharply, offering an acceptable view across the road and down into the Bowl. The fields there were managed by Maurice Botting, a crop circle believer, who gave Andrews permission to park the van and the caravan and erect the camera scaffolding in a barley field behind a hawthorn hedge over the road for a week.

On the afternoon of Saturday the tenth, when everything was finally in place, a few dozen people gathered beneath the camera scaffolding in the barley field. Several members of the press were there, and Colin Andrews explained to them that the cameras, collectively worth £28,000, would be operating day and night. Then Archie Roy stepped forward to say a few words, about how it would be the first major scientific cropwatch, though it probably wouldn't be the last. Terence Meaden said a few words, too, about how, despite their ideological differences, they all had a common interest in catching a crop circle formation on film. He explained to the volunteers who would sit before the video monitors how they should take hourly readings from the little meteorological station he had set up nearby, setting down the temperature and barometric pressure and apparent wind direction in the logbook. Finally Colin Andrews said a few more words, and then two volunteers took their places before the video monitors, and Operation White Crow was officially under way.

The afternoon passed without incident, and the night. Sunday came and went, then Monday, and Monday night, and in the early hours of Tuesday, the two circles enthusiasts on duty, Ron Jones and Terry Clarke, saw a strong orange light on the distant horizon. But it was there and gone, and no crop circles appeared. Tuesday passed without incident, and Tuesday night, and Wednesday, and Thursday, and Friday, and the bank of cameras atop the scaffolding recorded only the infinitesimal growth of Farmer Bruce's peas.

Saturday morning, as usual, Colin Andrews drove down from Andover. Ordinarily he came to find out what had happened overnight, but this morning he brought news of his own. He had just received an envelope, addressed to CPR, care of his address, and bearing the words: 'Utmost Urgency to Read. Very Urgent, Information re White Crow.' A card inside announced: 'A communication by our group, asked us to send this to you. Read before Saturday. COLIN ANDREWS: URGENT. WHITE CROW.'

There was also a two-page letter, in cryptic rhyming verse, written in a distinctive hand – narrow, wavy, and with a bizarre system of capitalization, reminiscent of that used hundreds of years ago:

Ring a Ring o Roses
A pocketful of Posies
tishoo tishoo the Corn Sat down

It has been Said that Crows are black
One White you Seek, is that your tack
If No white has Ne'er been Seen
Why Spend this time for one Pipe dream

If black they be, that's where be I
So Simple, flying in the sky
Black on Black, you Cannot See
Although you climb the tallest tree

Your Sight is Set for yards Apart
But Crows fly high, now check your Chart
Where I be is ALL Around, Listen hard
You'll hear my Sound

It seems you work from back to front
Looking for the Cause of such
Find us first, the next you'll know
ALL will be Clear for Rings to Sew

In your hands you have the key
to talk to us, we Are So free
One Soul is there. They have Signed in
Who has the Mind to link Within

Your machines you have Set up
Whate're they Cost is not enough
The human mind is what you need
to me you Can't See Wood for trees

The Chosen One you do know who
We Left our Mark at house of Jew

White Crow

Switch off my friends and Listen do
And I will tell you What to do

Get this Mind and Sit around
In quiet of dark upon the ground
Listen hard for every Sound
Not white of bird? But us Around.

To prove we Are the ones who know
Which one of you has hurt their toe?

Like eternity they have No beginning they have no end
Round + Round Like Atom chain

check your charts when you have time
Same Patterns are up in the sky

Andrews had made a few copies of the letter, and now he handed them around to some of his closer colleagues, such as Delgado, Don Tuersley, and Busty Taylor. None of them knew what to make of the thing. It had been posted from Rochdale, a suburb of Manchester, on Wednesday –

Rochdale . . .

No one said anything, but suddenly everyone knew. Harry Harris lived near Rochdale. He was a solicitor who took an interest in strange phenomena: crop circles, UFOs, alien abductions, and so on. He had been up at the White Crow site a few times, and had spent a night before the monitors. Harry Harris . . . Still, Harry didn't seem like the type who would send an anonymous letter. And in any case, what did the letter mean?

Colin Andrews turned to Rita Goold for help. Rita was a woman in her fifties who had appeared on the crop circles scene the previous summer. The mysterious triangular quadruplet at Oadby in Leicestershire had been just down the road from her house. After investigating it she had struck up a correspondence with several crop circles researchers, including Pat Delgado; and along with her husband Steve she had written several articles for *Flying Saucer Review*. Now, a year later, she was becoming fairly prominent in the crop circles and ufology worlds. But she was also reputed to be a powerful psychic. In a book called *Arthur C. Clarke's World of*

Strange Powers, she was mentioned as one of the world's only four 'materialization mediums'. At her seances in Leicestershire in the early 1980s, it was said, she had briefly brought to life, in solid form, numerous deceased individuals. Colin Andrews knew that if anyone could determine the meaning and the author of the mysterious letter, Rita could.

Rita had come down from Leicestershire for the cropwatch, and was staying with her husband at a nearby caravan park. On Saturday afternoon, Andrews showed her a copy of the letter. Could she help them figure out who had written it? She would try. As Colin sat beside her in her car, she put one of the copies of the letter to her forehead. She closed her eyes. Her brow furrowed. Andrews and the others waited, with the patient knowledge that psychometry, the divination of facts from a related object, was a difficult process, particularly when the object was only a photocopy of the original.

'No,' said Rita, opening her eyes at last, shaking her head. 'I'm sorry. Nothing.'

The day passed, and while Farmer Bruce's peas calmly swayed and grew beneath the cameras and the late spring sun, the discussions on the hillside became more urgent. 'To prove we Are the ones who know / Which one of you has hurt their toe?' Though awkwardly ungrammatical, it seemed to be a clear reference to Busty Taylor, who had broken his toe two years before, after tripping over a strip of barbed wire at Bratton. Not many people knew that story . . .

'Black on Black, you Cannot See / Although you climb the tallest tree.' What did that mean? Something invisible? Some unseen force? 'Read before Saturday.' Something was going to happen on Saturday. 'Get this Mind and Sit around / In quiet of dark upon the ground / Listen hard for every Sound.' This was obviously an instruction: they were to get 'this Mind', and then sit around somewhere, at night, most probably Saturday night. But who was 'this Mind'? Probably the same person referred to in the passages: 'In your hands you have the key,' and 'One Soul is there. They have Signed in / Who has the Mind to link Within', and 'The Chosen One you do know who / We Left our Mark at house of Jew.'

House of Jew? Well, that was an archaic way of putting things. It sounded almost anti-Semitic. It made the rest of them feel a little uncomfortable. Still, there was no getting around the fact that Harry Harris was Jewish . . .

But then so was Steve Goold, Rita's husband –

Of course . . .

It was obvious now. Why hadn't they seen it before? Rita, married to a Jew, thus living in 'house of Jew', was moreover a psychic – only she had 'Signed in'; only she had 'the Mind to link Within'.

That night, a chilly, moonlit night, six of them met for dinner at the Percy Hobbs, an old country pub a few miles down the road from the Punchbowl. Colin Andrews was there, with Delgado, Busty Taylor, George Wingfield, and Rita and Steve Goold. Don Tuersley was on duty back at the site, watching the monitors.

Andrews's plan was straightforward. They should all go up along the road, past the cameras and the van and the caravan, to a barley field where two crop circles had appeared a few weeks earlier. They would sit in one of the circles. Rita would go into a trance. They would keep their ears open. And they would wait for something to happen.

At first the idea had been to go up at about half past ten. But when the time neared, Andrews said he wanted to push things back a little while, closer to midnight. But Rita and Steve had hoped to drive back to Leicester before too long. It would be a four-hour drive. They didn't want to stay out all night. And neither did Wingfield. It was his wife's birthday, or their wedding anniversary, or something. He had promised to come home early, to take her out to dinner. Now, with the mysterious letter, and the plan for a seance . . . Well, he didn't want to miss out on what was going to happen. But all the same he wanted to get the thing over with.

Still, it was Andrews's operation, and they all shrugged and went along. No one wanted to risk Andrews's ire by complaining too loudly. Eventually they drove back to the caravan, and sat drinking coffee. Midnight approached, and Tuersley, fighting a cold, left for home. But Andrews wanted to hold off a bit longer. Why was Andrews delaying things like this? wondered Rita and Steve. Wingfield was annoyed, now, too. Even if he left now, he wouldn't make it home before one or two o'clock in the morning. His wife was going to kill him.

Finally, at about 12.15, Andrews said it was time, and they walked up the road and entered the field. The circles were only fifty yards or so from the road, up a footpath that ran along a hedge, and then to the left through narrow paths trodden in the barley. One circle was about twenty feet wide, the other about fifty. Rita suggested they sit in the smaller one; it seemed cosier. But now Delgado spoke up, and insisted they sit in the larger one. No one said anything. But the same question was on all their minds . . . First Andrews, with the delays; now Delgado, with the insistence on a particular circle. What were they up to?

They filed into the larger circle, and sat down towards one edge. Rita closed her eyes and began to slip into a trance . . .

'Wait,' said Delgado. 'There's someone missing. We need seven. We only have six. We need seven . . .' The others watched in silence as Delgado looked about anxiously. 'There's someone missing . . .'

'Ah!' he exclaimed finally. 'Yes, yes, it's all right now. That makes seven . . .'

None of the others could see the additional entity, but they decided it was best to accommodate Delgado, now that they had come this far. Rita closed her eyes again and began breathing deeply, then more gently, and at last she had entered the trance. Her eyelids quivered, and she murmured softly . . . distant echoes from the spirit world . . . The others tried to relax, closing their eyes, opening their minds . . . The moon and the stars shone brightly down on them, and the minutes began to pass . . .

'What the hell is that?' Andrews asked suddenly, anxiously, after about half an hour had gone by.

Wingfield wasn't sure where the noise was coming from. It seemed to come out of his head, out of everyone's head. It seemed to be everywhere and nowhere . . .

Nrrrrrzzzzzz . . . It sounded like a cricket, or a grasshopper, or a rattlesnake, or . . . high voltage electrodes, when the spark is about to jump . . .

Nrrrrrrzzzzzzzzzzzzzzzzzzzzzzzzzzzzz . . .

It was the same sound Andrews had heard at the Kimpton ring.

The Kimpton ring sound! The static electrical crackling sound he had heard in the summer of 1987, after asking God to tell him what was making the circles. 'Oh, God,' said Andrews now. 'Oh God!'

The noise grew louder, and now it was clearly outside the circle, on the other side, the side Delgado had moved them away from. But –

It was moving! *Nrrrrzzzzzzzzzzz . . . Nrrrrzzzzzzzzzz . . .* Moving around them, circling them! *Nrrrrzzzzzzzzzz . . .*

Delgado was on his feet now, fighting the force field . . . It pulled him away like a powerful wave . . . He staggered towards the centre of the circle, towards the noise. 'No!' he gasped. 'No!' The force field . . . the entity . . . Purest evil! It had him in its grip. 'No!' He faced the others, his face a mask of anguish. Dragging him away . . . 'Aagggghhhhh!' It bent him backwards at a horrible angle, yet somehow kept him on his feet, still dragging him, dragging him . . . It was too much . . . 'Aagggghhhhh . . .' He was at the centre of the circle now –

'Unnnhh!'

Delgado straightened suddenly. The force . . . the entity . . . It had relaxed its grip . . . Now he could get back to the others . . . Yes . . .

No! A wall! An invisible wall now lay between him and the others! His hands pressed flat against it, moved across it, seeking an edge, an escape . . .

Now Rita Goold got up, and walked towards Delgado. She seemed strangely unaffected by the force field. Her psychic powers . . . She –

She walked right through the invisible wall.

'Ahhhgggggggggggh!!!' screamed Delgado, as the awful release of energy hurled him to the ground. His back arched. Strange guttural noises came from his mouth. His head jutted unnaturally sideways. The entity . . . *The entity . . .*

George Wingfield felt as if he were somehow under hypnosis. It was all so unreal. He seemed to have lost his will . . . his free will . . . Something made him get up and join Rita at the far edge of the circle. The noise had stopped moving. It was close to them now, only a few yards away, down amid the stalks of barley.

'If you can understand us, stop!' said Rita.

And . . . it stopped . . . For an awkward moment there were only the muted noises of human gurgling and sobbing.

And then it began again.

Nrrrrrrzzzzzzzzzzzzzzzzzzzzzzz ...

Wingfield stepped forward to the edge of the circle, and addressed the noise. 'Will you make us a circle?'

Wingfield and Rita stepped out into the barley, to get closer to the thing ...

Nrrrrzzzzz!!! Down in the barley! Only a few feet away now! But it moved off again, and began circling, circling. Farther out ... Farther ... Like a wary animal, thought Wingfield ... Circling ...

But the worst seemed to be over. It looked as if it was going to be all right.

In fact, Delgado's crisis, his final test, had been passed. But for a few rough edges he was now a full-fledged shaman, a seer and a healer. He could handle the entities and their energies. He slowly got to his feet, and crept towards the edge of the circle. Andrews rose and followed him. At the edge of the circle, Delgado held Andrews, as Andrews leaned backward, far back, his hair touching the heads of the barley. He was sobbing with gratitude. Delgado held him with one hand, and scooped invisible energy from the heads of barley with the other, ladling it generously, medicinally, over his co-author and colleague ...

Ron Jones was forty-one that summer. He ran a hairdressing studio in Andover, and studied Egyptology on the side. He had been interested in the crop circles phenomenon for a few years, and had been a regular at Operation White Crow. When Andrews and the others walked up the road to do the seance that night, he was in the caravan, finishing a cup of soup. He wasn't officially on duty, but it was the final night of the operation, and he wanted to be there if anything happened. Ever since he had seen the orange light in the sky in the early morning hours of Tuesday, he had been waiting for something else ... And then this letter had arrived. He did wonder whether it might be some kind of hoax – someone having a little fun at their expense. But then again ... he didn't want to miss out on anything. He hadn't exactly been invited to join the others, but he hadn't been told to stay away either, and he knew where they were going ...

They had been gone for half an hour or so when Jones decided to leave the caravan and walk up the road. Even before he reached the gates marking the field where the circles were, he heard the sound. It was a penetrating sound, and loud, almost as if someone had brought an amplifier down into the field. He opened the gates, walked up the bridleway towards the field, and –

A bright pair of horns in the sky . . .

They seemed to hang above the circle. *A pair of horns* . . . Jones knew a thing or two about ancient rites, about gods and demons . . . He understood the significance of horns . . . and these looked just like the horns of . . . Isis . . . The ancient Egyptian Goddess . . . of fertility and farming . . . and of the underworld. The horns seemed to surround the moon, symmetrically, and they were high up, miles high, moonlit stratospheric ice, or ionospheric aurora-stuff . . . A natural phenomenon, to be sure, and yet . . . *the horns of Isis!* . . . And the sound! That awful chattering sound . . . It reminded him of the ritual rattle used in the Egyptian burial rites . . . The rites of Isis . . .

Nrrrzzzzzzzzzzzzzzzzzzzzz . . .

He walked along the hedge, as the field sloped down before him. In the distance shone the lights of Southampton, and . . . a fire . . . the great flaming breath of the Fawley Oil Refinery. And close to him in the moonlight, he could see the figures in the circle. By now, two more White Crow volunteers, Ken Smith and his brother-in-law, had heard the noise and had found their way to the circle. There were eight figures visible . . . The sound was clearly audible . . . Jones saw Delgado beckoning to him from within the circle. He walked down a narrow pathway through the barley . . . into the circle . . . Someone indicated where he should sit. Seven of them sat together to one side, while Delgado and Andrews stood apart. It was exciting, and yet . . . He felt like someone arriving late, cold sober, at a waning party. The rest of them listened hopefully to the noise . . . It was still there, but it seemed to have drifted away with Jones's approach.

The moment had passed, and after a while, the adrenaline began to run low. Delgado said that they should leave, and the rest of them readily assented. They quietly began to file out of the circle. They were tired. It had been a long day. The experience with the noise had been almost overwhelming.

'I can't get out,' said Delgado suddenly. The others turned and saw him, still inside the circle, wide-eyed, walking in his own tight spirals. '*I can't get out!*'

Andrews went to him, gently took his arm. 'Come on, Pat.' And they all returned to the caravan, as the sound receded behind them.

'We can't let the press get hold of this,' said Jones.

Delgado and Andrews agreed.

It was two o'clock when they returned to the caravan. Which meant they had been out in the field for about ninety minutes. To Wingfield, it hadn't seemed as long as that. It had seemed more like thirty minutes. He wondered whether they had experienced missing time. He knew that when people were abducted by aliens, they often experienced missing time ... And yet, he seemed to have a continuous recollection of the events of the night. But then so did a lot of people who had experienced missing time ...

Ken Smith's teenage daughter and her girlfriend had been watching the camera monitors in the van, but they could tell that something had been going on over in the adjacent field. They came over to the caravan. *What happened, Daddy?*

Oh, nothing, sweetheart. Only an odd noise.

Neither Ken, nor any of the others, was about to explain what had happened. It wasn't clear how they could explain it even to a mature adult. So they sat and drank coffee, and said very little. It had been a long, cold, exhausting, bewildering night.

After a short while Delgado and the Goolds and Ken Smith's brother-in-law left. Andrews, Wingfield, Busty Taylor, Ken Smith, and Ron Jones stayed in the caravan, talking, while the girls watched the camera monitors in the van. Wingfield suggested to Andrews that they go back and tape the noise. Andrews agreed. He had a tape recorder in his car, so they went over to the car-park. Jones followed, and slipped into the back seat as they were about to leave. They drove a few hundred yards down the road to the cattle gates, and got out. Andrews had his hand-held tape recorder. They went through the gates and on to the path. The sound was still audible, though now it seemed to have moved even farther away. They walked down the path, past the circles. *Nrrrrrzzzzzzz* ... It was hard to tell now where it was coming from. It seemed to emanate from the next field . . . a sea of wheat beneath the setting moon . . .

The path crossed a bridleway and stopped at the edge of the wheatfield. The thing was still ahead of them . . . Moving east . . . Jones wasn't sure he wanted to go further. He decided he would stay there, at the edge of the field. To stand guard. He watched the dark shapes of Wingfield and Andrews as they pressed on, walking single file down a wheatfield tramline, listening . . . listening . . .

NRRRZZZZZZZ!!!

Jesus! Ron Jones jumped. It was right beside him! Right there in the wheat! It sounded like someone crunching a pile of crisp packets together, all at once. But with a purpose! It was as if he were being . . . herded . . . ordered to move . . .

He ran along the tramline towards Wingfield and Andrews. It was embarrassing, but . . . he had nowhere else to go.

The three of them continued on down the tramline, down . . . down . . . the hill sloping gently down . . . to a barbed wire fence. And the noise was still there, tantalizing, in the next field now, still moving east. *Nrrrrrzzzzzzzz* . . .

But none of them had the heart to continue. It had been a long day, a long night . . . They would never catch it . . . Or perhaps it would still be there when daylight came.

Daylight . . . In fact, the eastern sky already shone dimly now, the high clouds catching the first vague refracted rays of a Sunday sun.

They walked back up the tramline, their shoes and trousers cold and wet from the dew on the stalks, their faces ashen from tension, sleeplessness, the cold. They reached the path, then the car, then drove quietly back to the caravan.

The girls had left, and Wingfield went over to sleep in the van. Taylor and Smith slept in the caravan. Jones and Andrews slept in Andrews's car. In an hour or two the sun was up and warm, and they awoke again, strangely refreshed, but in the kind of haze that turns to sleepless stupor before long. But the sun . . . A new day . . . And warm . . . They began to unhook the cameras, the batteries, started dismantling the scaffolding, cleaning the van and the caravan. A nice long sleep at the end of it –

But last night, they thought, it hadn't been a dream. It had happened . . . We had been there . . .

Round in Circles

They were drinking coffee at the caravan when a car pulled up at the lay-by. A young couple were in it. The guy was calling to them ... Hey ... Hey ... Trying to tell them something ... Something about a crop circle that had formed overnight ... A circle with a ring. In a field beyond the other two circles, far back from the road. To the east ... Had they seen it?

11

Circular Evidence

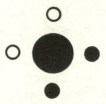

The greatest of all physicists, Albert Einstein, proved that photons exist, but they do not exist in time. In other words, they do not recognize time. He also stated that everything in existence is based upon the photon. The photon has an infinite lifetime, and can take any form it wishes as mass and anti-mass. With the anti-proton, or photon, which has no mass and no charge, an infinite lifetime is established as the vital bridge between the state of being (now) and the state of 'not being' in the physical world.

This would seem to support the theory that the circles are created by an unknown force field manipulated by an unknown intelligence.

— Pat Delgado, in *Circular Evidence*

By the time of the White Crow affair, review copies of *Circular Evidence* already had been distributed to the press, and news of its imminent arrival in bookstores had begun to spread. Circles enthusiasts, New Agers, aficionados of the paranormal, and the merely curious — all awaited it eagerly. And they would not be disappointed, for *Circular Evidence* was a handsome book. The first half featured large colour photographs of thirty-four circles formations from the period 1978–88, with accompanying text describing the apparent circumstances of circles formation, and any subsequent events, such as black flashes or angry farmers. The second half of the book featured lengthy and comparatively dry discussions of circles characteristics, various theories regarding circles formation, old saucer-nest cases, and additional anecdotes about paranormal experiences in the fields. But the book could easily stand on its picturesque first half alone.

Even so, Delgado and Andrews were taking no chances, and in the run-up to publication in July, they helped to keep the crop circles phenomenon in the news. Operation White Crow, for example, was widely touted as a success – the suggestion being that the mysterious noise had been the noise of a crop circle being swirled. 'Researchers from Sussex University,' reported the *Marlborough Times*, 'are investigating sounds produced when circles are created, said to resemble the noise made by a cricket. The sound was recorded by surveillance equipment worth £28,000.'

At the same time, Delgado and Andrews were telling the press that the circles-swirling energy wreaked 'molecular changes' in crops. Andrews had sent stalk samples to a private laboratory run by a New Age couple near Stroud; the lab had performed a kind of complicated crystallization process, and the microscope photographs seemed to show a difference between samples from inside the circles and 'control' samples from outside. Andrews wrote with these results to Nicholas Ridley, the Environment Secretary, requesting £50,000 in research funds, and warning of the possible dire consequences for the food chain if the circles phenomenon were not quickly understood. Ridley wrote back, apparently ignoring Andrews's plea for funding and suggesting that the circles were caused by wind. After further correspondence, Andrews received a letter from Richard Ryder, the Secretary of MAFF – the Ministry of Agriculture, Fisheries, and Food. Ryder told Andrews that the circles, rather than being swirled by some unknown force, were 'most likely to result from a combination of wind and local soil conditions', and were thus unlikely to involve any crop contamination.

Nevertheless, the fact that the issue had even been raised was news. The headlines included:

RESEARCHERS WANT BAN ON MYSTERY CROPS

ANALYSTS RING WARNING BELLS OVER CIRCLES

BAN ON MYSTIC CROPS URGED

Delgado and Andrews kicked off the book with a press conference in early July, in a crop circle on Longwood Estate, not far from where the White Crow seance had occurred. A dozen or so reporters were bussed out from London by Bloomsbury. Andrews gave a short speech, generally describing the phenomenon and his involvement in it, and Delgado followed with a speech of his own, and then the reporters asked their questions.

Don Tuersley was at the press conference, too, standing with Delgado and Andrews. He'd been working with Pat and Colin for three years now, and they were all good friends and colleagues. They were all part of the same team, as far as he was concerned. But somehow the Bloomsbury publicists didn't see it that way. When a reporter threw a question at Tuersley, someone interrupted from the back: 'Let the authors speak!' And Tuersley meekly retreated.

It could have been worse. Someone could have asked who had taken the photographs, which were obviously the book's strong suit – and ... Busty Taylor, who had taken most of the pictures, and who was not receiving royalties from the book's sale, nor even credit for his individual pictures, would have stepped forward ... But Busty was safely aloft that day. Pat and Colin had asked him to take a camera crew from SKY TV on an aerial tour of the circles hotspots.

Circular Evidence almost immediately made the bestseller list, and eventually reached as high as number three. It was reviewed, or its authors were profiled, in virtually every major newspaper in the United Kingdom, plus most of the local papers in circles-prone areas, plus a substantial number of foreign papers, including the *Wall Street Journal*, the *Chicago Tribune*, and a few of the big German dailies. And even if Delgado and Andrews themselves were occasionally portrayed as cranks, the reviews of the book were almost uniformly good, both in the tabloids and in the so-called quality press. Sean Thomas wrote in the *Mail on Sunday* that the book 'took at least this reader's sceptical breath away'. Alexander Urquhart wrote in the *Times Literary Supplement*:

If the circles are made by human beings (the argument against this is powerful and convincing), we might consider them a new ephemeral art-form; because they are not, their beauty acquires an extra, haunting quality ... That the authors are both trained electrical engineers gives credibility to their survey of the possibilities. They examine in detail many suggested theories from piezoelectric generation to hoaxing, and find them all wanting ... The case for the existence of this phenomenon stands well on the unembellished photographic evidence as well as the painstaking attempts at analysis.

Ralph Noyes, a former MoD undersecretary who was one of Archie Roy's colleagues in the Society for Psychical Research, wrote in *Country Life* that Delgado and Andrews's book was 'indispensable for its abundant illustrations', and offered 'an absorbing account of the many expeditions made in pursuit of cropfield circles by the book's two authors and their several colleagues ...'

John Michell, by now an icon of British New-Ageism, wrote in the *Spectator*:

> *Circular Evidence* is a beautiful-looking book. Its fine coloured photographs of rings and circles etched upon summer cornfields give good reason for the authors' delight in their subject. They feel nothing sinister about it, but they have come to suspect that physical science is not equipped to explain it. Their approach is nonetheless impeccably scientific.

Even Derek Elsom, a physics tutor at Oxford Polytechnic and an old TORRO colleague of Meaden's, wrote a reasonably favourable review of the book in the *Geographic* magazine. Perhaps out of embarrassment, Meaden had refrained from telling Elsom and the others in TORRO very much about his unseemly battles with the Delgadonians, and so as far as Elsom was concerned, Delgado and Andrews were merely fellow circles researchers, out to bring the phenomenon to the attention of the public. Even so, Meaden was staggered. 'Elsom's review was bland, bland, totally gutless,' he remembers bitterly.

*

Circular Evidence was more than just a book that received good reviews. It seemed to strike that deep chord in the collective psyche, the same one Orson Welles had touched with his *War of the Worlds* broadcast in 1938. Suddenly everyone was talking about . . . those circles in the fields.

Hansard recorded this exchange in Parliament on 11 July:

Mr Teddy Taylor: To ask the Secretary of State for Defence what progress has been made in the inquiries initiated by Army helicopters based in the south-west in investigating the origin of flattened circular areas of wheat; and if he will make a statement.

Mr Neubert: The Ministry of Defence is not conducting any inquiries into the origins of flattened circular areas of crops. However, we are satisfied that they are not caused by service helicopter activity.

A week later, Hansard recorded another such exchange:

MR MICHAEL COLVIN: To ask the Secretary of State for the Home Department if he will call for a report from the chief constables of Hampshire and Wiltshire on their investigations into the cornfield circles of Hampshire and Wiltshire; what is the estimated cost of these investigations; and if he will make a statement.

MR DOUGLAS HURD: I understand from the chief constables of Hampshire and Wiltshire that there have been no investigations into the cornfield circles by their officers.

The MoD declared its lack of interest, as did the Home Office, and yet . . . some of the photographs in *Circular Evidence* clearly showed an Army helicopter hovering over a circle at Westbury. On 9 July, the *Sunday Express* reported that Mrs Thatcher had read *Circular Evidence* and 'was passing a funding report to the Ministry of Defence'. On the 12th, the *Southern Evening Echo* reported that Mrs Thatcher would soon 'step in to help find an explanation'. And then in August, the *Wall Street Journal* reported that:

British agriculture and defence officials want to know more. So does Queen Elizabeth, who is said to have sharply questioned Prime Minister Margaret Thatcher about the circles recently. While those talks are kept secret, a Buckingham Palace spokesman says the Queen took a hurriedly published book about the circles to her summer palace in Scotland this month; as Britain's biggest landowner, she has every reason not to be amused.

Andrews and Delgado hardly had time for any serious circles investigation that summer. As sudden celebrities, their daily schedules brimmed with talk-show appearances, documentary filming sessions, and interviews with reporters from around the world.

Busty Taylor didn't mind at all. He recognized that most of the limelight, in fact just about all of it, was shining down on Colin and Pat. But he knew that that would change, because they were a team, and he had taken the pictures for the book, and everyone loved the pictures, and sooner or later . . .

One day a crew from some Australian TV programme arranged to interview Pat and Colin at Cheesefoot Head, and Busty was not invited. He found out about it later, and pressed Colin for an explanation. Colin explained that they had phoned him and Taylor's line had been busy – or that things had moved too quickly, and there had simply been no time to call. Taylor let it go by, but as the weeks passed, it seemed to him that these little coincidences, these little failures of communication, were occurring again and again, as German TV crews, Japanese TV crews, American TV crews, came and shone their lights around and left, while he sat expectantly by the phone in the living room of his council house in Andover.

Taylor began to question Colin and Pat more urgently, began to remind them that they were all in this together – all for one, one for all . . . began to insist, in fact, that as a team member he be allowed his share of the team's limelight.

'Busty's behaving very queerly these days,' Andrews would say to Meaden, on occasions when they would meet in fields. And Meaden would nod quietly, having earlier received an earful from Taylor on how Andrews and Delgado were allegedly depriving him of the recognition which he believed was due him.

Some time in late July or early August, when the public hysteria over the circles phenomenon was at its peak, Busty told Meaden he was going to force a showdown with Colin and Pat. At the same time, Colin told Meaden that he and Pat had decided to hold a meeting with Busty, to see if they could determine what was troubling him.

The meeting was at Colin's house in Andover, and the four of them were there: Colin and Pat, and Busty and Don. In the previous weeks, Don hadn't been as vocal as Busty about the alleged arrogation of the limelight by Pat and Colin, but even so, he had felt strongly about it, and had backed up Busty's suspicions with his own. The meeting began with Busty and Don complaining that throughout the summer Pat and Colin had been acting as if CPR were a team of two, whereas CPR was, in fact, a team of four.

But we did a lot of hard work on that book, protested Delgado. We spent a hard winter writing it. We deserve the reward we're getting now.

Busty asserted that his pictures constituted the most important part of the book, and that he had not received even a proper credit for them.

Andrews and Delgado disputed the value of the pictures, and Taylor and Tuersley disputed Andrews's and Delgado's valuation of the pictures, and finally, according to Taylor, Delgado said, 'After all, you two are just characters in our book.'

And the voices rose, and the tempers flared, and suddenly Andrews said: 'Right. We obviously can't agree on anything. CPR is hereby disbanded. Let's go our separate ways.'

And that was that.

Outside, as they walked to their cars, Tuersley asked Delgado, 'We'll still be friends, won't we?'

'Of course, of course, Don.'

But after a few weeks of unanswered calls and letters, it was clear to Tuersley what had happened. Demoralized by the experience, he more or less dropped out of circles research. Taylor, meanwhile, began to suggest that he had been promised, by oral agreement, a third of the royalties from the book, and for a time he lived with the idea that he would eventually receive this amount through the courts. To anyone who would listen, he would recount Delgado's and Andrews's alleged treachery, and would smile as he envisioned the day when everything was put right and justice was done. In the end he received £2,400 – an amount which Delgado and Andrews claim they had promised him all along, and which corresponded almost exactly, supernaturally, with the sum charged Taylor by an Andover solicitor for his consultations regarding the possibility of a lawsuit.

CPR was re-established that summer, with Colin Andrews and Pat Delgado as sole members.

One day, about a week or so after the break-up with Taylor and Tuersley, Delgado and Andrews were being filmed by a BBC-1 crew to provide feature footage for an upcoming edition of a popular talk show, *Daytime Live*. It was about three in the afternoon, on a hazy, warm, August day, and Delgado and Andrews stood in a massive 120-foot diameter circle near Beckhampton while the crew tried to sort out problems with one of their cameras – some kind of electrical interference, with noise bars on the scope, and red lights on the panel indicating a malfunction. The problems seemed to go away when they moved the camera out of the circle, then returned when they moved it back in again. Eventually they switched to another camera, and Andrews went out into the centre of the circle and delivered a short spiel, and when he was finished Delgado went out into the centre, carrying a small black bag. Delgado, like Andrews, wore a radio mike, a tiny little device fastened between the buttons on his shirt-front, and connected by a wire to a cigarette-pack sized transmitter in his pocket. At the edge of the circle stood Andrews, and the producer, David Morganstern, and the director, John Macnish, and a few cameramen, and a sound man, Richard Merrick.

'What's that?' said Merrick. He was looking at Delgado. 'I'm getting some kind of interference.' Apparently some kind of noise was cutting through Delgado's audio link.

'The noise!' said Andrews.

'It's an electric sparrow kind of noise,' said Merrick. It sounded like very high-pitched rushing air. *Shhhhhhhhhhhhhhhhhhhhhhhhhh.*

'I can hear it,' said Delgado, looking at the ground around him, then adding, 'I can feel it. It's right here.' He made a motion with his hands over the ground.

Delgado took a few steps to one side and the noise was gone. He walked back and the noise faded in again. After a while it stopped. Delgado reached down into his bag and retrieved a compass.

The incident was broadcast in October, and was so widely covered in the media – UFO BLASTS TV CREW IN CIRCLE, reported the *Sun* – that a few days later Delgado and Andrews and Richard Merrick came into the *Daytime Live* studio for a live interview about the event. Merrick explained that they had never figured out what had caused the camera to malfunction, but that it had required a complete rebuild, and as for the noise – well, the engineers and technicians and other experts had been mystified by that, too. Delgado managed to invoke *Circular Evidence* several times, and Andrews explained that for mankind it was 'ten minutes to midnight', and that 'mother earth was crying out'. And among the viewing public, many true believers were born that day.

12

The Mowing Devil

... the field has always been a grazing field since that time.

– Mrs Joan Tookey, in a letter to Terence Meaden about a crop
circle she had seen in a field in Kent in the summer of 1918

Meaden sent about 100 copies of his book to the press, and in some
cases it was reviewed, as he had hoped it would be, alongside
Circular Evidence. But on the whole it received far less attention
than his rivals' work. To the average reader, it was obscure and
technical, full of ion-leakages and Kapitza-type antinodal sites. And
its photos were small, dull, and black-and-white.

Professional meteorologists probably avoided *The Circles Effect*
for a different reason. To them it must have seemed like fringe
stuff, full of wild hypotheses and UFOs. What reviews it received
were seldom better than lukewarm. *Circular Evidence* would go on
to sell nearly 100,000 copies worldwide. Meaden's *Circles Effect*, by
contrast, would sell only a few thousand. Randles and Fuller's
Controversy of the Circles would sell about 700.

Not surprisingly, Randles and Fuller, and to a lesser extent
Meaden, spent the summer of 1989 fighting back. Through
interviews in the popular press, background advice to reporters,
letters to MPs and government officials, and articles in their own
journals, they pointed out Delgado's and Andrews's beliefs in alien

intelligences and unknown force fields, and the fact that both were consultants to *Flying Saucer Review*. They accused the two of deliberately misleading the public with the 'food-chain' scare, and with suggestions that the MoD, or MAFF, or Mrs Thatcher, were concerned about the subject. It was Fuller, in fact, who prompted his MP Michael Colvin to put forward parliamentary questions on the matter – hoping that the answers, by demonstrating government unconcern, would lay the matter to rest and expose Delgado and Andrews as cynical hypesters. Fuller wrote to 10 Downing Street, which similarly denied any interest in the subject.

Not that any of this mattered, with regard to the celebrity of Delgado and Andrews and the enormous success of their book. Fuller and Randles were like the proverbial voices crying in the wilderness. And even when the media might have had an interest in setting them against Delgado and Andrews for a debate on the circles, Delgado and Andrews were powerful enough – meaning, popular enough – to be able to insist that whenever they appeared, say, on a talk-show, they would not have to face any unpleasantness from the BUFORA duo. And they never did, although Randles did once manage to spar with Andrews long-distance. The forum was the *Gloria Hunniford Show*, a popular radio call-in programme on BBC Radio 2. Hunniford brought Colin Andrews on in early August, to talk about his new book, and for a while he did – until Randles called in. She began by mentioning Andrews and Delgado's association with *Flying Saucer Review*, and then berated them for allegedly having suppressed evidence that supported Meaden's theory . . .

RANDLES: . . . there are eyewitness accounts – which [Andrews and Delgado] studiously avoid mentioning in their book – of people who have actually seen circles being formed in daylight by wind vortexes.

HUNNIFORD: Let me stop you there, Jenny. Now what about this point, Colin?

ANDREWS: There are just so many, aren't there? I mean the lady just doesn't –

HUNNIFORD: Well, let's take that eyewitness report and the weather aspect.

ANDREWS: Yes. Yes, indeed, there's one eyewitness report [the Melvyn Bell case] –

RANDLES: There's more than one, many more than one.

ANDREWS: Well, I mean, we are directly involved in this every day, and not just as a journalist sat behind a desk up in London or wherever you are based. Ah, we've not yet seen you inside one circle, let alone the 218 that we've researched this year alone. Ah, you can indeed sit and make allegations, but I would suggest the most reasonable – the most responsible retort that I could make to that is that you have to respect the fact that, one, we are qualified people. We are working with thirty-five other scientists and not just one, as you are indeed yourself working with at the Tornado and Storm Research Organization –

HUNNIFORD: Let's pick up that other point, though.

RANDLES: Yes, the point.

HUNNIFORD: Yes, what of the theory about the weather –

ANDREWS: Yes, well, we're looking at this very closely. We're receiving all the weather data from Bracknell, and have done for a number of years. We have all the computer printouts. We're working with sixteen other Met bureaus in Europe, and we see no correlation with meteorology at all. Ah, let me say, this is not being done from a distance. We're working on a daily basis with Terence Meaden – Dr Meaden – who Jenny Randles is referring to, at Tornado and Storm Research. We ... we know of one, ah, *alleged* eyewitness account. And let me – I must say Gloria, this is very important, the only one, ah, one eyewitness account of a circle being formed during daylight hours, happened to be – isn't it a strange coincidence? – an employee of Dr Meaden's?

Meaden soon heard about it from Fuller, and demanded that Andrews apologize. Andrews admitted that he had 'mismanaged' his answer.

That seemed to be good enough for Meaden, who remained in frequent contact, phoning Andrews whenever he heard about a new circle, sometimes arranging to meet him and conduct a joint investigation. He had even been the one to tell Andrews about the circle at Beckhampton, where the *Daytime Live* episode occurred. In truth, he was willing to let a few black barbs go by, if only he could still remain connected to the Delgadonian network, which was now growing huge in the wake of *Circular Evidence*. But as August wore on, Meaden increasingly found himself examining circles that Andrews had been through long before. And he noticed that Andrews phoned him less and less, eventually ceasing altogether. After a while he stopped phoning Andrews, and the brief rapprochement of 1989 was over.

Unsurprisingly, Meaden's review of *Circular Evidence* in *J. Met.* was scathing. He lambasted its authors for their 'irrational and arrogant rejection of the application of the normal laws of physics and meteorology', and for the embrace of 'the questionable realms of thought of the paranormal and the hopelessness of the pseudo-scientific'.

He went into meticulous detail, contradicting the suggestion in *Circular Evidence* that Andrews had first met Delgado about the circles in 1983 – 'Colin Andrews and Pat Delgado did not know one another until Mr Andrews contacted Mr Delgado in summer 1986 at my suggestion.' He pointed out that several events related in the first person by Andrews had occurred when both Andrews and Delgado were absent, and only Meaden and Taylor, say, had been present. He complained about the glaring lack of mention of himself, TORRO, and BUFORA, who had all at one time or another cooperated with Delgado and Andrews. Above all, he took Delgado and Andrews to task for ignoring and suppressing evidence, and even hinted that they'd manufactured some:

> . . . The authors inhabit a world of their own in which observations inconsistent with their fantasies get overlooked . . . Admittedly, this might on some occasions be unintentional – the result of an inability to appreciate the significance of some of the clues passing before their eyes (the authors are not physicists or meteorologists) – but some omissions, as we shall show, are deliberate because evidence which they did possess has been knowingly suppressed . . . Can we deduce a reason for this? It seems that either it emanates from an unstoppable

desire to force a paranormal solution into the place of a natural one, or it is because the authors are astute enough to realize that high-volume sales depend upon feeding one mystery with further mysteries in order to distance the solution rather than approach it. This technique improves sales to a credulous public, but is unnatural and unworthy of investigators who would wish to claim they are scientists . . .

In what they have written there is so much that is erroneous, so much that is confusing and misleading, that many readers will be unable to tell the true statements from the false.

[Their] intention seems to be to attract the multitude and maybe deceive the gullible . . .

From a future historical perspective, one may be able to perceive some of the unusual opinions about the circles, including those intimated by the writers of this book, as providing a contribution to the study of modern myth-making. This aspect of the subject may then develop a usefulness to psychologists wishing to observe how myths commence and prosper.

It was a bitter summer for the Meadenites. But despite losing the war of words, they seemed to be winning in the fields, so to speak. At about midnight of 28 June, the caretaker of the West Kennet long barrow stalked out of his cottage beside the A4, after an argument with his wife. Outside in the darkness, he said later, he noticed something out of the corner of his eye. He turned and saw a dimly luminous sphere, orange-coloured and about thirty feet in diameter, drifting above one of the fields by the long barrow. It just drifted, moving west to east along the field, losing altitude like a spent balloon. It seemed to flatten at the bottom as it hit the field. It bounced up again, then winked out.

The caretaker told Colin Andrews about it, and Andrews recalled that the night before, he and a film crew had flown over the field, spotting two small circles and a ringed circle. That morning there was an additional quintuplet – albeit a botched one, with three satellites plus a small mashed patch on a tramline where the fourth should have been. It was generally agreed that the quintuplet had something to do with the luminous sphere, of which Meaden later wrote:

The observations of luminosity reported by the eyewitness are highly significant for the theory of plasma vortices as proposed by the author ... for one may conjecture that the peripheral brightness noted for the self-luminous ball accords with the position of the plasma-pause, the primary source of the electro-magnetic and radio-frequency emissions postulated for the radiating vortex.

Another case occurred at about half past one in the morning of 10 August, ironically the same day as the *Daytime Live* affair. Two youths, Wilfred Gomez and Simon Millington, were driving along a road near Margate, Kent, when, according to Gomez, they noticed 'a spiralling vortex of flashing light' ahead in a field. As they drew nearer, the thing began to look like 'an upturned satellite TV dish with lots of flashing lights. It appeared to brush the ground, then all the lights blinked out ...' It made a noise which Gomez later said he 'could not really describe'. Gomez and Millington stopped the car, walked into the field where they had seen the odd luminosity, and discovered two circles, one about fifteen feet in diameter, the other about sixty feet. The next day someone told a local paper about it, and somehow from there the news found its way into the crop circles research community. The *Fortean Times* later wrote that Gomez's and Millington's experience 'may well be the first incident in which the formation of a crop circle has been witnessed in direct association with the luminous aspect of Dr Meaden's "plasma vortex"'.

At about the same time, Jenny Randles received a surprising piece of information from a local historian named Betty Puttick, from St Albans, Hertfordshire. Mrs Puttick had just read Randles and Fuller's *Controversy of the Circles*, and it had reminded her of a seventeenth-century woodcut she had come across in a recent book on Hertfordshire folklore. The woodcut, which decorated the first page of a four-page pamphlet, depicted a small, black, horned figure, scything down oatstalks along a circular path, leaving what appear to be flaming stalks in his wake. The accompanying text, a charming example of early tabloid journalism, read as follows:

THE MOWING-DEVIL:
OR, STRANGE NEWS OUT OF HARTFORD-SHIRE

Being a True Relation of a Farmer, who Bargaining with a Poor Mower, about the Cutting down Three Half Acres of Oats: upon the Mower's asking too much, the Farmer swore That the Devil should Mow it rather than He. And so it fell out, that very Night, the Crop of Oat shew'd as if it had been all of a Flame: but next Morning appear'd so neatly mow'd by the Devil or some Infernal Spirit, that no Mortal Man was able to do the like.

Also, How the said Oats ly now in the Field, and the Owner has not Power to fetch them away.

Licensed, August 22, 1678

Men may dally with Heaven, and criticize on Hell, as Wittily as they please, but that there are really such places, the wise Dispensations of Almighty Providence does not cease continually to evince. For if by those accumulated circumstances which generally induce us to the belief of anything beyond our senses, we may reasonably gather that there are certainly such things as DEVILS, we must necessarily conclude that these Devils have a Hell: and as there is a Hell, there must be a Heaven, and consequently a GOD: and so all the Duties of Christian Religion as indispensable subsequents necessarily follow.

The first of which Propositions, this ensuing Narrative does not a little help to Confirm.

For no longer ago, than within the compass of the present Month of August, there hapned so unusual an Accident in Hartfordshire as is not only the general Discourse, and admiration of the whole County: but may for its Rarity challenge any other event, which has for these many years been Product in any other County whatsoever. The story thus.

In the said County lives a Rich industrious Farmer, who perceiving a small Crop of his (of about three Half-Acres of Land which he had sowed with Oats) to be Ripe and fit for Gathering, sent to a poor Neighbour whom he knew worked commonly in the Summer-time at Harvest Labour to agree with him about Mowing or Cutting the said Oats down. The

poor man as it behoov'd Him endeavour'd to sell the Sweat
of his Brows and Marrow of his Bones at as dear a Rate as
reasonably he might, and therefore askt a good round Price for
his Labour, which the Farmer taking some exception at, bid
him much more under the usual Rate than the poor Man askt
for it: So that some sharp Words had past, when the Farmer
told him he would Discourse with him no more about it.
Whereupon the honest Mower recollecting with himself, that
if he undertook not that little Spot of Work, he might thereby
lose much more business which the Farmer had to imploy him
in beside, ran after him, and told him, that, rather than
displease him, he would do it at what rate in Reason he
pleas'd: and as an instance of his willingness to serve him,
proposed to him a lower price, than he had Mowed for any
time this Year before. The irretated Farmer with a stern look,
and hasty gesture, told the poor man That the Devil himself
should Mow his Oats before he should have anything to do
with them, and upon this went his way, and left the sorrowful
Yeoman, not a little troubled that he had disoblig'd one in
whose Power it lay to do him many kindnesses.

But, however, in the happy series of an interrupted prosper-
ity, we may strut and plume our selves over the miserable
Indingencies of our necessitated Neighbours, yet there is a just
God above, who weighs us not by our Bags, nor measures us
by our Coffers: but looks upon all men indifferently, as the
common sons of Adam: so that he who carefully Officiates
that rank or Station wherein the Almighty has plac't him, tho'
but a mean one, is truly more worthy the Estimation of all
men, then he who is prefer'd to superior dignities, and abuses
them: And what greater abuse than the contempt of Men
below him: the relief of whose common necessities is none of
the least Conditions whereby he holds all his Good things:
which when that Tenure is forfeited by his default, he may
justly expect some Judgement to ensue: or else that those
riches whereby he prides himself so extravagantly may shortly
be taken from him.

We will not attempt to fathom the cause, or reason of,
Preternatural events: but certain we are, as the most Credible

and General Relation can inform us, that same night this poor Mower and Farmer parted, his Field of Oats was publickly beheld by several Passengers to be all of a Flame, and so continued for some space, to the great consternation of those that beheld it.

Which strange news being by several carried to the Farmer next morning, could not but give him a great curiosity to go and see what was become of his Crop of Oats, which he could not imagine, but what was totally devour'd by those ravenous Flames which were observed to be so long resident on his Acre and a half of Ground.

Certainly a reflection on his sudden and indiscreet expression (That the Devil should Mowe his Oats before the poor Man should have anything to do with them) could not but on this occasion come into his Memory. For if we will but allow our selves so much leisure, to consider how many hits of providence go to the production of one Crop of Corn, such as the aptitude of the Soyl, the Seasonableness of Showers, Nourishing Solstices and Salubreous Winds, etc., we should rather welcome Maturity with Devout Acknowledgements than prevent our gathering of it by profuse wishes.

But not to keep the curious Reader any longer in suspense, the inquisitive Farmer no sooner arriv'd at the place where his Oats grew, but to his admiration he found the Crop was cut down ready to his hands; and [as] if the Devil had a mind to shew his dexterity in the art of Husbandry, and scorn'd to mow them after the usual manner, he cut them in round circles, and plac't every straw with that exactness that it would have taken up above an Age for any Man to perform what he did that one night: And the man that owns them is as yet afraid to remove them.

FINIS

Aside from the fact that the oats were described as having been 'cut down', which in the context of the dispute between the farmer and the mower could easily have been a convenient misinterpretation, the Mowing Devil story was a perfect description of a crop circle. It was so good, in fact, that Randles thought it might be a hoax. In any case, she wanted to find the original account, or at least an older reference than the one she had. She hoped to elicit a comment on it from serious folklorists, before Delgado or Andrews – or worse, Gordon Creighton – got hold of it. If Delgado or Andrews started touting the thing, she worried, they might scare off serious researchers. And Creighton . . . Well, for the past few years Creighton had been suggesting that crop circles were swirled by 'djinns' – a kind of Middle Eastern satyr. Randles could imagine Creighton taking the whole account literally and claiming that it vindicated his djinn theory.

She contacted some people in the Folklore Society, and fairly soon she had established that the Mowing Devil story was genuine. Terence Meaden phoned her, having heard about it through Paul Fuller, and asked her if she would publish it in *J. Met*. He could get it out in a month, he said. He urged her to publish quickly. But she told him she wanted to wait – and meanwhile arranged to publish it in one of the Folklore Society journals.

Several weeks later, in early October, a crop circles enthusiast and *Fortean Times* correspondent, Bob Skinner, was browsing through some dusty old tomes at a Surrey flea-market, when he opened a book called *Bygone Hertfordshire* and saw . . . a picture of the Mowing Devil woodcut, along with the pamphleteer's introductory passage. Skinner bought the book, photocopied the relevant page, and sent it out with an accompanying letter to Andrews, Delgado, Randles, Meaden, Ralph Noyes, and Bob Rickard, the editor of *Fortean Times*.

Andrews's reply was interesting. He had been relatively casual in his book, and in the press, about repeating anecdotes, whispers, rumours, visions . . . but suddenly, confronted with an old case of a plain circle, he became the hard-nosed scholar. The account, he told Skinner, was interesting, and should be noted, but perhaps it was only coincidentally related to 'our circles phenomenon'.

[The account] does clearly refer to [the oats] being cut and mowed, as proposed by the sketch of the devil with his cutting tool. You would have expected to find different terms used by persons having inspected at close hand plants laid down in the manner in which we find them today. However I am still of a mind that we continue to experience an evolving phenomenon. Who knows how far it will go?

Delgado, on the other hand, unquestioningly accepted it as an account of an early crop circle, and gave a brief discourse on the hermeneutics of the paranormal.

If during the intervening night a crop circle or a number of them have been created, whatever would the poor landowner have gone through in his head on seeing the circles. Probably much the same as I did when I saw those three for the first time in 1981. The only difference is, that which I related them to, and that which he related them to – this would be totally controlled by the technical knowledge of our time. It is human nature to desperately try to relate it to something you know. In the farmer's case, as with most mysterious things of the period – what else? The devil.

Delgado noted with benign amusement that 'even in the so-called modern times', some people continued to attribute the crop circles to 'satanic forces'. But in any case, he agreed that the woodcut was fascinating. It was so fascinating, in fact, that he had decided to carry out 'a regressive historical information recovery'. He had dangled a pendulum over the photocopy of the woodcut, and had asked the pendulum questions. If it changed the direction of its rotation, that meant Yes; anything else meant No. Delgado asked a series of questions, and observed which way his little pendulum would swivel . . . and eventually he discovered not only the precise location where the Mowing Devil incident had occurred, but that there had been other crop circles nearby in that summer of 1678, including a good-sized quintuplet.

Bob Rickard saw the Mowing Devil case as a classic dispute between hapless Labour and monopsonist Capital, and, in a subsequent commentary in *Fortean Times*, pointed out that 'the pamphleteers of the period were at their best with the fantasy theme of retribution against the profligate or greedy privileged classes'. Which was not to say that such themes were always fantasy; in fact, Rickard seemed to wonder whether a supernatural explanation was all that far-fetched: 'Are we witnessing [now] a modern version of the 1678 fairy retribution, enacted on a larger scale to match the intensity of modern farming? Are the gods of corn and field showing us their stigmata? The commercial necessities of modern farming are the equivalent of the 1678 farmer's greed.'

Ralph Noyes, who was later able to track down the original pamphlet in the British Library, also responded to Skinner's message with a fairly lengthy analysis, noting the apparent rarity of the event, and raising detailed questions about the account, such as whether the woodcut was 'meant to represent the whole of the three half-acre field, or just part of it', and whether 'the flame-like points on the drawing are an attempt to indicate the reported luminous phenomenon', rather than a poor attempt to represent standing crops.

Noyes's nitpicking seemed odd. After his first *Country Life* article on the circles had been published, he had received reports from Hampshire residents of crop circles dating back forty years, and had later circulated a letter to the major crop circles researchers, noting of these old circles that 'the country people would not hand-reap them; they thought they were uncanny and had some devilish origin'. The Mowing Devil case seemed almost perfectly to confirm this observation. Yet in the aftermath of the 1989 season, Noyes had begun to believe that modern crop circles were *evolving* year by year. He was sure that some kind of intelligence was at work. The Winterbourne Stoke circle of mid August had finally convinced him. The Stoke 'swastika', as it came to be known, had a bizarre quadranted floor-pattern, with the wheat laid down radially in four directions, and a kind of rosebud swirl in the centre. It looked like some ancient Celtic symbol, signifying the sun, or the Wheel of Life. Noyes was certain that no natural mechanism could have swirled it, even if a plasma vortex, or whatever, had swirled the old crop circles. In fact, old crop circles might be another phenomenon entirely. Within the context of the modern formations, they no longer really . . . made sense. Noyes concluded that the 1678 account was 'very much a friend of a friend report', to be 'treated with the usual reserve which attaches to friends of friends reports'.

Meaden, naturally, assumed that the account was an early record of a plasma vortex visitation, with the moral tale tacked on to improve sales. He phoned Skinner and agreed to publish his findings in the next issue of *J. Met.* Randles, who had responded somewhat peevishly to Skinner's letter – complaining that she had already seen the Mowing Devil account, and had been keeping it under wraps while she researched it further – now also agreed to publish in *J. Met.*, alongside Skinner's report.

And so the Mowing Devil case was born. To Meaden, it was unimpeachable evidence that crop circles were a natural phenomenon. He believed now that, whatever the short-term successes and celebrities generated by the Delgadonian interpretation, his would win out in the end.

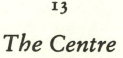

13

The Centre

On a summer solstice morning in the late 1960s, as the sun rose over the great heelstone of Stonehenge, and the assembled hippies and Druids chanted and prayed, one man stood apart. He was tall and dignified, with vaguely exotic features – broad face, blonde curly hair – that recalled both Peter Ustinov and, perhaps a little incongruously, Harpo Marx. His name was Michael Green.

Green had been trained as an architect and an architectural historian, but his role on this festive morning was primarily that of a policeman. As an employee of English Heritage, he was to see that things didn't get out of hand. Fortunately, the hippies were relatively well-behaved this morning, and the Druids ... well, there they were, a few dozen of them, having shed their workaday disguises as professors and stockbrokers and receptionists, standing there now in their white robes and white wellies, forming a circle, chanting in the pale orange light of dawn. And it occurred to Green, watching now with his historian's eye, that this annual Druid tableau was ... utterly bogus, for in truth no one knew the actual rites of the ancient Druids. The modern rites were based on the speculations of nineteenth-century dabblers.

Thanks to his work and his training, Green already knew something about Celtic religious practices, but now he resolved to dig further, to see if he could find out just what the Druids had done on the summer solstices. He had always enjoyed digging into the past – sometimes literally, for besides his library researches he had taken part in archaeological digs at two royal palaces and a Roman town in Essex. He was himself fairly religious, too, having been a member of a High Church lay order, the Franciscans, as a youth. He was curious to find out whether, as many suspected, the Druids knew more about the supernatural than they had let on to modern historians.

And so, as Green likes to tell the story, he set about investigating the Celts, examining the records of old excavations, searching for clues to the Druids and their mysterious rites . . .

. . . And one day, sitting in his flat in south London, he was paid a visit.

It was remarkably like the kind of visit that Colin Andrews would later claim to have had, except that these were not the Men in Black of ufologists' legend. They were from another tradition entirely. For one thing, they weren't men. At first, Green and his flatmate didn't know what they were. They seemed to be shadows . . . Shadows that shouldn't have been there.

After a few days they began to materialize, and eventually it became clear that there were three of them. They were very ancient . . . One of them even sported a pair of horns.

Yet they didn't seem hostile. They were merely curious. They wanted to know how much progress he had made, in his researches into Druidic rituals.

Green quickly summoned up a few prayers, exorcist-style, and eventually got rid of the beings. He hoped that that kind of thing wouldn't happen again. And yet . . . unpleasant as it was, this little ordeal had told him something very valuable. In the same way that Men in Black always confirmed the importance of ufologists' investigations, these demonic beasts had told him that his own supernatural researches were heading in the right direction.

So Green continued his work, began to dig deeper, and . . . a whole new world was opening up. His research began to take the shape of a general spiritual quest into the ancient mysteries, the ancient wisdom, bursting through the claustrophobic confines, as it were, of his previous Christian faith, into Druidism, paganism, dowsing, healing, astrology, sacred geometry, ritual magic, alchemy, channelling, the Qabbalah, Egyptology, Atlantis – the whole great alternative worldview. He found himself conducting a kind of second career as an enlightened archaeologist and architect, lecturing and writing and shamanically map-dowsing, and attending consciousness-raising workshops, and meeting people who shared his awareness of the supernatural, and his yearning to comprehend it all. He was quite popular within this alternative world, for his professional position gave him a certain gravitas, a certain reassuring, fatherly worldliness, that was often in short supply in mystical circles. His manners and his accent were also almost impeccable, and although he lacked none of the mystic's sense of the sublime, he seemed always to temper it with the English aesthete's sense of *comme il faut.*

In time, he began to celebrate the pagan feast days – Imbolc, Beltane, Lughnasadh, Samhain, plus the equinoxes and the solstices. Summer solstice 1989 he celebrated with several friends on Silbury Hill. They might have gone to Stonehenge instead, but by now, with the New Age well under way, Stonehenge was absurdly crowded around solstice time. Silbury was still relatively unspoilt, since it was surrounded by a fence with a locked gate, and fence-climbers were often arrested by the police. Green could let his friends in through the gate, because as an employee of English Heritage he had a key.

Anyway, Silbury had as much mystery and wisdom as one could find anywhere. It was also now obviously the centre of the crop circles phenomenon. Anyone who knew about Silbury Hill – meaning, every serious New Ager in the United Kingdom – knew about crop circles. Green certainly knew about them, and had seen immediately that many of the circles formations bore striking resemblances to Celtic and other pagan symbols, such as circles, circles with rings, and quintuplet circles. Obviously something tremendous was going on.

On Silbury Hill that night with Green were Isabelle Kingston, the channeller and crop circles prophet; Alick Bartholomew, who ran a New Age publishing house in Bath; Barbara Davies, a Welshwoman whom he'd met at the Oak Dragon alternative-education camps near Glastonbury, where they'd made spiral mazes on the ground with stones; and Beth Davis, who had a job taking care of historic buildings in Cambridgeshire. They sat in a circle and performed a ritual, a reasonably dignified one, what Green liked to call 'High

Magic', calling upon the Goddess – the neolithic Goddess that the Silbury Hill-builders had undoubtedly worshipped – and asking her to heal the earth, and to raise man's consciousness, and . . . to make more crop circles.

And as if in acknowledgement of their prayers, remembers Green, at dawn a shaft of energy shot down from a clear sky into the centre of the little circle of celebrants. A watercolour painting on the wall of Green's study commemorates the event, with Silbury Hill an emerald green, the sky a dawn blue, and the shaft of light a vivid yellow.

Later that year, somewhere on the New Age lecture circuit, Green ran into Ralph Noyes, and the two of them began to talk about the crop circles. By and by, Noyes voiced a complaint. He was plainly excited by the circles, but his efforts to find out more about the phenomenon had largely been thwarted. Terence Meaden had been relatively cooperative, despite his adamantly mundane theory. But Delgado and Andrews, who seemed to share Noyes's belief that the phenomenon was supernatural, had never even answered his letters.* It was beginning to seem to the rest of the circles research community that Delgado and Andrews were running a lucrative business, and wanted to divide the proceeds among as few share-holders as possible. Any further membership in CPR was obviously out of the question.

Noyes and Green decided to start their own group, the Centre for Crop Circle Studies (CCCS). Noyes would bring in some of his people, and Green would bring in some of his people, and together they would all form a tightly-knit, well-educated, well-spoken ruling council, to preside over a general membership that would be essentially unlimited – the more the merrier. And so as not to put a crimp on membership, or to seem cultish, there would be no corporate ideology. Even Terence Meaden would be invited to join.

Meaden eventually turned them down, but Noyes and Green were still able to sign up a plausible group of council members. Through Noyes's connections came Archie Roy and John Michell,

*Of Noyes's overtures Andrews had once remarked to his colleagues, 'They are all trying to milk us!'

while Green brought in his wife Christine (an archaeologist and Egyptologist), plus Alick Bartholomew, Barbara Davies, Beth Davis, a Hampshire socialite and channeller named Lucy Pringle, Richard Beaumont from *Kindred Spirit*, and an attractive blonde astrologer from Australia, 'Leonie Starr'. Archie Roy agreed to be President, while Lucy Pringle agreed to be Treasurer. Green would be Chairman, and Noyes the Hon. Secretary.

There were also a few refugees from the early days of circles research who could usefully be included. Don Tuersley and Busty Taylor were the most obvious, and although Tuersley had decided to give up active circles research in the wake of his defenestration from CPR, Taylor was still eager to get out into the fields again, and to get some recognition for his work. He gladly accepted the invitation to join. Richard Andrews and George Wingfield were also happy to find a home.

Wingfield brought a friend: John George Baillie-Hamilton Haddington, the 13th Earl of Haddington. He had known Wingfield at Eton and at Trinity College, Dublin, and he lived on a huge estate in Scotland. His interests ranged from alchemy to Zen Buddhism, but the circles had become his most recent obsession. He donated a few thousand pounds to get CCCS off the ground, and lent his name to the masthead, as the group's Patron.

In all this, of course, there was more than merely the idea of starting up a group to conduct research into a strange phenomenon. There were also ideas for literary ventures, including an official CCCS journal, the *Cereologist*, which John Michell would edit; and a book. As conceived, the book would be a collection of essays, perhaps a dozen or so, describing the phenomenon from a variety of perspectives. Almost everyone wanted to write something; in fact, some of those who had balked at joining the group were eager to contribute something to the book. Even Terence Meaden was interested. As he saw it, the book would be a kind of Trojan Horse, with his essay inside waiting to capture the imaginations of the tens of thousands of New Age enthusiasts who, while they might readily purchase a CCCS publication, would probably never have considered buying his own book.

So Meaden would write a chapter on his plasma vortex theory. Wingfield would write accounts of the 1989 and 1990 seasons, with a *tour d'horizon* of the crop circle theories. Michell would do more or less the same, hinting that the phenomenon was the effect, or the cause, or both, of a kind of Jungian change in collective-consciousness. Bob Rickard would write about the Mowing Devil account. Hilary Evans, a member of the Society for Psychical Research and a freelance sociologist of strange phenomena, would write about anomalies and mass hysteria. Richard Andrews would write about dowsing the circles and saving the planet. Michael Green would write about Celtic symbols and the meaning of the circles and the spiritual energy-entities, devas, which artfully swirled them. Lord Haddington would write about more Celtic symbols, and Jungian archetypes and chakras and Aurameters and Kundalini. Lucy Pringle would write a personal account of how a shoulder complaint, incurred one day by too much tennis, had been cured the next day by the energies in a circle. Busty Taylor would do the pictures. Archie Roy would write a respectable, scientific introduction. And Ralph Noyes would edit it all, adding a few essays of his own for good measure.

And, naturally, Alick Bartholomew would publish it.

The kick off – for the book and the group – was on Easter weekend, 1990, at Beth Davis's rambling house in Ely, Cambridgeshire. Everyone was there: authors and founders, dowsers and Forteans, eccentrics and esoterics. It was a regular country house weekend, with drinks and laughs and food everywhere and solemn parlour discussions about the circles. Busty Taylor loved it. He had neither seen nor heard anything like it in his life: all of these good-looking old-school-tie people with their high-toned accents. And he was right in among them, as an honoured guest. Except he couldn't help noticing . . . that when someone was needed to help in the kitchen, or to carry trays of food, or to do some spare-hand job, they would never ask John Haddington, or George Wingfield, or even Richard Andrews. They would ask . . . him.

14

Fly-fishing

'Sssshhhhhhhwwwwwwwwwwwwwwwwwwwwwwwwwwwwww-
wwwwwwwwwwwwwwwwwwwwwwwwwwwwwwww . . .' said the
wind-spirit. 'Sssshhhhwwwwwwwwwwwwwwwwwwwwwww
wwwwww wwwwww wwwwwwwwww wwwwwwww . . .'

'Who are you?' asked Lord Haddington.

'We are . . . We are . . . We are not a million miles away . . .'

And Rita Goold, between whose puffed cheeks the wind-spirit
was being channelled, held out one of her hands. 'We are not – Put
your hands out . . . Put it through our world . . . just through . . .
how near we are . . . just through . . .'

Several of the others obediently put out their hands.

'We are the highest being,' she continued. 'To hear us we must
slow down . . . And we arrange to hear us. Sssshhhhwwwwwwwww
wwwwwwwwwwwwwwwwwwwwwwwwwwwwwwwwwwwwwww-
wwwwwwwwwwwww . . .'

About a dozen crop circles enthusiasts were there that night,
sitting cross-legged on the dusty, hay-strewn floor of the little
barn at the foot of Milk Hill, a few miles south of Avebury. Just
about every night at this time Haddington and George Wingfield
and Busty Taylor and Michael Green, and half a dozen others,
repaired to the little barn to meditate and to beseech the Circlemakers to reveal themselves – or, as on this night, to communicate with them through a medium – before heading on up the
hill, past a fine specimen of a chalk white horse, to where the old

Saxon Wansdyke slithered along the ridge and one could see for miles.

The Wansdyke cropwatch was Haddington's brainchild. The year before, he had come down from his estate in Scotland to join Colin Andrews's Operation White Crow, but because of family obligations he had had to leave early, and the trilling noise experience, and the subsequent formation of the ringed circle, he had heard about only later, from Wingfield and the others. He was, to say the least, disappointed to have missed the experience. He decided that he would organize his own cropwatch for the next summer, so that if anything happened, he would be there. He was a keen fisherman, and saw the Circlemakers as something like a super-intelligent breed of trout, which would rise only to a well-tied fly – that is, to a close-knit gathering of the spiritually-minded.

The watch site would have to be near Silbury Hill, he decided, since Silbury Hill was now obviously where things were happening. During the autumn and winter of 1989 he made several short trips down from Scotland, touring the area, talking to farmers, assembling a group of like-minded cropwatchers from CCCS, and from the Fountain International Group – an organization he'd helped to establish a few years before, to bring people together to meditate and to think positive thoughts and thereby, hopefully, to bring about oneness and world peace. He finally obtained the permission of Farmer David Read – who generously donated a caravan – to camp up on the Wansdyke, overlooking the Beckhampton Downs to the north, and to the south, the sleepy and sinuous Kennet and Avon Canal, and the picturesque farming villages that lay along it: All Cannings, and Stanton St Bernard, and Alton Priors, and Alton Barnes.

On the appointed day, 8 June 1990, everything was ready. Haddington drove down from Scotland, with a carful of cameras and tape recorders and Gauss meters, and some icons and candles and incense and other paraphernalia relating to his esoteric brand of Buddhism, and a fellow Scotsman, a leprechaunish young man named Sandy Reid, who the previous summer had claimed to have witnessed a crop circle being swept out, as if by an invisible hand, at dawn in a field near Dundee.

Haddington and Reid and the others were confident. They felt that something *had* to happen. Each year, it seemed, the number and variety of circles formations had increased. The last year, 1989, had been the best yet, with over eighty formations in the Silbury area alone. Already this year, even before the end of spring, there had been dozens more. Most were singlets, but over at Baltic Farm, beneath Morgan's Hill, Farmer David Shepherd had found a gigantic Celtic cross – a quintuplet whose satellites were joined by a pronounced outer ring. Mysteriously, several other outer rings had appeared around the formation on a subsequent night.

Down in Hampshire, the formations were simply unprecedented. At Chilcomb, near Cheesefoot Head, on or about 23 May, Farmer John Guy had found a huge . . . symbol, of some sort. It started with a forty-foot circle, from which an eight-foot wide channel of swept wheat sped outwards, aligned almost perfectly along a tramline, narrowing suddenly to a four-foot width, running further, then stopping, leaving a patch of standing green wheat before the swept edge of another, smaller, circle began, only ten feet in diameter, like the dot in an exclamation mark. And on either side of the main channel, and parallel to it, lay two narrow rectangles of swept crop, almost like . . . ripples . . . vibrations . . . spreading outwards . . .

On 1 June, at Litchfield, north of Winchester, a similar shape had appeared, but with concentric arcs around the circle at one end . . . spreading out again . . . like waves of change . . . And on 2 June, at Hazeley Farm near Cheesefoot, another such shape . . . with one of the circles ringed – and trickling down from the ring were four curved channels, almost tentacular . . . but with a sad quality ('injured', Pat Delgado would write later) as though the planet were attempting to say something . . .

And then on 6 June, on Longwood Estate, a triple ringer – except that each of the two inner rings was interrupted, symmetrically, the interruption corresponding to the continuance of the other ring . . . It looked like some ancient symbol, perhaps Korean, or Chinese . . . When Andrews and Delgado first entered the formation, the energies were still so strong in the central circle that Delgado was thrown roughly to the ground. Later, Delgado phoned the British Museum and asked someone there if 'hieroglyph' was the right term for this new kind of shape. Delgado said they told him that 'pictogram' was probably a more suitable word.

pi'ctogram, n. pictorial symbol.

sy'mbol, n. thing regarded by general consent as naturally typifying or representing or recalling something (esp. an idea or quality) by possession of analogous qualities or by association in fact or thought.

During the evening meditations at the Wansdyke watch, Haddington and the others would leave their tape recorders switched on outside the barn, in case the Circlemakers happened by. After the meditation they would all go up the hill to the caravan and there would be coffee and tea and brandy and Haddington would get the incense going, and some of them would then retire for the night to campsites or bed-and-breakfasts or hotels, having served the early watch, as it were. The rest of them would stroll or sit or sprawl around the Wansdyke, watching for strange lights, listening for strange noises, telling stories, chanting . . . 'Come to us . . . Make us your circles . . .' and inevitably slipping into a deep, often alcoholic sleep while the cows and the sheep groaned and bawled on the hills all around them, and another summer night in the North Atlantic passed without incident.

But . . . on Tuesday morning, Michael Cox and Anna Scott, two of Haddington's friends from the Fountain International Group, played back the tapes that had been made while everyone was meditating the previous evening, and heard . . . the noise. The trilling noise. None of them had heard it during the meditation, and yet . . . everyone remembered that the meditation that night had been very serene, very together . . .

On Thursday, Rita Goold approached Haddington, and suggested that she might be able to contact the Circlemakers more directly, using her own channelling abilities . . . And presently a wind-spirit was whistling through her like a Fastnet gale.

'*Sssshhhhhwwwooooosssshhhhhwwwwwwwwwww* – I wish to say two things. We are so anxious at this sinful nation spreading lies about us. We do not come in machines, we do not land on your earth in machines . . . We come like the wind. We are Life Force.

Life Force from the ground . . . Come here . . . Come with love . . . Come to point . . . Come to heal the earth . . . We are so simple, but have the power of the breath of healing . . . the earth . . . such a beautiful place . . . Find the points of grametry . . .* The earth absorbs the healing breath . . . runs down the lines . . . the earth, the earth . . . it is not just for the point of our impact on earth . . . it spreads like a spider's web . . . it affects nations and people's minds . . . We have been before . . . We come to you once more . . . please help us . . . please . . . to get rid of the sore wound . . . spreads along the –'

'Where do you come from?'

'We are but a breath away . . . a breath away . . . we are not a million miles away . . . a Life Force that is larger than the energies in your body. But we meet at a higher level of life. We come to mean no harm.'

'Are you creating corn circles?'

'We are breath that blows on the land. The healing points are the patterns of time.'

'They are very beautiful. Does each pattern give a message?'

'You are very beautiful. Your light . . . I see your lights . . . You are beautiful. . . . The land is beautiful . . . Your bread of life is beautiful . . .'

'What name do you have?'

'We need no name. We are parallel to your world, alongside your world. We need not speak like you speak. *Sssshhhhhhhhhwwww-wooooooowwwwwwwwwwwwssssshhhhhhwwwwshhhhhhhhhhhhssssshhh hhhwwwww* . . . We are likened to your mechanical waves.'

'Magnetic waves? What do you call your world?'

'*Hummo* . . . how we call our world. I will tell you: *Sssshhhhhhhh-hhhwwwwwwwwwwwwwoooooooooooooooooooooossssssshhhhhhhhhh-hhsssshhhhhhhhhhhhhhhhhwwwwwwwwwwwww* . . . We have no

---

*Rita Goold's subsequent exegesis of the channelled text includes the note that this apparent neologism, *grametry*, 'is made up of the old English (now obsolete) term *gram* derived from the latin *graminens* meaning "grass or grassy", and the Middle English term *estre* (now also obsolete) meaning "being or condition" (it does not appear to refer to *metry*, "a process of measurement").'

speech or name for our world, but you would call – I can't think of a word that you would call . . .'

'You think . . .?' asked Haddington, somewhat sceptically.

'I am sorry my friend, we do not fight, we have no wars . . . our colour white . . . We are free to move through all of our worlds . . .'

'What are the purpose of your corn circles?' asked Michael Green, a good deal less sceptically. 'Why now?'

'The circles of corn are whorl-pools of energy. We breathe on your world and it runs like a spider's web and affects the minds of men whatever speech they hold. Have you not noticed in your decade how nations are getting on . . . There is plenty to do . . . three steps back and one step forward.* The walls are broken. Two men will rise from the past . . . the great bear . . . the world will be at peace . . . When the world is one, then we will come to you. Man will be ready to accept another existence of life . . . many forms of life in the whole of creation . . . I am just a humble part of that life. I must speak to you again and bring others too. *Sssshhhhhhhhhhh-wwwwwwwwwwwwwwwwwwwwweeeewwwwwoooooooooosssssss-ssssshhhhhhhhhhhhhwwwwwwwwwwwwwwwwwwwwwww* . . .'

Afterwards, they sat and talked in the barn for a while, then went up the hill to the caravan. It was an electric night. Something in the air . . .

Nrrrzzzzzzzzzzzzzzzzzzzzzzzzzzzzzzzzzzzzzzzzzzz . . .

The noise. It had come again. They stood quietly at the caravan, listening as it trilled . . . Tremendous! Like the trout rising to the fly! Haddington had done it!

But now there were . . . *lights* . . . flashing lights in the fields, from the noise . . . some of the lights orange, some red, some green . . . flickering rapidly . . . infinitesimal points of light . . .

And from the tops of the wheat . . . things that seemed to jump up and down in mid-air . . . they were dark . . . and they looked almost . . . rod-like . . . yes, like *rods* . . . *black* rods . . . some of them T-shaped, or Y-shaped . . . almost like the black

*Rita's exegesis also includes the suggestion that 'the entity may have meant this expression the other way round'.

Mystery Circles—Return Of The 'Thing'?

THE Warminster 'Thing' could be back. Speculation that the UFO, which hundreds of people claimed to have seen in the mid and late 1960s, began again this week after three circular depressions appeared in cornfields near Westbury White Horse.

The depressions have mystified local farmers and tourists to the White Horse and the Army could come up with no immediate explanation.

Two of the marks, which are perfect circles about 18 yards across, are clearly visible in a

Argentina Releases

1 Mike Seager, from Ian Mrzyglod's PROBE group, collecting a dirt sample from a circle beneath the Westbury white horse in August 1980. The samples were tested at Bristol University for spectroscopic anomalies and unusual radioactivity, but neither was found. (Photo: Ian Mrzyglod.)
Inset: The *Wiltshire Times* story about the Westbury circles, which marked the start, in the public mind, of the modern English crop circles phenomenon, and inspired Terence Meaden to begin his research.

2 Terence Meaden, the father of modern cerealogy, taking notes in a rapeseed circle. (Photo: Terence Meaden.)

3 Pat Delgado, founder of the Delgadonian school of crop circle studies, and fellow researcher Colin Andrews. Between them lies Delgado's cerealogical stethoscope – a tape recorder whose special microphone probe could be inserted into the ground within a crop circle in order to pick up the deep throb of the circle's energies. (Photo: Matt Page.)

4 Busty Taylor, dowsing, and Colin Andrews, filming, in a circle at Beckhampton, Wiltshire, in 1989, just before their split. (Photo: Terence Meaden.)

5 George Wingfield, electro-magnetically probing the centre of a circle. According to cerealogical dowsers, there were good energies, bad energies, positive energies, negative energies, male energies, and female energies, and they were generally most intense at a circle's centre. Be careful, George! (Photo: Pam Price.)

6 Richard Andrews, king of the circle-dowsers, crossing an energy line. (Photo: the author.)

7 Busty hoists his pole-mounted camera. (Photo: the author.)

8 The famous Alton Barnes double-pictogram of July 1990. Tim and Polly Carson, farm managers, collected more than £5,000 from visitors who paid £1 each to enter the formation. Key-rings, posters, and postcards were also available from a caravan at the side of the field. The formation marked the start of modern circles tourism. (Photo: Norman Lomax.)

9 Pat Delgado's pole was even bigger than Busty's. (Photo: Matt Page.)

10 The formation beneath Barbury Castle, near Swindon, in July 1991. John Haddington noticed that the design was similar to an alchemical symbol called the Golden Tripod; he had also seen it on an amulet around Shirley MacLaine's neck. Cerealogical alchemy seemed to have its dark side, however, for the rumour went around that a sheep had been sacrificed in the formation by black magicians, and at the Glastonbury Cornference in September, it was said that the Barbury Castle pictogram's energies had 'gone negative'. (Photo: Richard Wintle.)

11 George de Trafford, master of the Grid, measuring energy levels in the Stone Avenue Frog, August 1991. De Trafford's technique, similar in principle to an MRI scan, involved tapping the bowl to produce a tone, and then lifting a wheatstalk from the circle, feeling it resonate as it moved within the sonic field. By this time, de Trafford was no longer a threat to Delgadonian supremacy in cerealogy, and perhaps as a consequence was no longer regarded as sinister – after all, what true Templar would wear Levis and Docksiders? Colin Andrews (on de Trafford's left) was there purely by chance. (Photo: Matt Page.)

12 The author, July 1991, waiting for plasma vortices at the secret site. A low-light video monitor is on the left; a radar screen is on the right. The idea – my idea, anyway – was that a falling plasma vortex would hit close enough to the caravan to blow out the video and radar screens and awaken me. (Photo: the author.)

13 Dave Chorley and Doug Bower, in Bower's Southampton art studio. (Photo: Robert Irving.)

14 Paul, Bart, and Matt, members of the United Bureau of Investigation (UBI). John, another member of the group, became the CCCS database-keeper in 1992. Some of us wondered whether pictograms were appearing in the database before they were appearing in the fields. (Photo: Robert Irving.)

15 The author, giving biologist and meta-theorist Rupert Sheldrake a few pointers on circlemaking after the competition in West Wycombe, Buckinghamshire, July 1992. (Photo: Robert Irving.)

16 Summer's end. Note the pictogram symbol scrawled in the dust on the harvester's side. I rolled this formation (which is also featured on the back cover) in a field next to Silbury Hill on the night of 16/17 August 1992. CCCS chairman Michael Green, likening it to an Indo-Aryan mandala symbol known as the Dharmic Wheel, called it 'the most important crop formation of 1992'. You're too kind, Michael.
(Photo: the author.)

17 Soil samples taken by members of Operation Argus, an American-funded research expedition, from a crescent-within-ring formation (the 'Venus' or 'Cheshire Cat') at Alton Barnes, August 1992. It was hoped byArgus members, as it had been hoped by British ufologists twelve years earlier, that radiologic and spectroscopic analyses of soil samples, among other things, would enable researchers to settle the mystery of the crop circles once and for all. . . (Photo: the author.)

18 An alternative history of cerealogy, which appeared recently in the
Daily Telegraph's Young Telegraph section.

darts of Chilcomb, about which Colin Andrews had written so much –

'Thank you, Goddess!' someone cried.

But now the sound seemed to be drifting away across the fields, beyond the Wansdyke. Drifting away . . . Wingfield went after it. Michael Cox followed him. Michael Cox would catch it . . . he would catch it . . . It was so close –

Unhhhh! Cox went down suddenly, and crawled back to the edge of the field as the noise receded into the distance.

'What happened?' asked Haddington. 'Are you all right?'

Cox groaned. 'It hit me in the stomach.'

15

Oxonians

Michael Green, George Wingfield, John Haddington, Ralph Noyes, John Michell, Busty Taylor, Richard Andrews, Lucy Pringle, Leonie Starr, Barbara Davies, Beth Davis, George de Trafford, Isabelle Kingston, Rita Goold, Ron Jones, Pat Delgado, Colin Andrews . . . all of them, all of them, haunted Terence Meaden's private purgatory.

For Terence Meaden considered himself a scientist, considered his research scientific. He had once been a university professor, with tenure. He had once been surrounded by good, clean, sane, civilized, respectable, *revered* fellow scientists, fellow priests of the one true postmodern faith. But now . . . he seemed to have fallen into a grotesque Boschean abyss of dowsers and shamans and tabloid journalists and Goddess-worshippers and borough council handymen and perpetual-motion makers and mediums and astrologers and ufologists and Egyptologists and Forteans and undead Templars.

Not that he had much choice in the matter. He had left his professorship voluntarily, had climbed down, so to speak, from the ancient groves of Academe. And as a scientist studying a fringe phenomenon, he faced a long and lonely road back.

All of which explained why Meaden was especially eager to convert academics to his cause. John Snow had been the first, back at the TORRO conference in the summer of 1988, when he had been lured from his vortex test-flight centre high above the summery Auvergne. Snow had not only referred Meaden to the ring vortex idea, and the business of vortex breakdown, but had also begun mulling over the problem himself, and had even managed to interest his old PhD supervisor, Professor Christopher Church, at Miami of Ohio University. Church had begun to correspond with Meaden, and had begun to think about how to model the crop-covered hills of Wiltshire and Hampshire . . .

By the hysteric summer of 1989, Meaden had hardly needed to seduce scientists into the subject. They were turning up unannounced. One afternoon in July, Meaden was sitting in the customs offices at Dover, awaiting the completion of paperwork concerning an Austin Healey that he and his son Lionel had just shipped over from Belgium. The customs people were taking their time, so Meaden phoned home to explain to his wife that he and Lionel were going to be late. Well, said his wife, tell the customs people to hurry up, because there's a Japanese professor with a film crew camped on the doorstep, and he wants to see you.

The professor's name, it turned out, was Yoshi-Hiko Ohtsuki. He came from Waseda University in Tokyo, and was a plasma physicist, specializing in the rare and strange phenomenon of ball-lightning. He was currently on a world tour, visiting fellow ball-lightning experts and exchanging stories, and being filmed with them for a Japanese TV documentary. He had been in Amsterdam to meet a Professor Dijkhuist, and was on his way to America for a plasma physics conference, and had stopped over in London for a quiet couple of days to see the Fortean researcher Hilary Evans. Evans collected clippings of ball-lightning stories, photocopying them and sending them out semi-annually to a small group of ball-lightning aficionados, of which Ohtsuki was one. Ohtsuki was like Meaden, in that he had occasionally to work with non-scientists, or at least amateur scientists such as Hilary Evans – but unlike Meaden, he could return to the groves whenever he wanted.

In any case, Meaden's book had just come out, and Hilary Evans had just read it. He suggested to Ohtsuki that Meaden's plasma vortex idea might explain some of the larger varieties of ball-lightning (which tended to be ignored in the ball-lightning literature, falling instead into the UFO literature). So Ohtsuki and his camera crew drove straight out to the West Country, and parked outside Meaden's house, across the street from the auto-repair shop in little Bradford-on-Avon.

Meaden returned at about six o'clock in the evening, and once he understood what it was all about, he drove them all out to the Silbury Hill area, and showed them crop circles until the sun went down. The next day, Ohtsuki and his camera crew went off to America, to finish their tour, and when he returned to Japan, Ohtsuki continued with his ball-lightning work, collecting anecdotal reports and tinkering with different ways of creating the elusive glowing spheres of plasma in the lab – but now he also began to collect reports of swirled circular patches in ground-covering, mostly grass and rice, and started thinking about how to reproduce them in his laboratory plasma chambers.

Earlier that year, even before he had been approached by Ohtsuki, Meaden had met Kazuo Ueno, a reporter who worked for a Japanese newspaper group in London. Ueno, apparently a bit of a *manqué* scientist himself, had a love for the weird and sensational, and after the publication of *Circular Evidence* had interviewed Colin Andrews – mentioning to him, at one point, that his old physics professor back at Nihon University, Hiroshi Kikuchi, was interested in the circles phenomenon and wished to study it when he visited England briefly later in the summer. Andrews began to tell British reporters that he was now 'working closely with a number of Japanese scientists', and in fact Kikuchi did meet with Andrews when he came to England, and invited him to give a talk about the circles at an atmospheric physics conference he was organizing in Tokyo in the autumn. But Andrews, unable to escape his obligations to the Test Valley Borough Council, never made it out to Tokyo.* Instead, Meaden went.

---

*Under the headline, 'CORN CIRCLES CONFERENCE PLEA DENIED', the *Andover Advertiser* reported: 'Colin Andrews, the Andover local government officer in the front line of corn circles research, was scathing this week over his employers' refusal to let him chair a Japan conference on the phenomena. "I had three days' holiday left and requested two more days but I was refused. I think it's a pretty poor show," he said. "This is now becoming international research and the attention of the media all over the world has been caught, with Andover being at the centre of the interest, so the local authority must have done very well out of the publicity.

'"I got a flat 'No' as well as being told I could not have the time off without pay and could not be treated differently from anyone else.

Ueno had also introduced Meaden to Kikuchi, and with the discovery of two auspicious coincidences, the two scientists had immediately established a rapport. First, they discovered that they had the same birthdate, 6 May. Second . . . well, when Meaden had been a postdoctoral student at Oxford, old Professor Mendelsohn had asked him to take a visiting Japanese physicist, a Dr Shigi, under his wing for a year or two. Meaden had done so, and had got along well with Shigi. And Shigi had been grateful, because aside from Meaden he hadn't known a soul at Oxford – except for another young Japanese physicist, whom Meaden had somehow never met: Hiroshi Kikuchi.

Kikuchi's specialty was EMHD – electromagnetohydrodynamics – a new and highly theoretical field, but with obvious relevance to plasma and atmospheric physics. Kikuchi felt that a bit of EMHD theory might put some meat on Meaden's plasma vortex concept. He would start to examine the problem. In the meantime, Meaden should come out to Tokyo, to give a paper on his circles research.

Meaden accepted the offer, but before he left for Japan, another Japanese physicist contacted him. Tokio Kikuchi – no relation to Hiroshi – was a lecturer at Kochi University, on Shikoku Island a few hundred miles south-west of Tokyo. This Kikuchi, who earlier had quietly subscribed to *J. Met.*, faxed Meaden a letter that August, explaining that he would be in England and asking whether Meaden would be free to talk about the circles. Soon he was there, and Meaden drove him around, and showed him the big circle at Beckhampton, where the *Daytime Live* business had occurred, plus some little ones. Often in the little circles they would find a small clump of standing stalks in the centre, which Kikuchi realized could be the calling-card of a vortex at whose centre the wind velocity

---

'"I am disappointed over such inflexibility.

'"I consider that the growing scientific interest in the circles and my involvement should merit the same sort of treatment as, say, a top class athlete being released by a local authority to compete for his country.

'"I am finding it very, very difficult to run the research programme and without some flexibility from employers I shall have to consider how I can carry on."

'The head of Mr Andrews's department did not wish to comment.'

had been zero. Soon Kikuchi was talking about ring vortices and vortex breakdown, and Meaden suggested that he get in touch with John Snow, who was thinking along the same lines.

Meaden went to Japan in September for Hiroshi Kikuchi's conference – on Environmental and Space Electromagnetics – and after a summer of lost mud-battles with the Delgadonians, it was like a glimpse of heaven. At the conference, he was surrounded by fellow physicists, and when he gave his paper on the circles, the auditorium was packed. The press, too, practically mobbed him. In modern Japan, science had become almost the official religion. And when a scientist turned his attention to an oddball phenomenon, such as ball-lightning, he wasn't laughed at or ridiculed, as he might be in the West. He was clapped on the back, surrounded by eager followers, encouraged to go for it. Ohtsuki's ball-lightning work had made him a kind of hero among the Japanese.

Ohtsuki was at the conference, too, delivering a paper, and afterwards he drove Meaden out to his laboratory, showed him the microwave chamber where he generated plasmas and explained how he might one day simulate crop circles in the plasma chamber. It was very impressive. But the strange thing was, Ohtsuki's lab was nowhere near Waseda University; it was fifty miles outside Tokyo, on the campus of some minor aeronautical engineering school. Meaden eventually found out that the authorities at Waseda had forced the move, after Ohtsuki's first lab, on the Waseda campus, had experienced a terrific explosion.

TORRO had held two conferences, in 1984 and 1988, and Meaden decided the time was ripe for a third, this time exclusively on the circles. He had already formed a new branch of TORRO called the Circles Effect Research Group – or CERES, after the Roman grain goddess, a later version of Demeter – and there were now five academic physicists doing at least some work in the area: Snow, Church, Ohtsuki, and the Kikuchis. He would invite them all to come and give papers. He would invite the press, too, and the press would at long last see that the circles phenomenon was a subject for serious research. The press coverage, he believed, would attract the eventual interest of more scientists, and more press coverage, and so on – until Delgado and Andrews, and their country-house cousins at CCCS, would at long last be left behind ... in the infernal subcultural fringe where they belonged.

Meaden quickly lined up Ohtsuki to talk about his microwave plasmas, and Hiroshi Kikuchi to talk about EMHD vortices, and John Snow to deliver a paper that he and Tokio Kikuchi had written about ring vortices, and Christopher Church, who would be on sabbatical at the nearby University of Manchester, to chair the conference. But Meaden realized that even if he held the conference to one day, he was rapidly going to run out of speakers. So he arranged for Randles and Fuller to talk about UFOs, and for ... Frederick C. Taylor ... to discuss 'The Role of Aerial Reconnaissance in Circles Research' – which meant that Busty would show some slides of the prettier pictograms.

The conference, as with the two before, would be held in an auditorium at Oxford Polytechnic. Meaden didn't advertise the conference outside *J. Met.*, but he didn't have to. The crop circles grapevine hummed and buzzed in anticipation of the event, and well before the conference day arrived on 23 June, Meaden's TORRO colleague at Oxford Poly, Derek Elsom, had fled his office where the calls were coming in, and had left a message on his answering machine to the effect that the 150 tickets were sold out. Some of those tickets had gone to physicists and meteorologists, such as Professor Richard Scorer of Imperial College, London, and Dr Anthony Garrett of Glasgow University, and Dr Duncan MacLean of Cambridge. But for the most part, they had gone to ... the paranormal crowd, people like Michael Green and Colin Andrews. And although Paul Fuller had urged Meaden, had pleaded with him, to admit only Meadenites, in reality no such action was feasible. It was a public event. In fact it was almost an ecumenical event – for a founder member of CCCS, Busty Taylor, would be speaking.

The day before the conference, Meaden took some of the visiting scientists on a tour of circles sites in Wiltshire and Hampshire. Ohtsuki came along, with John Snow and Chris Church, and some British and German camera crews, and a gaggle of print journalists. They went over to Morgan's Hill near Bishops Cannings, and looked at the big quintuplet surrounded by rings, and then at some small singletons near the top of the hill, which particularly impressed John Snow. Then they went down to Hampshire, to Telegraph Hill near Cheesefoot Head, to see the odd dumbbell-shaped formation with arcs at one end, which looked almost like a symbol for an audio speaker, with sound waves coming out; and another dumbbell, the sad one with the trickling tear-tracks. The word *pictogram* was anathema to the Meadenites, but already it was clear that the shapes this year were ... bizarre. No one had seen anything like them before.

Day faded to night and night brightened to day, and the anxious crowd filed into the little auditorium at Oxford Polytechnic. Derek Elsom rose and said a few words, and introduced Christopher Church, who introduced Meaden, who launched into a lengthy history of the circles phenomenon, and the development of his plasma vortex theory. He made sure that the gathered Delgadonians got an earful:

> ... retrospective research has uncovered proof of around one hundred pre-1980 circles. The oldest which dates back to the year 1678 caused initial dismay to the paranormal and extra-terrestrial hopefuls who had been recklessly claiming, on baseless guesswork, that the problem was a modern, post-1980 one.

> ... it is indisputable that to produce the circles effect the circle-making agent must be a descending vortex ...

From time to time amazing things have been said – although on no firm evidence – about peculiar happenings or discoveries claimed to be linked to cropfield-circle events. Most of these have emanated from the indefatigable Delgado and Andrews and few have yet been acceptably substantiated either by them or anyone else ... as [Delgado and Andrews] believe in paranormal and poltergeist occurrences, they have admitted the likelihood that extraterrestrial forces may be involved (they have also intimated the contrary possibility that earth-sourced forces may operate instead, causing the corn to heel over from beneath!).

When Meaden had finished, Busty Taylor came forward and gave a kind of pictorial history of the phenomenon. He let the images do most of the talking. It was the first time he had ever stood up in public like this, and Meaden had to do all he could just to convince him to get up there in the first place. But the pictures were lovely, and Taylor's presentation went down well. A little incongruously, John Snow followed, and discussed vortex breakdown and ring vortices. Where Meaden had absolutely dismissed the idea that hoaxing was widespread, Snow was much more cautious:

We emphasize that any model put forth at this time is highly speculative since it must be based largely on circumstantial evidence.

... it is of concern that few similar events have been reported elsewhere [than in southern England].

There appear to be no ready explanations for many of the exotic details (such as the sometimes-multiple circumscribing rings) that have been documented. In fact, it is probably premature to attempt to formulate even speculative explanations for these.

Later on in the afternoon, Ohtsuki gave his own paper, starting out by describing an invisible object, apparently a huge fast-moving plasmoid, which had been tracked on radar* by a group of Japanese marine biologists in the Pacific in 1986. Then he displayed a video, taken in his lab a few months before, of plasma balls created in the microwave chamber. The little plasma balls glowed and danced, and then winked out as soon as Ohtsuki shut the microwave power down. It was difficult to follow what was going on in the video, but it was absolutely lucid compared to what came next – grey, diminutive Hiroshi Kikuchi, who presented a seemingly endless series of slides displaying unintelligible equations, accompanied by heavily accented commentary. Poor Professor Kikuchi had misjudged his audience so thoroughly – perhaps he thought it would be a British version of the conference he had chaired in Tokyo – that several of

---

*Radar bounces off electrically conducting materials, and since plasma is an electrically conducting material, radar should be able to track plasmoids. In fact, civilian and military radar operators have reported numerous incidents in which large but otherwise invisible objects have been tracked by radar.

the more boisterous crop circles enthusiasts began to laugh quite openly. Meaden was mortified.

Randles and Fuller finished things off with a discussion of the possibility that the UFO phenomenon was nothing more than the plasma vortex phenomenon. But time was short, and Randles and Fuller had to rush their presentation, and at the end there were only a few minutes left for questions from the floor – questions which could be directed to any of the previous speakers.

After a few relatively meek questioners had stood and been answered, Colin Andrews rose, and asked Meaden how his whirlwind theory could explain the strange new formations – such as the pictograms, or the quintuplet at Bishop's Cannings whose surrounding rings had actually increased in number since the formation had first been discovered. Andrews wanted to know how Meaden could reconcile his theory to the law of conservation of momentum, which – he thought – shouldn't have allowed a vortex to swirl a circle in one direction, and an outside ring in the same direction, as was often the case in the fields. Meaden replied that he was sure there was a natural explanation, and no need for extraterrestrialist fantasies. And Andrews came back at him, and demanded that Meaden's vortices comply with the laws of angular momentum. And Meaden responded to the effect that Andrews was a non-scientist, and it went back and forth like that, their voices rising in an unseemly and indecorous manner, as John Snow, and Yoshi-Hiko Ohtsuki, and Hiroshi Kikuchi, and Christopher Church, and Richard Scorer, and Anthony Garrett, and Duncan MacLean, and the rest of the representatives of the groves of Academe watched in silence . . .

16

Alton Barnes

Afterwards, a villager swore that he had heard a strange humming noise that night, coming from the field. Others recalled that dogs had barked and roof tiles had rattled, as if at the passage of some monstrous force. Still others remembered being unable to start their cars that morning, their batteries having unaccountably been drained overnight. And even several hours after the event, a local writer, Mary Killen, had her work eerily interrupted when a flock of birds flew into her study through a casement window. Perhaps strangest of all, as would be pointed out by George Wingfield and others, the medium Isabelle Kingston, during a map-dowsing session earlier that summer, had in fact predicted a major formation in that very field, East Field, which slopes breathtakingly down, in punchbowl fashion, beside the road running north out of Alton Barnes.

Alton Barnes, together with its Siamese twin, Alton Priors (within whose territory East Field technically lies), comprised about two dozen modest homes, plus a post office, a general store, a village hall, a primary school, two churches, and a several-thousand-acre farm. The farm was owned by New College, Oxford, and was managed by Tim and Polly Carson, a charming and handsome couple in their thirties. Polly was from the north of England, but Tim had lived in the Alton Barnes area all his life, and had seen wind damage, and had heard strange tales, but had never seen so much as a rough singlet circle on his land. Even so, on the morning of Thursday, 12 July 1990, Tim and Polly would find, swirled into the ripening winter wheat of East Field, the most spectacular formation in the short history of the crop circles phenomenon.

It began with a tiny circle, a few feet wide, slightly offset from one of the tramlines in the middle of the field. Fifteen feet along the tramline lay another circle, a little larger. Then another circle, this one about ten feet wide. Then – still running along the same tramline – a dumbbell pictogram, with the bars to either side, and one circle ringed, and the other circle sprouting, at an odd angle, some kind of appendage ... it looked like a skeleton key, or a crazed cubist fork, or ... a claw. It was very odd. But that was only the first half of the formation, because further along the tramline lay a second dumbbell pictogram, both of whose circles jutted with the strange appendages. Then still further along, and off to one side, lay a tiny double-ringed circle, and finally a tinier singlet. The entire thing, five circles plus the double-pictogram, was about 400 feet long.

Newspaper and radio and TV journalists soon found out about it, and inside of a week Alton Barnes had become a kind of New Age Lourdes. The little road beside the field became clotted with gawking cars, and the police were called in to keep traffic flowing. Even on a weekday afternoon, the formation was likely to be full of people. Some glowed with the energies, some became nauseous, some developed headaches, but most simply marvelled at the thing. Bird-harassed Mary Killen visited it and later said that the circles 'were perfect, as if they'd been made in one fell swoop. I mean, there was no possibility of a human doing that; it was too geo- metrically exact. Human error would have come into it if it had been made by a human.' Richard Ingrams, one of the founders of the satirical *Private Eye*, took a helicopter ride over the formation with his family, and came down a crop circles believer. The helicopter pilot, incidentally, was charging £15 a flight, and by this time the thoughts of Tim Carson also were turning to commerce. Having endured several days of his crops being gang-trampled by pilgrims, he decided to park a caravan by the field gate, with a hired hand to stand guard, and a sign that read:

ENTRY: £1

Within a week, he had made £1,000, and the little caravan at the gate was soon festooned with T-shirts, key-rings, glossy aerial photographs, all for sale. What with the hot, dry weather, the field had been due for harvesting in late July, but the crowds kept coming, and Carson held back the combines until the last week in August, even then harvesting around the formation, to preserve it for a few more weeks. In the end he made about £5,000, donating some of it to the village hall, and some to one of the local churches, and some to various other charities, but keeping a good deal of it, which amply compensated for his time and his trouble and the loss of only a third of an acre, or so, of winter wheat.

The Alton Barnes 'double-pictogram', as it became known, was not the only enormous new formation to appear that summer in the Avebury area. Similar shapes were found beneath Milk Hill, between the East Kennett and West Kennett long barrows, on Allington Down, and at Stanton St Bernard. Throughout England, in that hot summer, something like 700 individual circles were found, many of them attached to larger formations, and many also lying within a few miles of Avebury, or of Cheesefoot Head.

For Terence Meaden, it was a summer of unprecedented media attention, of countless interviews, microphones, glaring lights. And yet ... What could he plausibly say about these new shapes? That they were hoaxes? Not even he believed that. They were simply too complex, too well-woven. No human, nor organized team of humans, could have made such shapes within the four or five hours' darkness available on an English midsummer night. It simply couldn't be done. Moreover, the essential ingredients of these new formations remained circles and rings, both of which he had already explained. The new aspects – the interconnecting channels, the rectangular side-bars, the obvious alignment with tramlines, the sheer complexity of the formations themselves – he felt were also within theoretical reach, especially since there was so much unknown about plasma vortices anyway.

He told the readers of the tabloid *Today*:

A wholly logical explanation to this intriguing and important mystery will be forthcoming. It will be based on the laws of physics. These new symbols are the most extraordinary ever discovered, and will bring to light several exciting but natural phenomena.

And he told readers of *J. Met.*:

> While an understanding of [the pictogram patterns] will not be possible for some time, it may nevertheless be suggested that [they are] the result of instability, a consequence of an unstable and complex vortex (or double vortex) making a powerful impact with the crop and the ground. The mirror-image symmetry noted within the trenches [i.e. the flanking rectangles] is remarkable. Each trench from a pair on one side is mirrored by its opposite number with regard to the internal lie of the crop. In fact, despite the rectangularity of shape the quintessence of vorticity *is* present within the beds of these trenches. Because a rectangular mark in the crop is what would result from the translatory motion of a 'rainbow arc' or semi-circular arc across the field, trenches do in any event retain the quality of the vorticity which drives the system.
>
> I propose that the primary vortex if electrified – as indeed I have inferred it to be for other reasons anyway – sometimes finds itself attracted to tractor-line regions because of local electric field anomalies initiated by the repeated passage of tractors up and down the field ... To this novel phenomenon – the electric field anomaly link with tramlines – I have given the name *strange attractor* ... I suggest that one [reason for this phenomenon] is that repeated passage of heavy farm equipment leads to compaction of the thin chalk-dust laden soil to depths approaching the bedrock. This would affect the flow of sub-surface water and hence modify the electrical conductivity of the comparatively dry chalky soil.

That summer Meaden held an official CERES cropwatch, which he dubbed Operation High Hill. It ran for a month, from the inauspicious date of Friday, 13 July – also the day after the Alton Barnes double-pictogram – to 11 August, by which time most fields in the area had been harvested. An American network TV crew stopped by on the opening night, but in fact, despite occasional visits from the media, the operation was too dispersed and poorly organized to attract much attention. Besides Meaden, the core of Operation High Hill consisted of a half-dozen or so volunteers with binoculars and cameras, who on any given evening might decide not to attend, or if they did attend, might do so anywhere. There was no stationary base of operations, no command post which the media and onlookers could easily find. There was only Terence Meaden's cellular phone number. And despite the operation's lengthy duration, it passed without any circles formations being sighted – although there was one interesting incident: at about 2.30 on the morning of 25 July, one observer, wildlife photographer Richard Flaherty, who had been camping out in the area for several weeks, saw what appeared to be a column of light shining, for several seconds, from the clouds down into a field near Beckhampton – where an odd foetus-shaped formation was found after dawn.

There were other reports throughout the summer which convinced Meaden, and other circles enthusiasts, that the phenomenon remained for the most part genuine. At Bishops Cannings, on the night that the big four-ringed quintuplet appeared, farmhand Andrew Woolley apparently heard a strange high-pitched whistling noise, which lasted only long enough to awaken him from a sound sleep. At Gorleston in Norfolk, on the night that a ringed circle surrounded by ten satellites was formed, a nearby farmer saw over the field a glowing ball of light, 'a red central glow with a thinner red outer ring'. At Preston Brook in Cheshire, at about 1 or 2 a.m. on the night that a seventy-foot circle was formed, witnesses heard 'a high-pitched screeching wail coming from the direction of the field'.

It seemed obvious to Meaden that not all of these could be hoaxes. Nor could hoaxers work so widely – for circles were reported that summer not only from Wiltshire (426 circles), and Hampshire (56), but from Oxfordshire, Somerset, Sussex, Staffordshire, Devon, Avon, Norfolk, Yorkshire, Cheshire, Buckinghamshire, Warwickshire, Nottinghamshire, Herefordshire, Leicestershire, Essex, Lincolnshire, Worcestershire, Shropshire, Lancashire, Tyne and Wear, Humberside, Durham, Llanidloes, Dyfed, Perthshire, the Isle of Wight, Ireland, the Netherlands, Bulgaria, Japan, Canada, and the USA.

There were also two valuable eyewitness reports of circles from previous summers. One was from a Miss Kathleen Skin, who wrote a letter to the *Sunday Express*, describing an event she had witnessed in 1934. Then only fourteen, she had been sitting in the shade of a farm hedgerow on a hot, windless July afternoon at Eversden, near Cambridge, when with a sudden crackling sound, a whirlwind descended into the nearby field, spinning dust and loose stalks into the air above one patch of grain before moving rapidly across the field, pausing, and spinning up more dust and debris. At each place where the whirlwind had paused a circle had been swirled. The laid stalks were still hot to the touch. Later, the farmer who managed the field told her that the whirlwind circles were nothing strange or special; they were simply something that happened in the area from time to time.

There was also a very interesting report from Woolaston, on the west bank of the Severn in Gloucestershire, describing an event that had occurred in 1988. A farmer, Tom Gwinnett, who had contacted Meaden after a local radio station broadcast a programme on the circles, claimed to have seen a circle form, with sound and light and dramatic electromagnetic interference, on a warm night in July of that year. According to Gwinnett, he had been driving past one of his fields at dusk when his car suddenly stopped, the ignition cutting and the headlights winking out. Gwinnett got out to check beneath the bonnet for a loose battery connection, but found nothing amiss. The car, a 2.3 litre Vauxhall, was only three years old, and nothing like this had ever happened to it before. He closed the bonnet and was about to try to start the car when he noticed something odd. A sound . . . A whirring, humming sound, almost mechanical, like an old foot-cranked Singer sewing machine. Then, through a break in the hedge, he saw suspended over the field a dull red ball . . . not much larger than a football . . . except that it wasn't really a ball, or something solid. It was a kind of swarm . . . of sparks . . . red sparks . . . which jumped up from the heads of the surrounding wheat, in a spiral swirl . . . feeding into the dull red spherical swarm in the middle . . . and all the time the bizarre Singer sewing machine sound was going –

Whhooooooommmmmmwhhooooooommmmmmmwhhooooooo oooooomm . . .

Gwinnett was frightened, but also mesmerized, and he watched it for what seemed like a minute or two, until it suddenly winked out – the sparks, the sound – and his car headlights came on.

Gwinnett continued to watch the field, until he had established that it wasn't on fire, and then he drove home. He remembers telling his wife, 'I don't know what happened in the field there, but there was these sparks flying about in there.'

'Oh, dear!'

'But nothing gone afire or anything, so that's all right.'

Gwinnett revisited the field the next morning, and wading into it found a twenty-foot diameter crop circle where the ball of light had been. He had seen such circles before, in fields beside the big road that ran along the Severn, between Lydney and Gloucester. And he remembered that the field in which his circle had appeared was the same field into which a whirlwind had descended dramatically thirty summers before, when he was a young man helping his father harvest hay. The cut stalks had lain in neat rows, waiting to be baled, and one hot, calm afternoon the whirlwind just . . . appeared . . . and inhaled a great lungful of hay, at least a ton of it, took it up in a great spiral, as if carrying it up a winding staircase, and then let it drift for five or six hundred yards before dropping it back down again, in an oddly intact clump, atop several unreachably tall trees that belonged to a neighbour, while his father cursed angrily, and young Gwinnett shook with helpless, awed laughter.

17

Blackbird

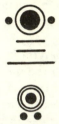

One morning in late July of 1990, several weeks after the Alton Barnes double-pictogram had arrived, BBC breakfast-time viewers were jerked awake with the news that the entities which created crop circles had at last been captured on film, in a field beneath the Westbury white horse . . .

COLIN ANDREWS: (*on the grassy hilltop overlooking the site*) Well we do have a major event here . . . ah, very much excitement, as you can imagine. We do have two major ground markings which have appeared in front of all of the surveillance equipment, performing absolutely to form for us. We had a situation at approximately 3.30 a.m. this morning. On the monitor a number of orange lights taking the form of a triangle . . . it's a complex situation, and we are actually analyzing it at this very moment, but there is undoubtedly something here for science.

NICHOLAS WITCHELL: (*BBC newsreader, in the studio*) I'm sure you have the nation agog. Are you quite sure you couldn't have been the victims of some elaborate hoax last night?

COLIN ANDREWS: No, not indeed. We have high quality equipment here and we have indeed secured on high quality equipment a major event . . . We do have something of great, great significance . . . Yes, we have everything on film and we do have, as I say, a formed object over the field ... We are doing nothing more now until we have helicopters over the top, to film in detail what we have, before anyone enters the field.

NICHOLAS WITCHELL: Gosh, we had better let you get on with it. We look forward to seeing the pics.

And the tense, emphatic visage of Colin Andrews faded from the screen, leaving all of England in suspense ...

The previous year had brought so many successes for Colin Andrews – Operation White Crow, *Circular Evidence*, the *Daytime Live* affair – that when it came time to put together a cropwatch in the summer of 1990, he had no shortage of support. Both the *Daytime Live* producers and Japan's Nippon Television Company became involved, underwriting the provision of special night-vision and video recording equipment that was worth several tens of thousands of pounds – although Andrews, in numerous statements to the media, estimated it to be worth £1 million. There were said to be starlight image-intensifier cameras, short-wave infra-red cameras, thermal infra-red cameras – and, inside a large caravan, a bank of monitors and video recorders. And all of it lay grandly above the Westbury white horse, overlooking the picturesque Vale of Pewsey.

A few days into the operation, at dawn on 25 July, the young volunteers manning the Blackbird site noticed several dim shapes in one of the fields about a half-mile to the north. The shapes were crop circles. They immediately rewound the videotapes, and found that an hour previously, at about 3.30 a.m., a thermal imaging camera had recorded a triangular formation of lights hovering for twenty minutes over the field in question. Nothing more could be discerned from the film, and at about 5.30 a.m., Colin Andrews and Pat Delgado were telephoned.

Andrews and Delgado hurriedly dressed, got into their cars and sped to the site from their homes in Hampshire. What adrenal thoughts leapt through their minds at such an hour, on such an occasion? Most likely, historians will never know, for Delgado and Andrews are nowadays quite reticent on the subject of Operation Blackbird. But reportedly, during a major portion of the trip along the A303 from Hampshire to Wiltshire, Colin Andrews's cellular telephone was occupied, as he dialled, one after the other, at least several dozen major media organizations, from Reuters, to the Associated Press, to ABC News.

At the hilltop site, Andrews continued to dial journalists, and began to give interviews, while the growing crowd of onlookers took turns gazing through a telescope at the circles. The circles were very well-defined, and they definitely seemed to have been arranged in a symmetric pattern. At the top of the formation three circles lay in a row, the central one larger than the others, and dramatically ringed. Parallel with this row of circles and directly beneath them, were three straight lines, running perpendicularly to the field tramlines. Then further down were three more circles, arranged in a triangle, again with two small ones and one large one, the latter doubly-ringed. It was all very precise and neat. And there seemed to be something more involved, for within each circle . . . well, no one could quite make out what they were . . . but, they were . . . things . . . blue things . . .

Blue things? The word started to go around. *Blue things inside the circles* . . . But somehow, Andrews seemed not to notice, what with the distractingly bright buzz of klieg lights and cameras and questions from journalists who had themselves been telephoned out of bed by anxious editors, or in some cases by the distinctive brogue, with Tom Clancy syntax, of Andrews himself . . . 'We've had a major event . . . We're going in at ten o'clock.'

Ten o'clock. And of course that had been the plan all along. Andrews had written it all down long before, had impressed it deeply upon every member of the Blackbird team. If circles were swirled in his absence, he, Colin Andrews, was to be notified at once. No one else was to approach the thing. He was to be notified and he would then take appropriate measures. That had been the plan, and, as anyone could see, the plan was working. The reporters and gawkers and paranormal pilgrims had charged up to the hilltop site like an army, and when they had reached the summit, they had looked down into the Vale and had seen the field where the circles lay, not terribly far off, but nevertheless impenetrable, thanks to the stolid Blackbird volunteers who guarded every entrance.

After a while, the reporters tired of gathering quotes, and began to mutter and grumble and look at their watches. The BBC News people were particularly annoyed. They wanted the videotapes from the night-vision cameras, to broadcast on the midday news, but their brethren at *Daytime Live* – who had intended to keep Operation Blackbird to themselves – were refusing to part with them. The BBC News people became so frustrated that they began to threaten *Daytime Live*'s John Macnish and David Morgenstern, informing them that they would, if necessary, go over their heads at Beeb headquarters to force them to give up the sensational tapes. Macnish and Morgenstern got on to the phone with their bosses at BBC Pebble Mill, but anyone who could help them was away on holiday, it seemed, and finally Macnish and Morgenstern packed the tapes into the boot of a young assistant's car. If Delgado and Andrews went into the circles and declared them genuine, as presumably they would, the assistant would drive back to Pebble Mill with all haste, and BBC News would be informed that the tapes, alas, were unavailable pending 'analysis'.

Of course, little backstage dramas like these were as nothing compared to the promised main event, around which an international audience was quickly gathering. The Reuters wire, for example, informed the newsrooms of the world that:

> Excited scientists said they recorded evidence on Wednesday that could solve the centuries-old mystery of circles in English cornfields which have aroused speculation of visitors from outer space.
>
> Scientist Colin Andrews said the circles could not be a hoax. 'We had many lights ... a complex arrangement doing all sorts of funny things. There is undoubtably something here for science.'

'I hope this isn't a hoax,' Andrews confided to Delgado when the cameras and microphones had briefly turned their attention elsewhere.

Shortly after ten o'clock, all was ready. As the crowd hummed and swelled with anticipation, Andrews and Delgado, with John Macnish and a film crew from NTV, drove down to the distant field, and parked on the side of the road. Delgado and Andrews prepared to enter the field alone, armed with a radio mike and small video cameras. It was a momentous event, and neither of them wanted any shamanic monkeying-about. Their next few minutes would be as scrutinized as the first lunar landing had been. 'This is the first time any human has entered these circles,' Delgado said to the cameras. 'We want to take it carefully, step by step, as we approach the formation, to see what exactly is lying in front of us, so that there will be a sequential report coming back from us, as we go in, right through the formation to the other side.' As they went in, Andrews sent back the reports. 'It's a ripened field of wheat . . . We're about thirty, forty feet, now, into the field . . . Turning my own video on . . .' No detail was too insignificant. Andrews even filmed his own feet walking in the tramlines. *This is one small step for a man . . .*

Finally, just as they entered the first part of the formation, three small aeroplanes zoomed in low overhead, sprouting cameras. By the time the planes had passed, Andrews had reached the centre of the first circle, where something blue had caught his eye.

The throng on the hilltop muttered and buzzed impatiently, watching Andrews and Delgado, who were now two little ants in a distant circle of swept wheat . . . two little ants staring down at one of the little blue things. They stared at the little blue thing, and then they stared at it some more. They stood there staring at it for what seemed to be, and in fact was, a very long time. What was it? What had they found? What were those little blue things? Why weren't the two famous crop circles experts rushing back with the news . . . ?

And inside the circle, as the sun danced crazily on the surfaces of what were, in fact, six little blue 'Zodiac' board games – each placed neatly in the centre of a circle, beneath a pair of crooked sticks – Colin Andrews was trying to convince a reluctant Pat Delgado that the thing was a hoax.

And up on the hilltop, the multitude muttered and buzzed and grumbled, and took turns looking through the telescope at the two little ants and the little blue things. Look! They're moving! They're inspecting the circle! It's all right! It's genuine! And as the crowd on the distant hilltop watched, Andrews and Delgado began crawling and poking around the circles, closely examining the laid stalks, the sharpness of the circles' edges, the overall symmetry. They poked and prodded and examined and measured, and conferred, and nodded, and shook their heads, and conferred some more, and then drove to a nearby pub to confer further with Macnish and the NTV people, and . . . a full two hours later . . . carrying the little Zodiac games and the crooked sticks, they drove back to the hilltop, and faced the expectant crowd.

Andrews did most of the talking. 'As soon as I saw the edge of the first circle,' he told the press, 'I knew it was a hoax. It was damaged and ill-formed and the wheat had just been broken down. The game being left in the middle was just like someone's calling card . . . I saw at once that we had an obvious hoax. The pattern is not consistent with the development of this perfectly genuine phenomenon, and an inspection on the ground showed very severe damage to the corn – bruising, severance, and disturbances consistent with human feet. This is quite unlike the pattern one sees in genuine circles . . .

'I suppose we were already suspicious because of what we had seen on the video recordings. For a start, it took about twenty minutes for the circles to form when our research shows that real circles are there within seconds. But I feel very sad that someone has sunk to these depths . . . Whoever created these circles has demonstrated to young people that it is no bad thing to go on to private property and destroy crops, and to hoodwink a serious research project . . .

'This affair has just improved our credibility, however. We had £1 million worth of equipment which did its job. We were able to identify a hoax for what it was within seconds . . . our equipment can tell within seconds whether a ring is a hoax or not. The equipment even detected the heat from the bodies of the perpetrators . . .

'Somebody has had a laugh. They have had a joke. Frankly, it is probably funny for about sixty seconds. Then I find it very very sad. They have only set the research back . . . This hoax was totally irresponsible. It was only funny for about ten seconds . . .'

18

The Tractor-driver

The newspapers naturally had a good long guffaw over the Blackbird affair. HOAXERS RUN RINGS AROUND CIRCLE OF EXPERTS, snickered the *Independent*. SUMMER MADNESS OF SUPERSTITIOUS CELTS, snorted *The Times*, which quoted a spokesman for the Met Office at Bracknell: 'We have people looking at these things in their spare time, and the general consensus is that they are a glorified hoax.'

A glorified hoax. So this was how the summer of the pictograms would end. Even if they did derive a secret chuckle or two from Andrews's and Delgado's public embarrassment, Wingfield and Green and the rest of the CCCS chiefs – and even Meaden and his camp – were fairly bitter about it, because Andrews and Delgado, by their actions in this one highly-visible case, had invited scepticism about the entire phenomenon, scepticism which reflected adversely on all of them. 'Colin's initial statements,' wrote Wingfield in the *Cereologist*, 'were undoubtedly ill-advised, perhaps even unwise in the extreme.' Meaden, writing in *J. Met.*, was less restrained:

It had taken seven hours for the nature of the trick to be realized, five hours of which were daylight hours – a dismal performance by any standards although not unexpected of nonscientific publicists who had worsened matters for themselves by proclaiming for three hours on live television that 'this was a major, a really significant breakthrough'. In the absence of prior testing and application of the scientific method the alien-intelligence believers had been unable to tell the difference between humans on the ground and thermal-images in the air. Instead of inspecting a doubtful situation without delay they had advertised their desired success in a wholly unscientific manner.

In any case, the thing was done and past. The only thing now, as the cereology community saw it, was to lament Andrews's and Delgado's particular foolishness, to admit that hoaxing occasionally occurred, and to contrast the hoaxed formation with its genuine, gently-swirled, and aesthetically much more pleasing cousins at Alton Barnes and Beckhampton and Stanton St Bernard and Longwood Estate and Chilcomb and wherever else the pictograms had appeared that summer. In fact, almost nothing that summer looked like the Westbury hoax, except possibly a three-in-line triplet – a practice run? – which had been seen near the Warminster by-pass a few weeks before. It would be nice to find the Westbury hoaxers, and to get them to admit to having done it as a one-off. Then cereology might become respectable again.

Wingfield decided to take up the investigation, and soon found a promising lead: on the day after the hoax, it turned out, Colin Andrews had received a letter which read:

> Colin,
> the circles on Wednesday were just a hoax,
> but we can't help to play jokes.
> Inconvenience caused? We're sorry.
> Catch us, you'll have to hurry.
> Yours, in total control,
> the Justified Ancients of Mu Mu – the Jamms.
>
> Try not to worry too hard.
> We find it very funny,
> While you sit back and rake in the money.

Down at the bottom of the page, as a further postscript, was the cryptic message '25 31 Wiltshire', with a symbol resembling a portable stereo player, a so-called ghetto-blaster, superimposed upon a pyramid. The symbol, as Wingfield soon established, was the logo of the acid-house band KLF, also known as the 'Kopyright Liberation Front', also known as 'the Timelords', also known as ... 'the Jamms' – which at the time of the hoax had just released a new album called *Space*. Wingfield's sources apparently reported that someone resembling Bill Drummond, a member of the group, had been seen near the Blackbird site on the night of the hoax, disguised in 'a long straggly beard ... a blue ladies' suede coat, [and] a skirt and bowler hat'. And in early August, or perhaps on the night of 31 July, the KLF logo was swirled into one of David Read's fields north of the Wansdyke, not far from where the Haddington watch had occurred. Busty Taylor and Richard Andrews duly reported that the formation 'didn't dowse', and in fact Farmer Read confirmed that the thing had been done by humans – two members of KLF, plus one of their wives, plus a film-maker friend of the band, Bill Butt, who had flown over the area in a microlight aircraft on the 24th, and had later paid Read £350 for the privilege of creating 'landscape art' in one of his wheatfields.

Case closed. KLF had hoaxed the Blackbird circles. Except that Farmer Read told Wingfield that the KLF circle, though made in daylight, had taken the group six exhausting hours to complete. The Westbury formation had been swirled in less than an hour, in darkness. And according to Wingfield, although the group was rumoured among pop-rock aficionados to be heavily involved in circle-making, they strongly denied having done the Westbury hoax.

To complicate the picture, there was George Vernon, a middle-aged man from a seedy section of Bristol, who occasionally went by the moniker of 'Merlin the Magician' and had long been claiming the ability to make crop circles, either by remote psychokinesis or by directly rolling around in fields. He apparently told a reporter for the tabloid *Sunday Sport* that he had fabricated the Westbury circles using the latter method, and he noted that the Zodiac board game, copies of which were found inside the circles, had been his own invention, and in fact bore the stamp: 'Copyright 1990, George Vernon'.

Case closed, again. Except that ... how could Vernon have swirled such a precise formation so quickly, so ... professionally? And why would he have done it? Wingfield began to ask himself who else might have wished to plant the Zodiac board games in the faked circles. Obviously not a bona fide occultist, who would never have come near the prying cameras of Blackbird. But perhaps . . . someone who wished to discredit the phenomenon as the work of bizarre ritualists. But who? Who would have wanted to discredit the phenomenon?

To Wingfield, the professional precision of the circles was one clue, as was the fact that, although absent on the night of the hoax, the military had been present beside the Blackbird site thereafter. In any case, according to Wingfield, he soon received a call from a knowledgeable informant, who, in Wingfield's words, 'had supplied sensitive information in the past which had always proved to be good'. The alleged informant allegedly told Wingfield that the Westbury hoax had been 'ordered from a high level in the MoD', had been 'carefully planned, practised in advance, and then executed swiftly and precisely in total darkness at short notice', in 'utmost secrecy', by a 'specially set up detachment of the Army'. 'Our source,' wrote Wingfield in both the *Cereologist* and *Flying Saucer Review*, 'had even spoken to an officer involved in the planning of the operation, which was carried out in utmost secrecy.'

To understand the motive, one has to appreciate the extraordinary situation which had arisen at the end of July. With the advent of pictograms, and the giant formation at Alton Barnes in particular, Circles hysteria had almost risen to fever-pitch. Yet the government said nothing, did nothing, and was probably as perplexed as everybody else. Somehow the situation had to be defused, and the best way of doing this was to make the populace believe that the Circles were no more than hoaxes. To do this, an elaborate hoax had to be executed, which appeared the equal of the real phenomenon, and yet could be seen to be a hoax. Blackbird [with its attendant publicity] was the perfect opportunity . . . But why the Horoscope board games and the wooden crosses? To achieve its objective the hoax had to be seen to be a hoax. There was always the ghastly possibility that Andrews and Delgado might proclaim the hoaxed circles as genuine, thereby defeating the purpose of the whole exercise, and redoubling public fervour for the Circles. Therefore, these artifacts were placed, with tell-tale military precision, at the centre of each circle, the items having been chosen to implicate a very different group of people from those actually concerned.

Despite the success of the operation, said Wingfield, the government was still worried over how to respond in 1991, when the circles would undoubtedly begin again. 'Proof of this,' he wrote, 'is demonstrated by a report' – from the same reliable source, apparently – 'that a secret cabinet level meeting was called in recent weeks to discuss the subject.' At the meeting, according to Wingfield's informant, the idea that the circles were generally caused by hoaxers or whirlwinds had been raised . . . and dismissed. The problem of public hysteria had also been discussed, as had the possibility of spreading 'disinformation'. And in the end, the matter had been placed in the hands of the MoD, which would, suggested Wingfield, no doubt have something up its sleeve the following summer.

The year 1991 was a few December weeks away, and the summer of 1990 a warm but fading memory, when the Leon Besant case came to light. Leon was about twenty years old, and worked on a farm at Stanton St Bernard. He lived with the family that ran the farm. They had taken him in when he'd left home a few years before. He was a shy young man – seldom went out, seldom spoke.

One hot, sunny afternoon in July 1990, while the cameras of Operation Blackbird still whirred and circles tourists still roamed the Wiltshire countryside, Leon had been driving a tractor through a field of barley beneath Milk Hill. In an adjacent field lay one of the big double-pictograms, and beside it a kind of mini-pictogram – a circle with one of the claw-like appendages, perhaps symbolic of the earth, mankind, reaching out.

Suddenly Leon noticed a strange object coming at him from one of the other fields. It was shiny, bright, indistinctly shaped . . . but at least a few inches across . . . It moved past him, over the tractor, glinting in the sun, like a piece of tin-foil, but moving with an unreal speed through the hot, listless air . . . And then it was away across the fields, climbing higher . . . up the slope of a distant hill, and . . . gone.

The Tractor-driver

Leon rushed home to tell his adopted family. And ... they laughed at him. *Leon saw a flying saucer! Beam me up, Scotty!* And so on.

Leon shut up after that and didn't mention the experience again. But the word got around, and soon the people of Stanton St Bernard and the surrounding villages all had heard the story. *Leon saw a flying saucer! Beam me up, Scotty!* Word also got around that Leon, frightened by his UFO experience, would no longer go outside at night.

One day, about six months later, Colin Andrews arrived in the village and asked if anyone knew of a tractor-driver who had seen a shining object flying over a field near Stanton St Bernard the previous July. Someone had videotaped it all, explained Andrews, and the tractor-driver had been there in the film.

It turned out that the videotape had been made by a man named Steven Alexander, from Gosport on the Solent. Alexander and his wife had been in Wiltshire on that day in July, having heard about Operation Blackbird, and had decided to take a look at the circles for themselves. They drove to Alton Barnes first, and saw the big double-pictogram, and while there were told about the similar formation below Milk Hill. So they walked along the ridge from Alton Barnes towards Stanton St Bernard, and videoed the Milk Hill formations. Alexander and his wife were about to leave when they saw the object in the field below them, moving about as if under intelligent control, before suddenly turning and zooming over a hedge and past the tractor, and away into the ineffable blue yonder.

Andrews showed Leon a copy of Alexander's video, and pretty soon the news spread through the village of Stanton St Bernard. Leon noticed a curious thing. Folks who a few months before had been taunting him mercilessly would now come up to him and clap him on the back and buy him drinks and say, *Aw Leon, we believed you all along.*

19

Professor Fireball

One thundery summer evening in the early 1960s, while ten-year-old Yoshi-Hiko Ohtsuki sat in the bathtub at his family's house in the city of Kakuda, Japan, a silent orange globe of light drifted past the bathroom window outside. It was, according to Japanese folklore, a fire-spirit. But to the science-minded young boy, for whom it would eventually become the focus of a career, it was ball-lightning.

Ball-lightning remains a mystery. It seems to range in size from the diameter of a grapefruit to that of a hot-air balloon. It can be white, or orange, or bluish, translucent or opaque, hot or cold, dim or bright. It can bounce, or float, or spiral, or flutter. It can move against the wind. It can pass through walls, windows, and other electrically non-conductive obstacles, while conductors seem to pique its interest – it tends to hover around them, often meandering along the paths of buried wires or pipes . . . before suddenly disappearing into them with a violent explosion. Several reports describe the destruction of entire houses. As for human conductors, ball-lightning seldom does any harm – one observer simply brushed away a ball that had clung to her chest – but there are reliable accounts of severe burning and explosive dismemberment, and a link with spontaneous human combustion has long been suspected. Moreover, in a recent large-scale survey of cases in Asia, Ohtsuki found hints of a subtler hazard: nearly a third of the ball-lightning or 'fire-spirit' accounts appeared to be associated with unexplained deaths among the elderly.

Ohtsuki also found that, contrary to widespread belief even among professional researchers, ball-lightning is not exclusively associated with thunderstorms. Nine of the ten cases he surveyed occurred in calm weather. Nevertheless, the glowing globes occasionally seem to behave remarkably like their more common linear cousins, as in these British accounts:

> I saw a ball of pearly white light drop vertically but gently from the cloud to disappear in a few brief moments behind the horizon.

> . . . the lightning seemed to consist of three large balls of about three feet diameter, one above the other, which corkscrewed down from the sky to strike the roof of the house, the first ball exploding on contact, and nothing more was seen of the other two.

Hypotheses that have been developed over the years to explain the elusive phenomenon include swamp gas, rogue collections of electrostatic charge, and slowly burning 'aerogels'. But none of these concepts is able to account for, among other things, ball-lightning's ghostly yet indisputable ability to pass through walls and windows without causing damage.

In a famous paper in 1955, Peter Kapitza, a Russian physicist who for other work would later win a Nobel Prize, suggested that ball-lightning might be primarily an electromagnetic wave phenomenon. He postulated the existence of naturally occurring short radio waves – say, in the 1 metre range, not far from the FM band – which at certain frequencies, and at certain points (called 'antinodes') where wavefronts interfered constructively and created an area of super-high intensity, would ionize the air molecules. The ions and their dissociated electrons would tend to move away from the antinode, to areas of lower electromagnetic field intensity, but eventually the surrounding air pressure would force them into an equilibrium – a glowing shell of plasma surrounding a spherical standing radio-wave. The shell would effectively trap the high intensity wave, while the wave, oscillating in synch with the surrounding radio-frequency field, would keep the shell energized and glowing.

Kapitza and other physicists argued about and expanded upon

this concept over the years. Some said it would never work. Others said it covered not only ball-lightning, but also ghosts and UFOs. In any case, it seemed to explain the odder aspects of ball-lightning behaviour: as the radio-wave field antinode moved (in any direction, and potentially at the speed of light) the plasma shell would follow, in effect reconstituting itself from the surrounding air wherever it went. When the antinode passed through a wall, its surrounding plasma shell would disappear on one side and instantaneously reignite on the other. And when the antinode hit a well-grounded conductor, the field would 'spike' (in the hand-waving slang of physicists) and suddenly concentrate its energy, explosively, into the earthing point.

One major objection to the theory had to do with the supposed naturally occurring short radio waves. Where were they? What made them? Several suggestions were put forward: Peter Handel, a physicist at the University of Missouri, proposed in the early 1980s that a short, sharp electric field pulse, from lightning or from some other less obvious meteorological process, might excite a relatively high proportion of local atmospheric water molecules, pushing their outer electrons into higher, less stable orbits – until these electrons fell back, releasing radio-frequency electromagnetic photons, which would collide with other excited water molecules, causing them to de-excite and release more radio photons, and so on in a sudden cascade of high-intensity radio-frequency energy which physicists call a 'maser'.*

Other researchers pointed to the long association between strange electromagnetic phenomena and seismic activity – such as balls of light spouting out of the ground during earthquakes, or, in seismically quieter times, the disproportionately high frequency of UFO sightings near fault lines. Perhaps some seismic process could occasionally, without any other obvious manifestation, generate the required electromagnetic waves. But no one really knew.

*

*For Microwave Amplification by Stimulated Emission of Radiation, which by convention refers not only to microwaves but to all sorts of radio waves. Incidentally, the maser, when it was discovered/invented, immediately suggested what has become a much better known device – the light-amplification 'laser'.

Ohtsuki himself was primarily an experimentalist, and he decided more or less to try everything – electrical discharges, aerosol combustion, fuel-gas combustion … And after several trials and errors (one of which forced the move to the suburbs) he turned to plasma tests, setting up a magnetron which would feed strong radio waves into a metal cavity. The waves would interfere, antinodes would be set up, and presumably, plasmoids would spring to life and dance for the cameras. He would have liked to use ordinary VHF radio waves, which would have been in accord with the Kapitzian theory, and should have produced ordinary-sized plasmoids – or 'plasma fireballs', as he liked to call them – but a VHF generator of the necessary power would have been too expensive, and the cavity would have to have been huge. In the end he settled for a souped-up microwave oven – a 2.45 Gigahertz microwave generator, and a simple six-by-fourteen-inch cylindrical cavity made of metal plate. His plasma fireballs would have to be in miniature.

The creation of plasmoids with radio waves wasn't new, of course. Fusion engineers routinely used radio-frequency radiation to heat deuterium gas to the plasma state, and for years physicists had been demonstrating, sometimes inadvertently, how plasma could form at the antinodes of electromagnetic fields. But no one, using radio waves in ordinary air at ordinary temperature and pressure, had yet created plasmoids which could last for any significant length of time, and which could demonstrate the full repertoire of ball-lightning behaviour.

Until Ohtsuki. His plasma fireballs glowed and danced for hours on end, in white, orange, red, and blue. They hovered at the main antinode, they buzzed crazily around the cavity, they ducked into the waveguide, they drifted insouciantly through a ceramic plate, and against an airflow created by a fan, and in roman-candle multiples along a metal bar. One of the little plasmoids was so robust it burned through the aluminium-foil wall at one end of the cavity and popped out into the lab, lasting a few moments on its own, *à la* Frankenstein's monster, even after Ohtsuki's startled students had shut off the power.

Several months of experiments followed, and then Ohtsuki wrote everything up in a paper and sent it to the interdisciplinary science journal *Nature* in London, which duly sent it out to several academic physicists around the world for peer review. One doubting Thomas refused to believe Ohtsuki's claim that the fireballs had passed through the ceramic plate – until Ohtsuki sent him the video. The paper was finally published in March 1991 and created a sensation, not merely within the fraternity of ball-lightning researchers, who generally had already learned of the experiments, but among the wider community of physicists, where fascination with oddball phenomena was seldom allowed to be indulged. Ohtsuki was swamped with requests for further details of his research, and the American Physical Society voted to create a new branch especially for the study of such weird atmospheric electromagnetic phenomena.

Meanwhile, Ohtsuki was busy topping the plasma fireball experiment with an even stranger one.

In Japan, swirled circles in grass and rice had been reported in the popular press and the UFO literature since the late 1970s. Ohtsuki, who began to scrutinize these accounts a decade later, noticed a link with reports of ball-lightning. Folklore also suggested a connection; one classic children's tale from northern Japan involved sky-maidens dressed in bright kimonos who would descend to the rice-fields at night to dance.

On the assumption that ball-lightning was indeed a radio-frequency plasmoid, and with the help of some fairly dense mathematical physics involving three-dimensional Schrödinger equations and soliton wave solutions, Ohtsuki hypothesized that the ball-lightning plasma shell might sometimes have enough surface tension to enable force to be exerted against obstacles. Thus, although the ball could go through walls – or could seem to – it might occasionally resist, deforming elastically upon impact, and perhaps leaving a mark.

One day early in 1991, Ohtsuki received a telephone call from an official who worked for the massive Tokyo underground railway system. It seemed that some maintenance workers had been seeing strange things down in the tunnels. Little circles . . . inscribed in the soot and dust on the walls. Perhaps Professor Ohtsuki would be interested.

One morning a few weeks later, at about 2.30, the Tokyo transit authority cut power to the system, and Ohtsuki, decked out in a subway jumpsuit and hardhat, descended into the bowels of the city, accompanied by Tokyo transit officials and a TV camera crew. Soon it was clear that the little circles were everywhere – on the walls, on concrete ledges, beside the electrified third rail, horizontally, vertically, diagonally. Most had one or two rings, some had three or four or five, and some seemed aligned together, like the linear multiplets seen in the fields of southern England. To Ohtsuki, it was easy to see what was happening. The high-voltage chaos of the underground railway line was somehow spawning little plasmoids, which like soap bubbles would fly around until they hit a solid surface. When they hit, the plasma shell would leave its imprint on the soot and dust. One ring implied a single plasma shell; two rings implied two shells, and so on.

Unfortunately, there was no telling how often the little plasmoids were formed. The subway walls hadn't been cleaned in a quarter-century. But less than a month after the subterranean discovery, Ohtsuki was able to duplicate the little plasma graffiti in the lab. It was an experiment he had been planning all along, in an effort to prove what was causing the crop circles, and it did more than anything to erase the media scepticism that had set in after Operation Blackbird. 'Good news!' Ohtsuki wrote to Meaden. 'On 17 March 1991 we succeeded in creating the circles effect on thin aluminium powder distributed over a metal plate set in our plasma chamber. The circles range from 2 to 10 mm with ring! You can see our photographs. So, your idea has been confirmed experimentally!'

20

Chaos

•

Researchers who ignore these basic facts and attempt to rational-ize away what is becoming increasingly obvious can only be described as *totally unscientific*.

– George Wingfield, in *Crop Circles: Harbingers of World Change*

This is a serious scientific subject, utterly polluted by the fantasies of these ill-educated people.

– Terence Meaden, in conversation

I see no indication that there has been any attempt to apply the scientific method, no rigorous testing of hypotheses. Instead – and this applies to all the major protagonists – there has been a haphazard accumulation of what might loosely be called 'data', and the construction of vast and shaky edifices of speculation.

– Martin Hempstead, of the Wessex Skeptics, in the *Skeptic*

The idea of a method that contains firm, unchanging, and absolutely binding principles for conducting the business of science meets considerable difficulty when confronted with the results of historical research.

– Paul Feyerabend, philosopher of science, in *Against Method*

A few months later Ohtsuki came to England again, and there were the stories in the papers about the thirty-nine British and Japanese scientists, and the secret site, and another crop circle season got under way.

Not long after midnight on 2 July, residents of Alton Barnes and Alton Priors briefly heard a loud roar, as if, they said, a Hercules transport aircraft had flown over. In the morning, a new pictogram lay in the Carsons' East Field. It consisted of three circles, two of them ringed, all of them linked by an avenue. No claws jutted out, but two smaller circles lay neatly nearby, well away from tramlines.

Three days later, on a glorious morning that promised a hot summer day, I drove out to East Field, armed with map and tape recorder and camera, and a pound coin for the farmhand who sat in the cool shadow of Tim Carson's caravan, beneath dangling crop circle T-shirts and key-rings and glossy pin-ups of 1990's cereological beauties.

I noticed now that there were two formations in the field. The farmhand explained to me that the smaller one, a little ping-pong bat-shaped dumbbell down in the bottom of the bowl, had only just been discovered that morning, and was closed to the public until the scientists had made their analyses. But I was welcome to visit the other one.

I walked east along the edge of the field to the sign marking the appropriate tramline, and then south along the tramline, a narrow down-sloping path of packed earth and chalk pebbles, as if through a shallow but perfectly parted beige sea. The tramline reached its nadir, began to slope upwards again, then suddenly gaped open – and for the first time in my life I stood within a crop circle.

I was unable to sense any residual energy, any electrostatic tingling, but there was clearly something hair-raising about the place, something surreal . . . as if I had been caught up in a kind of terrestrial whirlpool. I walked along the edge of the circle, and snapped a photo looking down the 300-foot length of the formation. I wondered whether the camera would work at the very centre. Even then, barely a day after my initiation at the secret site, I knew about the demon that had bewitched Delgado and Andrews at the centres of circles. And according to his most recent book, *Circles from the Sky*, Terence Meaden had experienced the beast, too, in the form of 'weak electromagnetic effects [which] persist in the vicinity (in particular the earth and perhaps straw) for some time afterwards'. Meaden's camera had malfunctioned in 1990, in the centre of a double-ringer at Bratton. It had worked anywhere, and when pointed in any direction, except when he brought it to the centre, and pointed it downwards.

I walked to the central circle and pointed my own camera downwards and . . . *ksshheeeezzzz* . . . It worked fine. I moved a few paces away, pressed the record buttons on my tape recorder, and holding the thing in front of me, calling out the distances so I would know precisely when the electromagnetic effects began to take hold, I slowly approached the centre again . . . 'Five feet . . . four feet . . . three feet . . . two . . . one . . .'

It was then that I noticed the tape recorder wasn't working. The record buttons were down, but the tape wouldn't budge. The machine was brand new, and I had checked it out in the store. I checked the tape, which was also brand new, and the brand new batteries. I slapped the thing. Nothing.

Ignoring the faraway farmhand, who was chatting with several sun-struck tourists at the caravan, I climbed the long narrow tramline and continued further east, then down again, to the bottom of the field where a half dozen young men had gathered at the edge of the new formation. It was only a few hours old – still hot, so to speak. The stalks, as yet untrampled by pilgrims' feet, lay messily half-up, half-down, springing upright in unruly clumps here and there, although the general dumbbell shape of the formation was unmistakable. Had anyone seen anything overnight? No, came the reply, but two ingenuous-looking fellows in their late teens said they had come up from Sussex to camp out on Adam's Grave – a round barrow atop the steep hill that overlooked the field – and had planned to watch for circles seraphs . . . but their tent had blown down in a high wind, at about midnight, and after an hour of struggle to re-erect it, they had collapsed exhausted in their sleeping bags, oblivious to any goings-on below in the field.

There had also been fog that night, just before dawn, a fact which reminded me of something.

I had been alone in the caravan at the secret site, at four o'clock on the previous morning, facing the surreal green radar image of the surrounding landscape, and feigning consciousness, when someone from a cropwatching caravan at the far side of the hill – theirs was a full-fledged Kon-Tiki motor home – paid a visit. He was John Macnish, and his group in the Kon-Tiki had dubbed their enterprise Operation Chameleon. Macnish, of course, was one of the BBC people who had been present at the *Daytime Live* affair, and so was one of his Kon-Tiki colleagues, David Morgenstern. But the BBC connection with Operation Chameleon was unofficial, said Macnish, because the Beeb had been embarrassed so badly the previous year at Operation Blackbird. We talked for a while about cropwatching and the unfortunate rivalry between the Meadenites and the Delgadonians, and the *Daytime Live* incident, and what might be causing the circles. Macnish also told me about a little dumbbell formation that had appeared in the field below the Kon-Tiki the previous Friday morning. The fog had come in thick, and then after dawn it had risen and risen until there had been one little patch left – and the formation had been there. The barley field, said Macnish, had been covered by a very sensitive directional microphone on top of the Kon-Tiki, operating in the ordinary sound range as well as in the ultrasound and infrasound ranges. The sides of the field where the tramlines into the field could be accessed were covered with some kind of sophisticated infra-red-beam intruder alarm system that his friend Mike Carrie, an entrepreneur with a company called Cloud-9, had set up. If any hoaxer had come in via the tramlines, he would have had to cross the beam – or, presumably, he would have eschewed the tramlines and left a trail of his own in the field. But the alarm hadn't sounded, and in the morning, when the fog had risen, the field had looked clean. Except for the circles.

Why would plasma vortices form in fog? And wouldn't an infra-red beam be cut by fog? These questions drifted back to me on that bright morning in East Field, as I stood at the edge of the new formation.

Next to me, an earnest young man in his late twenties dangled a lump of crystal on a chain at the edge of the circle.

'What's he doing?' I whispered to one of the Sussex campers.

'Pendulum-dowsing,' he whispered back. 'Measuring the energies.'

The minutes pendulated past, and the energies slowly waned, and we waited for the scientists to arrive. Who were the scientists? I asked. 'Dr Terence Meaden, and a Japanese professor,' said a slightly officious man who was wearing a robin's-egg blue jacket, a robin's-egg blue railway-engineer's cap, and a white goatee. He carried a clipboard, a tape measure, and two L-shaped metal rods with white plastic dowels around the short ends – dowsing rods, with plastic handles that permitted a freer swing.

The railway engineer eventually grew impatient. He tip-toed along the far edge of the smaller circle, knelt, and then stretched himself out towards the centre, carefully inspecting the tangled singularity from which – like a hairy cowlick, or a hurricane's eye, or a galactic hub – the stalks all swirled outwards. Soon the others joined him, tape-measuring, dowsing, photographing at the wide-angle from a tripod held overhead. I checked my tape recorder again; it still didn't –

Oh. The pause switch. The little switch that lay snugly along the side of the thing, practically hidden. I must have accidentally turned it on before leaving the car.

A short time later Meaden appeared, with Ohtsuki and two gaunt young Japanese. Ohtsuki, a short, pleasantly moon-faced man with large-framed glasses, was brightly dressed in a striped blue button-down shirt, bright white trousers, and an even brighter white floppy beach hat. A fluorescent yellow video camera dangled from a strap on one shoulder. He entered the formation, followed by his silent, solemn, attentive students, and measured the dimensions, and checked the stalks and the ground, and commented occasionally in quiet Japanese, and videotaped everything. There were several smaller circles farther back in the field, to the south, and these were also of interest, having apparently arrived simultaneously with the dumbbell. They were in pristine condition, without tourists' trails leading to them from the surrounding tramlines.

In an hour or so, Meaden had had enough, and after making arrangements to meet Ohtsuki later, he walked back up towards the caravan. I walked with him, and as we passed the caravan, an elderly local asked Meaden, 'Is it a hoax?'

'It is not a hoax,' said Meaden authoritatively. 'Not at all. There are eight circles, five of them away from the tramlines. I very much doubt that hoaxers would have gone to the trouble to make all those.'

*

'This was a hoaxing,' one of Ohtsuki's students told me that afternoon. We were sitting in the CERES caravan at the secret site. The student's name was Kondo. He was a physics undergraduate at Waseda University. He had helped to run several of Professor Ohtsuki's plasma fireball experiments. And that morning, he and Professor Ohtsuki and the other student, Tanaichi, had determined that the new formation at Alton Barnes was man-made. According to Kondo, there were several giveaways. Firstly, there was a footprint at the edge of the circle. (I remembered the goateed railway engineer stepping gingerly around that edge, but said nothing.) Secondly, many of the stalks were broken, as if by a solid weight. Thirdly, the dumbbell when viewed from above was . . . less shiny, more scuffed-looking, than they had come to expect of genuine formations.

In truth, Kondo was unsure whether plasmas were ever involved in the creation of crop circles – though there had been one mysterious incident, a few afternoons before, which seemed to confirm the plasma hypothesis. A film crew from TV-South had been jammed into the tiny caravan, filming Kondo and Tanaichi as they watched the radar scope (which was ordinarily used only at night) when suddenly . . . a shape . . . not too large, about aeroplane-sized on the scope . . . but moving incredibly fast . . . and in a few sweeps of the antenna it had crossed the eight-mile span of the screen.

A hypersonic plasmoid?

Kondo shrugged.

That was a Friday, and Ohtsuki stayed on until Sunday. He had a fairly busy schedule while he was in England, examining circles, supervising his students' all-nighters in the caravan, pulling a few of his own, and above all talking to the press. In those few weeks, he was interviewed, photographed, and/or filmed by dozens of newspaper, radio, and TV news and feature reporters, plus documentary film crews from National Geographic, the BBC and Channel Four. He had also imported his own press – in the form of Nippon TV, Tokai TV from the suburbs of Nagoya, and a young reporter from Playboy Magazine of Japan who apparently had been following the intrepid professor around for several years. On that Friday afternoon the pasture surrounding the Meadenite caravan was every bit as amok with reporters and producers and cameramen and scurrying gofers as I had imagined in my original Spielbergesque fantasy. The only things missing were a few dozen jumpsuited scientists, and a few million pounds worth of high-tech equipment, and of course the howling cherubim.

On Saturday, in an upstairs room at the Devizes Museum, surrounded by Bronze Age bric-à-brac and delayed forty-five minutes by someone's forgetting a VCR remote-control switch, Meaden held an informal meeting on the crop circles. It would later be referred to as the Devizes Workshop. Word of it had got around the CERES grapevine, and a few dozen people turned up. There was Ohtsuki, and Kondo and Tanaichi, and Nippon TV and Tokai TV and the Playboy reporter (who introduced himself blandly as a member of 'the magazine press'); and Mark something, an independent TV producer who was doing a documentary about ball-lightning; and Greg, a Canadian physicist and circles-tourist; and George, a retired engineer; and Peter, a retired engineer; and Jean-François, a Belgian engineer; and a few young Meadenites such as Paul Fuller. I was there, too.

Meaden started out with a long, and largely extemporaneous, defence of crop circles science:

> As scientists . . . we do have this advantage over non-scientists of being able to look quite rationally at things which, when they're not understood by non-scientists, appear to be very mysterious, if not mystical. And for those who are quite religious, something which is mystical, looks to be perhaps paranormal – certainly deeply religious people are able to accept anything that goes, if it's not easily understood, by any reasoning that pleases them. So there are lots of people in this field who are inventing their own answers to the circles problem just to satisfy themselves . . .
>
> The complex shapes which we know to exist, and which we have authenticated, anyway – that's something we would have liked to have left for a few years, and work out the easier ones first. But the public are attracted by the complex shapes, and the press, and the entertainment media in particular, are attracted to the complex shapes, and they want answers to those. I think Professor Ohtsuki would agree with me that, in

principle, there's going to be nothing impossibly difficult, regarding the complex shapes, that cannot be handled by physics and mathematics and meteorology . . .

Of course what we really want to do is to see circles form. And that is something which might happen this year, or will happen in the future. That's going to be the one thing which will convince those remaining scientists who have said we're probably dealing with some sort of massive hoax, and that we're all being fooled, because there is somebody around who is cleverer than we are . . . creating circles. I'm saying that all the ones I've authenticated are real. The great sceptics are even sceptical of those cases. But they don't have the advantage of having been in — the first person in — so many of these circles . . . It's very different from just reading about it in somebody else's book. I have found that where I've been able to get a scientist along to look at circles just after they were formed, he's been pretty well convinced afterwards. The ones who aren't so convinced are the ones who remain back in their armchairs, and haven't yet moved into the field. There's no great problem there, in the end, in the long term — we're bound to win through — because we know that the phenomenon is genuine, despite the fact that a few carefree people have made some simple circles, by way of experiment or deliberate hoax. But they are awful affairs, which don't deceive anyone. But when it comes to a real circle, then there is just *so much in it* that is immediately recognized and understood by scientists, but which the ordinary ignorant hoaxer wouldn't know . . .

After Meaden had finished, Ohtsuki rose and played a videotape made from a Japanese TV documentary about his work. The videotape showed Ohtsuki down in the Tokyo subway, and Ohtsuki in his lab, and the little plasma fireballs dancing around inside the microwave chamber, and occasionally dipping down on to the little aluminium-powder cornfield, emitting dramatic flashes and large captions in exclamatory Japanese.

Paul Fuller followed, with a solemn discussion of UFO cases and the likelihood that many could be explained by the plasma vortex hypothesis – either Ohtsuki's or Meaden's, though for diplomacy's sake the two were never distinguished. Finally there was a congenial free-for-all in which questions and speculations and stories meandered around the room. Jean-François wondered whether UFO abduction cases could be explained by some plasma-induced local increase in the relative concentration of nitrogen, causing nitrogen narcosis, the well-known scuba-diver's demon. Peter mentioned that there seemed to be a statistically significant correlation between crop circle locations and the locations of geologic faults, although this correlation disappeared when only active faults were considered. Greg the Canadian physicist related a report he had heard concerning enormous and inexplicable holes in the ground in Switzerland, tens of metres deep and tens of metres wide, with neat cylinders of excavated earth sitting quietly nearby. Meaden passed around a glossy black-and-white photo of a circle in ice, in Turkey in 1975. Ohtsuki mentioned a recent case from Japan in which two young boys had seen a bright tube descend from a cloud and emit a smoking orange ball, which had then fallen to the ground, swirling a rough circle in the grass. He mentioned some rice-paddy cases, too, where water had mysteriously disappeared, and revealed that he had already patented his plasma vortex – or plasma fireball, or whatever – and that his work was funded by several Japanese industries interested in two particular applications of the technology. The first would be a little plasma chamber in the exhaust system of diesel engines, to plasmify toxic nitrous oxide into harmless nitrogen and oxygen. The second would be some kind of plasmoid spectrometer which by its colour-sensitivity to chemical changes in the ambient air could serve as a handy pollution monitor in industrial and other processes. There were apparently other applications, unstated – perhaps something to do with his recent visit to London, during which he had conferred with scientists at British Petroleum; or perhaps something to do with nuclear fusion, questions about which he deflected with a shrug and an inscrutable smile. I had another Spielbergesque vision – of the 'Mr Fusion' device featured in the film *Back to the Future* . . . and Ohtsuki as the richest man in the world.

Are there any military applications of this technology? someone asked, and Ohtsuki mentioned human combustion, simulations of which, in his plasma chamber, were planned soon with lab rats. 'This will not be so comfortable for the weaker student,' he said with a grin at Kondo and Tanaichi.

Ohtsuki also noted the apparent connection in some cases between ball-lightning reports and mysterious deaths of the elderly. He speculated that atmospheric plasmoids might somehow generate, or otherwise be associated with, large magnetic fields which could even at a distance induce rogue electrical currents in blood and tissues, interfering with delicate nerve signals and triggering seizures or heart attacks. He also noted that UFO cases sometimes included mention of automobiles being dragged off the road or into the air, in Death Star tractor-beam fashion. This was in accord with his favourite atmospheric plasmoid models, which predicted – by arcane and debatable physics which are not worth going into here – substantial forces being exerted on nearby metal objects.

With some help from a supercomputer, the models also predicted, or could be coaxed to predict, elaborate shapes formed by the impact of plasmoid with cornfield, such as triplets and quintuplets and multiple-ringers. Ohtsuki believed that a cylindrical plasmoid – i.e. the descending bright tube which appeared so often in the UFO literature – was responsible for most of the complex formations, with a core cloud of ions swirling out the central circle, and screaming shells of electrons downing the rings and the satellites.

And what about the pictograms?

'I'm sorry,' he said, smiling, shaking his head, 'I have no idea.'

A few days later I phoned Meaden to find out if there were any new circles. He wasn't at home so I tried his cellular phone, and after a few rings his voice came on the line. He was standing, he said, within a formation just south of Swindon. It was 'gigantic', but 'of dubious authenticity' – a mess of broken stalks. National Geographic were also standing there in the gigantic formation, waiting to film him.

The next day I went to see the formation, which was beneath an Iron Age hillfort called Barbury Castle. The formation, which would eventually have about the same visual impact, culturally speaking, as the Alton Barnes double-pictogram had done the year before, looked remarkably like the work of an entity that had studied geometry. In the middle was a circle, surrounded by two broad, neat rings. Superimposed around these was a triangle, or more accurately a two-dimensional overhead representation of a pyramid – an ordinary triangle, plus three lines from the vertices to the centroid. At each vertex of the triangle had been swept a ring: one was a simple ring, another had six curved spokes, and the third turned into itself with a kind of stair-step spiral effect. One of the triangle sides had a kink where it bent outwards to avoid crossing one of the inner rings, but otherwise the creation looked geometrically flawless.

I also inspected some new formations along the road between Marlborough and the village of Broad Hinton. The fields there were perfect for circles-viewing – low and sloping up away from the road. Cars dotted the grassy shoulders, their occupants wielding binoculars and cameras. One formation seemed to be an exact replica of the 2 July formation at Alton Barnes. A farmer's wife, Debbie something, advised me that it had probably been caused by the military, firing Star Wars weaponry from helicopters. An old country codger reckoned it was of American origin. 'The Yanks always have something up their sleeves.' I drove further along, stopped by a clump of cars, and saw in a distant field a formation comprising two circles within a single pan-shaped outline. I had a sudden craving for fried eggs.

I asked Meaden later about the fried-egg formation. 'It was quite disturbing to see that,' he said. 'But there wasn't much damage' – to the swept stalks – 'so I have to accept it.'

Next I asked one of the young Meadenites, a bearded Bristolian named Peter Rendall. He frowned, shifted uneasily on the caravan seat, and said with a touch of irony, 'Well . . . Terence thinks it's genuine.'

In all there were four young Meadenites who regularly attended the secret site: Rendall, Roger Davis, Jacqui Griffiths, and Paul Fuller. Rendall worked for British Rail, drove a gruff 1984 Capri with a CB radio, and had become interested in the circles through a general attraction to Earth Mysteries and other paranormal subjects. He had read *Circular Evidence*, and had been unhappy with what he considered to be its lack of objectivity, and with the subsequent media hysteria surrounding its authors. He was led to Meaden's *Circles Effect* book by a local newspaper story and subsequent correspondence with Meaden himself. In the late summer of 1989, a friend saw a rough circle apparently swirled by a minor whirlwind in a field in east Bristol. Rendall interviewed the witness, investigated the circle with a fellow Earth Mysteries enthusiast, wrote up the report, and sent it in to Meaden, who published it in *J. Met.* Roger Davis, who also drove a muscle car with a CB, was the Earth Mysteries chum. Jacqui Griffiths was the whirlwind witness. The three of them began to correspond regularly with Meaden, and had put in some time at the High Hill cropwatch of 1990. They were now, along with Paul Fuller, a kind of Revolutionary Guard for Meaden, pulling all-nighters in the caravan, running around measuring and inspecting circles, and handling the minor press when Meaden was busier with bigger things. I guessed that they were all in their mid twenties, but I was some years off. Rendall and Davis were thirty-eight, and Fuller was thirty. Crop circles keep you young at heart.

'If,' said Peter Rendall, 'a circle were swirled in front of all of us, in front of all the crop circles researchers, this is what would happen: CERES would go out and measure it. Delgado and Andrews would bow down and worship it. And CCCS would call a committee meeting.'

Nights at the secret site were like that – full of jibes and stories and general breeze-shooting ... about 'Fandango and Condrews', and Goddess-worshipping Michael Green, and Richard Andrews, and George Wingfield, and beleaguered Busty Taylor, and all the foolish names and foolish faces on the other side. Fandango and Condrews by now had had their second book published, *The Latest Evidence*, and it, too, was climbing the bestseller lists. CCCS's book was already out in paperback, and selling well at such places as Tim Carson's caravan at Alton Barnes, where neither Terence Meaden's nor Fuller and Randles's books were on offer. To add insult to injury, Fuller and Randles's German publisher, Goldmann Verlag, had without consulting them published their latest book, *Crop Circles: A Mystery Solved* with a foreword by Erich von Daniken, the *Chariots of the Gods* guru who believed that extraterrestrials had visited the planet thousands of years ago. Obviously Goldmann wanted to catch the eyes of bookstore-browsers with a famous old name, but to Randles and Fuller it was an outrageous distortion of their message.

The commercial advantage enjoyed by the Delgadonians and their ilk reinforced among the young Meadenites the sense that they were the underdogs, the oppressed, doomed to play the straight men for the other side's disingenuous and demagogic mocking. In *The Latest Evidence*, for example, Andrews had described his Oxford Conference confrontation with Meaden as follows:

[The appearance of a fourth ring around the big quintuplet at Bishops Cannings in early 1990] was a point I put to meteorologist Dr Terence Meaden at a conference on the circles held in Oxford in July. He became highly embarrassed and blatantly personal when words failed him in front of a packed assembly of scientists and media representatives from many countries. They had come to listen to Dr Meaden's claim that he had solved the mystery, concluding that stationary whirlwinds were responsible, as they produced electrically charged vortices, called the plasma vortex, an effect due to certain weather conditions close to hills. I appeared to agitate him further by asking how he accounted for the new pictogram formation[s] in terms of the law of angular momentum, a law of physics which must be complied with for his plasma vortex theory to be credible. He refused to reply. Finally, when I asked why he had not informed the conference of other important questions associated with re-visits to existing formations, it became clear that this British weatherman had been, as it were, undressed on stage. The whirlwind explanation was now seriously ill.

What was worse, according to the young Meadenites, was that they were often unable to return fire. Most tabloid and local paper journalists seemed to *want* a mystery to surround the circles. Moreover, there were Dutton, Gregory & Williams, Delgado's fire-breathing solicitors, to worry about. 'I'm still under threat of a libel suit,' Paul Fuller would often remind me, the idea being that until the statute of limitations on his alleged 1988 libel expired, four or five or six years hence, he was obliged to keep more or less mum in public about Fandango and Condrews. This despite the sensational dirt he had on them, occasional hints of which would drop, pseudo-anonymously, here and there, in the *Cropwatcher*, a Fuller-edited monthly about the circles scene, copies of which also lay scattered about the secret-site caravan. Its circulation was 60, compared to 1,000 or so for John Michell's (newly renamed) *Cerealogist*.

The ultimate insult, as far as the young Meadenites were concerned, was the business of the secret site. I had noted with surprise the fact that the CERES caravan was tucked away on the wrong side of the hill, on a gentle slope behind the western end of the Wansdyke, above a rumpled vista which was much less observable than the neat arena of barley beneath Macnish's Kon-Tiki. In fact, I was told, the relevant farmer had originally agreed to give Meaden the plum site on the steep side of the hill – but had suddenly changed his mind, claiming to be worried about too much publicity and too many circles tourists trampling his land, and had pushed the Meadenites back to their inconspicuous, and largely ineffectual, secret site. Shortly thereafter the Kon-Tiki had appeared in the preferred location, beneath a copse at the summit of the hill, and a seventy-foot stalk bearing a wide-angled camera had sprouted in one of the barley fields below, and one of the Kon-Tiki boys had been heard to say, while in his cups one night at the Crown Inn at Bishops Cannings, that the displacement of the hapless Meadenites had cost only a hundred quid.

Ironically, Meaden might later have been thankful for the secrecy of the secret site. If it had been more visible, the throng of visitors might have been unbearable. As it was, it was almost inevitable that when he arrived in the evening with fresh batteries, and sat in the caravan to chat with the young Meadenites, someone with an interest in circles would arrive . . .

'Is that Dr Meaden?'

. . . and strike up a conversation which would generally result in the newcomer's revelation that he (or, much more rarely, she) believed that flying saucers were responsible. There would then be a tense, silent moment, after which Meaden might launch into a refutation of his visitor's ideas, but more likely would only sigh and gaze out of the plastic window of the caravan at the hopelessly glorious midsummer sunset, or down at his watch, murmuring, 'Yes . . . It's getting late . . .' And then with a gleam of irony in his tired eyes he might add, 'Ahhhh . . . can you stay and watch the radar tonight?'

The Duty Site Operations Officer's Log records the result of one such encounter.

Thursday

2205: Yves Choisson and Robert Fischer arrived to see the site. We done the survey all night long.

Friday

0355: Radar Stops. Low voltage!

0740: Battery changed. Radar works! (Tune only 4 1/2!) Brought to 5. OK!

0800: (+/− 2 min): A small dot seen on screen, 171deg, distance 1.3 nm, during more than 10 minutes. Disappeared.

0811: 1 spot 313deg D = 1.6 nm
1 spot 302deg D = 1.3 nm during 3 or 4 seconds. Maybe a 3rd one very briefly (less than 1 second)

0815: the spot at 171deg appears again. seem to be a ground reflexion.

0822: 2 spots very close each other. 315.5deg D = 1.682 nm.

0823: Farmers arrived.

0831: Hercules flight over the site. Just above the clouds. Not seen on radar screen.

0838: Another Hercules. D = 1.3 nm. Seen on screen.

0839: A remaining spot appears at 324.5deg D = 1.3nm. Never seen before. Not moving. (No aircraft.)

0842: A new spot 216deg D = 1.438 nm. Very shortly.

0844: The spot at 324.5deg disappears.

0855: Aircraft flight over – not seen on screen.

0857: Spot at 273.5deg D = 1.8 nm. Very shortly.

0915: Aircraft over. Not seen on screen.

0917: Jet over not seen on screen.

0920: We leave – radar off.

Best of luck and many thanks
See you later
(signed)
Yves
Robert

In the autumn of 1989, when *Circular Evidence* still rode the bestseller charts, and the mysterious *Daytime Live* affair had set people talking all over England, a small group of people gathered at a house near Beckhampton – where the *Daytime Live* incident had occurred – to discuss the circles, their significance for the planet (the Iron Curtain was then crumbling), and the possibility of setting up a group to study them. Among those present were Alan Rayner, a systems analyst; Dennis Wheatley, a local dowser and writer; and a parson and his wife, the Weavers. The Weavers were put off by talk of dowsing, which they considered too occultish, and quickly withdrew from the group, but Wheatley and Rayner kept on, and eventually formed the nucleus of what would come to be known as the Beckhampton Group. By the summer of 1991 the group had a few dozen members. In terms of numbers, it was almost insignificant by comparison with CCCS, which by then had a membership in the several hundreds. But CCCS's members were spread thinly, often far from circles-prone counties, and indeed seemed only to exist as a kind of captive audience for CCCS books, magazines, and lectures. And though CCCS was officially a scientific research organization, with no 'corporate view' as to the cause of the circles, in fact the chairman of CCCS, Michael Green, believed that he knew exactly what spiritual entities were causing the circles, and that surveillance was virtually pointless. Though the perseverent cropwatcher might catch an occasional glimpse of multicoloured sparks, or jumping black flashes, or might hear a tantalizing burst of pan-pipes, the Circlemakers themselves would never be seen. Some CCCS members, being unaware of this, spent as many summer nights as possible on the hills south of Avebury, but most of these enthusiasts lived in the area, and also belonged to the Beckhampton Group, to which, generally speaking, they owed their first loyalty. A small core of perhaps a dozen regulars, by keeping in touch with each other, and with local farmers, and with local pub-keepers, and with Delgado and Andrews and CCCS – and even, through acceptable intermediaries, with Meaden – managed now to be first on the scene whenever a new formation appeared.

The Beckhampton Group met every Friday night at an old pub near Silbury Hill called the Waggon and Horses. It was a congenial place, with good food, friendly managers, and an authentically horsy décor which included, at one habitual table near the door, a group of eerily child-like jockeys who worked at the nearby race-training stables. And on weekends in the circles season, it became a roaring, drunken, sweating, backslapping, international crop circles convention.

I went over one Friday in the middle of July, forewarned by Peter Rendall and Paul Fuller that I would meet only lunatics. But by now I had wangled an assignment to write a story on the circles for a magazine, and I wanted some colour, some quotes. I arrived early, when the place was still uncrowded, and struck up a conversation with two older fellows, one of whom turned out to be Dennis Wheatley. He told me about dowsing, about how it was all to do with a fifth force, which was somehow related to electrical and magnetic forces, but had other units, such as Lithons and Petrons, in which were denominated the energies that flowed between megalithic stones. He suggested books to read, and insisted that nine out of ten people could dowse – those unable to do so having 'a screw loose somewhere'.

Later I was wolfing down a quick dinner when George Wingfield entered and walked up to the bar, dressed in a business suit and a loosened tie, having just arrived in a smart orange BMW from his job at IBM in Bristol. Someone told him I was writing a magazine story, and he came over to my table. He introduced himself and sat down. I dutifully opened my notebook. I asked him what he thought of Meaden's theory.

'Meaden's theory is crap.'

I thought that was a good start, but then a stocky blond American walked up to Wingfield and interrupted him with some urgent diagrams of crop formations that resembled insects. 'We call these curly-grams, or insectograms,' Wingfield explained to me, with what I imagined was a trace of embarrassment. Then a circles-tourist couple sat down at the table. They were from Los Angeles. Mr was a mellow, indulgent English expatriate, and Mrs was an energetic, wide-eyed Californian. It had been her idea to visit Wiltshire. 'I'm on a personal mission!' she told me, only half-jokingly. A couple of German backpackers started to pull up chairs around the table, and then the doughty Frenchman, Yves Choisson, came over ... The little table suddenly seemed to have become the nucleus of a fast-growing organism.

I suggested that we move elsewhere, and Wingfield led us into one of the side rooms, to a long table by a big bay window.

Wingfield sat at one end, and held court. Most of the discussion revolved around the wildly geometric formation beneath Barbury Castle.

'So I went to see this thing on Wednesday,' said Wingfield to the assembly which was rapidly filling the small smoky room. 'And I ran into Terence Meaden there, and I said, "Terence, you don't really believe this was made by an atmospheric vortex, because it's just not possible, is it?" And he looked very worried, and he said, "I don't like it, I don't like it." I said, "Why don't you like it, Terence?" He said, "Well there's some broken stems, there's some broken plants, they're not all truly bent." I said, "Well, all the ones I can see are bent." And he said, "Well, there's damage. There's a lot of damage." So he showed me two or three plants which were actually snapped and broken, and I said, "Well, yeah, we've seen this before, this is not unusual." And he really couldn't show me anything else. And then the people from the *National Geographic* magazine arrived, and they had a lot of floodlights, and wanted to put Terence and me together. And Terence fell silent, so I had to do most of the talking. I was a bit unkind to him. And he kept saying, "I don't like it, I don't like it." And I said, "Terence, this is *exactly* the same as any other formation I've seen. It's not the same, but the characteristics are the same, you look at the crop, you look at the way the stems are bent, sometimes exploded, almost as if they've been microwaved. It's all the same ... Why don't you like this? Is it because it completely ... *blows your theory out of the water?*" [Guffaws from the table.] Well, he didn't like me saying this, so the next day he issued a press release, saying this is a fake, and he could see it was made by rollers and all this sort of thing. Well, it's all a lot of bullshit, frankly ... Busty Taylor's been there today. He's dowsed it, and its very strongly dowsable ... It's not a fake. It can't be a fake ... This one is for real. It is the most elaborate and the most extraordinary one we've seen. And I daresay there'll be more.'

'On the other hand,' ventured a timid-looking man at the table, 'Meaden has said that a vortex could do some complex shapes.'

Wingfield laughed derisively. 'Well in that case someone's driving the vortex –'

'Yeah, that's right, that's it, that's it,' said the man, nodding his head submissively, regretting his foolish counterpoint.

'– I mean, what sort of thing is this vortex?' Wingfield continued, to the table in general. 'Maybe it's a UFO.'

The stocky blond American spoke up. 'What Meaden is doing is typical of any scientist when his theory runs into trouble. Any time he runs across any objections, or any exceptions, or anything that will disprove the theory, then immediately it's called a hoax.'

Wingfield reported that three people had seen strange lights in the sky on the night before the Barbury Castle formation. The people had been standing in a lay-by along the A4, about a mile west of Beckhampton, and the lights had passed overhead without sound, without accompanying shapes, with only pulsating colours . . . green, red, white, in that order . . . It went on for an hour. Six objects in all were seen. And then there was a dark object . . . The observers 'were quite badly scared', said Wingfield. 'It was quite close to them . . . They were quite shaken by it . . . And this guy said to me, "You know, I've been on plenty of watches, and I've never seen anything like this. This was something out of *Close Encounters of the Third Kind* . . ." You're talking UFOs. But UFOs are not necessarily little metal spaceships with little green men inside; they're a lot stranger than that.'

Later I asked Wingfield about Ohtsuki and his laboratory crop circles.

'Well . . . Ohtsuki's a smart guy. But what has he done? He's created this plasma, and then he's dropped it on to aluminium powder. And he's made these little *craters* in aluminium powder. Those aren't crop circles. If they are, then I can make crop circles, too. I can go and throw a stone in a pond. There! I've made crop circles!'

I spoke with the stocky American, whose name was Jon Erik Beckjord. He lived in Malibu, and worked as a freelance cameraman, and was curator of something called the Crypto-Phenomena Museum. He asked if I'd seen the recent news item regarding the discovery that a small cluster of hills on the planet Mars bore a striking resemblance to the face of Senator Edward Kennedy. As a matter of fact, I had. He informed me that, as curator of the Crypto-Phenomena Museum, he had been helping to bring this item to the attention of the media. He was good at seeing patterns where others couldn't. 'I want to show all of you something strange in this picture,' he said, waving an aerial photograph of a pictogram. 'This is something that is not exactly in the crop circle, but it's nearby, and some of you may see this, and some of you may not. But I find these in most images of crop circles. Right here, this white thing. It's the face of a man. A large face, probably fifty feet across ... And some of these trees look like human heads as well, but this one is very prominent – here, he's got a sour expression and he's got low brows. Right here ... And I don't think it's a coincidence.'

The rest of the evening I remember – and my tape recorder remembers – as a kind of smoky aural haze, involving almost every Anglophonic accent imaginable, although most of the time Wingfield's asserted itself theatrically above the rest.

'... Ninety per cent of people don't look outside the window, because their attention is solely focused on the television in the corner, and they're not aware of anything which goes on outside the house. Ninety-*nine* per cent of people ...'

'Some vicar, driving home, saw a very bright light in the field ...'

'Just past Silbury, on the right-hand side ...'

'Anyone want to join CCCS?'

'Busty was in the formation yesterday. Busty says that's for real. And I'll tell you that's interesting because Busty is very sceptical ...'

'The one shaped like a ring, with two circles inside it?'

'I'm not suggesting a UFO sat down and made that. But it probably has symbolic significance.'

'It would take a few days to decipher.'

'If we're dealing with something intelligent, it can make any pattern ... It's not magic. I mean, we could make that. If we determined to make that pattern, we could make that pattern, with our laser beams or whatever method.'

'Technology from a thousand years ahead of us will look like magic ...'

'We don't know what form of energy is involved ... All I'm saying is that it's intelligently produced.'

'I'm thinking of the scientific aspect of a beam coming down from a UFO, and inscribing this pattern ...'

'I'm not saying it's necessarily an energy beam coming down from a UFO –'

'I'm saying it!'

'It definitely traces out a blueprint that is put there in advance . . . There's something moving around at ground level. Whether it's an energy field or what, I can't say.'

'I had this vision on the M5 . . .'

'The national papers are thick as numbskulls, and can't cope with this sort of thing . . .'

'You won't get in there, the farmer will blast you with a 12-bore . . .'

'. . . about four circles, ringed circles, and a line, and a hand coming out at the end . . . It looks like no other formation . . . And these little wiggly lines . . . I can't tell whether they're coming in or going out. It looks like a whole spaceship full of . . . little wee beasties sort of got out and made their way into the corn. Two or three hundred tiny little tracks . . .'

'George, can I just . . . I heard a rumour, the last time I came down here, that you'd been to see the Hopi Indians –'

'I have been to see the Hopi Indians.'

'– and that you'd shown them pictures, and that they'd reacted quite strongly.'

'Uhm . . . They did appear to recognize certain symbols, and they said, "Yes, I know this one." But . . . you know I wasn't really there for long enough to reach really any conclusive results.'

'I think this rumour must have got blown up a lot because they said that the chief had broken down in tears, and that he'd said –'

'That wasn't when I was there. That was Alick Bartholomew's story. He wept a tear when he saw the Alton Barnes pictogram, and he said, um, "I know this sign."'

'And it means "Beings of Light" or something, right?'

'Well, I don't know . . . the story's getting better.' [Laughter.]

'. . . that lot rather than the other lot . . .'

'. . . the mother of all pictograms . . .'

'. . . but I mean, the symbols we recognize are only a tiny fraction of the whole.'

'. . . it's an infra-red rainbow . . .'

'. . . it looks Masonic . . .'

'Gurdjieff had a symbol like that . . .'

'Tuesday would probably be best, Tuesday, Wednesday. I'll call you Monday. I've got to write some material, so I have to get away from this place and I have to take the phone off the hook, and I have to actually write, so that's what I'm doing over the weekend . . . I can't keep up.'

'So you come here every summer?'

'No. Usually I go to Loch Ness.'

'Jürgen!'

'George! I'm so astonished that you're still here. I'm quite glad to see you, but –'

'I'm trying to go but I can't get out!'

The next day, a fine hot sunny day at the secret site, Paul Fuller told me that a woman who had recently seen an odd luminosity would be coming by to give him an interview for the *Cropwatcher*. In a little while she drove up, and emerged from her silver sedan on the pasture by the path, wielding, I remember with an odd clarity, a large crop circle key-ring. She was short, plump, matronly, with electrically frizzy white hair, a stage-strength voice with a faint Liverpool accent, and a pleasant, polite volubility. We sat in the caravan and she gave us both an interview. Her name was Rita Goold.

She told us she had been cropwatching on Thursday night the previous week – as she had been doing for much of the past month – with two young locals, Tom and Roy, and an itinerant taxi-driver from Nottingham, Nick. They had been sitting on patio chairs outside the caravan at East Field in Alton Barnes, with the intention of watching the area until dawn. At three o'clock Roy declared his exhaustion and entered the caravan to lie down. A few minutes later the wind dropped to nothing. There was a brief burst of birdsong, a false dawn chorus, and then East Field was eerily silent.

'And all of a sudden we looked, and it just came out, like a tube out of the sky – we went, "God Almighty!" I mean, I leapt up in the air and I said, "We got it!" – and it was . . . it was a cloud . . . and out of this cloud came this white tube. It was not a beam of light – now, everybody's saying, "You saw this beam of light." That's different, a beam of light is different – this was a white tube, of cloudy – Let me show you . . .' She pointed to a passing cumulus. 'Right. You see that white cloudy substance – cotton wool? Right? It was full of that . . . It was a solid gas. And it came down and it grew. And we were going, "God Almighty!"'

'But it was illuminated somehow?' I asked.

'It was luminous. It was like the moon. It didn't shine the valley up or anything like that. It was just against the black . . . It was absolutely luminous. And it was so big, that . . . I mean my heart raced, I thought, "My God, what is this?!"'

The tube descended over two hills to the north-east, Tan Hill and Golden Ball Hill – the latter so called, I learned later, because of a peculiar variety of yellow flowers which had once covered its summertime slopes.

'. . . And this tube came down. It missed the field. You see, it hit the hill. It came straight down. And I mean if it had come into the field, we would have seen [a pictogram] form. And just before it got to the top of the hill, as it came down, it shot out two arms, and this covered the two tops of the hills – must have been eight hundred feet across – and, and, in each arm, all this stuff was pouring in, finding rivulets, and clouding, and making formations – and I thought "God!" – and as it was doing it, the tube was emptying. We could see it pouring out the bottom. It funnelled, and it just poured into it, and did it. And then the tube collapsed and it just vanished into the hill.'

The entire event had taken about eight seconds. She would have tried to take a picture with her camera, she said, but Nick had spilled tea on it and she had put it away in her car. She and the others had hiked up to the hills the next morning, and had found nothing. But she was sure that what she had seen was the same mechanism which produced the complex crop formations. 'I could see that the tube would make the central ring. And it hits in the middle and disperses out, so if that had been in the field, that would have been . . . whatever we want to call these formations – I don't like the word "pictogram", but let's say that's what it would have been, because it did that, and it seemed to shoot out as if it was finding . . . it was finding . . . little rivulets, and things like that, but it was in the air, it formed in the air before it sank to the ground, it didn't form when it hit the ground. If it hadn't done we wouldn't have seen it.'

Rita was sure she had seen a natural phenomenon, a plasma

vortex. 'As Terence Meaden was saying to us, these are hitting all the time, we were lucky to see it, it just did not hit – it hit the hill . . . If it was intelligent, there would have been no point in hitting the hill where no one could see anything afterwards.'

Nevertheless, it was majestic. 'I'll tell you what it was. This may sound very strange . . . It affected Tom a little bit, because . . . Tom described it as "biblical". And I've seen the same effect in a film. It was a Spielberg film, *Raiders of the Lost Ark* – he had it absolutely just the same: this thing comes down [on the Nazi-guarded Ark] and goes *wham*! The might of it! It *was* biblical . . . It was awesome. But of course it was plasma. It was spinning.'

Spinning cherubim! Plasma seraphim! My own Spielbergesque vision, I realized, was a common one.

Rita explained, somewhat apologetically, that she had once belonged to the other side – the Andrews and Delgado side, the CCCS side. She had long investigated UFOs, Earth Mysteries, ghosts, poltergeists, and so on, and had initially suspected that the circles might be the work of aliens. But increasingly she had been disenchanted with the crop circle paranormalists. 'I'd been with such a lot of people, and had seen such a lot of rubbish going on. And people making religions out of it. And the hype getting to such extraordinary levels. And superstitions – And all in a decade! I've never seen legends grow up so quickly. It takes hundreds of years for legends, or myths, to evolve. And seeing the calibre of the stuff that was going on, I thought, "Just a minute. This is just not on. I'm going to just take three steps back, because I'm not going to go down in the whirlpool of nonsense that's going on."' She began to correspond with Meaden. He explained his theory to her. She attended his Oxford Conference, and was impressed. She maintained her membership in the Beckhampton Group and CCCS, but then the luminous tube came out of the cloud . . . 'I was dancing around, shouting, "We've got it! Terence Meaden was right!"'

I spoke later to Tom, who, while agnostic on the Meadenite–Delgadonian dispute, and unsure that the phenomenon he had witnessed was responsible for making pictograms, nevertheless thought it unlikely to have been intelligently controlled. Roy told me that, having been inside the caravan at the time, he had experienced nothing other than the reflected excitement of his friends. Nick, according to Rita, had resisted the plasma vortex explanation, asserting that he was 'never going to give in to Terence Meaden', and suggesting that a 'mother ship' hidden in the clouds may have been the origin of the luminous tube. Nick then had apparently phoned George Wingfield, and had informed him of Rita's interpretation of the event. 'And so,' said Rita, 'George has phoned me every day – and even threatened me . . . I've had a lot of flak this week.'

'From the CCCS people?' I asked.

'Anonymous. Threatening. I've been threatened that if I don't take it back, I'll be *done over* in a crop circle in the middle of the night. That's how bad it's got . . . And there was a *Leicester Mercury* reporter with me last Monday morning, sitting in my house, and we were chatting . . . and he was sitting right next to my phone. And it rang, and I went, "Hello?" and this *voice* boomed out, "How *dare* you say it's a plasma vortex . . .!" This man was bellowing down the phone. And my friend couldn't believe it! You'd think there was millions of pounds involved! Really, megabucks!'

Rita told me other things as well. She told me about the former goalkeeper and TV sports announcer, David Icke, whom she had seen in the Alton Barnes formation the previous Monday, at dusk, kneeling in prayer. 'I'm waiting for a message,' he had reportedly said to her. 'Something's going to happen.'

She alleged that George Wingfield had gone west, to America, to meet the Hopi Indians and to lecture on crop circles and the coming New Age and had ended up falling off Shirley Maclaine's yacht into the sobering Pacific – and that some other time, while travelling at 90 m.p.h. along some lonely Wessex road and gazing anxiously out over the fields, his eyes lured by the crop circle Sirens, he had smashed his car head-on into another and escaped serious injury only by a miracle.

She told me about the youngsters in Avebury who had swirled a smiling-face figure near the double-pictogram at Alton Barnes the year before, running and jumping, drunk and on acid, and in the process doing a remarkably competent job, with complex layering and lightly-laid stalks. She told me some very interesting ghost and poltergeist and demonic-infestation stories. She told me about the night when she and some others had heard a noise, a strange trilling noise, which they had taped, and which had apparently accompanied the making of a ringed crop circle they had found the next morning . . .

By the summer of 1991, there were more circles tourists in Wiltshire than ever before, and some were even coming over in organized groups, with buses and guides, and scheduled talks and tours with experts. Two such experts were Richard Andrews and Busty Taylor, whom I followed one day as they introduced a largely North American crowd to the wonders of Barbury Castle.

Richard and Busty bussed them in in a large chartered coach, and a minivan, and a few straggling cars, unloading them and herding them in along the narrow tramlines, splitting them off into two halves – Richard taking one, Busty the other – and then demonstrating effortlessly, their rods swinging out, in, out, in, as they walked over trampled and dying stalks, how strong the energies remained. It was a fine day. Sheep noises . . . *baaaaaaahhh . . . rrrrrgggggghhh* . . . sounded from the hillside above us. There was the faint malt smell of crushed wheat, and, as before, the whirlpool sensation of the swirled stalks – moderated in this case by the sharp angular geometry of the thing, a segment of which Busty was busy describing as a Sistine Chapel tour-guide might point out a famous frieze or fresco.

'. . . It isn't actually a ring, in a sense, because it doesn't form a ring, though it looks like it. It isn't joined up. It's very cleverly designed because it finishes up here. And how that's done is unbelievable – You can see the size of it . . . It's nearly a hundred feet across . . . So you can see how large the formation is. It's three hundred feet from that edge, to the edge of the circle there, and the same the other way. So you see it's quite large. And if we move on up, before the next people come on up, we'll get into the far ring . . .'

Dowsing lessons were also given, and brief anecdotes were related about crackles or flashes or knocks or noises. A woman in pink placed her hands over the centre of the formation, feeling the radiant energies. A man in a turtleneck and a floppy white hat did the same. Then a group gathered around the spot, and held hands, and closed their eyes and meditated.

There was a break for lunch at Avebury, and Busty unexpectedly had to leave for the airfield to go up and inspect a new circle that had been found near East Kennett. I caught up with the group at Alton Barnes, in a field opposite East Field, where a week before a new pictogram with jutting 'fingers' had appeared.

The group sat comfortably on the swept wheat in the afternoon sun. Richard Andrews was talking in a quiet, earnest, hypnotically confident voice. The vicar's voice.

'I'd just say to you today: look at what you have here. You don't have to try and understand it. But I'd say enjoy it for what it is. You can see we're all happy; there's no one here that's making it a hard time . . . We have had people who've come out and have made it a hard time, and found out how difficult it was to come all the way out here, and how hot it is, and there's no cooling breeze and all the rest of it. But this is the country and this is where, really, you can have the freedom . . .

'What I would say to you – it would be nice for you to go down to the other end, and have a look. Have a good look at the fingers, and . . . any one of you who wants to feel any benefit of different energies, you will feel them down there . . .

'If you're walking with [dowsing rods along] the [energy] line, you'll notice something else. As I walk forward, you see how [the rods are] pointing in and swinging out? Now on all energy lines, when you walk with the line, you get them going in. When you walk against it, watch what happens now. They are going out, and not going in. You get a regular pulse, like the pulse of a heart. That is what you get on all these lines. Now this configuration will be dowsable in five, ten years' time. The energy will be here exactly like this. This is what we now call a fixed pattern . . .

'We're also, you notice, close to trees. And in amongst those trees you'll see a line of trees that are dying. And over the last fifteen years, billions of trees have died – it is not pollution, as we call it. A lot of people think that acid conditions of the air – yes that does strip off a lot of them . . . but in amongst all woodland now, you will see lines of dead trees. Those are trees that have died on the lines that these [crop circles] form on. So a lot of things have found themselves unable to sustain their life on the lines . . . And we know that lightning strikes on these lines . . . Energy does strike from or to an exact point. It is not random . . . And they all change every day. All of these node points change ... So it's something that's happening. This is a living world that we live on. This is not dead matter ...

'So look around today, enjoy this, and see what's happening ... I've called it The Indicator ... We just have to find out what it is indicating ...'

The crop circles tour that day was part of a weekend package, based in Glastonbury. Other events included songs, slide shows by Busty Taylor and George Wingfield, healing workshops, a lecture concerning the circles and the Grid by George de Trafford, and an evening dance. It was all held in the 'Glastonbury Experience', an enclosed little quadrangle off the town's High Street. It was a nice quiet world of its own, with gift shops, a café, and little rooms tucked away here and there for hire. They must have overbooked that weekend, because the little room slated for Wingfield's and Taylor's slide shows was absolutely packed, a sweltering mass of circles tourists – plus one young journalist. They warmed us up, as if we needed it, with a few tambourine-and-cymbals groups who encouraged us all to sing along. I fled after a half-hour or so, on the point of hypoxia, but one refrain comes back to me even now from that hot little room in the Glastonbury Experience:

> Round and a-round it goes, yeah
> Round and a-round it goes
> Round and a-round it goes, yeah
> Round and a-round it goes
> (Repeat)

Jon Erik Beckjord also attended the Glastonbury Experience. I asked him about it later, expecting him to praise it. He didn't. 'Look,' he said, 'I'm not into this ultra gentle, ultra ... metaphysical approach. This idea of – you know, just being passive, sitting back on your ass, letting things happen in your mind. I don't go along with that bullshit. When I was in Glastonbury, this guy came up and started telling me about how he'd been in contact with the twelve elders of the outer rings of the planet. I mean, I'm tired of listening to all this crap.'

The problem, according to Beckjord, was that the English were averse to serious research. They were, in fact, 'flat-out lazy'. They would never get anywhere. Beckjord, by contrast, was not lazy. Nor was he averse to serious research. In fact, he had already established why the circles were appearing, and he was about to take appropriate action.

But first things first. Beckjord had known from the beginning, instinctively, that the circles were messages from a non-human intelligence – or 'NHI' as he put it. The messages were in some kind of code, but Beckjord had quickly broken it. After poking around in archaeology books, searching for ancient pictorial languages – 'earth languages' – that might bear some resemblance to the circles formations, Beckjord had discovered a 4,000-year-old North American Indian petroglyph language called 'Tifinag'.

To hear Beckjord tell it, Tifinag was absolutely tailor-made for deciphering pictograms – a veritable Rosetta Stone. It involved circles, loops, rings, curves, dashes . . . The neolithic redskins who'd invented Tifinag had had a fairly limited vocabulary, by modern standards, but by extrapolating slightly (about five words for every one actually translated), Beckjord had been able to crack a few of the pictograms from recent years: 'THIS IS THE PLACE OF THE DEVIL,' said one. And another explained: 'THE TRIAL BY THE LAW SAY THE SECRET WRITINGS.' Still another warned: 'THE DRAGON FROM PEGASUS, FROM THE OUTSIDE, COMES TO GIVE A TRIAL TO THE EARTH-GLOBE.'

It sounded bad, very bad. But Beckjord believed that the NHIs were merely giving us a friendly warning – a conversation-starter, really. What we needed to do now, he believed, was to let the NHIs know that we understood them. 'Roger that, Alpha Centauri' – or the equivalent.

But since Tifinag was somewhat primitive for conversations between planetary cultures, and since the NHIs presumably were bright enough to cope with modern earth languages (perhaps Tifinag had been the lingua franca the last time the NHIs had visited earth), we should, said Beckjord, answer back in the most earth-wide modern language there is: English. And in English, we should explain, in no uncertain terms, that we were listening – or watching, or whatever.

Everybody should be doing it, Beckjord told me. Mowing it into every lawn, painting it on to every housetop – 'TALK TO US!'

*

Sometime towards the end of July 1991, a Wiltshire farmer named John Hussey received a telephone call from someone he later described as 'an American who said he was the curator of a museum in Los Angeles'.

Beckjord had wanted to know if he could cut the message 'TALK TO US!' into one of Hussey's barley fields. The deal was, Beckjord would use a heavy-duty weedcutter to clear out some letters, and then he would take the cut barley and stack it where Hussey could later process it with the rest of the harvest. The barley was ripe anyway, and would be combined in a few weeks, so Beckjord's little project wouldn't cost Hussey anything.

Naturally, the farmer was dubious. But Beckjord lectured him about broadmindedness and galactic responsibility and so on and so forth, and Hussey . . . well, Hussey was no goggle-eyed mystic, but he'd seen a few strange things in his day, lights that hovered and zoomed over his land, and already that summer he'd had a good-sized triplet pictogram turn up in one of his wheatfields, right under the white horse at Hackpen Hill. He had been one of the first ones in, naturally, and had immediately felt peculiar. Oh hell, he told Beckjord, go ahead.

July 24 dawned grey, cold, and drizzly. Beckjord and four others drove out along one of the rutted mud roads that criss-crossed Hussey's farm. They pulled up at the barley field, and got out. Beckjord thought he was going to catch pneumonia. Perhaps another day would be better. But then someone yanked the starter lanyard, and with a ferocious little snarl the portable barleycutter came to life.

It was hard work. But Beckjord had chosen good men. There was the little Frenchman Yves Choisson, who was absolutely devoted to the cause, a true believer, because he was a *convert* – an ex-member of VECA, a French group of paranormal sceptics. God knew what job Choisson held down in France, but in any case, he had certainly spent most of his July in Wiltshire.

Beside Choisson toiled another Frenchman, Thierry Pinvidic, and an Alsatian, Giles Munsch. And finally there was Arthur Mills, the lone Englishman of the team, and the rising young star of the Beckhampton Group. Arthur's strange quest had begun on the day, six or seven years before, when on a walk in the Wiltshire woods he had seen two white globes jump up in front of him, like startled grouse, and whizz silently off through the trees.

TALK TO US! There it was on the graph paper, the letters starting to run a little in the rain. Yves had mapped it out the night before, seated at the cramped desk of his room at a nearby bed-and-breakfast, or perhaps in Meaden's caravan, meticulously drawing, shaping, diagramming the cuts that they would make.

They began at a tramline, using it as a base. Yves and Thierry held up stakes with a string strung between, as a guide for the cutter. First the T. Easy enough: a straight cut in, like mowing a lawn, and then rearrange the stakes, and move back and forth with the stalk-slicer, and then cut to the left, and back and forth, and then rearrange the stakes, and then cut back right. In fact, it was precise work; the least slip, the slightest shiver, and a straight line would become a snake. And the barley was tough; one could hear the cutter gnawing through every stalk. At this rate, it would take them three days . . .

All right, listen up, announced Beckjord. There's no point in being super-neat. Let's just make it legible. Yves, his carefully graphed plan becoming soggy and tattered in the rain, was in no position to protest, despite the possibly dire consequences of sloppy interstellar handwriting. He was soaked to the skin. So was everybody. And there was mud everywhere. And it was cold – that English cold, that works its way into the bone . . . And the sky was just a thick grey pall coming in low over the hills, drizzling down on them . . .

In all, the inscription took four hours to complete. It was a little wiggly, but it was legible, and the '!' at the end was unmistakable. Each letter was about twenty-five feet from top to bottom, and the entire exhortation was 250 feet long.

Beckjord didn't catch pneumonia. The hard work had kept him warm. The others had worked hard too, Arthur Mills perhaps hardest of all – Arthur Mills, a veritable Paul Bunyan in barley, single-handedly giving the lie to the myth of the lazy Englishman. Beckjord was proud of him.

Later, when the weather had cleared, they hired a helicopter and went up to view their handiwork. They took a video camera and a Polaroid. They circled the field, videotaping, snapping shots with the Polaroid. Beckjord would want pictures for the press releases he would issue later. At one point, though, Beckjord accidentally dropped one of the polaroid photos out of the helicopter window ... And as it drifted down, he leaned out to see where it would land ... and his sunglasses slipped off his nose ... a prescription pair, a hundred California dollars ... spinning sightlessly down into the muck and the barley.

When the helicopter set down again at the airport Beckjord and the others got into their cars and drove back to John Hussey's farm. They trundled out through the rutted muck to the barley field, wielding their dowsing rods, asking the rods for ... the polaroid ... and the sunglasses ... But something was wrong. The energies were uncooperative. They couldn't find anything. The dowsing rods were dithering all over the place. They were about to give up when someone noticed a flash of white in a distant part of the field. The white edging of a photograph. They went over and found the polaroid snapshot. It had landed right side up, like a cat, perfectly OK.

But they never found the sunglasses.

It was at about this time that I began to go out regularly, two or three nights a week, to watch the fields – not so much to catch spinning cherubs, but to catch hoaxers. I was fascinated by the idea that two or three groups of people, perhaps half a dozen people in all, working the areas around Avebury and Cheesefoot Head, could keep this massive craze going. Perhaps they had even started it.

I also enjoyed the social aspect. I would often go down to Alton Barnes, to sit by the caravan with Rita Goold and the usual crowd she attracted. She always had a thermos full of tea with her, and a few beach chairs, and a million stories, most of them gleaned from her work in the paranormal world. 'Now this is absolutely true ...' she would say, as preamble, and with that we would all gather round and listen, while the stars winked and the night tiptoed past.

I was fairly serious about catching hoaxers, though. One night I went down to the caravan, and Rita was there with Matt Page, a photographer from a local paper in Warwickshire. A journalist from a German magazine was there, too, with a girl who someone said was a reporter for the *Observer*. The German and I began to talk about the circles. I maintained that while there were obviously many hoaxes, there were also some genuine ones, probably swirled by a natural mechanism. I quoted him the Mowing Devil case, and several eyewitness cases, including Rita Goold's. The German shook his head. 'No, zey are all made by people.'

'All hoaxes?'

'No, not hoaxes. Zey are "Land Art".'

He went on in this vein for a while, explaining how he was interested in the sociological aspects of it, and how people would always see what they wanted to see, and how the New Age –

'But how could they all be hoaxes?' I interrupted. 'Surely the first hoaxer got his idea from *somewhere*.'

'No, no, it iz not nezessary for zis. Sings can arise out of nosing. You have heard of ze Chaos Seory?'

Chaos Theory ... Well, that was pretty fancy, but he hadn't convinced me. We argued a little while longer, and gradually he spoke less, and more quietly, and spent more time looking out over East Field. Sometimes he would look at his watch. He seemed to be waiting for something to happen. His girlfriend from the *Observer* eventually dragged him away, but I decided that he knew something I didn't: the hoaxers would strike that very night, in East Field.

The German hadn't been gone long when I saw a fog gathering to the south-east. The Pewsey Vale was like a bathtub, and when the fog started up it was as if an invisible faucet had been turned on somewhere; the fog would spread out quickly and flood the entire valley, running like a ghostly tidal wave up against the sides. Soon we would be immersed, and blinded, and deafened by the sound-absorbing vapour, and any hoaxers would have free run of the field, while we sat obliviously at the caravan. I decided to go down and wait for them in the middle of the field. Fog-stealth could work both ways.

Matt Page, the photographer, came along, and we made our way down to the first big formation – the 2 July pictogram. Now amid the expanse of the dark field it was a strangely comfortable place, reminiscent of the soothingly wombish hideouts one builds as a child – tree-houses, snow-forts, couch-pillow castles, and so on. We stood and waited as the fog rolled in. We felt first a warm breath driven before the chill, and then a cold mist that swept across the wheatstalks with a faint hiss, and the moon dimmed, and finally we were bathed in a grey featureless haze.

Now was the time when the hoaxers would move. I held my breath, the better to hear what I guessed would be the distant sound of stalks being swept down –

Kshunk, kshunk, kshunk, kshunk.

'Matt!' I whispered. 'Can you hear it?'

'Uh . . . hear what?' he whispered back.

I pointed east, where the noise seemed to be coming from, and we listened again.

Kshunk, kshunk, kshunk, kshunk.

'Can't you hear it?' I whispered again. 'It's so loud!'

'Uh . . . I'm not sure.'

'Come on,' I said, and we went east through the field, towards the 5 July formation, the little ping-pong bat shape, along a narrow path, perpendicular to the tramlines, that some lazy circles tourist presumably had made. Every so often I put up my hand, military-fashion, and we stopped and crouched low and listened –

'Can you hear it yet?' I would say. 'You have to be able to hear it!'

'Yes . . .' Matt would say. 'Yes, I think so.'

We made our way down to the little ping-pong paddle. It was empty, but the sound still drifted to us from the east. We crossed the formation, stopped at the far side. Beyond us lay wet, trackless, virgin wheat. I looked at myself. My trousers and coatsleeves were soaked with dew. But what did it matter? We were about to catch the hoaxers who had been fooling the world for so long. I had my little instant camera ready, whining ultrasonically, its flash pumped. They would never know what hit them.

I decided to pause, to get a final bearing on the sound before we charged.

I turned my head to the south.

And to the north.

And to the west.

It seemed to be coming from all around us. Well, perhaps that was only the effect of the fog. Fog could play strange aural tricks . . .

Kshunk. Kshunk. Kshunk. Kshunk . . .

It seemed to be slowing now. Perhaps they had heard us. Or perhaps they were finishing already – my God, they worked fast! No wonder they had never been caught. Yet . . .

Kshunk. Kshunk.

It was funny. Now that I thought about it, the sound seemed to run in synch with . . . I felt my wrist.

Kshunk. Kshunk. Kshunk. Kshunk.

And I realized I had been chasing the sound of blood – rushing, pulsating, in my own excited ears.

Much of the road between Lockeridge and Alton Barnes lies in an ancient stream-bed. Cars flow there now, and the eerily liquid night fogs, and the fields, once stream-banks, slope dramatically up and away from you. In one of those fields, just outside of Lockeridge, early on 30 July, a large new crop formation appeared. It was a slim ellipsoid with bisected rings at each end, and two curving spurs from its midriff. It was garishly visible, and it attracted crowds. I went there one day and was accosted by a giggling child. 'Mister,' the kid said to me, spotting my notebook, gesturing at the swirled stalks around us, 'Mister, you've got to write that this was made by people!'

'Why?'

'Because it looks like a man!'

His guess was probably as good as any, but I thought it could more easily have been a cubist woman, or an ear-ringed female fertility symbol, or an uncomfortable bicycle, or . . . a fish.

'We've been expecting fish!' Wingfield said triumphantly to the gathering at the Waggon and Horses that night. In the previous issue of the *Cerealogist*, the Earl of Haddington himself had predicted 'figurative designs of animals, fishes, dragons and serpents'.

The day after the Lockeridge fish, an almost exact replica appeared at Steven Horton's circles-prone farm at Beckhampton, visible from the A4 and the A361. And on the next day a smaller version, without fins (it resembled a peanut, or a frog, or a motorcycle), appeared in an upsloping field along the Avebury Stone Avenue. That day was a Friday, and I arrived in the afternoon. Ohtsuki was back in the country briefly, escorting his own group of circles tourists – a group of coach-driven Japanese schoolchildren, whose schools had presumably paid Ohtsuki's way. I followed Meaden and Ohtsuki around, and interviewed them for another article I was writing. We ended up in the Stone Avenue frog, where Ohtsuki posed smiling for photographs with his overheated charges, and Meaden was mobbed by them for autographs. Later, after Ohtsuki had left, Meaden and I sat in the frog and talked about his new book, *The Goddess of the Stones*. A product of his archaeological researches (which apparently had been occurring in parallel with his circles work), its thesis was that the circles had appeared in neolithic grainfields, had been attributed by the farmers of the time to the ubiquitous neolithic Goddess, and subsequently had been commemorated by circular Goddess temples, made of stone. Such as Avebury and Stonehenge. It was a pretty ambitious theory, but to someone like me, who knew almost nothing about archaeology, it sounded half-way plausible. I learned later what trouble he was having with the book. A manager at one of the big bookstore chains, who himself was a believer in the circles (and a worrier: he thought the circles might be marks left by gigantic invisible aerial beasts intent upon sucking away Wiltshire's water supply), told me that Meaden had been pestering him for weeks, trying to get him to buy more copies, trying to arrange public readings. The only reading, somewhere in Bath, had been disappointing. Meaden had given a crisp pedantic lecture on the circles and at the end of it someone had spoken up from the back of the nearly-empty room, in a rank cockney accent, 'So they're not made by spaceships, then?'

Now we sat in the late afternoon sun, Meaden and I, and talked about science and the inertia of orthodoxy. Ohtsuki was soon going to send him the draft of a paper, describing the aluminium powder experiments, which they would together send to *Nature*. Meaden wasn't sure it would be accepted by *Nature* – arguably the most prestigious scientific journal in the world – since the experiment itself was not all that substantial. But someday, somehow, the plasma vortex theory or a near variant would be accepted by the scientific community. It was just a matter of time, of collecting enough evidence, of continuing forcefully to make his case. And when that day came ... Would he accept an academic post? Oh, yes, yes – if he could be permitted to continue his research work, of course.

Meaden told me about his confrontation with George Wingfield at Barbury Castle. '"There is evidence of intelligent planning here," Wingfield said to me. And I said, "Yes, *human* intelligence."' Meaden laughed at the recollection.

I wondered whether the group that had made Barbury Castle might have videotaped their work as they made it, in order to prove its origins and embarrass any researchers who had pronounced it genuine.

'Oh, I'd be very glad,' said Meaden, 'if in a month or so someone produced a video.'

A portly young man approached us. He was Arthur Mills. He produced a plastic bag which contained what appeared to be several igneous rocks. The rocks, he said with a quiet gravity, had been found atop the swept stalks of a pictogram at East Kennett. On behalf of the Beckhampton Group, Arthur was donating this portion of the mysterious rocks to Dr Meaden for his own independent analysis.

'Very interesting,' said Meaden, and accepted the bag. After Mills had left, Meaden asked me with a sly smile what I thought the little stones were. I shrugged ignorantly. 'Plasma-carbonized limestone?' Meaden laughed, shaking his head at the little plastic bag full of rocks. 'It's clinker,' he said, meaning the stony residue of burnt coal – meaning nothing extraterrestrial. Meaning someone was having a laugh on the Beckhampton Group.

A reporter from the *Marlborough Times* came by. 'Dr Meaden? Just a few questions, please ... What do you think of this formation?'

'It looks good,' he said jauntily. 'We can explain it. There is nothing in there that is unsettling in the least. It's just another nice system.'

'Do you think there are many hoaxes this year?'

Meaden smiled, shook his head in polite exasperation. 'There are as many hoaxes this year as in the other years put together.'

'What about the formation at Barbury Castle?'

'Definitely a hoax. The stalks are damaged as if hammered down with rollers. Everything is broken, smashed up. It's the worst mess I've ever seen.'

'But you think this is genuine?' asked the reporter, pointing to the frog-like formation on the hillside.

'Oh yes. I was able to get into this one early to study it, before it was trampled by tourists . . .'

While Meaden was talking with the *Marlborough Times*, I was looking at the map, and when he finished, I showed it to him. There seemed to me to be a deliberate symmetry in the placement of the two fish and the frog. One more frog (everything was coming in twos this year, like Noah's Ark) in the right place would form, when one connected the points, a top-down representation of a pyramid: the same motif as the one at the heart of the Barbury Castle formation. The thing was, the fishes had arrived on consecutive days, and the first frog had arrived last night, which meant that the second frog . . . would be made tonight.

Meaden wasn't impressed. For one thing, he didn't think the fishes and the frog were hoaxed. There was too much that was vortical about them, and the stalks seemed relatively undamaged. For another, one could always discover symmetries if one joined enough points. Anyway, it was getting late. Meaden had promised his wife he would be home before dinner. It was their son's birthday. He had to drive back to Bradford-on-Avon. But perhaps in his absence I, a young Meadenite, could make myself useful. A farmer, Chris Cutforth, had some potentially interesting information regarding hoaxers. Meaden hadn't yet had time to get the details. Perhaps if I had the time, he suggested, I would go over and speak with Cutforth myself. He would introduce me.

We drove down the road between Lockeridge and Alton Barnes, turned off on to a private road which led up to Cutforth's place, and Meaden introduced me and went on his way. Cutforth, a genial man who had lived in the area all his life, explained that at 4.30 on the same morning that the Lockeridge fish had appeared, he and his wife had been awakened by the sound of a car driving over their cattle grid. His partridges had been agitated, and at dawn the partridge keeper had found a pair of tyre tracks leading from the private farm road across a long pasture to a hedge. Cutforth and I now drove over to the hedge, parked and got out, crossed through brambles and thistles to another field, and after a few minutes' searching picked up a distinct narrow trail through the field to another hedge, on the other side of which was his neighbour's field, in the middle of which, at the end of still more trails ... was the Lockeridge fish.

I took some photos, thanked Cutforth, and drove to the place where, according to the pyramidal symmetry, the new frog would appear. The spot was in a naked wheatfield about a mile east of Avebury. Now I was certain.

I drove up to the secret site, but found it deserted. I drove down to Bishops Cannings and by phone managed to rouse Peter Rendall, Roger Davis, and Paul Fuller for a night of hoaxwatching. They seemed reluctant, and Rendall was even a little suspicious – I had, after all, been regularly consorting with the enemy at the Waggon and Horses. But they were also impressed by my urgent confidence, and when we had all gathered in the caravan, and I showed them the map, they understood why I had called them.

We went out at about midnight, parking in the Avebury car-park and walking along the road that leads east from the town. There was no moon, and the paved road soon turned to rutted dirt, causing us often to stumble; but I discouraged the use of torches. This was to be a stealthy operation. No talking either – sound carries at night.

By the time we reached the naked field, it was obvious to the others that we were, by comparison with other circles sites, in the middle of nowhere. Only an aircraft, or a random rambler, would have found a formation in that field, and in any case few people would ever take the trouble to visit the thing. But I was reluctant to admit defeat, and while the young Meadenites shivered and grumbled on the Ridgeway overlooking the field I climbed down towards it, through what seemed like four or five barbed-wire fences, and sat and listened for the sounds of hoaxers ...

Mmmmmuuuuuu ...

Rrrrgggghhhhh ...

Baaaaaaaahhhhhh ...

And in the morning, there was a brand-new frog – at Beckhampton, beneath the fish at Firs Farm.

*

In the summer months, the tabloids received numerous letters-to-the-editor regarding the crop circles. The *Sunday Mirror* probably received the greatest proportion, because it had offered a £10,000 reward for proof of what caused the phenomenon. Most of the letters contained speculation about what might be behind it all; others contained alleged eyewitness accounts of circle formation, perhaps by a spaceship, or by nesting birds, or by drunken youths, or by any of a great variety of alleged mechanisms. Relatively few of such letters were ever printed, but the *Mirror* would occasionally send them, *en masse*, to its designated judge in the £10,000 competition, Terence Meaden. Thus it was that in February of 1991, amid a pile of prize-aspiring correspondence, Terence Meaden discovered the Tomlinson case.

The Tomlinsons, Vivienne and Gary, were a couple in their thirties who lived in Surrey. He was tall, pale, thin, and quiet, and worked as a garage mechanic. She was short, dark, plump, and garrulous, and managed the household. Meaden told me I should hear their story, and put me in touch with them. A few days later I was standing with them in the very wheatfield where, they said, they had been caught up in a plasma vortex.

It was one of a group of pleasant little fields making up a few dozen acres behind a churchyard in the little Surrey village of Hambledon. Trees surrounded the fields on most sides, opening up to more fields and a broad flat rural vista to the north-west.

Vivienne did most of the talking. She was initially concerned about what I might do with their account. 'I want you to promise me,' she said, 'that we're not going to be exposed to the point that – OK, I would like to sell my story to the tabloids. I have bills . . . We are just average, working, hard-working people.'

According to Vivienne, the event had occurred on or about Thursday, 17 May 1990. Gary had come home after a long day at the garage, and she had asked him to take her out for a walk. She had been decorating the house, and wanted to get some fresh air. 'We argued,' she remembered. 'He wanted to go and do the shopping. I wanted to come for the walk.' She laughed, 'And of course eventually I won.'

They set out across the field, heading for a nearby hill which was their usual destination. The sky was overcast. The air was humid and breezy. As they walked along the narrow public footpath which split the field they noticed a few small circles of swirled wheat nearby. 'Nothing big,' remembered Vivienne.

'We thought it might have been foxes,' remembered Gary.

They reached the hill, and then turned back as dusk began to fall. They were passing the field where they had seen the circles. The sun was sinking beneath the clouds, colouring the tips of the wheat a lovely orange as the breeze rippled the field in liquid-like waves. 'I stopped to admire the beauty of it,' said Vivienne.

Then at either side of the gap to the north-west, the trees began to sway with a sudden gust of wind. 'Those trees were really blowing,' said Gary. 'You could tell it was much stronger than normal.'

'And then the wind started really coming on,' said Vivienne, 'and you could see the trees were really going . . . it was surging forward. We could feel the air changing . . .'

And then an odd channel of wind seemed to head straight at them through the gap, about twenty feet wide, moving in a narrow streak across the field. 'Really pushing the stalks down,' remembered Vivienne . . . 'It was a full river of air, pushing . . . And suddenly we could hear a high high high high-pitched sound, very very high-pitched, you know like when a plane is taking off . . . almost like pan-pipes . . . My ears were popping . . .' They wondered whether a helicopter might be over them, but looking up, they saw nothing. 'And the next thing, we just found ourselves, *whooshh*, being pushed, and we were tossed and turned, because we were in its path.'

'It was very quick,' remembered Gary.

'And everything seemed to slow down . . .' said Vivienne. 'And not being able to get out, and trying to get out . . . suddenly this feeling of being trapped . . . And during this time I was trying to talk to Gary, but he couldn't hear me. There was so much noise. You couldn't even hear the high-pitched sound any more.'

'It was a weird sensation,' said Gary. 'You can't believe how strong it really was. It's almost hard to explain it.'

'We were frightened at this stage,' said Vivienne. 'We were just being tossed and turned, there was nothing we could do about it. It all happened so quick. And when I was trying to talk to Gary, I looked at him, and I noticed that his hair was standing all on end

... all spiked up ... We had a funny tingling sensation all over. I'd never felt anything like it. There was *this tingling*, all over. It felt rather strange. And the next thing, we found ourselves in a circle. And the wind we were in ... sort of split into two, and the other one sort of whooshed off to the side, dropping the corn as it whooshed, and then zig-zagged away, and started spinning not too far off, and forming another circle. And it was very hazy, very hazy looking, you know, like a mist.'

'Glassy,' said Gary.

'You could see through it,' said Vivienne. 'And there was a shimmer ...'

The two whirlwinds quickly died, but mini-whirlwinds seemed to remain. 'When I looked down,' remembered Vivienne, 'I noticed that little spirals were forming, and the circle was being made from in to outwards. And we just stood, looking at this, and I mean I was just fascinated by what was going on.'

The little whirlwinds, which also seemed to shimmer vaporously, wound slowly around the outer edge of the circle, gathering the stalks in bunches, and laying them down, gradually widening the circle.

I asked Vivienne and Gary what these little whirlwinds looked like. 'Like little tornadoes,' said Vivienne. 'They were all like fog ... like mist, all shimmering.'

How large were they?

'They were about – I would say four inches apart, and about the breadth of the height ... They were quite, ah ... They seemed to be going up, but the height was, ah, the breadth of the ...' She made a face, looked at Gary, leaned down, made a spiral motion with her finger above the ground. 'They were about, you know like little tornadoes, about like this ... They were about that size.' About six inches in diameter.

Extending how high?

'Going up, I think they were just about levelling with the corn, you know, about ... because when we went into the corn –'

'Well they appeared to be inside what we were in, wasn't it?' said Gary.

'Yeah, yeah,' said Vivienne. 'When they sort of went into the corn, you failed to see where they ended.'

Vivienne and Gary say they stood and watched the shimmering little tornadoes as they spun around the perimeter of the circle, gathering bunches of stalks and laying them down, widening the circle. It went on and on. 'Turning around the corn, and dropping,' said Vivienne. 'Turning around the corn, and dropping. And they were shimmering. They seemed to be going round and round.'

After fifteen minutes of watching this spectacle, remember Vivienne and Gary, they grew bored and left.

For some reason, they never photographed the resulting circles, and the farmer doesn't recall seeing any in his fields that summer – or any summer.

One fine day at the Stone Avenue frog, a television production company called Juniper were filming various circles personalities for Channel Four's *Equinox* series. A very thin man with a white beard and earphones plugged into a little metal box was demonstrating for the cameras how he detected residual Orgone Energy in the circles. Orgone Energy, the man explained, was something which orthodox science did not yet accept. Michael Green was standing by, having just given a demonstration of dowsing. The Juniper people finished with the Orgone Energy man, and he and Green left, just as Terence Meaden walked up the long tramline that sloped from the road.

The frog had a spiral motif throughout, and its layering was as complex as in any formation, but for the cameras Meaden preferred to discuss a simpler shape if possible: a nice small simple circle. Fortunately, these often lay scattered near the large pictograms, usually in groups of two or three; they were known as 'grapeshot', or 'signatures of the Circlemakers'.

After much trampling of wheat and trailing of wires, a simple circle was found a few dozen yards above the frog. The Juniper producer, a woman named Jill, conferred briefly with Meaden as he took his place within the circle. This would be merely a short rehearsal, she explained. A sweaty, bare-torsoed sound man hoisted a furry boom-microphone over the tableau; and the camera rolled.

'Simple though this is,' said Meaden, looking down at the little nest, 'this is typical of, ah, genuine crop circles. It's the sort of thing I've been looking at for years. And, ah . . . For the first ten years, I really didn't see anything more complicated than simple circles.'

The cameraman said something to Meaden, and Meaden changed his position within the circle and continued.

'Well, we've got here a circular perimeter, an outflowing spiral from the centre, sharp edge to the circle . . . It's a pity it's cut by this tramline . . . The gapseeking effect which a tramline produces is evident here, because [grasping several horizontal stalks] this just collapses into the tramline, instead of being out here if there had been no tramline.' He walked to the centre of the little circle, paused. 'Two metres diameter. This one is anti-clockwise –'

'Uh, I'm not seeing anything,' the cameraman said to Jill. 'I don't know what the hell I'm looking at. I need to get specifics, otherwise I'm just going to do what I did last time, which was point in the general direction of what he's looking at.'

The sound man was having trouble, too. Wind noise was obscuring Meaden's voice. 'Terence,' said Jill, 'we're going to put you on a radio mike now . . . assuming that the radio mike isn't that affected by the wind. And you need to be more detailed than you were there. I mean that was just a quick whizz through. You need to really use this as a sort of test case, to sort of show how you use your evidence. I mean, I'd like to actually hear you sort of talking about circular axial symmetry and things . . . and then explaining what you mean by that.'

'I don't mind seeing it, if it's necessary,' said the cameraman, referring to the radio mike. 'But you probably want to hide it . . .'

'Ian,' said Jill to one of her researchers, 'I haven't actually got my list of things; if you can be sort of ticking off the ones he's dealt with . . . Oh actually Charlotte's got my stuff; if you look through there, somewhere in there . . . inside the back of the folder is a list of "Points to be Covered by Terence".'

The cameraman was talking to Meaden, trying to put him at ease, telling him he didn't think the little circle was a hoax. 'I mean, why would they bother to come up here, and just throw one of these things down?'

'Yes, why would they bother?' laughed Jill.

After a few minutes Meaden was wired with the radio mike, and the researcher returned with the checklist.

'So should we start with Terence just walking down there and into the circle?' asked the cameraman. He turned to the sound man.

'Unless it's really bad we'll just stay with the radio mike. Unless it really gets bad. If you get the odd blow, don't worry.'

'Twenty minutes,' called out Charlotte, indicating the time left before the cameraman and the sound man, both contractors, went overtime, knocking Juniper overbudget.

'Okay, when you're ready,' said the cameraman.

'Watch out for the crop circle,' said Jill.

'Are we on?' said Meaden.

'Running,' said the cameraman.

Meaden walked along the designated path, entered the circle, looked down with an air of confident recognition. 'Simple though it is,' he began, 'this simple circle has all the characteristics of its bigger brothers. This one is anti-clockwise; about half the ones we find are clockwise. Ah, notice the sharp, circular perimeter, the central area from which a spiral outflow has taken place, and the way in which the corn falls into the perimeter area – and in this case, because there's a gap there, it falls [clutching the laid straws again] quite heavily into the gap area, instead of remaining out like this. The, ah, bigger brothers are a bit more complex, because there are layering effects in those, and sometimes twin centres. But here, we've got the standard evidence for descent of a vortex. Implied by the centre here is axial symmetry; the whirling vortex that made the circle came down and in a matter of probably less than a second, spun out this simple circle.' Then he paused, regarding the simple little circle, his index finger resting across his mouth in the desperately pensive manner of an actor who has forgotten his lines.

'Remind me . . . I guess I'll start again.'

'No, that's all right,' said Jill. 'We can, uhm, uhm . . . Can you make more clear the sort of perpendicular sort of . . . the undamaged corn, and the damaged corn, the sort of, the sort of clearness of distinction . . .'

Meaden nodded, started again. '. . . You find this sharp edge, the sort of thing which electrified air, rather than non-electrified air, is likely to, ah . . . it was probably because of the plasma content of the air, and you do get this sharp edge, and also you wouldn't get a sharp edge if the thing wasn't descending vertically –'

'Do you want to make the point there about contrasting it with ordinary wind damage?' said Jill.

Meaden nodded. 'By contrast, ordinary wind damage, which is often coupled in fact with heavy rain, doesn't give any of the ordered structure we see here. The, ah, wind and rain combined usually flatten the corn in a single direction and there is no ordered structure as we get in these plasma vortex circles . . .'

Jill turned to Ian for the next item on the checklist.

'Circular hollows, central pyramid,' said Ian.

'Yeees . . .' said Meaden uncertainly. 'Not applicable in this case.' There was neither a hollow nest nor a conical pyramid at the centre of the circle.

Ian looked down at his list for the next item. 'Uh, the differences between the effect in ripe and unripe corn.'

'That's a good one,' said Meaden, nodding.

'And [the differences between] laid flat or merely bent,' continued Ian.

'Yes,' said Meaden. 'That's a good one, too.'

'Carry on,' said Jill.

'This corn was ripe when it was hit down,' said Meaden, 'and the flattening has really occurred in the base . . . but, ah, early in the season, when the corn is green . . . one finds a more gradual bending over, from the ground . . . and this is something which, when it comes to hoaxing, cannot be replicated at all . . .

'Ah, there is, at the centre of this circle, the remains of a very minor cone. The stalks here are wrapped around rather tightly, but while it's very very small, it does indicate that a ring vortex was at work here, as in other circles where the central cone looks a lot better. Occasionally [pointing to a clump of stalks which stuck up slightly] we find standing stems, such as here. These were better rooted, and were probably bent over quite a bit, but were able to recover afterwards . . .'

Ian looked at his list again, and Meaden discussed further aspects of the phenomenon, and the clock ticked down. Eventually the cameraman's videotape ran out. While he reloaded, he said aside to Jill, 'I don't know how you're going to cut this. I mean I'm just in one position, but he's changing position on me . . . And most of the time he's just demonstrating with his hands . . .'

'Is there a cone left in that big one?' asked Meaden, referring to the nearby frog, or as he called it, a peanut. 'Because there was a huge cone there last week.'

'Is there any layering in the other one?' asked Jill.

'Yes there is,' said Meaden.

'Very good layering,' said Ian.

'We'll do a bit of layering in the other circle,' said Jill, adding with exasperation: 'And then it's forty minutes sitting in the van.'

'And a quick stop to get a long shot of the fish,' said the cameraman.

'We're calling it a peanut,' said Meaden.

'I think it looks a bit like a frog with fat legs,' said Jill.

'There are two peanuts and two fishes that we know of,' said Meaden.

As we walked down from the frog/peanut/fish I mentioned to Meaden that Wingfield said he'd been expecting fishes.

'Yes . . . he was expecting loaves as well.' He chuckled at the joke. 'Oh yes . . . loaves and fishes.'

We fell a little way behind the Juniper people as we walked down. Meaden's voice turned confidential and pedantic, and for a moment he was Sherlock Holmes and I was a notebook-wielding Watson. 'My conclusion, for a lot of reasons, is that all four fishes, or two peanuts and two fishes, are genuine.'

Meaden by now knew all about the trails through Chris Cutforth's fields to the Lockeridge fish, so I didn't argue.

Ahead of us, Jill was talking about layering.

'Terence,' said Ian, walking back to us, 'I mean, where's the best layering?'

Jill was right behind him. 'I mean layering is the really important sort of thing.'

Juniper interviewed Rita Goold about her luminous tube, and Vivienne and Gary Tomlinson about their shimmering little tornadoes. They interviewed astronomers and sociologists, dowsers and pagans, journalists and farmers – and one day, while I tagged along, they interviewed the Wessex Skeptics.

The Wessex Skeptics were a group of about half a dozen young research scientists and technicians, most of them based at the University of Southampton. Like many such groups around Europe and the US – and their spelling of Skeptics betrayed an American influence – they had come together in the 1980s as a kind of immune response, on behalf of scientific orthodoxy, against what they considered to be the pseudo-scientific claims of the New Age movement. Most orthodox scientists simply ignore such claims, at least in their day-to-day work, but some are sufficiently interested, usually because of a previous flirtation with fringe science or the supernatural, that they set out actively to debunk it. Among the Skeptics' targets have been firewalking, dowsing, and homoeopathy. Crop circles, when they became big news in 1989, were an obvious addition to the list.

The Skeptics started out on Meaden's side, supporting his attacks on the Delgadonians and even attending his High Hill cropwatch of 1990. But after Meaden declared the Alton Barnes double-pictogram to be genuine, the Skeptics decided that Meaden was just as unscientific as the Delgadonians, and began to promote the hoax theory. By the summer of 1991 the media had begun to turn to them as experts, just as they turned to Meaden for quotes supporting the meteorological theory, or to Delgado for the paranormal theory. The National Geographic crew interviewed them at length, and even paid them to make a few crop circles, in support of their contention that hoaxing was relatively easy.

Juniper decided to do the same, and one grey and blustery August afternoon at David Shepherd's Baltic Farm, on the downs north of the now-abandoned secret site, I watched as the Skeptics swirled several circles into a field of wheat. Martin Hempstead, a moustachioed physicist, used a big green plastic garden roller to knock out a big circle. Chris Nash, a bespectacled optoelectronics technician, and David Fisher, a tall bearded don from the University of Cardiff, swirled a ringed circle nearby with a smaller roller. Robin Allen, a Southampton physicist soon to join the parapsychology department at Edinburgh, was crouched somewhere in the field with cardboard panels strapped to his feet and hands, immersed in his own little spiral creation. The Juniper crew filmed from a dirt road fifty yards away. The National Geographic crew had brought over from the States a large and high-tech fishing-rod type device to crane the camera for this kind of shot, where a high angle was needed; but Juniper didn't have that kind of budget, and had to make do instead with Farmer Shepherd's bulldozer, inside the raised shovel of which Jill and the cameraman sat shivering.

'What is Robin doing?' someone asked.

'A hand job, I think,' said someone else.

'Don't make jokes,' said Jill. 'We're in a dangerous position for laughter.'

The Skeptics finished their work within a half hour or so. The initial laying of the stalks took only a few minutes; most of their time was spent tidying up the edges, removing damaged stalks, creating odd layering effects, and sculpting the centre to suit Meaden's theory.

'Yes, with a nice cone in the middle,' said Jill.

After they had finished, the Skeptics tip-toed along the seed lines to the safety of the tramlines, swishing up fallen stalks behind them to cover their tracks. Now it was time for the second act of the show.

Meaden arrived, with Peter Rendall. Being interviewed for television documentaries was one of the perks, the bonuses, of being a young Meadenite. Meaden doled these opportunities out carefully, and only to his staunchest, or most potentially useful supporters. Rendall had done yeoman work over the summer, putting in long hours at the secret site, and ideologically-speaking he was the staunchest of the staunch. Now was his turn for a little limelight.

Meaden and Rendall went into the field, inspecting the formations as the cameras rolled, and Meaden started to tick off the problems he found: the broken stalks, the absence of proper spiral patterns, a tell-tale footprint . . . On the whole it wasn't a bad job, he conceded disarmingly, but to the trained eye, it was an obvious hoax.

Then Martin Hempstead was brought in to confront Meaden. But Meaden made a pre-emptive strike. 'Actually we suspect you of hoaxing other circles,' he said to Hempstead, his voice rising with indignation. 'There've been so many done, this year. We know you've made some, and we suspect you've made others you've not told us about.'

'You've seen the ones we've made,' replied Hempstead nervously, referring to a set made overtly, with farmer Chris Cutforth's permission, for *National Geographic*.* 'We made them at Chris Cutforth's

---

*The Skeptics' formation at Cutforth's farm was not the same as the

farm; I assume you've been there, or somebody in your group has been there. Our point is that –'

'But you've made others, too,' pressed Meaden.

'– you have created – You have given us – You are now giving us criteria –'

'Look, have you made any or not?'

'Yes, at Chris Cutf –'

'Other than – Other than the ones at Chris Cutforth's farm and these.'

'Have we made any other than those? Yes, I've – I've made – made some.'

'Ahhh? Ohhh? I wond –'

'However –'

'We'd better have a –'

'The POINT is,' said Hempstead angrily, 'we are now learning – '

'We're suggesting that you are the hoaxers –'

'– we are now learning how to hoax them better.'

Rendall weighed in, 'Don't you think that that's a damned irresponsible thing to do?'

Hempstead gave a poor imitation of laughter. 'We're stuck in Southampton. We have very little time –'

'No, no look, you admit you make circles,' said Meaden. 'We've never made any ourselves. We're finding them –'

'Well maybe you should try to make them –'

'– and we've found – and we've found – and we've found some hoaxed circles, and we think you've made more than you've told us about.'

They had. Earlier I had overheard Robin Allen talking to Jill on the road by the field, discussing what would be filmed. 'You haven't got me before,' Allen had said. 'Well,' Jill had responded, apparently referring to some other, nocturnal, occasion, 'we got your silhouette. We heard you whispering –'

Jill had seen that I was listening, and had swallowed the rest of the thought.

*

Lockeridge fish, which despite the hoaxers' apparent access through Cutforth's land had occurred on an adjacent farm.

One day, to collect some material for a newspaper story I was writing, I interviewed Delgado at his house in Alresford. We sat in his living-room for an hour or two, and drank tea and munched biscuits, and discussed the crop circles, and the people who studied them. He started off on Meaden. People like Meaden, he said, would always come along and prematurely try to solve a mystery. 'People need a prop – it's like a religion.' All this without a trace of irony.

He said that Ohtsuki was 'a very rational man', but that even Ohtsuki would surely agree that little craters in aluminium powder did nothing to explain the pictograms, which were unambiguously evolving. In fact, the phenomenon itself was all about evolution. There was another realm out there, the realm of a higher intelligence, and we were evolving towards it, under the guidance of the higher intelligence. 'We are all controlled by the higher intelligence,' Delgado told me. This had implications for governments, and for religious leaders. 'I'm sure the Vatican is very interested in this' – because in the end, the phenomenon would take us beyond religion, beyond science, beyond human institutions, beyond human language.

But it was still worthwhile to run an occasional cropwatch. 'It helps. People like to see something going on, something being done about it. Not all sitting back waiting. Although sitting back and waiting, really, I can see is quite sensible, because you can't accelerate this phenomenon. There's nothing you can do to accelerate it. It's evolving at its own pace. And if you take note of the pace, and what is happening while it's evolving, there's a lot to be studied. If you go out, with cameras, and magnetometers, and infra-red cameras, and do biological studies and crop soil investigations and plant investigations, you only see the result of what has happened but it leaves you in greater confusion because you don't know *why* it happened.'

After I finished my questions and turned off my tape recorder, he sat me down at a table in front of an unkempt heap of letters, videotapes, and unsolicited book manuscripts which people had sent him. He looked at it all wistfully, commenting on the unifying nature of the phenomenon and at the same time on the unlikelihood of his ever catching up with all of his mail. Then he explained how for the past two and a half years he had been following a parallel career as a healer, having discovered that the crop circles energies could be channelled for therapeutic purposes. Recently at the Arthritis Society in Winchester, for example, he had brushed away the malfunctioning energies from an elderly woman who had subsequently been able to discard her neck brace. Another elderly woman had been able to shed her crutches. It was the higher intelligence, working through him. Sometimes it even spoke through him. He would be discussing a subject and suddenly he would utter something that ... he hadn't known before. And then he would realize that he was under the control of the higher intelligence.

'Now that might sound a bit daft to you,' he said, with a benign chuckle.

After interviewing Delgado, I drove out to Cheesefoot Head to see some of the insectograms, and then drove back up to Wiltshire, to Adam's Grave – the long barrow atop Walker's Hill, overlooking Alton Barnes and East Field. Nippon TV was running another cropwatch up there, called Operation Black Swan, with a caravan and a familiar cantankerous generator and a small arsenal of low-light cameras. Colin Andrews was up there, too.

Delgado had warned me that whereas he, Delgado, was secure in his position as the world's first crop circles investigator, and didn't mind keeping a low profile these days, Andrews was more 'into the media type thing' – perhaps, I thought, because he had just quit his job at the Test Valley Borough Council and was now forced to make a living from crop circles, come what may. But Andrews didn't strike me as being hungrier for press attention than Delgado, although the caution in his comments suggested a public shrewdness that Delgado could have used more of. Andrews seemed curious to know what Delgado had said to me, explaining that Delgado's spirituality, while certainly well-intentioned, could sometimes be 'off-putting' to those who were unused to it.

But otherwise their views were harmonious. There was a spiritual component to the phenomenon, said Andrews, and a possible link with ley-lines, UFOs, megalithic sites, and the Gaia hypothesis. There was even possibly a link with plasma physics, although of course any circles-swirling plasma would be under the control of a

233

higher intelligence. He didn't come right out and say 'higher intelligence', however. He would only go as far as to say that 'the evolution of the circles demonstrates behaviour' – and not human behaviour, either, although certainly there had been some hoaxes.

I paid several more visits to the site over the course of Operation Black Swan. The hilltop wind necessitated winter clothes, and exacerbated my hay-fever, but Adam's Grave was a far better vantage point for cropwatching than the East Field caravan had been. One could see for miles into the Vale of Pewsey, and up the stream-bed road to Lockeridge, and back past the Milk Hill white horse along the farms and villages straddling the Kennet Canal.

One Sunday night, the penultimate night of the Black Swan watch, I drove up to Adam's Grave with Rob Irving, a photographer from Bath. Earlier in the summer, with three or four others, Irving had seen an odd light zooming and hovering over the fields nearby. He wasn't sure that it was connected with crop circles, but in any case he had since become one of the regulars at the East Field caravan. I told him about the Adam's Grave site, and we went up one night with our cameras.

It had been a strange weekend. The harvest was in full swing, and yet the excitement among crop circles enthusiasts was as high as ever. On Friday night, a group of young German circles tourists had videotaped a strange lightform drifting over a wheatfield near Marlborough. The Germans would drive around and show people the footage, through the viewfinder of their video camera. Everyone at the Waggon and Horses was talking about it. Even the Nippon TV crowd had seen it, and had been impressed. Some wet blanket types said the thing was just a thistle-spore, of which there were trillions drifting around just then, but others swore that it demonstrated behaviour.

And then there had been the new crop circle formation in a field south of Cambridge. It was a masterpiece – a giant cardioid, with little circles sprouting from it in a strikingly complex symmetry that many instantly recognized as a representation of the Mandelbrot Set. The Mandelbrot Set was the name given to data generated by any of a family of deceptively simple non-linear equations – in which variables feed back into other variables, so that changes in one variable would flutter and reverberate throughout the whole system of variables. In tabular form, the data seem an inchoate mess, but when graphed, variable against variable, a lovely complexity emerges, with cardioids and circles and paisleys sprouting and spinning off *ad infinitum*, in what has become the most popular symbol of the endless, almost metaphysical possibilities of ... Chaos Theory.

Of course it went without saying that the formation was unhoaxable. Certainly John Martineau thought so. Martineau was part of a small group of young, New Age, vaguely millenarian cropwatchers who called themselves UBI, which publicly meant 'United Bureau of Investigation', but privately meant 'United Believers in Intelligence' – i.e. non-human intelligence. Whenever Andrews or Delgado needed volunteers for a cropwatch, UBI were happy to oblige. They had been at Blackbird in 1990, and had paid a few visits to Macnish's Kon-Tiki watch earlier this summer. Now they were helping out with Black Swan, watching the monitors and waiting for something to happen. Irving and I chatted with Martineau on the hilltop, that Sunday night. The previous morning, at about three o'clock, Martineau and the others had seen and videotaped an odd red light moving about on the horizon – not an aircraft, nor an Army flare, nor a shivering TV tower, nor the planet Mars. Something unknown. Otherwise they had nothing to show for their pains. But Martineau was absolutely certain that the crop circles were a genuine phenomenon. We stood out on the windy hilltop at midnight, and he told us that things were coming to a head. There had been, he said, electrical shut-outs in many of the nearby villages, often coincident with the appearances of crop circles. The MoD had sealed off some villages altogether, to prevent word getting out, to forestall public panic. But there was little the MoD or the government could do, in the long run. A massive electrical shutdown of Western society was coming. It was coming from the earth, as perhaps it had come in millennia past ... a kind of back-EMF, an omnipresent, magneto-voltaic opposition to man-made circuitry ... until everything simply stopped. The circles were merely a manifestation of this process.

Some time after midnight, Martineau went back into the caravan to get warm, leaving Irving and me outside with our cameras. At about three o'clock the wind slowed to ten knots or so, and soon the white wave of fog came from the south-east, lapping against the sides of the hill, blanketing the valley. The little generator droned on, and the watchers in the caravan talked and played cards, their faces a tired, cathode-ray grey. At four o'clock, about a mile distant, near a road beyond the far end of East Field, a light suddenly appeared in the fog. Over a few seconds it brightened, like a climaxing firework, then it dimmed and vanished. None of our cameras had been pointing in the right direction.

At about five minutes to five, the light returned, but this time it continued to brighten, and beneath its diffusing blanket of fog, began to move.

'It's a car,' I said.

But then it seemed to swing violently, from side to side, in great hundred-yard high-speed zig-zags that no human machine could have executed. I felt a deep shiver of xenophobia.

The light ran for a quarter-mile or so, throwing chaotic shadows into the fog, until the projected image of a dying tree suddenly emerged enormously before it, swung crazily from side to side, and vanished with the light that had made it.

Irving's camera had not been pointing in the right direction. Mine had, but I soon discovered that the film had been wound on improperly. Nippon TV had also drawn a blank, the light having run its course within a minor gap between two cameras' high-tech fields of view. 'It always happens that way,' said Martineau, nodding sagely.

A half hour later, as if some magic meteorological wand had been waved, the fog suddenly dispersed, and Irving and I went down to inspect the path of the light. We found that it did indeed correspond to a road, which at the initial location of the light took a sudden sharp turn towards Adam's Grave, running straight for a quarter mile, before taking another sharp turn away, in front of a large and dying tree. The road and the tree were unscorched, and as far as we could tell, the surrounding fields, where harvesting machines here and there lay in suspended animation, were heavy with dew but free of crop circles.

21

Magic

The Nippon TV crew was long gone on the evening that Tim Carson's combine-harvester finally swept through the main East Field pictogram. I was there, with about half a dozen other passers-by who had stopped to watch the poignant scene. And at the last minute, just before the slow-rolling harvester made its first, fatal cut, a helicopter swooped down out of nowhere, a daredevil camera-man hanging by a strap out of its side, and recorded the event for posterity.

At night now on Adam's Grave, the fields lay naked below us, their pictograms so much blurred stubble. A few brown fields remained uncut, but the final push was on, and some nights my camera would track the lights of a distant harvester, working round the clock, racing rot and frost, chasing the season's sad end.

On Friday evenings I would drive down to the Waggon and Horses, and Rob Irving would be there, with Ute Weyer, a pretty young circles tourist from Germany, and Adrian and Paul Dexter. The Dexters, twins in their twenties from Somerset, were members of the Beckhampton Group, and had been among Rita Goold's favourites on the East Field cropwatches. We would have drinks, and dinner, and coffee, and then would drive down to East Field and hike with our gear up the hill to Adam's Grave, where we would wait for rogue lightforms or hoaxers, or just for dawn, and would talk about the circles, and who could be making them, and why, and we would shiver and wipe the dew from our camera lenses as the night deepened and the stars fell in a grand arc over Alton Barnes, and the fog reached surreally from the western part of the valley down over East Field, in slow tendrils, like the grasping fingers of a ghost.

One night at the Waggon and Horses, Irving and the Dexters took me aside and told me that they had a theory, the essence of which was that the crop circles, although made by humans, were not a hoax. That is to say, they were made not by mere pranksters, but by an entirely different class of artist.

The evidence was only circumstantial, but it was significant. In some circles they had found small areas in which the heads of wheat had been removed by a sharp instrument. In others they had found not the Meaden-predicted pyramidal cone but instead an effigy, a 'corn dolly'. Both findings pointed to harvest rituals, symbolic sacrifices which echoed the deep pagan past of rural England – a past to which, spiritually speaking, many English obviously wished to return. Irving and the Dexters believed that the crop circles were being made by modern pagans either as some kind of complicated mystical rite, or, more likely, as a kind of cosmological terrorism, a surreptitious attempt to proselytize the larger population, to shake up its sclerotic, Piscean, Christian worldview, paving the way for an enlightened Aquarian one, through the use of mysterious symbols with pagan or at least non-Christian significance. The design for the Barbury Castle formation, as by now everyone knew, had virtually been lifted from a seventeenth-century work on alchemy. The key-like appendages bore a resemblance to runic script. The two eggs in a pan were really a plan of the Avebury henge and stone circles. The frogs and fishes employed as a basic motif the *vesica piscis* shape, the 'vessel of the fish', which John Michell had described in *The New View Over Atlantis* as 'that basic figure of sacred geometry and architecture ... [which] represents a state of perfect equilibrium between two equal forces, and in the symbolic vocabulary of the old geometers ... was an image of the interpenetrating worlds of heaven and earth, spirit and matter, and other such complementary elements'.

All right, but who, specifically, was doing it? Who was behind this massive and secret Aquarian Conspiracy? Neither Irving nor the

Dexters knew, but over the next few weeks, the picture seemed to become clearer, thanks largely to Rita Goold.

Rita had recently been confiding in Adrian Dexter with regard to a series of anonymous letters that had followed the initial White Crow letter. Several had been sent to such people as Busty Taylor and Richard Andrews over the summers of 1989 and 1990, and now this summer she was receiving them. Written in the same rhyming verse and in the same hand as the White Crow letter, they continued to pose various obscure riddles:

> A move of Chess. Is it the Queen?
> Whatever, it will Sure be Seen
> A Nightingale is out of Light
> A spinning Top goes out to Fight
>
> Eight silver Coins will play their Hand
> Again I say, Right on the Land
> Another clue: Right up might
> Did you not Understand our Plight?
>
> Every Weight has Bouncing Bomb
> Like Bratton they will make a Song
> Keep your Nose in the Air
> Beware, Beware, of Red Light's Flare

Other letters she had received that summer, probably from the same source, had been of a threatening nature. Most had arrived via the post, but one had been left beneath her car windscreen wipers outside her bed-and-breakfast in Winterbourne Monkton; the message had been written in blood, and apparently had included grotesque sexual innuendoes concerning herself and Terence Meaden, and the caravan at the secret site.

The people we were after, said Rita, were the people who had written those letters. They had written the White Crow letter, and had, presumably, made the noise and the circle that night. They were also, apparently, the same people who had written a series of threatening letters to the occult writer Andrew Collins in the wake of his most recent work, *The Black Alchemist*, which among other things had discussed a Sussex-based group known as the Friends of Hekate.

*

To the ancient Greeks, Hekate (or Hecate, as she is usually spelt) was the great chthonic goddess, combining her underworld attributes (hell-hounds, crone-like appearance, sacrifices performed at crossroads) with attributes of fertility; she was closely associated with Demeter, the Greek counterpart of the Roman grain-goddess Ceres. As such she was fairly close to being an earth-mother birth-death figure, and played much the same role that Isis had for the Egyptians. But alas, the Friends of Hekate did not worship Hekate; instead they worshipped a god better known to the Judeo-Christian world: Satan.

The Friends of Hekate apparently had conducted their black magic rituals in Clapham Wood, a forest near Worthing which by the middle 1980s had begun to develop a certain reputation. Strange lights were often seen there at night. Sulphurous odours were smelt. Dogs and horses would vanish there without trace, and four unexplained human deaths had occurred in the area, including that of Harry Snelling, the retired vicar of Clapham and Pinching, who disappeared on the afternoon of Hallowe'en, 1978, and whose skeletal remains were not found for three years.

Among satanists, it was said, Christian priests made the best ritualists, and the best sacrificial victims. And in fact, a local investigator, Charles Walker, apparently claimed that in a clandestine meeting in the late 1970s an initiate of the group confirmed to him the Friends of Hekate's involvement in the Snelling murder. According to the account in Collins's book, the initiate said more:

'We hold meetings in Clapham Wood every month and dogs or other domestic or farm animals are sacrificed,' the voice revealed. 'It all depends on what is easy to obtain at the time.'

Charles had then remembered the various dog disappearances in the woods. Were any of these connected to their activities?

The response was sharp. 'We have already told you that our cult demands a sacrifice at every meeting. You are very close to a site that has been used.' However the initiate added: 'But if the weather is bad we make other arrangements.'

So how long had the Friends of Hekate used the woods? Charles asked next.

'We have been using this area for ten years and plan to continue using it for another ten,' was the response from the dense undergrowth. 'After which time we will select other areas from which to spread the word. We use Clapham Wood because it is the most convenient for our members and because the atmosphere of the wood is right for our purposes.'

Exactly what *were* their purposes? Charles had queried, feeling that such a question might push his luck a little too far.

The answer came in the form of a stern warning. 'There are people in high places holding positions of power and authority who are directly involved and will tolerate no interference. We will stop at nothing to ensure the safety of our cult.'

Then there was only silence. No further statements came from the concealed initiate, implying that the meeting was now over and that Charles should go.

That had been in late 1978, just after Snelling's disappearance. Nine years later the wood was severely damaged by the memorable hurricane of October 1987, and according to Collins the group moved on to a new, unspecified location. Rita Goold thought she knew where it was: West Woods, a several-square-mile forest south of Lockeridge in Wiltshire. West Woods, it seemed, had everything a modern satanist could want. Though accessible by car it was deep and dark and primeval, with a segment of the pagan Wansdyke snaking through it, and a long barrow near its southern edge. And it was only a few miles from the raw and tremendous energies at Avebury, which a group skilled in ritual magic could tap and control in the same way that hydroelectric engineers could pull power from a great rushing river.

Rita had been somewhat reluctant to tell us this. She said that she had been working on the case for many years, and that there were great dangers here in which she would prefer not to involve us. The Friends of Hekate had money, power, and wide influence. And they would brook neither opposition nor inquiry, because they sincerely believed that they were 'spreading the word' – that is, preparing the way for the coming of the Antichrist.

And she believed that they had come to West Woods. If so, they would have arrived in late 1987 or early 1988 – just before the area had become the world's hotspot for crop circles.

That might only have been a coincidence, but there was also the symbolic imagery of the circles – the vesica shapes, the obvious ritual-magic connotations of the Barbury Castle formation (which we now saw contained numerous geometric references to the number 6). Even the chaos-evoking Mandelbrot Set took on significance. Throughout the eighties, Chaos Theory had been popular among young maths enthusiasts, but it was now also very much in vogue in the occult world. 'Chaos Magic', a term referring to a particularly bizarre and *laissez-faire* style of occult rite, dated back to Aleister Crowley, the notorious ritualist of the early part of the century. 'Chaos' symbols as known to modern mathematicians were now increasingly being co-opted as totems of the Chaos Magic style, and diagrams of Mandelbrot Sets had become a frequent adornment to books on magic, the occult, and paganism.

And there were the sacrifices – and not merely the symbolic ones involving corn dollies and sheaf-cutting. A sheep had reportedly been found near the Barbury Castle formation, its throat slit, and the warden of the Castle had found his flock unusually on the south side of the hill on the morning of the formation, as far away from it as they could get. Rob Irving, Ute Weyer and the Dexters and I also found a dead sheep one night, on a farm road near Alton Barnes; its throat had been slit, and its genitals had been removed with a rough V-shaped incision. And practically everyone had heard the story about the white stallion at Operation Blackbird in 1990, which was said to have been found early one morning entangled in a barbed wire fence, with one ear and its penis missing and a horrific foam coming from its mouth.

Even so, the Friends of Hekate themselves had been somewhat elusive. Rita told me: 'I've tried to research all these years these people who've moved to Avebury – this black magic lot – but I've never found them. Until I came across those people on the Wansdyke.'

It had been on one of the nights of Lord Haddington's watch, back in June of 1990. Rita and her husband Steve had been driving up Milk Hill from Stanton St Bernard. They had, she said, taken a winding side-route, not easily visible from the hill itself. Nor had anyone been expecting them, for that night the plan had been to meet at the Silbury Hill car-park, after dusk. Anyway, near the top their car headlights had suddenly swung across a group of four black-cloaked hooded figures, seated in a circle. As the headlights hit them they clambered to their feet.

Rita and Steve stared at them from the car. The hooded figures stared back. Then one stepped forward, threw back his hood, and with a disarming smile said, 'Oh, helloooo, Rita.'

It was Michael Green.

'These are very good against the cold,' Green allegedly said, indicating his cloak.

The confrontation had passed without further comment. 'I played stupid,' Rita told me. 'But from that time, Michael Green turned funny on me.' After her barn seance at the Wansdyke watch, she said, Green had hugged her, downplaying the talents of Isabelle Kingston and suggesting that Rita's mediumship should be relied upon more often. 'We've got the oil rag when we could have the engine driver,' she said Green told her. Requests for her psychic talents increased. In the spring of 1991, Green phoned and tried to get her to come out to Cambridgeshire, to 'clear' an 'evil spirit' who was guarding a particular field. Rita begged off, assuming it was another subtle attempt at recruitment.

And then, she said, there was the time a wealthy divorcee in Melton Mowbray had phoned her, asking her to remove a sample of dirt from a circle near Leicester and to send it airmail to George de Trafford and his Maltese Esoteric Society. The Pope was coming to Malta and they wanted to be ready for him. An energy-drenched clump of dirt, apparently, would be to the de Traffordians what a ton of Semtex would be to the IRA.

Rita said she had even met de Trafford in person, at the Melton Mowbray woman's house. She and her husband Steve had been invited for dinner, and upon arrival, had been led through a series of rooms and halls – doors locked ominously after them – until they came to a room where George de Trafford and several others sat. De Trafford was in his usual distracted, vibratory mode, unnerving Rita and Steve who, although they had heard the stories about the undead Templar and so on, were witnessing the phenomenon for the first time. Then de Trafford produced an

Aurameter, and leaning over towards Rita, began prodding her with it.

'What are you doing?' demanded Steve.

De Trafford muttered unintelligibly.

Steve grabbed Rita and they left. But de Trafford had apparently been successful in recruiting others. Wingfield and Haddington had flown to Malta in the spring of 1991 to join de Trafford's very exclusive, very secret 'Circles Seven' group. Haddington, according to Rita, had later disparaged it, and had cautioned against too deep an involvement in these areas, but Wingfield, perhaps glad to be distracted from his marital troubles, had returned from Malta full of enthusiasm for his new esoteric pursuits. 'George is very naïve,' Rita told us.

According to Rita, Delgado's odd behaviour might also have had a little help from the de Trafford magic. Shortly after the business of the horseshoe and the Grid, said Rita, she had received a call from Pat's wife Norah, who sweetly explained that an entity known as Zirkka wished to speak to her. Pat had allegedly come on the phone, using a strange mechanical-sounding voice, and had proceeded to harangue her with oblique demands that she get out of circles research. The calls continued for a while until Rita's husband Steve had a serious heart attack, and tactful Zirkka decided to desist.

These were the stories we heard from Rita, but there seemed to be other evidence besides: one day the story went around the Beckhampton Group about the time Stanley and Sue Morcom, two comparatively level-headed group members, had visited Michael Green at his London flat. Green had suggested a little map-dowsing, to determine the locations of next summer's circles. Well ... all right, said the Morcoms uncertainly. They sat down before an ordnance survey map, and Green got out his little crystal pendulum – and for good luck, ha ha, a little female effigy. The Morcoms allegedly made excuses and left.

CCCS was clearly a religious organization, with a decidedly pagan flavour to its conferences and belief systems. A pagan motif was also distinctly evident in the CCCS-associated journal, the *Cerealogist*, which featured on its front cover a dancing satyr — complete with horns, cloven hoofs, an obvious erection, a cut stalk of wheat, and a burning torch (another attribute of Hekate). The figure stood within a crop circle, surrounded by dancing humans. At the edges of the scene were two corn dollies.

The *Cerealogist*'s editor, of course, was John Michell, who in 1989, in *Fortean Times*, had remarked of the crop circles: 'There have been tricks, puns, and red herrings, and these, together with the impish, teasing conduct of the phenomenon towards its investigators, typify the behaviour of Robin Goodfellow, the old English spirit of mischief.' And Robin Goodfellow, of course, sprang from the same satyric source as Old Nick, the devil.

From the late sixties through to the present, Michell had written dozens of books on UFOs, ley-lines, Atlantis, sacred geometry, Glastonbury, megaliths, Druidism, Forteana, and why Britain should resist metrification. These had helped to inspire what is now an enormous and still-growing social movement. And like many of those associated with the New Age, he seemed to have had a difficult relationship with Christianity. In 1977, as the fourth in a series of underground 'Radical Traditionalist Papers', he had written an essay entitled 'To Represent Our Saviour as "That Great Cock" is not Blasphemy but Eternal Christian Orthodoxy'. The essay had been in defence of a poem by James Kirkup, published in *Gay News*, several lines of which had drawn a blasphemy ruling in court. Michell had argued that, far from being blasphemous, Kirkup's sentiment reflected the ancient and true Christian orthodoxy. 'In only one detail does the poet deviate from the most authoritative representations of Jesus Christ: in that he attributes to Our Saviour the possession of a "great cock", whereas, according to the early sources, Jesus did not just have a big cock, he was a big cock.'

As Irving and the Dexters and I reviewed this kind of material, the following hypothesis presented itself. There was a secret satanist organization which called itself the Friends of Hekate. The Friends of Hekate enjoyed covert links with, or controlled, other, overt organizations, 'front' organizations through which it (a) attempted to recruit new members, and (b) attempted generally to undermine orthodox religion, through seemingly innocuous appeals to 'ancient wisdom', etc. The Centre for Crop Circle Studies was apparently one of these front organizations.

The Maltese Esoteric Society, we hypothesized, was another such front organization, with particular value as an apparently unrelated 'third party' through which the deep recruitment of senior crop circles researchers such as Delgado and Andrews and Haddington and Wingfield could take place. If suddenly horrified at what he had got into, the would-be recruit would disparage only the expendable de Traffordians. (Green's venture with the Morcoms, by this reasoning, had been a foolish indiscretion.) But all spokes ended at the same hub – the diabolical Friends of Hekate, which perhaps was itself only another dark spoke leading to another dark hub.

And Rita Goold knew this. And they knew she knew this. And they had attempted to recruit her, to bring her within the fold. And she had resisted. And so, it seemed, they had begun to take other measures.

Some time in the middle of July, according to the official CCCS version of the story, Michael Green had received a telephone call from a Mrs Robinson, a Wiltshire landowner. The woman had complained about a trespasser in one of her fields. Apparently she had confronted the trespasser, a plump, middle-aged woman with electrically frizzy hair, and the trespasser had rudely explained that she was a member of CCCS, entitled to trespass in the name of scientific research.

'That sounds like our Rita,' responded Michael Green, assuring Mrs Robinson that the incident would not be repeated. He had then sent Rita a letter of reprimand, which mysteriously had received a very wide circulation, discrediting her in the eyes of many.

And that, apparently, was only the overt part of the campaign. The covert part included the anonymous letters, the innuendoes in blood. As time went on, Rita began to tell us about other incidents. Her car had been broken into while parked at Alton Barnes, and her address book had been stolen. One morning at home in Leicestershire she had run out after the postman to give him a misdelivered letter, and had badly cut her slippered foot on nails which had been strewn across her front step. Sometimes the harassment came in the form of telekinetic 'psychic attack' – as on the day she found the contents of her wardrobe strewn mysteriously across the room.

*

One night at a hotel bar in Glastonbury, Rob Irving ran into Andy Collins, the author of *The Black Alchemist*. Irving introduced himself as a crop circles enthusiast. Collins too was interested in the circles. Irving mentioned the White Crow letters. Collins had received some similar letters, which he would be glad to show Irving.

At about this time, Irving and Adrian Dexter (Paul Dexter had dropped out of the chase, on the insistence of his pregnant wife) were contacted by George Wingfield, who expressed his desire once and for all to get to the bottom of the White Crow business. He gave Irving and Dexter copies of the first White Crow letter, with the understanding that they, with their subtler connections, would find other copies. Irving and Dexter regarded this offer warily, but were happy to get a copy of the letter. Irving and Dexter then visited Andy Collins at Collins's home in Essex. Collins showed them some of the strange letters he had received, discussed some of the pertinent background, and for Irving and Dexter, the situation suddenly became clear.

For Andy Collins, the story had begun in 1982. He had then been a twenty-five-year-old occult journalist with a self-published book to his credit: *The Sword and the Stone*, an account of 'psychic questing' for buried historical artefacts such as swords and grails. One day he'd received a phone call from a strange woman with an upper-class accent. Presumably acting as a medium, she had channelled over the phone to him a message, in cryptic rhyming verse, which he had duly transcribed. 'Who are you?' Collins had asked the voice. 'We are Shadow,' had come the reply.

The message, among other things, instructed Collins immediately to get in touch with a Leicestershire medium named Rita Goold, whose phone number was provided. Collins hesitated, but within a few minutes the phone rang again. It was Rita Goold. She had just received a strange channelled message over the phone, instructing her to get in touch with Collins.

Thus began the Shadow Quest. It soon became clear that Shadow was not, strictly speaking, a person. It was a group of entities which Rita Goold channelled. Sometimes she would channel messages from them over the phone. Other times she would go into a trance in Collins's presence, and would begin to dictate a Shadow message by ethereally guided 'automatic writing'. On other occasions, one of the Shadow entities would be speaking through her and she would suddenly produce, or 'apport' from the ethereal plane, an already completed letter from Shadow – a typed letter, usually with bad grammar and misspellings.

Since the Shadow entities were interested in psychic questing, the messages usually provided clues to the whereabouts of this or that historical artefact, which Collins, Goold, and occasionally other occult journalists would then set out together to find. The letters would get them close, and subsequently Goold, with her psychic powers, would direct them to the exact spot, where they would discover something which . . . alas, always turned out to be cheap antique-shop stuff.

The Shadow entities included a number of vaguely demonic figures, one of whom, on at least one occasion, appeared to possess Rita, causing her to speak backwards in Latin and produce other unpleasant noises. But always opposing this dark side was the relatively pleasant entity known as Norman, also known as Raymond Lodge.

Raymond Lodge, who died as a soldier in 1917, had been the son of the physicist Sir Oliver Lodge, a contemporary of Einstein's who rejected relativity but embraced spiritualism – even more so after a medium began to channel messages from the deceased Raymond. Lodge had written a lengthy book about the experience, entitled, *Raymond, or Life after Death*.

Sometime in the late 1970s, Rita Goold had somehow discovered her psychic ability, and, giving up her job with the Haymarket Theatre in Leicester, had begun to practise mediumship. One of the first entities she produced at a seance was Raymond Lodge. What was remarkable about Rita's ability in this regard, however, was that to those present, Raymond would not simply be a voice trickling ectoplasmically from the Beyond. Raymond would be there in person, in uniform – six foot four and fifteen stone. Of course it was all done in the dark, but one could touch him, talk to him, ask him difficult questions. Occasionally he would don luminous clothes and move about the room. And soon he was joined by other entities: Albert Schweitzer, the philanthropist; Helen Duncan, a Scottish medium who had perished from the dread ectoplasm-backlash in the 1950s; Russell B—, a nine-year-old who had died in the 1960s and whose parents were frequent visitors to the seances ; and several relatives of Rita Goold, including Laura Lorraine, apparently a young and lovely Edwardian opera singer. In early 1983, an anonymous female caller tipped off journalists at *Psychic News*, and soon the paper's headline read:

MATERIALIZED FIGURES APPEAR AT HOME CIRCLE
Materialized Form Appears in 'Complete Military Uniform'

Somewhere in Staffordshire at the time, another medium was calling forth Raymond Lodge. The other medium, informed of the Rita Goold seances, claimed that Goold's Raymond was an impostor. Goold claimed that the other medium's Raymond was an impostor. The issue was never resolved, but Rita Goold's seances continued and her fame grew.

Most of the seances occurred in the home of Pat and Barry Jeffries, friends of Rita who had, she said later, been instrumental in getting her to become a medium. Records of many of the seances are preserved in post-seance written form (the entities forbade tape-recordings). One account, from a forty-five-year-old Bristol gentleman named Michael, who came to speak with a nineteenth-century relative named James Arthur Findlay, includes the following remarks:

Barry asked me to be very still when Rita went into trance but said that once the people from the unseen universe arrived I could relax and join in the conversation. Barry then put the candle out.

Helen Duncan spoke first. 'Michael you are very welcome, it is a great privilege to have you with us.' She then said some very complimentary remarks about me to assure Barry and Pat that I was perfectly trustworthy . . .

The small table was moved across the room and came to rest very gently against my legs. A young girl's voice said 'Laura'. A hand gently touched my knee. Then Laura broke into a beautiful song, with great feeling. She was standing only about two feet from me. It seemed that she was singing this song especially for me as a newcomer.

Raymond Lodge then put on an illuminous jacket and boots that Barry had also provided ... With one of the drum sticks he hit his body, arms, and legs to show me how solid he was. He then walked back and forward straight through the table.

A voice says 'James Arthur Findlay here, Michael.' He grips me firmly on my left arm.

Laura then came to me and then sang another beautiful love song, holding my hands most of the time, sometimes stroking the backs of my hands. She also kept throwing her dress over my head and pulling it away so that my hair was pulled forward. All the time there was this delightful smell of hyacinths. I have never experienced such a feeling before in my life of overwhelming love ... I fell desperately in love with Laura.

Often, at the end of a seance, or during one of the many intermissions, sitters would discover an apport that the entities had left. This might be some little knick-knack such as a stuffed mouse, or a small plastic Snoopy figure. But sometimes the apport was a letter.

Andy Collins, who attended some of the seances after his involvement with Goold began in 1982, received several such letters, ostensibly from Raymond Lodge. The handwriting of the letters, the archaic system of capitalizations, and the cryptic rhyming verse style were clearly identical with those of the White Crow letters.

After this discovery, which instantly dissolved our Friends of Hekate fantasies, I visited Rita Goold at her home in a small village south of Leicester. As gently as I could – somehow I found her tricksiness endearing – I confronted her with the business of the letters.

She hadn't expected this from me, and for a time she was at a loss for words. But she admitted that the Shadow letters had been similar to the White Crow letters. 'When Colin Andrews showed me that letter I said to Steve, "My God, it's a Shadow letter. What can we do?"' She admitted that the Raymond Lodge letters had also been similar to the Shadow letters. 'I don't know, maybe Shadow is Raymond Lodge.' Then she suggested that Shadow was a group of people, headed by 'an unknown man', which had been formed to combat a resurgence of black magic in England. She denied having written the White Crow letters. She denied having been the mysterious 'Mrs Robinson' who had phoned Michael Green. She denied inventing the threatening letters and phone calls which she had allegedly received. She also defended herself against less imaginable charges. 'I swear,' she said, hand and hanky on a Bible, 'that I did not hoax Barbury Castle.' At one point a decorative iron fireplace instrument, shaped like a pitchfork, fell off the brick wall by the hearth and nearly speared her cat.

I still wonder about that pitchfork.

22

The Circlemakers' Surprise

At Alton Barnes one evening, towards the end of August, a woman and her daughter asked Meaden if he could yet fully explain the crop circles phenomenon. 'Yes,' he replied, 'between six or seven of us, we know everything there is to be known at the time. There are a thousand others who don't know anything.' The 'thousand others' was a reference to CCCS, whose membership total had just gone into four figures. Meaden was supremely confident. His theory had survived another summer, and in the quality press now, he was the reigning expert, while the Delgadonians, with their increasingly obvious supernaturalism, had become little more than a sideshow. And when an article appeared on the leader page of the *Daily Telegraph* in late August, arguing that because it was easy to hoax a circle, all the crop circles were hoaxes, Meaden dismissed it as 'quite an abomination'.

Meaden was nevertheless slightly wistful at the pace the phenomenon had taken. 'It's too bad that we got it all at once,' he said to me. 'It would have been better to have only simple circles for a long time, so that we could have had adequate time to develop a theory for them.' In any case, he was glad that the summer was over. He could rest at last, and think about the shapes that the latest season had brought. First he would spend several weeks at his country house in France. He felt that he owed it to his wife, after his long and frantic summer in the public eye.

Just before he went to France, Meaden gave another interview to Juniper, in his spartan office over the garage in Bradford-on-Avon. The producer, Jill, asked him about a series of crop circles which Meaden had previously observed at Clench Common near Pewsey. Meaden enthusiastically pronounced them genuine:

> The circle formation on Martin Pitt's land consists of simple, round circles, which pleased me very much to see, because they were so typical of the ones I've been looking at all these years. They didn't have those complex strange shapes which so many other systems have had, this year and last year. But in detail, they had a lot of complex structure, a kind of petal effect, a braiding, a plaiting, and a layering, which showed the difficulty which any hoaxer would have, to manage to contrive to follow, if he wished to copy it. In fact it was a system that was too hard to copy, and yet was of a simple variety nevertheless. Genuine in every way.

Subsequently Jill informed Meaden that the formation on Martin Pitt's land was in fact a hoax that had been perpetrated for Juniper by the Wessex Skeptics, with Martin Pitt's permission. It had been the one Jill had referred to obliquely within my earshot, that day at Bishops Cannings.

In his response to this news, later broadcast by Channel Four Meaden struggled to remain composed, and slowly leaned forward - in pain, or as if unsure he had heard Jill correctly:

> So ... you are telling me ... that ... the circles on Martin Pitt's farm ... are hoaxed circles made by the Wessex Skeptics ... I have to admit that some people, at least, if they are scientifically trained, are capable of perpetrating at least one hoax. That does not, however, negate all of the positive evidence which has been gathered over the past ten years in favour of genuine circles ...
>
> When a scientific theory is complete then it would be possible to distinguish between hoaxed circles and genuine circles. But we're not yet quite at that stage. The theory is undergoing development, and modification according to the incoming data.

Busty Taylor also had been caught out by the Wessex Skeptics over the Clench Common circles. He apparently had dowsed them successfully, saying, 'We have a really complex one here. It's absolutely amazing what this is telling us here . . . it's really a cracker.' When informed that the formation was a hoax, he was distraught, although when Juniper did eventually film his response, he seemed to shrug off the matter:

> Owing to the fact that we are producing books, with photography showing the lay of the corn, it would be possible for individuals to go out and recreate circles. It isn't off the cards. It's on the cards. That is highly possible. But not all of them. No way, too many. Seven hundred and fifty in Beckhampton last year – that's a lot of work. All night. Worldwide? How do they do that? It's just one of those things. I regret it. The farmers definitely regret it. And I just wish [the hoaxers] would come to their senses and realize it is a waste of time.

The same defiant confidence shone from Glastonbury on the weekend of 7 September, when John Michell hosted the *Cerealogist*'s First Annual 'Cornference'. The price of admission was a steep £30, but with the understandable exception of the Meadenites, everyone who was anyone on the crop circles scene turned up, along with the usual Glastonbury crowd. For most of the lectures, there was standing room only.

The Cornference stage was draped grandly with white and yellow banners depicting pictograms, and the stone-walled hall was lined with tables displaying everything from mandalas to crystals to manuals on crop circles dowsing to massive monographs on the coming of the flying saucers.

Pat Delgado and Colin Andrews, the grand old men of supernatural cerealogy, were undoubtedly the early stars of the show. In a beatific gesture, they offered to heal the rift between CPR and the rest of the supernatural camp by working, from now on, with CCCS. Michael Green, in response, eloquently praised Delgado's and Andrews's years of work, and offered them platforms at CCCS lectures, and space to write in the *Circular* – a monthly that in the wake of a split between Green and Michell had supplanted the *Cerealogist* as the official CCCS journal. 'It is my intuition, here,' said Green, 'that if we work as a team . . . working together, we will get a positive response from the crop circle makers themselves.'

Whether or not that would be the case, it was clear that Delgado and Andrews no longer had any reason not to join CCCS. Financially, they had everything to gain from CCCS's organizational power – its journals, its lectures, its built-in market for books and videotapes. And ideologically, they fitted right in, having in the past two years managed to conform their message to the careful blend of Aquarian hope and eco-apocalypticism to which New Age audiences seem particularly receptive.

Andrews, mindful of the recent Juniper revelations, began by exhorting the audience, 'Hold your ground . . . Because even if the world hasn't yet awoken, you are at the dawn of a new era. We are at the beginning of a very very important period, where I believe time is going to appear to stand still . . . England is the New Jerusalem, in many ways.' Later, he switched to the apocalyptic theme, insisting that 'This planet is in very severe trouble. You can ignore that at your peril. Our planet is dying . . . What you are looking at is the reaction of a planet in very severe trouble . . . The Hopi Indians have said this. Mother is crying. *Mother . . . is . . . crying . . .*'

Delgado noted that some of the pictograms resembled dolphins, and remarked that it might be a warning about the dolphins dying in the seas because of pollution. Then he brought up the matter of the higher intelligence. '*We* don't take the initiative,' he claimed. 'The subject takes the initiative . . . It is always one jump ahead of our thinking and our predictions. It's probably even more than that – it's programmed two or three jumps ahead of us . . . This energy is controlled by some high level of intelligence. This intelligence controls everything else, including us . . . this subject has evolved, and drawn us along, like the pied piper, or like throwing crumbs in front of ducks at the poolside, and they're all going after them.'

Delgado and Andrews seemed to get along well on stage, although there were occasional hints of discord, or at least jostling for position. Delgado opened his remarks, in fact, by implying his priority over Andrews: 'I would just like to say, as the founder member of this subject in the early eighties, I was a very lonely man. Because at that time I had very great difficulty in even getting one or two people to take some interest in this subject.' Andrews, for his part, interrupted Delgado half a dozen times – once when Delgado started to discuss his healing ministry, and at least three times when Delgado, pointing to a photograph on the screen, began casually to note the presence of the little 'signature' circles . . . which seemed to accompany a strikingly large percentage of pictograms, implying a common authorship.

Delgado and Andrews agreed on one thing, however, and that was that the Juniper sting had been most unfortunate. 'This hoax,' said Delgado, 'that was sickeningly perpetrated with one purpose in mind – and that's to make somebody [Terence Meaden] look a fool – even if they are endeavouring to prove something – which, no way will they be able to find a conclusion – I felt so sorry, and I put myself in his shoes, that, the day before yesterday, I tried to phone him – he's on holiday. I spoke to his secretary, I said, "I don't know if you know me, I'm Pat Delgado." She said, "Yes, I know you very well, because of what was going on between you and Terence." I said, "Well, on this occasion, I want you to pass on to him my sympathy, that he is a victim of this vicious and unfunny hoax." And she couldn't believe what she was hearing, coming from me. But I was sincere. I felt very emotional about it.'

That Busty Taylor had been duped by the same hoax was not mentioned, although when it was Taylor's turn on the stage, he did refer to it obscurely: 'Unfortunately, later on this year, you'll see something on television which is embarrassing.'

Taylor and Richard Andrews did their own slide show of the 1991 circles, and talked about their upcoming lecture tour of nine US cities, which would start in Fort Collins, Colorado, where a colloquium or symposium on New Science was being held. 'We're going to give them the facts,' said Richard, who later, from the stage, dowsed the audience, walking from right to left as his rods moved out, then in, denoting the boundaries of an energy line that ran straight down the central aisle. He asked us all to meditate for a moment, suggesting that if we were sufficiently spiritual, our collective energy-line would widen. It did, as Richard demonstrated, to gasps and applause. 'That's what prayer is all about,' said Richard. Later he said that although it might regrettably curtail some of the public's ability to participate in the phenomenon, he hoped that next year only experts such as himself would be allowed into crop circles, to facilitate scientific research.

John Michell discussed the sacred geometry and symbolism of the Barbury Castle formation, relating its proportions to those of the earth and moon. Michael Green gave a lecture entitled 'Breaking the Code of the Agriglyphs', in which he established a connection between the Agriglyphs – or pictograms – and petroglyphs from South America and Atlantis. He said that the Barbury Castle formation was merely the two-dimensional imprint of an incoming beam of energy – 'like a three-pronged plug'. A handsome white-haired woman named Delphine Starr delivered a comparatively bland lecture on behalf of the absent, indisposed George de Trafford. A London correspondent for the German newspaper *Die Zeit*, Jürgen Krönig, gave a talk entitled 'Mass Phenomena and the Interests of the State', and spoke darkly of ministerial meetings and disinformation.

In fact, everyone seemed to be worrying about disinformation. Andrews insisted that there was 'a high level of disinformation coming from the British media'. Delgado described the Juniper hoax as having been perpetrated by 'the dirty tricks department'. It was George Wingfield, however, who spun the most elaborate conspiracy theories, describing the piece in the *Daily Telegraph*, which had been authored by the nephew of Nicholas Ridley, as 'just one instance of disinformation by HM Government'. Wingfield also alluded to 'the gentlemen from MI5 who are with us today', and an apparent spy within the CCCS ranks: 'Earlier this year, I was told that a certain circles researcher was working for the government. I will not name this person.' Wingfield explained that he had not initially believed the story, but that subsequent events had 'served to confirm' it.*

*Apparently the alleged spy in question was Rita Goold. The story Wingfield told privately was that a Catholic priest from Norfolk had contacted him, claiming to have heard Rita describe her espionage activities to him in the confessional. When pressed about his source, Wingfield said that he had been

Everyone also seemed to be talking about changes in consciousness, and the crop circles as a prerequisite, or a catalyst, or a stimulus, or a by-product, of this change. The flip side of this sentiment was a certain ambivalence towards the idea of hoaxing. Crop circles were only important in so far as they affected human consciousness. It didn't particularly matter how they were made. Richard Andrews referred to hoaxers as 'those who are so impatient that they go out and make them on their own'. Michael Glickman, a London-based inventor, suggested that we should merely 'Enjoy . . . and leave a thank-you note in the fields'. It often seemed as if some kind of half-baked Aquarian Conspiracy were under way after all.

The conference was harmonious, even oppressively so, but there were a few glitches. During a panel discussion, someone noted from the audience that the energies of the Barbury Castle formation had 'gone negative', and that a dead sheep had been found nearby, apparently the victim of a black magic sacrifice. Richard Andrews tried to get rid of the microphone, but eventually addressed the point: 'Once a good thing gets going, it shows how it can, as it were, develop an opposition . . . Everything that is magnificent, something will try to drag it down. Never take anything for granted.' Someone also pointed out that each pictogram had a narrow underlying layer of swept stalks leading from the nearest tramline to the centre of the formation. The clear implication was that this was how tiptoeing hoaxers began their artwork. Wingfield fielded it neatly, though, saying, 'Yes, we see this quite often. We're not quite sure what it is.'

At one point a New Age Traveller, dirt-smeared and with long scratches on his face, stood and began to exclaim loudly to the effect that CCCS was bogus, a massive con, that crop circles were simply made by people. He continued in this vein until he could no longer stand the amassed indignation of the crowd – an almost palpable thing, though no one touched him – and he walked out. I followed him into the fresh air and blinding sunlight, and he

---

meaning to track down the priest, but hadn't yet had the time. Alternatively, it is possible that Wingfield's Cornference reference was to Terence Meaden, whose activities on behalf of MI5 were also widely alleged as the only plausible explanation of his faith in the plasma vortex theory.

explained to me, in an increasingly mad rant, that he knew people, other New Age Travellers, 'The Convoy', who practised white magic and black magic and made crop circles – some by walking in circles, and some, he thought, by magic. They read old books on the Celts, on alchemy, on sacred geometry, to get the designs. They went up to the Glastonbury Tor at night. Sometimes they stayed at Gordano Services on the M5. Sometimes they made circles near Avebury. He himself had been oppressed by these people. Jürgen Krönig followed us outside, and began to interrupt my questions with his own, uttered so fast, and in such a rapid-fire manner, that the poor Traveller was quickly disorientated. Then a fellow named Graham, a maths teacher from Frome who had earlier said that Chaos Theory should be put on the secondary school curriculum, approached us angrily, his features working, and warned me, a journalist, to 'give equal space to the other side's point of view'.

Such incidents were quickly forgotten and the Cornference seemed to fade serenely into the Sunday afternoon. Wingfield took several people home to Shepton Mallet with him for drinks, including Michael Green; and an attractive young couple from Oxfordshire who marketed crop circle T-shirts; and Shauna Crockett-Burroughs, the editor of *Global Link-Up* magazine. They sat in the Wingfields' backyard and talked and drank and joked. It had been a fine day, and a fine weekend, and a fine summer. A new book would be coming out soon from Alick Bartholomew's Gateway Press, *Crop Circles: Harbingers of World Change*, to which Wingfield had contributed two articles, 'Towards an Understanding of the Nature of the Circles', and 'The Circles Spread Worldwide'. Other articles, by such people as Michael Green and Lucy Pringle, were about such things as 'The Language of the Circlemakers', and 'The Voice of the Earth', and 'Nature's Timely Intervention'. It was certain to be a success. The first CCCS book, *The Crop Circle Enigma*, had already sold close to 50,000 copies to British, American, and especially German circles enthusiasts.

As the sun set and the stars came out, Wingfield showed his guests a letter he had received from the Prime Minister, John Major, although he concealed its contents. The implication seemed to be that it was a letter of encouragement. By now it was well known, though spoken of only discreetly, that Delgado and Andrews often received such letters from enlightened authorities, such as the Queen, the Duke of Edinburgh, and of course the Prince of Wales.

Wingfield and his guests had been drinking and talking for about an hour when the phone rang. Gloria Wingfield went in and answered the phone, and came outside again saying it was Pat Delgado, asking for George. He had sounded very strange, said Gloria. His voice had seemed 'mechanical', as if it were coming through some kind of electronic voice-changer. George went in and took the call. After a moment he asked Green to join him inside. When the call had finished, they came outside again, and conferred on the lawn, out of earshot of the others, and away from any possible government listening devices in the house. Green seemed very concerned. Finally they came over and explained to everyone what had happened. Apparently Delgado had been very nervous about something, and had insisted, without elaboration, that they all meet secretly at a hotel in Winchester the following Tuesday night. It was all very strange. The phone rang again and it was Lord Haddington, ringing from Scotland. Delgado had phoned him with the same message: meet at this hotel in Winchester on Tuesday night. No one knew what was going on.

More drinks were poured. The conversation resumed. Wingfield quipped that they would all come back from Winchester with government-performed lobotomies, as plasma vortex-believing Meadenites. It was a variant of a joke he had just used at the Cornference, but everyone laughed anyway, grateful for the comic relief. After another hour or so, the party broke up. Wingfield, Green and Gloria went out to dinner. They returned home just before Colin Andrews phoned and broke the awful news.

I heard the news at eight o'clock the next morning, on BBC Radio Four. The announcer blandly reported that, according to a story in the tabloid newspaper *Today*, two men from Southampton, Mr Doug Bower and Mr Dave Chorley, were claiming responsibility for the crop circles phenomenon, and had been making circles in English fields since 1978.

It sounded as if these two men were claiming all of the crop circles over the past decade, which was about as plausible as the notion that Santa Claus could distribute, in one night, toys to every child on earth. The *Today* story, and the buzzing crop circles grapevine, made things only a little clearer. The two men, both in their sixties, had apparently dreamed up the idea as a prank in 1978, and had started swirling simple circles with an iron bar near Cheesefoot Head, eventually spreading to other areas of Hampshire and Wiltshire. They claimed to have made all of the circles in the early years, and then a decreasing proportion of the total as other hoaxers began to imitate their work. But they had remained innovative to the end. A *Today* photograph showed them in Doug Bower's picture-framing shop in Southampton (both men were artists) with a paper cut-out of an insectogram.

Bower and Chorley had apparently made an insectogram for *Today* the previous week, in a field at Sevenoaks, Kent. *Today* had then called in Pat Delgado, who after inserting audio probes into the ground inside it, had pronounced it genuine, declaring, 'In no way could this be a hoax; no human could have done this,' and adding, with perverse prescience: 'This is without doubt the most wonderful moment of my research.'

The *Today* reporter, Graham Brough, then brought Bower and Chorley to Delgado's home on Sunday afternoon. Delgado, who had just arrived back from the Cornference, greeted them warmly, recognizing Bower and Chorley as circles enthusiasts he had often seen at Cheesefoot Head, or having a pint at the Percy Hobbs pub nearby. Brough, Bower, Chorley, and the *Today* photographer were ushered in, and were given tea by Pat's wife Norah. They then explained the situation, in a manner convincing enough to elicit the following comments from Delgado:

We have all been conned. Thousands of lives are going to be wrecked over this.

What does make me upset is the thousands of people whose lives are going to be shattered because of this, if everything you say is true. I'll look a fool.

I admire your courage for coming forward. I find this quite hilarious really. It's quite a relief it is all over.

You've done so much good in this world. You have brought millions of people together over this.

Thousands have said that the corn circles have changed their lives. You're going to upset an awful lot of lives by blowing this now. Couldn't you just tail it off with a couple more next year?

On the moral side, you have caused a considerable amount of trouble for the police and the Army.

My reaction is one of wonderment at the artistry that they have done in such a manner that their work could be considered as something out of this world.

They have to be admired in the way they have conducted their nocturnal escapades which made it look as though there was a real intelligence that we don't understand. From this simple prank has developed one of the most sensational unifying situations since biblical days.

If everything they say is correct this is a lesson to us all that we should look and listen to the beautiful and small things in life.

We have all learned one of the greatest lessons of our lives because of the actions of two country lads who started this off as a joke.

At one point in the meeting, Delgado's daughter Jan intervened, saying, 'I think we'd better get Colin Andrews.' She phoned Andrews, who arrived shortly thereafter, reportedly delayed by a speeding ticket. 'Sit down,' a shaken Delgado told him. 'This is bad news. This is 100 per cent bad news.' Yet Andrews refused to give in as easily as Delgado had, and in fact reprimanded Delgado for apparently having swallowed the two hoaxers' tale. 'Do you realize what you've said, Pat?'

To Graham Brough's questions, Andrews responded stiffly, 'Pat has accepted that the phenomenon is over.'

By the next afternoon, when Bower and Chorley made another insectogram for the international press in an overripe field at Chilgrove in Sussex, the counter-attack had begun. Andrews and Delgado arrived after the formation had been completed (apparently having got lost on the way), and traipsed through it briefly, avoiding Bower and Chorley altogether. 'Straight away,' Andrews told the waiting press, 'we saw everything we would expect to see in a hoax. The plants were broken. It is extremely ragged and obviously a fake. There is nothing here to impress us at all except two very fit sixty-year-olds.' Delgado, after his bucking-up by Andrews, was now also defiant. 'Yesterday there were circles discovered on a prairie in Canada. Have these guys been out there?'

Meaden, too, joined the battle, speaking to reporters from his vacation house in France. He invoked old historical accounts, such as the Hertfordshire Mowing Devil, and modern eyewitness cases, such as the Tomlinsons', to suggest that Bower and Chorley had not ended the mystery. His comment to the *Daily Star* was typical:

> To suggest these two men have done them all is nonsense. We have realized for some time that there were hoaxes going on and there were more than ever before this year. These two men clearly made the shape last week and I dare say they made a few last summer and a few last year and they could have done a few earlier than that. But other people have come up with this sort of claim over the years.

Meaden, like everyone else on the crop circles scene, had strong suspicions regarding Bower and Chorley. Although the *Today* story had included the declaration: '*Today* has paid no money', no one believed it. *Today* has paid no money to whom? And what if Bower and Chorley were paid off later? 'It can be one thing,' Meaden told me, 'to say you haven't got any money, when it [really] means you'll get paid by cheque on a monthly basis.'

It was assumed by most circles enthusiasts that Bower and Chorley had invented, or had at least exaggerated their claims, and had then sold them to a gullible tabloid. A rumour then began to circulate that Bower and Chorley had embarked on a long and lucrative world lecture tour, including an extended sojourn in the USA, where they would, of course, completely disrupt Busty and Richard's own planned visit.

After a few weeks, Meaden softened his views on Bower and Chorley, admitting that their claims, which were not so grand as the *Today* story had made them seem, were probably genuine. He eliminated from the scope of his theory most of the formations he had studied over the previous decade, telling Juniper:

> We are now quite certain that all the most complex systems, the pictograms, are definitely fakes – because these are the very systems, the complex systems, which were always going to be difficult for a scientific theory to grapple with. We are really only left with the simple circle cases, as being those which are likely to be quite genuine.

But for the Delgadonians to relinquish the pictograms would be suicidal. CPR and CCCS fought on. Wingfield began to suggest that Bower and Chorley were outright crooks. They had, he told me, apparently been prosecuted 'on some charge involving fraud three years ago'. According to the story, the prosecution had occurred in Brighton, had made the evening news, and had somehow involved a Dutch brewery, Grolsch. It was also alleged that Chorley had had a hush-hush job with the military. Eventually, it was declared by Wingfield, Green, Andrews, Delgado, and just about the entire Delgadonian network, that Bower and Chorley were agents in a government disinformation campaign – the campaign that had begun with the Operation Blackbird hoax and was now aiming for a knockout blow.

The clue, they believed, was in the first *Today* story, the one which had appeared on Monday the 9th. At the very end of the piece, after '*Today* has paid no money', was a copyright symbol and the words 'MBF Services'. This suggested that MBF Services was a news agency which had sold the story to *Today*. Wingfield had friends in MI5, he said, who informed him that setting up a front news agency to sell phoney stories was a classic disinformation technique. The faithful at the Waggon and Horses were told that *Today* had flagging circulation, and scoop-hungry editors who wouldn't look too closely at a story. It had obviously been 'targeted', as Jürgen Krönig told me. Wingfield persuaded a friend, a Nottinghamshire man of Middle Eastern extraction who was variously known as 'Henry Azadehdel', or 'Dr Armen Victorian', or 'Dr Alan Jones', to phone *Today* and find out about MBF Services.* One of

---

*The *Independent* of 22 August 1992 reported: 'The most famous success

Today's editors, Lloyd Turner, fielded the call, and suggested vaguely that MBF was an agency that *Today* used from time to time, but refused to give out MBF's address. Azadehdel somehow came up with an address in Somerset, which turned out to be that of a scientific and technical consultancy, based on a farm, Maiden Beech Farm, on the outskirts of the small town of Crewkerne.

Wingfield, Haddington, and some other CCCS members reconnoitred the place. It seemed suspicious. Next Jürgen Krönig drove down, and reported back that the owner of MBF Services, a Dr Andrew C——, had not been home. At this point I decided to have a look for myself, driving down to Maiden Beech Farm one afternoon in early October. It was a sprawling place, fairly ordinary as far as I could tell. I pulled up in front of the new-looking brick Manor House, approached the open door, and was howled at by dogs before a striking blonde in pink riding breeches appeared and shooed them away. Her name was Shan. She was Dr C——'s wife. Dr C—— was not at home. Briefly, I described the allegations of a link between the crop circles story in *Today* newspaper and a news agency known as MBF Services. 'Oh, yes,' she said, with languid amusement, 'some German was here asking the same thing. I really don't understand what this is all about.' She and her husband, she

---

Customs and Kew [Gardens] had against the [rare plant] traders was in 1989 with the prosecution of Henry Azadehdel, a Soviet Armenian insurance salesman living in Britain. In his search for plants to feed a lucrative demand among collectors in the West, Azadehdel found the habitat of the rare *Paphiopedilum rothschildianum* – Rothschild's Slipper Orchid – on the slopes of Mt Kinabalu in Borneo. He ravaged the crop and went on to find the location of several other species, discovering a new one as he did so. He made no secret of his activities and after an international police investigation, which cost the taxpayer around £30,000, was caught ... He pleaded guilty and was sentenced, for the first time, to a prison term. Conservationists were delighted. But on appeal, his sentence was suspended. Mr Azadehdel's whereabouts are unknown but at the time of his release after six weeks in Pentonville prison he said he would continue "the quest for new species of orchids".'

In a meeting at the London kickoff of the *Harbingers* book in late 1991, Wingfield mentioned that Azadehdel was working for him. Ralph Noyes threw up his hands at the mention of the name, shaking his head in pained exasperation. Rob Irving, who was present, remembers that Wingfield replied: 'Sometimes you have to make a pact with the devil.'

said, were directors of an engineering firm known as MBF Consultancy, which was named after the farm. They had nothing to do with news agencies, nor with crop circles.

I believed her, but Wingfield apparently didn't. In lectures and radio talk shows around the world, and in articles in *Flying Saucer Review*, the *Cerealogist*, and the *Circular*, he began to detail the government conspiracy, alleging that MBF Consultancy was a suspicious organization, and that Dr C—— performed work of a defence-related nature for the government. But as time went by, Wingfield admitted privately to associates that the waters were murky in this case, and suggested that the investigation of MBF Consultancy was temporarily at a dead end.

The last I heard of the case, Wingfield was on the trail of an MBF rubber stamp manufacturer, somewhere in Scotland.

23

Doug and Dave

Who can say where something begins? All we know is that one day around about 1968, Dave Chorley walked into Doug Bower's modest picture-framing shop in Southampton. Bower had just bought the shop, and Chorley had come to pick up a painting he had left with the previous owner. Chorley was an artist in his spare time. Bower, who was also an artist, praised Chorley's work, and after a while the two began to discuss art in general. Bower, who had recently returned with his wife from an eight-year stay in Australia, had few friends in the area, and suggested that Chorley meet him now and then for a pint, and to talk about painting. They have been meeting every Friday night for a pint – or two, or three – ever since.

Bower and Chorley were a little like the symbiotic Felix and Oscar of the *Odd Couple* film. Bower was thin and fastidious, always planning ahead, always a little nervous. Chorley, an electrician and a former dockworker, was tough-looking, terse, careless, and ironic to the point of cynicism; any exuberance he cloaked in a perpetual cloud of cigarette smoke.

Of course, they wouldn't restrict their pub discussion solely to painting. Sometimes their conversations would veer into photography, or wildlife sound recording, or the war, or current affairs, or . . . strange phenomena. Doug was particularly interested in UFOs. Ever since his younger days, in the late 1940s and early 50s, when the UFO mystery had first become popular, he had assumed that somewhere, among the hundreds of trillions of other solar systems out there, a higher intelligence existed. He had hoped that some day, before he died, its representatives would descend to earth overtly, unambiguously, and make themselves and their purpose known. But as time went by and he grew older, he masked his hope within a jovial scepticism.

One summer evening in the mid-1970s,* after several customary pints at their customary country pub, the Percy Hobbs, Bower and Chorley were taking the air on a bridle path on Longwood Estate, near Cheesefoot Head. They were talking about UFOs. The Warminster Thing had some life in it yet, and occasional reports of sightings still reached the tabloids and local papers which Bower and Chorley read. Bower now also recalled a case which he and his wife had read about when they were living in Melbourne, in early 1966. A tractor driver in Tully, north Queensland, had reportedly seen a flying saucer ascending from a nest of swirled marsh-grass.

'What do you think would happen if we put a nest over there?' Bower joked to Chorley, pointing to a nearby wheatfield. 'People would think a flying saucer had landed.'

Chorley liked the idea – the two often pulled pranks like this – and the next week, after a few extra pints to stoke their courage, they walked out to the field with a heavy steel bar that Bower used to latch the rear door of his shop. They walked into the field along a tractor path, and then into the virgin wheat, leaving a narrow trail. At a certain point they planted one end of the bar, and pivoting around that point with the rest of the bar, swept out a small circle, shifting the bar out and sweeping around again to enlarge the radius. They both held the bar, and worked on their hands and knees, occasionally popping their heads above the wheat to see if anyone had detected them. No one had, and in a half-hour or so they finished a thirty-foot diameter circle, with neat flat swirls, a precise perimeter, and their entrance trail concealed beneath the laid stalks. In the car home, they were exultant. There was something about it, something about being out in a field at night, under the stars, making something in secret . . . It was no more than

*Bower and Chorley did not keep records of their circle-making activities, but Chorley now remembers that their first circles were done when his son was still at school, which, he says, would have made their first circlemaking summer 1975 or 1976, rather than 1978 as first repoorted.

an adolescent lark, a practical joke, and yet their delight seemed ineffable somehow, ancient, ageless: the pride of the creator, mingled with the pride of the spy.

They made a dozen or so circles that first summer, around Cheesefoot Head and near Headbourne Worthy.* They made a few the next summer, too, and the next summer, and the next. But no one seemed to notice. There was never any mention in the papers, nor on the television. By the end of the summer of 1979, the two men were on the verge of giving up circlemaking.

Then in the months before the summer of 1980, they decided to use a different approach. The iron bar method was too exhausting, and caused excessive damage to the stalks. They would instead use planks, each about four feet long, and tied with rope at each end to enable them to walk upright, holding the plank beneath their feet and swishing down a four-foot swathe with each step. They could work much faster now, and longer, for the planks were comparatively light.

They now also decided to make circles only where people could easily see them, and where people would naturally associate them with UFOs. The area beneath the Westbury white horse, a few miles north of Warminster, seemed the ideal spot. One night in May they drove up from Southampton, parked amid young lovers' cars at Bratton Castle atop the hill, crept over the earthworks and down the escarpment past the chalk horse, and entered the fields. It took them only a few minutes to make the first circle in Geoff Cooper's wheat, and they raced back to the car. 'It was like a commando raid,' Dave remembers. In July they placed two more circles beneath the white horse, in John Scull's oatfield, and several more in wheatfields beneath Cley Hill in Warminster.

Strangely enough, the two men never knew it when the *Wiltshire Times* story broke. They read only the London tabloids, and the local Southampton papers. It was only the next year, when with what might have been their last effort they swirled the three-in-line triplet in the Punchbowl, that they saw their work in print. And in

---

*Colin Andrews later claimed, on the basis of a farmhand's testimony, that the Headbourne Worthy circles of 1978 formed a quintuplet, but Bower and Chorley insist that they began making quintuplets only several years later.

1983, when they devised the quintuplets – 'to make it look like a four-legged spaceship had landed,' Doug says simply – their work became internationally, though anonymously, famous.

Secret celebrity didn't seem to faze Dave, but it made Doug as nervous as ever. On Friday afternoons, he would scarcely be able to work, his anticipation would be so great. And when, after a few pints at the Percy Hobbs, or wherever, he finally reached the chosen field, his anxiety could sometimes reach down to his bowels. He had to start bringing toilet paper out to the fields with him.

But Doug also was organized, and he devised a simple method for making the quintuplets. He and Dave would swirl a main circle first, then set a small crosspiece of wood in the centre. Dave would tie one end of a string to the crosspiece, and Doug would hold the other end, walking in a narrow arc through the stalks outside the main circle, starting at a tramline. Dave would sit in the middle of the central circle, watching the string and the crosspiece. When the string became parallel to a leg of the crosspiece, Dave would shine a tiny red flashlight at Doug, who would stop, unsling his stalk-stomping plank, and swirl a satellite circle, continuing on until he had moved through another 90 degrees and Dave shone the light again, and so on until four satellites had been laid down. It generally took about half an hour. Most of their time was spent driving out to the site, and walking to and from the car, which was often parked a mile or so away, to avoid suspicion.

The suspicion of Doug's wife Ilene was not so easily avoided. She began to notice the heavy mileage on the car, and one day in the summer of 1984, she confronted her husband. There was another woman, wasn't there? She imagined that Dave might have had something to do with it. Despite his age, Dave was always running around chasing women. He was a bad influence on a married man.

Doug realized that the time had come to divulge the secret to his wife. He sat her down, showed her his album of corn circle press clippings, explained to her that he and Dave were the ones making the circles, the circles everyone had read about in the papers, and had seen on television. Yes, he and Dave were the ones. That was where they went on Friday nights. They had hoped to keep it a secret, but . . . well, now she knew.

She didn't believe a word of it.

Doug was taken aback by this, but eventually he brought her into the back room of the shop, and showed her the paraphernalia that he and Dave had accumulated: the crosspiece, and the stalk-stompers, and the string, and the little flashlight, and the detailed maps, and the step-by-step diagrams, often drawn lovingly in watercolours – with the number and direction of rotations noted, and the positions of the nearest tramlines.

Ilene still wasn't convinced, so the next Friday night, Doug and Dave brought her along, and she waited in the car on some lonely country road while the two men, laden with planks and ropes, went off to make a circle in the darkness. The following Sunday, they drove out to admire their handiwork, and at last Ilene believed.

By 1986, Doug and Dave had become familiar with the otherworldly theories of Pat Delgado. It gave them no end of pride and amusement to hear him refer to their creations as the work of a 'higher intelligence'. That was what they had wanted all along. And to be fair to Delgado, he did at least recognize that there *was* an intelligence at work. The meteorologist Terence Meaden, on the other hand, thought that whirlwinds were to blame, not only for the simple circles, but for the triplet in the Punchbowl in 1981, and the quintuplets they had made since 1983. This was the last thing they had expected – to have their work, their careful artistry, attributed to a non-intelligent, meteorological mechanism.

They decided to teach Meaden a lesson, by making a formation that his theory couldn't possibly digest. One night they crept down into the Punchbowl, and after they had swirled a simple clockwise circle, Doug hurdled into the wheat beyond the perimeter. He unslung his stalk-stomper, and swirled an anti-clockwise concentric ring. It was the first ringed crop circle, and naturally it caused a sensation, baffling even Meaden for several years.

Doug and Dave also decided to oblige the enthusiasm of the Delgadonians with a strange creation at Wantage. They made a circle with a ring, and then a 'runway' jutting out from the ring, at the end of which they dug a small hole, as if aliens had landed and then had taken samples. That Colin Andrews could somehow conjure a poltergeist out of that hole hadn't occurred to them in their wildest dreams.

The years went by, and Doug and Dave increasingly spread their creations around the week; it had been too obvious, they felt, when the circles appeared only on Saturday mornings. On the other hand, Saturday had been convenient. People would go out for their Saturday drives, and would see the circles, and would stop their cars to gawp and take photographs, and crowds would gather, and someone would always call the newspapers or the television stations. Sometimes Doug and Dave would go out on weekend afternoons themselves, to admire their works in the light of day, and mingle with the crowds, and feign innocence, asking people what they thought was making the circles, biting their tongues to keep from laughing at the answers. Eventually they became regulars around Cheesefood Head, and became well known to Delgado and Andrews and Taylor and Tuersley – to whom they were merely two old-timers enthusiastic about circles, so much so that they would occasionally assist in photography, or measurement, or in evaluation of the swirl patterns . . . Oh yes, Doug and Dave had a grand old time for themselves.

Dave didn't take it all as seriously as Doug did, however, and as their secret celebrity mounted, this personality difference created an increasing strain. On Christmas Eve, 1988, Dave failed to pay his customary visit to Doug's picture-framing shop, and the two broke off relations. When the summer of 1989 began, Doug was on his own, putting several small circles and ringed circles in the fields of Longwood Estate. And when Operation White Crow came along, he knew he couldn't resist. He drove up to Cheesefoot Head on the last night of the operation, at about eleven thirty, and leaving Ilene in the car at the Cheesefoot Head car-park, simply walked a few hundred yards up the A272 to the bridle path, entered a field beyond the surveillance caravan and his earlier circles, and swirled a new ringed circle. He and Ilene were on the road back to Southampton before Andrews and the others left the caravan for their seance. The 'trilling noise', when he heard of it later, he recognized as the song of the grasshopper warbler, a nocturnal, field-dwelling bird whose call has a peculiar, piercing, ventriloquial quality.

Some weeks later, after doing four more circles on his own, and feeling increasingly lonely, Doug decided to try to make it up with

Dave. But since Dave lived on the south side of the city, was often not at home, and had no telephone, it took Doug a month to find him. After some initial embarassment, they shook hands and renewed their friendship. They celebrated with the weird, quadranted circle at Winterbourne Stoke. Dave had had too much to drink that night, and spoiled some of the special plaiting effects that Doug had planned; and half-way home to Southampton, Doug realized that he had left the stalk-stompers in the field, and had to turn the car around. But in the end it didn't matter. The formation confounded Meaden, and converted Ralph Noyes to the paranormal hypothesis, and the Delgadonians celebrated it as the jewel of the season. That the design of the thing might have resembled some ancient Celtic symbol was utterly unknown to Doug and Dave – although mystical ideas had not been completely alien to them. They had often wondered why, of all people, *they* had decided to do this thing which had captured the imaginations of so many.

Of course, by the end of the summer of 1989, they were no longer alone. A group in the Avebury area was now obviously active, and had been for several years. They had even ventured into Hampshire as far back as 1986 – causing Doug and Dave to inscribe, despairingly, WE ARE NOT ALONE at Cheesefoot Head. The encroachment of the Avebury gang, plus the grotesque success of Delgado's and Andrews's book, plus the ingenious tenacity of Meaden and his new plasma vortex theory, forced Doug and Dave to take radical measures. In the winter of 1989–90, they began to devise a series of patterns that, they believed, would not only maintain their supremacy as circlemakers, but would create absolute pandemonium in the Delgadonian camp, and would finish Meaden off once and for all. The first pattern was inspired by a 1920s modernist painting in one of Dave's art books. The scene involved a triangle, and some flanking rectangular bars. They eventually discarded the triangle motif, but the side bars – which they assumed would be the bane of any vortex theory – they incorporated into their first design that summer, at Chilcomb: the first pictogram. Doug even devised a new piece of circlemaking gear for the occasion – a wire sighting device attached to a baseball cap, with which he could stalk-stomp in a straight line, orientating himself by lights or silhouetted objects on the horizon.

And of course the pictograms created a sensation. Doug and Dave were back in the driver's seat. The Delgadonians were agog. Meaden, about to launch his scientific conference, was stunned. And as always, it seemed that Doug and Dave could do no wrong. One night they went up to Hazeley Farm, near Cheesefoot Head, and made what should have been a fairly ordinary pictogram, with side bars extending straight down from one of the ringed circles towards the other circle. But to Doug's annoyance, Dave again had had two or three pints too many. The sidebars were a mess, not straight at all, and the ring was an abortive oval. Doug barely spoke to Dave as they drove back to Southampton. But the formation was an astounding success. Meaden, to whom its irregularity was the sign of an unstable system of vortices, included it on the tour he gave to visiting scientists. Delgado remarked famously that it displayed 'a sad quality, as though something has been hurt'. Green, Wingfield, and the other CCCS luminaries dubbed it 'the Gaia formation', because for them, or for the people whom they imagined would buy their books, it might have symbolized the destruction of the earth.

In the winter of 1990/91, Doug devised the insectograms. By now, thirteen years after he had started, he and Dave were beginning to tire of the yearly charade. They were almost begging the crop circles researchers to recognize that they were looking at merely human artistry. The insectograms, they thought, would be the height of ridiculousness. Early in the year they began to put them down around Cheesefoot Head and Stonehenge, always including two little half-rings nearby, aligned with tramlines in such a way as to form two signature Ds, for 'Doug and Dave'. The Meadenites, though they embraced virtually all other forms as genuine, quickly dismissed the insectograms as hoaxes. But the Delgadonians enthused all the more. A picture of an insectogram near Stonehenge appeared on the cover of the *Cerealogist*. Inside, George Wingfield described how the strange formations had attracted the mystified attention of Mick Jagger's brother Chris, Lord Haddington, and even Lord Carnarvon. Wingfield himself saw the insectograms as simply another step in the circles' evolution: 'At every stage the circles phenomenon stretches and tests our perception of reality. Those of us who are unable to escape from the prison of our preconceived ideas will be left hopelessly behind, protesting that the insectograms are a hoax because they don't fit our concept of how crop circles should be.'

It was, to Doug and Dave, naturally incredible that their work could be so regularly elevated from the ridiculous to the sublime. What was even more mystifying was that although they visited the same sites again and again, no one ever caught them.

There had been a few close calls. One rainy night, in a field by the Long Man of Wilmington in the early eighties, they had been preparing their stalk-stompers for action when a New Ager, part of a crowd that was meditating nearby, happened upon them without warning. 'Are you trying to put up a tent?' he asked. 'Yes,' they said. 'Hard work.' The fellow wandered off, obliviously wishing them well.

Another time they thought they would be killed. They were down in the Punchbowl late one night when Farmer Bruce and his men suddenly opened up with 12-bores from the woods on the edge of the Bowl. Doug and Dave dropped their stalk-stompers and lay flat in the tramlines. Eventually, as it became clear that the shooting was coming no nearer, it occurred to them that they were not the targets (rabbits were, apparently) and when the gunfire subsided, they resumed their work – somewhat shakily.

Still another time Dave was holding the crosspiece in the centre of a circle when the string suddenly slackened. Dave looked up and saw that Doug had disappeared. His first thought was that his friend had collapsed of a heart attack. His second thought was to worry about how he was going to carry the body out of the field without being noticed. When he went over to the body, he realized that it wasn't a heart attack. It seemed as if Doug had been shot, somehow. In the dark, it felt as if the poor man's brains were oozing out of his forehead. Then Doug groggily regained consciousness. When they reached the car, and illuminated the situation, they realized that Doug had been the victim of an indignity with almost supernatural improbability: the slushy, malodorous remainder of an aircraft toilet discharge had hit him smack on the head.

It was in June of 1991 that the police finally caught them. A patrol car pulled up alongside a field where they were about to create a new insectogram. It looked bad. But they quickly discarded their stalk-stompers, and when confronted by the policeman, used the cover that they had always held in reserve. They walked with the policeman to Doug's car, and Doug produced his wildlife sound recording equipment, plus several letters from the British Library of Wildlife Sounds which noted the fact that Doug, as an amateur wildlife sound recordist, had provided the Library with several aural snippets from the English countryside. The policeman apologized for having disturbed them.

Doug and Dave realized that they probably wouldn't get away with it again. Not only were the police alert to circles hoaxers, but the number of cropwatchers was increasing every summer. The odds were starting to weigh against them. They decided to end their career as hoaxers.

There were other reasons of course. One was that they felt a certain amount of anger, or perhaps envy, towards Delgado and Andrews and Green and Wingfield and the CCCS people, for having reaped fame and fortune from their anonymous creations. Another was that with the pictograms at Alton Barnes* and Barbury Castle, the focus of the phenomenon had shifted permanently to the Avebury area. They decided that they might as well get out while they still had a worthwhile story to tell. The last reason was their age. Doug was sixty-seven. Dave was sixty-two. Even if they wanted to, they couldn't keep up the pace much longer. And it was clear that unless they stopped it now, it would never end. No matter how improbable their designs, someone would always believe in them.

On Tuesday morning, 3 September, with Dave beside him in the little picture-framing shop in Southampton, Doug telephoned the news desk of the *Daily Mirror*. He asked the editor who answered if he was interested in knowing what made the crop circles. The *Mirror* man said that, alas, he was uninterested, Doug then phoned the news desk of *Today*. An editor answered, and after obtaining a few details, suggested a meeting between Doug and Dave and a *Today* reporter at the Wessex Hotel in Winchester the following

---

*Which had provoked Doug and Dave to make their only north Wiltshire formation, a series of large letters which spelled 'COPYCATS' in a field near Avebury.

day. Doug and Dave and Ilene were there the next day, when *Today* reporter Graham Brough arrived. He grilled them for a half-hour or so, and then pronounced their story genuine. The insectogram demonstration at Sevenoaks was arranged, Delgado was contacted and duped, and on Sunday evening, Brough, Bower, and Chorley broke the news to him. After a sleepless night for Doug and Dave, the story appeared in *Today* on Monday morning, and the media frenzy began. Doug and Dave and Ilene were put up in the Wessex Hotel again (the picture-framing shop was closed for a week), and from there they fielded calls from all corners of the globe, from Nashville to Sydney. In the next few weeks, they appeared on television talk shows in Rome, Cologne, Amsterdam, and Manchester. The *Mail on Sunday* hauled them out to Cheesefoot Head, dressed them in spacesuits, and filmed them romping around amid a dry-ice fog.

But by the middle of October, the frenzy had subsided. And curiously, as in the biblical paradox that a prophet is without honour in his own country, the media attention seemed to have been much greater from abroad than at home. Aside from *Today* and the *Mail*, and a few quick interviews on BBC and ITV, they received relatively little coverage from the British media. In fact, among the British media, and among the British public in general, there was a certain amount of scepticism regarding their claims – which had been widely misinterpreted, thanks to *Today*'s sensationalism, as implausibly encompassing all of the crop circles that had ever appeared in England. Juniper, for example, in their otherwise informative programme which appeared on Channel Four's *Equinox* series, appeared to dismiss the claims of Doug and Dave as 'contradictory'.

There was another factor, more subtle but probably just as powerful – an indignation, on the part of so many among the intellectual classes, at having been fooled for so long, and in such a grand and embarrassing fashion, by two old men, humble Doug and Dave, whose own highest aspiration had been merely . . . the ecstasy of art.

Epilogue

The Delgadonians therefore did remarkably well in surviving the revelations of Doug and Dave, and a surprising number of people were willing to believe the charges of fraud, espionage, and general discreditableness that were levelled at the two men from Southampton. But the Delgadonians also came up with more positive pieces of evidence in their favour – namely, two American analyses of pictograms around Avebury. The first analysis, by Marshall Dudley, a systems engineer for Tennelec/Nucleus, a government contractor at Oak Ridge, Tennessee, concluded that soil samples from several pictograms, including the Barbury Castle formation, displayed anomalously high, or in some cases anomalously low, alpha and beta radiation counts – by comparison with control samples taken from outside the formations. The second analysis, by a private plant physiologist, W. C. Levengood, of Michigan, concluded that the wheat seeds and wheatstalk growth nodes from several pictograms, including the Lockeridge fish, were abnormal compared to controls. An American circles enthusiast named Michael Chorost summarized the findings in a report that was widely circulated throughout the crop circles community, and concluded that 'The work of Marshall and Levengood points to a cause which pumps energy into the plants, leaving them intact but causing damage within. This kind of damage is almost impossible to cause by trampling.' CCCS issued a press release with similar conclusions in October, a few days before Juniper's critical programme was aired on Channel Four. Confidence was high that CCCS, and the crop circles research community, would weather the storm.

But further storms were to come. In December it was revealed that one of the leading members of the Beckhampton Group, a fellow I will call R, had perpetrated a major hoax eleven years before, when he had been a member of the UFO research group SCUFORI in Swindon. Shortly after he had joined SCUFORI, other members of the group had begun to receive anonymous calls, anonymous letters, and message-carrying audio tapes, purporting to be from a member of an alien mission to earth. The messages warned SCUFORI members to cease all UFO research at once, or else. At least one message included a death threat; another threatened to 'blow up' SCUFORI members' homes. After R showed his colleagues pictures of a bogus UFO (which turned out to be part of a sewerage system), they became suspicious, and set a trap for him, leaving a message for 'the alien' in a secluded wood, and making sure that R knew the location. R went to retrieve the message, was photographed automatically, and after briefly claiming that the aliens had forced him to act as an intermediary, left the group. In the summer of 1991, one of his former SCUFORI colleagues happened to see him in the Avebury area. Wondering if R could be responsible for hoaxing some of the crop circles, the ex-colleague decided to attend a Beckhampton Group meeting in the Waggon and Horses, where, before leaving hurriedly, he saw that R was a high-ranking member of the group. Upon exposure, R denied that he was a circles hoaxer, and insisted that the SCUFORI incident had been merely a psychological experiment conducted for a course he had been taking at the time. But his arrival on the circles scene had been preceded by the appearance of a crop circle outside his house near Swindon, and within a few months he had managed to become not only Treasurer and Membership Coordinator for the group, but also Cropwatch Coordinator. He had planned to hold a summer-long cropwatch at East Field, where, he said, he was sure the circlemakers would oblige him. He had explained to fellow members of the Beckhampton Group: 'I reckon they're going to try to do something right in front of me. Right under my nose.' After the revelation about the SCUFORI incident, Polly Carson refused to allow him on her farm, and R was forced to resign from the Beckhampton Group.

Another blow fell early in 1992, when a CCCS member and former circles believer, Ken Brown, obtained the opinion of a wildlife expert, based on Colin Andrews's tape of the White Crow trilling noise, that the noise was, as Doug Bower had long claimed, the song of the grasshopper warbler.

The story of Rita Goold and the White Crow letters made the rounds as well, and to top it all off, in January 1992 Marshall Dudley abruptly withdrew the bulk of his radio-isotope results, citing an improper statistical analysis of the data by another firm's computer. Although this disappointing turn of events was immediately conveyed to CCCS, some of the organization's officers continued to cite Dudley's work, in their lectures around the country, as evidence for the validity of the crop circles phenomenon.

The 1992 season got under way with a circle in oilseed rape at Sutton Scotney in Hampshire, in full view of the A34. It was quickly followed by rape-field circles at Lurkeley Hill outside East Kennett and at Avebury Trusloe. The latter was never visited by anyone, other than its maker, and from aerial photographs it was judged to be genuine by CCCS. The East Kennett job was more accessible, and was generally considered to be a hoax. Citing the broken stalks and messy swirl, Terence Meaden declared it the work of a rank beginner.

Well, he was right. But before I embark on a description of some of my own and others' circlemaking adventures in that short, sad summer of 1992, I should explain that it all started innocently. I was looking for hoaxers – the Wiltshire hoaxers, the Avebury gang, the team that had done the Silbury quintuplets in 1988, the East Field double-pictograms in 1990, the fish and the frogs in 1991, and presumably everything else in the Avebury/Silbury/Alton Barnes area in the past several years.

I – or rather we, for Rob Irving and some others also were involved in the chase – had decided long ago that the Avebury gang must have at least one member in a major crop circles group. How else would they have known, and so quickly, where Mary Freeman had seen the light coming down from the clouds? and where Isabelle Kingston had predicted the double-pictograms? and where to put a massive fish — no, a whale — in a field near Alton Barnes, under the apparent flight path of the light phenomenon* Rob Irving and I had seen at the Black Swan watch, a few days after the event? How else would they have known the designs for which the Delgadonians were clamouring?

One suspect, naturally, was R of the Beckhampton Group, who with his past infiltration of SCUFORI seemed a likely Kim Philby. And although we had long ago abandoned the Friends of Hekate conspiracy theory, we still considered the possibility that the hoaxers were big fish, Aquarian Conspirators out to change world consciousness, like Michael Green or Pat Delgado, or Colin Andrews . . . who had been in particularly close touch with Isabelle Kingston in the early years. The idea of such a conspiracy was by now beginning to be mooted, quietly, at Beckhampton Group get-togethers. Some even seemed to approve of the idea, such as the Beckhampton Group regular who wrote a plaintive note to Doug and Dave, asking them secretly to make her a pictogram, somewhere near Avebury, in the shape of an Egyptian ankh.

But R had only been around for a year or two, and the Aquarian conspiracy . . . well, somehow I couldn't picture Michael Green in a wheatfield in the dead of night, puffing and panting as he swirled out occult symbols with a garden roller, stumbling occasionally on the hem of his dew-soaked wizard's cloak.

Our main suspects were a group of young people surrounding and including John Martineau's UBI. They had long been Delgado's and Andrews's right-hand men, and had later managed to cosy up to Wingfield and CCCS, and seemingly had always been willing to pull an all-nighter for a cropwatch. Through Colin Andrews and others, members of the group had been well connected to Isabelle Kingston, and thus could have heard about, and could immediately

---

*This phenomenon was almost certainly a pair of car headlights, viewed through the distorting lenses of fog and fatigue. Tired eye muscles find it difficult to track smoothly a point-source of light in the darkness, and the result — what Rob Irving has called 'cropwatcher's eye' — is the violent zig-zag effect which I have seen, at other times, in objects which a squint could quickly immobilize.

have acted upon, not only the Mary Freeman sighting in 1988, and Isabelle Kingston's prediction of the Alton Barnes double-pictogram in 1990, but also the sighting Irving and I had had from Adam's Grave in 1991.

There was more direct evidence, for a UBI member named Paul, a short, sleepy-eyed kid of about twenty, who looked as though he should have had a skateboard tucked under his arm, had confessed in 1991 to having made additions to a dumbbell near Avebury. With a beatific-looking fellow named Matt, and a barefoot lad named Bart, an aspiring thespian who claimed also to practise 'Red' Magic, Paul also was seen one night early in the 1992 season, coming out of a circles-filled field near Lockeridge; next morning, several new grapeshot circles were found, and their perfect swirls, their delicate, nest-like centres, were lauded by the crop circles community as having been the work of the true Circlemakers.

As the summer wore on we discovered further clues. Paul told Rob Irving that earlier in the season he and Matt had made a pictogram in oilseed rape outside Matt's village of Urchfont, near Devizes. The formation had originally been a large circle with a key – expertly done, considering the difficulties of working with brittle rapestalks – but then had been enlarged to include five or six circles and interlinking avenues. Several individuals close to UBI also let slip, perhaps to divert attention from themselves, that Matt had been making circles since 1989. Matt told me he had been interested in circles since the early 1980s, but that his circlemaking activities had been insignificant; the real circlemakers, he seemed to suggest, were people like Paul and John.

At unguarded moments Matt and Paul and the others would express amusement, and perhaps a touch of pride, at the things people would find in pictograms, such as dowsable energy or radio-isotopes, and this seemed at odds with their public belief in the phenomenon. John Martineau even suggested to me, half-jokingly, that he might avenge himself against a certain sceptical journalist, who owned farmland in the north of England, by putting dozens of circles into his fields.

But beneath the inevitable touch of cynicism which one might expect from those who lead a double life, there seemed among some of the members of UBI to be a sturdy layer of belief: that the circles were a sign, a sign of the end. The more an individual could do to hasten this end – by producing chaos, disorder, cosmological confusion, strange signs upon the earth – the more he would earn his place among the chosen. The chosen, in accordance with this fairly common apocalyptic motif, were those who would ascend aloft in alien spaceships, to witness Armageddon and back-EMF and the general terrestrial combustion from a safely high orbit. To prepare for this eventuality, Paul and Matt and some of the others had built a UFO landing strip at Cley Hill, near Warminster, in the autumn of 1991, marking out a runway with candles; Colin Andrews, among other luminaries, had paid a visit.

Shortly after Doug and Dave's story appeared in *Today*, Terence Meaden received a strange letter, filled with biblical and apocalyptic references, which lamented the likely decline in belief in the circles, and suggested that the author of the letter was a member of the group that had been making circles in Wiltshire ('You have even been fooled by children' the letter-writer said, and indeed some of the UBI groupies were remarkably young). The letter warned Meaden to cease his research or face further public ridicule. Later, Paul told Rob Irving that he and some of the others had periodically put Meaden under surveillance, had broken into the secret site caravan on at least one occasion, and were thinking about tapping his home telephone.

Rob Irving and I, and Pam Price, a member of the Beckhampton Group who now believed that virtually all of the circles were man-made, decided that it would be fun to catch UBI in the act of making a circle. So around the beginning of June we laid a trap, spreading the word that someone had seen a UFO over a field near Lockeridge. It was a good field for a formation, because it sloped sharply up from a road – passers-by couldn't miss a formation appearing there – and because, since it had never been hit by circles before, a circlemaker wouldn't expect cropwatchers to be around the place at night. We called it 'the virgin field', and after the story about the UFO had spread, Pam and Rob and I began to sit inside it at night, waiting with our flash cameras ready.

Well, one night went by, and another, and another, and after the better part of a week the field was still a virgin. We decided to leave UBI alone, as far as cropwatching went. Indeed, having made a few experimental circles by that time, we had begun to feel a certain solidarity with Matt and Paul and John and the others. What was the use of exposing circlemakers? we asked ourselves. Why should it matter who, precisely and incontrovertibly, had made this or that formation? We decided that there could be better reasons for losing sleep and being chilled by the Wiltshire mist. We could do it for art's sake, for instance.

Now first of all, I should point out that the act of making a crop circle causes little or no material damage. I have heard it said countless times by circles-prone farmers that, unless a formation has been severely trampled by tourists, it can be harvested without loss merely by lowering the blades of the harvesting machine. Anyone who doubts this should hire a plane and fly over an untouristed or even a moderately touristed formation, just after the harvest, and observe how its downswept stalks have disappeared with the rest of that field's crop. Only the formations which draw crowds up until harvest time will be so flattened as to be unreachable by the harvester, and these will have amply compensated the farmer for the damage caused. For example, the formations in and around East Field in 1991 could not have amounted to an acre of flattened wheat altogether. An acre of wheat sells for about £350. The receipts from the thousands of tourists who visited East Field that year, at £1 per head, must have run to at least ten times the value of the lost wheat.

All that having been said, it remains true that circlemaking can be an annoyance to farmers who do not like having crowds drawn to strange shapes in their fields. Even farmers such as the Carsons, who welcome 'genuine' pictograms with open arms, have threatened to prosecute anyone whom they can reasonably accuse of hoaxing on their land. The police at Pewsey and Devizes, under pressure from the Carsons and other farmers, have been obliged to growl and squint and vow that they are on the case.

Therefore I shouldn't be too specific, although even with Polly Carson and the police in hot pursuit I am unable to repress a few frank memories of circles swirled by myself or by my artistic colleagues: for instance, that set of big circles at Lockeridge, formed in lovely, soft, moonlit green barley with a garden roller and some string, and energies which were still powerful enough, a day later, to cure an old woman of her arthritis pains ... The triplet near the town of Wroughton, so well-wrought that George Wingfield said of it, 'If this is a hoax, I'll eat my shirt in public' ... The rough-hewn ring, beneath which, according to the newspapers, an expert dowser detected a buried stone circle ... The 200-foot pictogram that appeared on the crest of a hill above Ogbourne St George, like a message from God, with a single pristine grapeshot for signature ...

I remember also the long night of the circles competition organized by John Michell, in a field above the caves of the old Hell Fire Club in Buckinghamshire, and the morning when it became clear that I had beaten, among others, a team fielded by UBI ... I remember the crescent moon shapes, and an alchemical pictogram that a bearded Californian carved into stone and sold for £100 ... And a narrow ring on a hill opposite the Silbury mound, and pop music rising up through the mist from a radio in a caravan on the A4 – where several young New Agers from the outer orbit of UBI drank and talked and slept ... I remember a hot night with thunder in the air, and a mysterious quintuplet in a field by Isabelle Kingston's house ... I remember pitch darkness under a ridge of hills, with the raindrops drifting down in slow motion, and above on the ridge, UBI's torches occasionally searching skyward, while beneath them grew a perfect swirled circle with an outstretched hand, the hand of God ... And another night, when suddenly – car headlights and voices, and the terrible adrenal pulse of the hunted hoaxer (who escaped, naturally).

I remember one night, which I swore would be my last, when I made several formations in separate locations, and how lightning flashed all night and I thought it was only artillery practice on Salisbury Plain until an opaque downpour suddenly burst over my cereal canvas, shielding me from cropwatching eyes as I made my valedictory pictogram ... and I can still see myself afterwards, trudging a mile to my car, soaked to the skin, shivering in the pale blue light of dawn, hungry, thirsty, tired, triumphant – and also knowing helplessly that only the harvesters could free me from this addiction.

Actually, for all the supposed otherworldliness of the pictograms, making them requires more nerve (or lunacy) than dexterity or design skill. It took me less than two months to move, on the cerealogical scale, from obvious hoaxer to superhuman intelligence, and by the end of the summer, despite the steadfast efforts, I assume, of Matt and Paul and Bart and John and other apparent veterans, a few other beginners and I had fully replaced them in the role of 'Wiltshire Circlemakers'.

There are three basic implements I used in knocking down stalks: the first, which I prefer for all jobs requiring a large area to be flattened, is a garden roller. It flattens stalks only in the direction one is rolling, so it doesn't give one much of a swirl, but it allows one to work very fast and is perfect for doing rings, avenues, the edges of circles, and even the insides of circles, if one doesn't mind a strictly tangential lay of crop.

The second, the Doug and Dave stalk-stomping plank method, I prefer for making circles themselves because it allows one to flatten stalks somewhat radially (that is, both away from and around the centre, giving a lovely spiral effect) even as one walks tangentially. Of course, one has to practise this to understand it fully. The drawback of stalk-stomping is that, depending on the length of one's plank and one's stamina, it is much slower than using a roller.

The third and most obvious method is to use one's feet – which incidentally is more comfortable, in a chalk and flint-strewn field, when one's feet are inside shoes. This method I generally use only for very small jobs, such as grapeshot. There are at least two ways of making grapeshot. One is to plant a pole in the wheat, extend it at arms' length, walk sideways around it once, and then continue walking sideways in an inward spiral to the centre, as if mowing a circular patch of grass from the outside in. The other way is to walk sideways around once, and then to reach into the centre, fashion a nice central nest with one's hands, and step-swirl the wheat from there in an outward spiral, as if mowing a circular patch of grass from the inside out. For larger circles, of course, the perimeter can and should be defined using a pole at the centre (or a friend) and a string of the appropriate length, stepping sideways while holding the string taut. But for larger circles I seldom use my feet, simply because it is such a slow method.

On one occasion I was more or less forced to use my feet. I walked a mile from my car, crept into a field with a stalk-stomper, got soaked from the heavy dew, and promptly lost the stomper to a field-nymph in the darkness after being distracted by an Army flare to the south. I made the circle with my feet, trudging slowly sideways in ever-wider spirals, taking about half an hour to make a simple twenty-five foot circle. The stalks crunched ungenuinely under my shoe soles, and I could tell that I was making a mess. But I felt that I had to do something – my creative urge wouldn't let me leave a virgin field behind.

In the morning, the circle was found by several cropwatchers. They rousted the farmer out of bed and went in and – well, the cropwatchers were sure it was a hoax. The stalks were covered with muddy footprints.

However, it was still quite early in the season, and there was cerealogical excitement for even the smallest circle, and pretty soon Michael Green came roaring out from London with some other CCCS officials. They went into the circle and looked at the footprints and the layering of the circle and the breakage of stalks, and the cropwatchers explained how it was all a hoax, and how they had gone in at first light and found the footprints –

'My boy,' Green told the cropwatchers, 'we have ways of telling a genuine circle from a hoaxed circle, and this circle is *genuine*.'

After I heard that story, I wondered whether Green or some other CCCS officer might find my lost stalk-stomper, and experience a terrible epiphany. But I needn't have worried. Green and his colleagues apparently did find it, but decided it was some other researcher's measuring rod, and promptly lost it.

Such is the magic of art.

Colin Andrews was almost invisible in the summer of 1992. He had released a video in September of 1991, had gone to Australia to promote it, and then had returned in December and had split with Delgado, taking the CPR name and logo for himself. Pat Delgado announced the news briefly in his monthly newsletter:

> Colin is now working full time on crop circle research and as it was Colin who initiated the title of CPR he will be retaining sole use of it for his business from now on.

Delgado changed his newsletter's title to Circle Lines, and his logo was changed to resemble not 'CPR' but 'CPD'. He wrote a third book, *Crop Circles – Conclusive Evidence*, without Andrews, and although Bloomsbury, in the wake of the Doug and Dave story, were said to have cancelled plans for a book by CCCS officials, they nevertheless agreed to publish this, Delgado's third book, in the spring of 1992. The book was not a bestseller, and in July Delgado announced in his newsletter that:

> Something does not seem right about the crop circle phenom-
> enon this year. There have been a large number of hoaxes and
> quite frankly, I am not prepared to say that any of about thirty
> I have examined are genuine.

Delgado went on to suggest that there was little point in cata-loguing more circles, and that the phenomenon would shortly move into a new and more profound stage. Meanwhile, Delgado was suspending his newsletter, although, he said, it would be 'resur-rected' when the new phenomenal stage was reached.

Andrews had issued a press release in January, announcing that he would be holding an enormous cropwatch in Wiltshire in July. According to newspaper accounts, the cropwatch would include £1 million worth of equipment, would be sponsored by several media organizations including Nippon TV, and would be attended by several dozen scientists, including Japanese scientists, and scientists from the United Nations. A few weeks later, Andrews was said by friends to have declared that the market for books on crop circles was played out, and that he would in future concentrate his work on UFOs and poltergeists. Dropping hints that he was going away to prepare for the rapturous End, he left in the spring of 1992 for the UFO lecture circuits in Australia and America. He returned in June, and was seen on television avowing that his cropwatch would go forward as planned. He promised that there would be Alien Contact. In July, a group of Americans calling themselves CSETI, or the Committee for the Search for Extraterrestrial Intel-ligence (no relation to the quasi-governmental SETI, which boasts associates such as Carl Sagan) arrived and pitched camp at Woodborough Hill, overlooking Alton Barnes from the south. For several weeks they, with Colin Andrews and a few others, shone lights into the sky at night, hoping to draw attention and induce contact by alien craft. One night several CSETI members did report a large 'structured craft' moving slowly beneath the hill, along the Kennet and Avon Canal, blinking its lights in response to their own signals. It wasn't the rapture many had been preparing for, but it was exhilarating none the less, and the CSETI crew had something to tell their colleagues when they went back home. Colin Andrews went with them, or to Connecticut anyway, where he now lives with an American woman and lectures, researches, and writes about strange phenomena.

Busty Taylor's and Richard Andrews's lecture tour of America in the autumn of 1991 was a near-disaster ('Everybody wanted to hear about Doug and Dave,' remembered Busty), and when Busty brought out a book in the spring, featuring lovely photographs of 1991 formations, it sold poorly. He continued to photograph circles in the summer of 1992, from planes and from atop his long pole, but he was more wary now, believing that a large percentage of circles were man-made, and he began to be concerned that too much attention to the circles was hurting his driving-school business.

I saw him late in the summer of 1992, and with some friends we went flying above the circles-filled fields of Wiltshire. It had been a long day for Busty – as on most Saturdays, he had worked hard hours at Thruxton Airport, towing gliders into the sky with a powered plane. He had made twenty-eight takeoffs and twenty-eight landings when we arrived in late afternoon, and a strong storm front was fast moving in from the south-west. But he cheerfully consented to take us aloft, and soon we were drifting over Alton Barnes, Silbury Hill, the Avebury Stone Avenue, and points in between, Busty putting the plane into tight turns so I could more easily photograph mine and others' creations. Some were only marks in the stubble, and some had already been turned under the dirt, but some gazed happily back at me through ripe, wind-blemished fields, at the edges of which there might be a tiny car, or tiny humans, with their insignificant motions, or toy villages, with papier-maché trees and sheep-flecked green hills and painted brooks, and a grey little cloud reaching towards us from the horizon, emitting a lovely, rainbow-ringed shower. I could see why Busty loved to fly, and I was glad that, when one summer the crop circles no longer cared to appear, and his erstwhile colleagues scurried off to environmentalism or poltergeists or Atlantis, Busty would still be able to drive over to Thruxton and take a plane from the flight line and roar confidently down the runway and into the sky, above it all.

After a reasonably successful lecture tour in America in the spring of 1992, George Wingfield had a hard summer. Some of the formations looked very good to him, but as the season wore on, he grew suspicious. It seemed that every time a new formation appeared, Rob Irving would ask his opinion of it. And whereas Irving before might have argued with Wingfield if he declared something genuine, he now seemed only to enjoy a special, private pleasure. Pride of authorship, Wingfield guessed, and he began putting it about that a police investigation was under way, with plenty of evidence implicating Irving. He even phoned up poor Adrian Dexter, and suggested that if Dexter would only cop a plea and testify to the circumcereal misdeeds of Irving, he would get off lightly. The idea of this scheme, which although it was leaked to us by insiders was supported by a surprising number of CCCS officials, was to prevent Irving from exposing his hoaxes and thereby embarrassing Wingfield and CCCS.

Rob Irving was interrogated by the police one day, but only because they thought he had information about other people who were hoaxing circles. Alas, he didn't, and in a telephone conversation that ensued with a Pewsey policeman Irving tried to explain that there were many hoaxing groups, and that all of the formations were hoaxes. There was a moment of stony silence, and then the policeman said, 'I don't want to get into a philosophical discussion with you, but they can't all be hoaxes.'

By the end of the summer, though otherwise still unprosecuted, Rob Irving and I managed to join Doug and Dave and MBF Services and other shadowy figures in the Wingfieldian pantheon of government spies. One day Wingfield's friend Henry Azadehdel phoned up Irving, pretending to be an African gentleman, a 'Mr Ntumba', who was interested in crop circles. Was Mr Irving working for any intelligence organization? asked Ntumba innocently. Irving replied with equal sincerity that he did consider himself to be intelligent. Eventually, Ntumba phoned me, asking whether Irving was a spy, and I discreetly let on that we were both members of a secret organization spanning the globe and comprising, among other sub-agencies, the CIA, MI6, the Vatican, and the Trilateral Commission. Azadehdel taped it, and passed the tapes on to Wingfield, who began to send out faxes hinting that he had cracked the crop circles conspiracy at last. Eventually I explained to Wingfield that the whole thing was a wind-up.

But Wingfield refused to believe me, and stormed across the cerealogical and ufological lecture circuits of Britain and America, denouncing Rob Irving and me as spies (Pam Price was annoyed that she had been left out). Some of Wingfield's colleagues who dared to question the conspiracy theory became, in Wingfield's eyes, co-conspirators. The episode ended with a split between Wingfield and his last ally, Azadehdel, whom Wingfield now suggested had also been part of the conspiracy.

'Plato said, "The gods give us paranoia, that we might occasionally glimpse the truth",' was John Michell's enigmatic comment on the whole Ntumba episode. He had seemed to take the crop circles phenomenon less seriously in 1992, and in the pages of the *Cerealogist* (renamed the *Cereologist* early in the summer, and re-re-named the *Cerealogist* in 1993), articles about hoaxing or the possibility thereof had begun to appear with remarkable frequency. Michell and his partner Christine Rhone together began to seem an oasis of calm good humour in the hot, heaving desert that crop circles research had become. In Michell's earlier writings, I might add, I no longer saw anything sinister, only a combination of puckishness and scholarly eccentricity which, several decades later, has mellowed to a charming, rumpled perspicacity and can regularly be found, for example, in his column in Richard Ingrams's magazine, the *Oldie*.

Rita Goold spent a good part of the summer of 1992 in the fields around Avebury and Alton Barnes, clad in camouflage and waiting (alas, in vain) for hoaxers. She now believes that the circles phenomenon is largely due to pranksters, and she is said to be returning to her old career. According to a story in the newspaper *Psychic World*, 'Rita Lorraine Goold of Wiltshire,' accompanied by 'Mr Arthur Mills, her close friend and manager,' recently hosted a seance featuring Helen Duncan and other famous spiritualist figures. The article noted that Rita and Arthur were currently researching a book about mediumship.

Richard Andrews wasn't seen much in the summer of 1992, but when he did appear he looked healthy enough, and in good spirits. I heard somewhere that he was working with researchers from some university, I forget which one, researching ley-lines and energy lines and their ecological and electro-atmospheric effects. I also heard that he had met and gotten engaged to a UFO abduction researcher somewhere in California, and as far as I know they are living happily ever after.

I haven't heard much about Michael Green, except that last summer he asked Andy Collins's psychic girlfriend to become one of his 'priestesses'. George de Trafford failed to show up for a crop circles conference in Glastonbury in July of 1992, because of ill-health it was said. Little has been heard from him lately, although occasionally his wisdom (which, like Green's, is as far as I know completely benign) seeps out in the pages of the New Age magazine *Kindred Spirit*. Go well, George.

Ralph Noyes took part in a summer-long expedition in Wiltshire, called Project Argus.* Organized by the American Michael Chorost, the project involved a team of circles enthusiasts, based in a cottage at Polly Carson's farm, collecting samples of soil and stalks from circles that appeared in the area, for later analysis by everything from gamma ray spectrometers to electron microscopes to magnetic permeability indicators. The idea was to build upon the 1991 findings of Dudley and Levengood. I haven't yet heard what their results were, but Chorost didn't seem too happy when he flew home early to the US in August, and by September, Noyes had begun to talk about closing down CCCS. The Beckhampton Group had just folded, many of its key members having decided that even the most beautiful formations were likely to have been man-made. Not that Ralph Noyes had become a complete sceptic, for Rob Irving and Pam Price saw him one night just before the harvest, sitting in his

---

* Argus was Odysseus's blind dog, the only one to recognize his master when he returned from his epic journey. Unfortunately, according to the legend, the dog died immediately thereafter.

car on the road above East Field, just gazing out into the darkness, waiting . . .

Doug and Dave were relatively quiet in the summer of 1992, and early in the summer, when I asked Doug whether he had been out in the fields at night, he said: 'No, no. David and I have hung up our swords. We're finished.' I didn't believe him, and in July, when a formation appeared in Hampshire which seemed to incorporate two copies of the letter 'D', I knew I had been right. It turned out that Doug and Dave had been doing an encore performance, this time with the farmers paid and the camera rolling. Behind the camera was John Macnish.

Terence Meaden continued to receive strange reports from *Journal of Meteorology* correspondents and tabloid editors, for example this one which arrived via the *Sunday Mirror*:

On Sunday 21st July 1991, I was fishing in a match at Stathe Drain [Somerset]. At 1.15 p.m., I was conscious of a movement in the far bank to my right. The movement was initially reeds waving violently 45 yards away where the drain is 20 yards wide. At this precise moment a violent burst of activity took place. A central column of water, rotating rapidly, with a clearly defined core, approximately 2 feet in diameter rose above the surface to approximately 3 feet high. This central column was surrounded by dense spray covering a diameter of about 4 yards and was rotating at speed. The duration of the occurrence was about 3 seconds. The miniature 'whirlwind' appeared to be stationary for 1 second, then moved rapidly across to the near bank in a second, causing a large surface disturbance, remained there for a further second, and then was gone just as quickly as it had started. During the 3 seconds the rotational speed was rapid and obvious. I was not aware of any noise, but there may have been. There was no after effect and there was no evidence that the 'whirlwind' had continued on its way. The energy had been completely discharged.

Meaden remained confident that despite having chased the creations of Doug and Dave for twelve years, his basic concept of a circles-swirling vortex had been correct. It began to seem possible that Bower's and Chorley's sensational hoax, which after all had been based on an apparently genuine event in Australia, had simply drawn attention to a phenomenon too rare to have attracted it otherwise. Yoshi-Hiko Ohtsuki, the Kikuchis, John Snow, and Chris Church, to whom Meaden now left any further elaboration of the theory, also expressed their faith that some simple circles swirled into ground cover might be genuine, despite Doug and Dave. Converts were even added, as when a physicist in Moscow grew interested in the subject, and reportedly procured a large microwave chamber for making Ohtsukian plasmoids.

In February 1992, Ohtsuki sent Meaden a brief account of a ten-metre circle which had recently appeared in grass inside a fenced area near a Radio Nippon transmitting tower outside Tokyo. An electromagnetic noise warning alarm had switched itself on an abnormally large number of times between 2.00 a.m. and 2.40 a.m. on the morning the grass circle was found. Ohtsuki's cover letter read in part:

> Dear Terry,
> Enclosed is the contribution to your *J. Met*. This is the report on the 'real' circles effects recently appeared in Japan, and we concluded that this is not hoaxing!
> I want to visit [England] this summer, once again, to see real circles effects . . .

But as the summer of 1992 approached, Meaden began to grow distant from the crop circles scene, and although he did visit one or two formations, and did submit to one or two press interviews, he became increasingly preoccupied with the promotion of his new book, *The Stonehenge Solution*, which was released by Souvenir Press shortly before the solstice. A distillation of one of the archaeology theses that Meaden had been working on for several years, the book purported to explain the ancient and secret rites performed at Stonehenge. It had, he told me, nothing whatsoever to do with crop circles.

Author's Note

I wish there were some way to thank properly all those who made my work easier during my crop circle days. I should mention in particular: Doug Bower, Ilene Bower, Dave Chorley, Adrian Dexter, Jill Freeman, Paul Fuller, Rob Irving, Jayne Macnish, John Macnish, Ian Mrzyglod, Yoshi-Hiko Ohtsuki, Matt Page, Pam Price, Stuart Rae, Jenny Randles, Peter Rendall, Busty Taylor, Don Tuersley, Peggy Tuersley, Alexandra Villing, Ute Weyer — and especially, Terence Meaden.

I also should acknowledge a number of previous books about the circles, the most important of which are *The Circles Effect and Its Mysteries* and *Circles from the Sky*, written and edited, respectively, by Terence Meaden; *Crop Circles: A Mystery Solved*, by Paul Fuller and Jenny Randles; *The Crop Circle Enigma*, edited by Ralph Noyes; and finally, *Circular Evidence* and *The Latest Evidence*, both by Pat Delgado and Colin Andrews.